# MY DARLING
# DAVIS
## HOW REAL IS YOUR LOVE?

Created in the United States of America

ISBN:  Softcover              978-1-64908-986-1
       eBook                 978-1-64908-985-4

Republished by: PageTurner Press and Media LLC
Publication Date: 05/03/2021

**To order copies of this book, contact:**

PageTurner Press and Media
Phone: 1-888-447-9651
order@pageturner.us
www.pageturner.us

# MY DARLING DAVIS

## HOW REAL IS YOUR LOVE?

An Online Romance Scam based
on a true story

T.G. Diamond

# Contents

I would like to Thank all of my Friends who tried to protect me from myself and who stood by me throughout my whole ordeal.

For answering my questions and helping me with my research, I would like to Thank Randy Reed, Matthew Bernier, and Derrick Vallieres.

My Family for their love, encouragement, help and continuous support, most of all I would like to Thank my Two Sons and my Daughter, all three I Love very much.

A very special Thank You to Beth King for preparing the cover art.

And a special Thank You to William Bohmer my friend.

# 1

# LIFE WITH STEVE

I think of myself as an average woman, and like most women, when you are with your (boyfriend) partner of 4 years, it would be nice to hear the words I love you, and it would be nice to know that the person you are with thinks of you as someone special and interesting. When you are in a relationship and you don't hear those three big words and the person you are with treats you in such a way that it makes you feel like they are indifferent to you . . ., you tend to become . . . oh what's the word?, . . . they should have a slang word other than one starting with the letter f that describes how you become indifferent yourself, immune, numb, let's just say I learned how to accept things for what they were and I learned how to really love myself because other than my kids, the love wasn't coming from anyone else. I was in such a relationship with Steve. Steve, who stated his guidelines when we first started seeing each other; I never met anyone with relationship guidelines before, they comprised of—he would never tell me he loved me, he would never compliment me, he would never ask me to move in with him and he would never marry me, oh and that his kids would always come first. Which is a given fact with anyone who has kids, but he felt it necessary to list it. Well he managed to stick to almost four out of the five guidelines. Steve helped me out when my daughter and I needed a place to stay for six months; he invited us to stay with him for that amount of time.

I asked myself several times throughout our relationship why am I staying with him? We did break up a couple of times for short periods. Once, it was for a week. I phoned and told Steve that I didn't think

1

it was fair to me or to him, for us to see each other if he wasn't really interested in me. Steve would walk by me downtown, without saying hi; he would just raise his hand bending his elbow at the hip in an effortless wave. He wouldn't call me, I would call him . . . He sounded surprised when I mentioned that this bothered me, to him. Then, just like a man, he started showing interest in me . . . phoning me, inviting me out and over to his place and there we were again, spending time with each other.

Steve had a lot of really good qualities, he was extremely intelligent. He had a dry sense of humor, but none the less he did have humor, he could make me laugh. He was very competent in everything that he did. He made me feel safe and underneath it all, we did have fun together, oh and one of Steve's best attributes was that he could cook. He was an amazing cook who taught me a few things in the kitchen.

I wanted to believe that he did love me, he just couldn't say it. After his wife left him, he had issues. Why is it, as we try to meet men later in our lives, divorced men all seem to have issues. As women, have we screwed up our men so much during a marriage that now they suffer what I consider to be, post ex-wife stress syndrome? Anyhow getting back to Steve, what else can I say as to why I stayed with Steve for all of those years other than the cooking, the interesting times, the fun times and of course, mainly it was the sex. We had an amazing sexual relationship that worked for both of us.

Steve was there for me when I needed him. Going against his own guidelines he offered his house and his help, until I could get my feet back on the ground and buy my own house. We even had a contract, yes a written contract. I wrote one up because Steve mentioned to his friends that I was moving in for six months and they told him "oh you had better be careful, not a good idea, she can take you for half of everything once you've been together for six months". None of his friends knew me personally, and some of them had only met me briefly on different occasions. My biggest question here is, why do people think of the negative right away? I guess it goes back to people not having any faith or trust in others because they've had it happen to them or they've seen it happen to others around them or that is what they would do if they themselves were put into that same situation. Needless to say, I got pissed off, and wrote up a contract that stated . . .

I, Tess G.Diamond would be at Steve's house for six months and that when I moved out after the six months, I would only be taking with me what ever I brought into the house that belonged to me personally. I signed it and gave it to Steve to do with as he pleased.

After living with Steve for six months, and that in itself is a story, all I can say is that I survived and I only had to go to a healing counsellor once. I stayed with Steve during this time mostly because I had no where else to go at least that is what I felt. When my daughter and I first moved in with Steve, things were really good at the beginning and then family dynamics happened with one of his cousins who came to visit from out of town. This particular cousin, who was like a sister to Steve, was rude and mean to both my daughter and me. When she would say snide or mean, rude comments to me or my daughter, I would immediately want to say something to her, ask her why she was like that. Steve told me that if I were to ever confront her Steve would point to the door and say "There is the door." Or tell me water off a ducks back. I guess I was the duck. Steve told me that he may not agree with his cousin but that blood is thicker, and he would have to stand by his family, no matter what. Our stay went from good to bad when the cousin came to town and then it went from bad to worse as Steve would become distant and cold to me when his cousin was over at the house visiting.

There was one time, while living with Steve, a couple of weeks before my birthday that I asked Steve if he would take me out to dinner for my birthday; now it is important to understand that Steve was one who never believed in buying me gifts for birthdays or Christmas. Steve's reply was, " If I do that, you can't ask me for anything else". I agreed to this, I felt excited; we were going out for my birthday. During the next week, I watched Steve talking with one of his neighbours, as he said goodbye to her, he reached over and gave her shoulder a squeeze. I realized as I watched this that he never did that to me, he only gave me a hug goodbye when he left in the mornings and that was when I stood there and would look at him; he would only then reach out, give me a hug and a pat on my shoulder. During that week, it seemed that he hadn't touched me or hugged me; I was getting jealous of him petting the cat. He was showing the cat more affection than what he was showing me.

At the end of the week we went out to the local pub and as we were playing our second game of pool, I came up to Steve as he was finishing making his shot and I asked him if he would do something for me, Steve turned his head with distinction, looked directly at me "What" was his reply, I asked him if he would touch me, just touch me every once in a while. I told him that I was jealous of his cat for Christ's sake. Steve looked at me, and said" If I do that, do I still have to take you out for your birthday dinner?" I looked at him, turned and walked out. I didn't start to cry until I got into the vehicle, I just sat there, then the pain took over and the tears came. I had a good cry. There was so much pain from the indifference, the coldness and the cruelty that I was shown from Steve and his cousin. It felt as if everything was letting loose, holding myself, I sobbed. I very rarely cried, but this time, I couldn't hold it back and then I saw Steve walking towards the vehicle; I took a few deep breaths and managed to stop the flow of tears and the sobs. I dried my eyes. Steve got into the passenger seat, he looked at me, never saying a word, I had nothing to say, I was empty. We drove home in silence, nothing more was said. A long time ago I learnt to accept Steve, his ways and the way he treated me, I also had nowhere else to go. I tried to find another place to live, however, that wasn't easy given my situation at that time, so I put my feelings aside, accepted Steve once more for the way he was and why, and we continued on. We made love that night when we got home.

We went to The Klondike Rib and Salmon BBQ for my birthday dinner, and we did have a good time. Life continued. Throughout my stay at Steve's he showed me a lot of indifference, I would often ask him if we were going to continue to see each other once I moved out, his reply was always, "we'll see".I told him I didn't want a we'll see, I wanted either a yes or no . . . he could never give that to me.

I remember Steve saying to me about the fourth month into staying with him, (I always thought this came from his cousin), that he wanted me to do more around the house. More, I thought, lets see, I already wash and hang to dry all the clothes for all six of us, Steve had his three kids with us every other week, I wash the dishes after all the meals, I keep tiding up the house, vacumming, clean the bathrooms and wash the floors, feed the cat, give his Mother her baths, her pills, help her get ready for bed and dressed in the mornings, drive the kids to where they needed to go, take his eldest daughter out driving and I also paid him money to stay there, it wasn't much but at least it was something. Steve's brother was over one evening and after helping make supper, doing the dishes, putting their mother to bed I went over to Steve and I asked him "what else do you want me to do for you before I go to bed?"

4

Steve looked at me with a questioning look I reminded him of his earlier statement.

"You told me that you wanted me to do more around the house, so I was wondering what more do you want me to do for you?'

Steve never mentioned that to me again.

I guess I played with Steve at times just to get back at him, I never believed in throwing words back at people, however it was my only way of getting back at him at times. When I first moved in with Steve he said to me that his decision would be the final decision, I could come up with ideas but he had the final say. So when he would ask me simple things such as what I wanted for dinner, I would simply say, "what do you want?"

This after awhile frustrated Steve and he said to me, "you make the decision' why can't you make a simple decision for yourself?"

"But Steve, you told me that you would make all the decisions around here, so . . ."

My best one ever that I did for Steve was the gift that I gave to him the Christmas after I moved out. Steve never wanted me to buy him any gifts what so ever. In fact, around the second year that we were together I went on a trip and I brought Steve back a bottle of hot sauce, because he liked hot foods. When I gave the bottle of hot sauce to him, he got upset with me and told me that I should have bought him a jar of pickles then at least his kids could eat them. He told me that if I ever bought him anything again, that it would be the last thing I would ever buy him. (he did take the bottle of hot sauce home with him)

One thing I enjoy about a relationship is being able to see something in a store or make something with my own hands for the person I'm with and give it to them. It's a way of sharing myself with that person and Steve wasn't ready for that. Anyhow, after I moved out of Steve's it was coming up to Christmas and I got Steve a gift subscription for the Readers Digest Magazine. It was the gift that keeps on giving. Every month he would get a gift from me. In a way it was my payback for not being able to give him gifts over the years and I got a chuckle out of it too.

At the end of our six months I managed to buy a house. A couple of months after we moved out, Steve and I had come to an arrangement, our relationship was one of convenience. Until one of us found someone else that we wanted to be with, we would spend time with one another when it was convenient. It was mostly for the sexual pleasures that we shared and sometimes for the companionship.

I felt a love for Steve, even though he couldn't say to me he loved me, I often felt, that deep down, he did feel something for me. He did tell me he loved me on a couple of occasions, two to be exact. Once, just shortly after I moved in to his house, he was lying in bed, his back was to me as I climbed in next to him, and he rolled over, kissed me and looking into my eyes, said to me, I do love you. He kissed me again and then he rolled back over. I smiled to myself, and hugged him. The next morning, he said he couldn't remember anything from the night before as he was drunk. That was guideline number one that he almost didn't stick to. Getting drunk and saying it doesn't count.

I had joined eharmony just after moving out of Steve's house. I felt so lonely, and eharmony was a safe and secure online dating network. They ask you so many questions, in fact they will match you on twenty-nine different criteria, and you do pay for their matching services. I did meet a couple of men on eharmony that I went through the whole communication process with, the questionnaires, the waiting for responses, the continuous matches that a person receives ; I could have spent hours just checking out the men that eharmony was sending me for matches. There was this one guy I met who was not from Whitehorse, who seemed so eager and sounded so wonderful, he wanted to send me flowers for my new home. He managed to contact a friend of mine by phone. After talking with him, she told me he sounded very sincere, and very interested in me, then she hesitated, and asked me if I had ever talked with him on the phone myself; I told her no, that we just had emailed each other, she mentioned to me that there was something about him that made her feel uncomfortable when he spoke, she mentioned obsession, which I too felt in a couple of his emails. There was something about the guy that didn't seem right, so I listened to my intuition, my friends would have been proud, and I stopped communicating with him. Anyhow, after having a couple of bad experiences with online dating, I felt somewhat leery but I didn't give up, I knew that true love had to exist somewhere, see I'm a complete romantic and I do believe that there is someone out there, you just have to find him. For me, someone who doesn't meet a lot of single men, online dating seemed to be the way to go. So I kept my subscription to eharmony, after all the couples on the commercials seem happy and I had talked with several people who had met their partners/ wives/husbands online and were in happy loving relationships, there was hope. So no, I was not going to give up. Except for the fact that I was getting about twenty matches from eharmony a day, of which I deleted, I wouldn't even look at them anymore. Steve and I had basically found that comfort zone in our relationship of convenience; however, after close to ten months of this, I felt that I wanted something more, I wanted a boyfriend. I wanted to have that special someone with me, to share my life with and that someone who would spend time with me and my daughter and do things together; I wanted a family that, dare I say it, I wanted the husband and wife scene. I wanted to meet someone who wanted to marry me, make me and my daughter a part of their life, and us a part of theirs. I guess I had heard so many people telling me that they were going to weddings here and there or that they were getting married and lets face it, I'm forty four years old, I want to get married and have that secure feeling with someone. That this is the person that I matter to and that I will be supporting and be supported by for the rest of our lives, and together we would work towards that common goal, such as taking a trip to some exotic tropical island, or doing renovations to a house . . . taking care of the yard together, cutting wood together for our fireplace . . . It's funny but when I think of having the privilege of calling someone my husband or having someone call me their wife, those labels, and yes they are labels, that label would give me, at least I think that the label would give me a sense of belonging, and that was what I was wanting. I knew Steve would never give that to me. So the day that I received a notice from eharmony notifying me that I had a match requesting 'fast track communication', I opened up my email and what really caught my eye was that the guy was from home, from where I lived, so yes I was interested, after all Whitehorse is such a small city surely I knew this guy or someone knew him, and we would be able to meet. I didn't delete him; instead I read his email.

# 2

# GETTING TO KNOW YOU

**Messages between you and Davis**

Sender: Davis

Date: 08/06/2008 05:19PM PDT

Message: Hi Tess,

It's nice to come across your profile. I joined this sit in search of someone I can start a new life with, someone who I can trust and who is honest. I have read your profile over and over again, and like what I have read about you. It is interesting. I hope we will be very honest to each other and open. I really want to know everything about you and will tell you everything you need to know about me. Hope to hear from you soon, Take care.

Davis

Sender: Tess

Date: 08/06/2008 05:27PM PDT

Message: Hi Davis,

Your message has intrigued me, to be honest, I have not read any of your profile, so I know nothing about you other than your age, height and you love your mom. Always a good sign. I am a very open and honest person, so much so it has sometimes gotten me into difficult

8

situations. I would like to know about you as well, one question I should ask you I guess is who are you? What do you do? What do you enjoy?

Looking forward to hearing from you, Tess

Sender: Davis

Date: 08/07/2008 05:34AM PDT

Message: Good Morning Tess,

It's nice to hear from you, I hope you had a good sleep. First of all, I want you to know I find you really pretty. AS I told you earlier, I truly want the opportunity to get to know you, all of you. I was raised by a strong catholic mom and being an only child she taught me so much about caring for people and accepting them as who they are—. respect, honor, dignity, honesty, compassion, and love were some of the strongest features that were instilled in me.l like to take things at their natural rhythm when it comes to relationships. I adore the arts, having been involved in them in one way or another since I was little. Love the movies, walking, riding in my sports car. I tend towards shyness at times, but when I am comfortable with the people around me, I'm a lot of fun. I like my peace and quiet—too much noise/activity around me can make me anxious. But I can also adjust/adapt quite quickly to new circumstances. I am deeply romantic, optimistic, hopeful, wise, smart & stubborn. I have a good, honest heart and don't like being lied to. If you are straight with me from the get-go, I'm more likely to grow to care for you. I am affectionate by nature, but believe that trying to sense the boundaries of others shows caring, sensitivity and a willingness to look beyond yourself to see that person instead of only being concerned with your own desires and needs. We all have a right to be selfish at times, but if you are truly going to relate well to someone else, you have to be willing to acknowledge the compromises inherent in any relationship and if you truly care for someone, wanting that person's happiness and well-being should be a high priority this is how i feel . . . I've been extremely candid and hope to hear from you and learn more about your likes/dislikes as well as more about your life. Take care and enjoy the day.

Davis

Sender: Tess

Date: 08/07/2008 08:32PM PDT

Message: Hello Davis,

I've just spent the last half hour writing to you and I think that it never went through, so if you have received two letters from me, one sounding as if it is repeating itself, I apologise, but I wanted to say Thank You for your letter. Your mother sounds like a wonderful woman. I too have had three strong women in my life that have instilled morals and qualities that I live my life by. The qualities are trust, respect, honesty, love and humour. I believe that in any relationship, these qualities must be there to have a good lasting relationship. The saying 'truth may hurt, but lies destroy', is very true. I believe in the truth. I also believe in building a good strong relationship built on the qualities of trust, honesty, respect, love and humor. I'm a very affectionate and caring person. I believe in others and I believe in the good of others. I have been selfish lately in focusing on my daughter and myself, however I feel that we needed to have this time together. I agree with you as well in regards to being able to compromise in a relationship. I find though that with the foundation of respect in a relationship, that compromise comes easy and it works both ways. I wish I hadn't lost the first letter that I wrote to you, as I now have to get going, there is more that I want to tell you, however that will have to wait. I did want to say that you do look familiar to me, I don't think that we've ever met, you have a memorable look to you, so I may have seen you in passing. I will be going away for the weekend, so if you e-mail me I won't be able to get back to you until after the weekend. I do look forward to hearing from you again, you are a wonderful writer . . . Have a great weekend

Tess

Sender: Davis

Date: 08/08/2008 02:50PM PDT

Message: Hello Tess,

It feels so good to hear from you again. I hope your day is going well. I didn't get the first e-mails, but hope you can get time to tell me more about yourself. My dad came to Italy to do business, and that was how he met my mom. I was born in Italy on the 5th of October, schooled

10

there. Two years after they met, dad went back to the US and we didn't hear from him again. When I was nineteen years I decided to take a trip to the US to see my dad for the first time, and that was my first time of being to the US.

I first lived in New Mexico, then moved to Arizona to stay on my own, then later I moved to Dallas, TX just in search of my dad. While in Dallas, I met a man who liked me for my ways and was interested in doing business with me, so I had to move to Chicago with him. I moved back to Dallas where I started to do my own business. Then I heard my dad was working for an oil company that was located in Canada's Victorian Oil Town at a point in time, so I later moved to Ottawa then, Alberta, where I saw my dad for the first time. It was much joy to see him but we would not relate to well. I was very happy I saw my dad but I decided to find my way and started doing my own business again. I was interested in the oil business, and was introduced to it by one of his workers. I see my business as a responsibility, and a dream come true, I thank God I have made it this far and thank my mom for her support through the hard times and for having taken care of me till I was able to stand on my own. My dad's worker though my dad introduced me to something that has brought me much wealth, but my mom introduced me into something that no one can ever take from me. She showed my how to love and care, how to accept people as they are and always be there for them. How to be honest and to sincere. She always said Davis, no matter what, never lie to anyone, for the truth will always set you free. Even if the truth will kill you, let it kill you. Always be honest in all your ways. And today, I realized all what she showed me is helping me in all my ways and to be the best man I can be. I have always had it in mind to do my own business since I was a kid. I never had my dad around, so I saw it as a challenge to make something for myself and my mom who had to do all she could to make me who I am today. I started to import raw materials when I was in the state, and I sometimes bought their finished product and exported it.

Later I went to study project Planning and became a project planner. I realized my interest was in the oil business, so I opened my consulting firm with the idea I have in planing and oil. I later started mining oil and still does enjoy mining it. It's all I know how to do best. I am a very honest, understanding, caring and lovely Davis.

I have never married, but I lived with a woman once. She had to leave because of her unfaithfulness. I try to have the most time for my partner, no matter how busy I can be most of the times. I have no kids but love kids so much. Oops, have to go now, I hope I have been as open as I could, and hope to hear from you too. I will be leaving to Orlando on Sunday. If you are ok with us talking on phone, please let me have your number and I will call you. Take care.

Davis

*I wrote to Davis telling him a little bit more about me, unfortunately I lost this one e-mail somewhere in cyberspace. In this e-mail I told Davis about my "friendship with Steve. That we would spend time together but we were not in any type of committed relationship, in fact just after sending this email to Davis, Steve and I went to Skagway for the weekend. It was during the weekend, while going through the Skagway gardens alone, Steve didn't want to join me, that I walked around the gardens thinking it was such a romantic spot, it would be so nice to be able to share this with someone, holding my hand, sharing the moments. I felt empty inside, knowing that I would never share moments like this being with Steve. I thought about a man named Davis.*

*I gave Davis my hotmail account so he could e-mail me without having to go through eharmony. I have to tell you that Davis's picture on his eharmony profile showed him to be a very distinguished, handsome gentle man, ( his eyes were gentle looking). A picture I had no difficulty looking at what so ever. His response to my—email I received in my hotmail account. eharmony was no longer  needed.*

From:Davis

Sent: August 12, 2008 5:43:28 AM

Good Morning Tess,

I hope you had a good sleep and are getting ready for the day. It's 8:32 here in Orlando, I guess it will be about 5AM back home. I am glad to know this much about you, it seems we have all had over part of experience, and as long as life still goes on, we are yet to have a greater and good experience. A happier one than before. I look forward to getting to know you that much. You got me a bit scared when I read about you having someone you see once in a while. I want to know if you are ready for a committed relationship, and why you don`t want to be committed to the one you see once in a while. I am glad to know you are in good terms with your children's father. By doing that, you let go all the past and look forward to the future. You kind of share one thing with my mom, and I know how it felt at that time. I am talking about the man who went and never came back. It hurts, and it only takse a woman with a very strong heart to go through it. I respect you for that and respect all mothers who have to go through such experience. I really appreciate mothers because I think they are the best thing God has ever created. I feel so very sad when I travel to some part of the world and meet kids who have no mothers, that is why I am working on having an NGO to take care of these kids. I am almost through with it and will start working once I am done with this last consignment I am working on. I will retire so I can have time for my family and those kids who need mothers. I am a very caring, understanding, honest and lovely person to be with, and hope I can share that part of me sometime soon. I am getting more interested in knowing more about you, I look forward to meeting you sometime soon. I wanted to talk to you on the phone because I thought by doing that, we can get to know each other a bit better so once you are with me, we will be able to relate much better. But I respect your decision and will let things be the way you want it to go. I am a very goa—orientated person who believes goals are an important thing to want to achieve. This is what keeps us moving forward. I am an avid car guy, Formula 1 racing is a must see on TV and in person. I'm not a wrench—head, that's what mechanics are for. Love to drive top of the line exotics like Ferrari and Lamborghini . . . I have traveled to Europe (London, Paris, Frankfurt) and Asia often for work; one of my favorite places is Singapore.

I love to cook, listen to a wide range of music. Don't like to watch sports, or television really, unless it's in a hotel room. I love cities, travel, road trips. I get lost on purpose. I can be spontaneous, in fact I'm sometimes better at living in the now than I am at planning. I'm a problem solver by nature. I thrive in absurd situations, they often make the best stories. I have to get going, have a meeting coming soon. Take care and hope to hear from you soon.

Davis

On Tue, Aug 12, 2008 at 10:12 PM, Tess wrote:

Hello Davis,

How was your day? My day was filled with meeting new people. You asked me about whether or not I'm ready for a committed relationship, I am, I just have to meet the right person and hopefully I'm almost there. You also asked me why I don't want to be in a committed relationship with the one I see once in a while, I'll call him my friend. We were in a committed relationship so to say; we've known each other for over four years now. Just over three years ago I was working and I hurt my arm, causing a lot of damage to the soft tissue in my shoulder, wrist, elbow and neck. I ended up being off from work for a few months, I was covered by a compensation plan for a while and then they sent me a letter stating that I was better, which I wasn't. Unfortunately, once they stop compensation, they stop even helping you to get back to work, so I had to turn to my work's staff accommodation dept. to get put into a position that I could do without having to do any heavy lifting. My job requires a lot of heavy lifting, nursing it involves transferring and moving people all the time. Anyhow, my work did not have anything for me, and at the end of December I was running out of money, I lost my house that we were living in. I was, unable to pay the rent. I did help out a friend of mine who was going through cancer treatment at that time; she had a supportive living home. Unfortunately it wasn't enough.

So my friend offered my daughter and I to move in with him for six months until I got myself back on my feet so to say. I put everything I had into storage and my boys had to find their own place to live and my daughter and I moved in with him. It was ok; there were family dynamics at work. His mother wasn't doing very well and being that I was off work, I spent a lot of time with her, taking her shopping, to appointments. I checked her blood pressure and blood glucose levels as she was a diabetic. I also did regular foot care on her. Unfortunately my friend's cousin who was like a sister to him, who didn't live in Whitehorse did not like me helping her aunt, so this didn't help matters. During this time, I did discover that yes, my friend appreciated my help. His mother moved in to the house during the time my daughter and I were there, however his cousin's mannerisms towards me and my daughter were really nasty, she was up for about a month at this time. People can be so cruel, anyhow it was during this time that I realized that I wanted someone who would support me in a relationship, and support

14

me as a person. We knew each other, saw each other for close to four years at this time and during that time, even living together, this seems petty, but he only gave me a Christmas gift and a birthday gift once, and that was our first Christmas that we had together just after we met. It's nice to get a gift or even flowers or even a card once in a while just as a symbol, a gesture saying that you are thought of. That never happened. I don't want a relationship like this. He also has issues from when he got divorced which I see as a reason for his behaviour. You may be wondering as to why or how I can still call this guy a friend, let alone spend time with him once in a while. I have come to terms with the way he is, how he is, I understand where he comes from and I have accepted the way he is, but I haven't accepted him as a committed part of my life. He also, would never include me to share a part of his life. This was very evident when we were together; if his cousin didn't want me at a family get—together I didn't go. So that is why I am not in a committed relationship with him, I'm honest with him, he knows that I am looking to meet someone, and he has stated to me that he hopes that I do find someone who will treat me right, he's told me in the past that I deserve to be treated nice. So that's that.

During this time I did get a job at a doctor's office as a nurse, it was a great experience and I learned a lot from the doctor and have developed a respect for what doctors have to go through.

Shortly before October, which was the end of our six month agreement, I won my appeal with compensation and was awarded back pay, which enabled me to buy my house, so my daughter and I now have a place to live, our very own place. I also received a call from my work shortly after Christmas and they finally found a position for me that did not require heavy lifting, and that is doing the job that I'm doing now. My arm is getting better, stronger. I have kept positive throughout my whole ordeal, I never gave up, I don't believe in giving up, and I believe in going for what you want and fighting for it. I also believe that things happen for a reason, and no matter how negative things may seem, you have to look for the positive and for a lesson learned.

I'm getting very interested in getting to know you as well. You sound like a wonderful person, full of experiences that I would love to hear about. Things you've seen and things you've been able to do, I could only imagine. I would love to hear about your experiences some time. The closest I've ever come to seeing a Lamborghini is at a car show in

Calgary. Nice . . . I also like the fact that you believe in helping others, kids that need help, you're a very impressive sounding person.

I have sponsored for a few years now, two kids with World Vision, one in Chile and one in Thailand.

I enjoy cooking, music, dancing, and a lot of different things. I have just started to travel, nothing exotic as of yet. I did go to Las Vegas with a friend of mine.

I too enjoy getting lost, I believe that you really see the place only when you discover you're lost, and you have to really look around. I like to work with my hands. I enjoy doing pottery, watercolour painting and writing. One of my goals is to get published a children's story that I wrote a while ago, it's been a goal of mine for years and I'm getting to where I'm ready to start the process. Sending in this story to a publisher, I find a very difficult thing to do: it's my creation that I'm sending away and the first thing you're told is to be prepared for is rejection. I keep telling myself that Dr. Seuss got rejected two hundred and thirty two times I believe, so I need to just push myself and send it off.

I still am wondering about you, and when you came to Whitehorse and why? I had better get going, I do hope to hear from you again soon, Tess

From: Davis

Sent: August 13, 2008 7:20:13 AM

Hello Tess,

Nice to know this much about you. I hope you had a good sleep and ready for the day. I have waited onto God, to give me someone so special, someone so sweet, and someone I can share everything with. I have been alone all this time because I kept myself working hard and not thinking of going into relationships anymore. I have not shared this with anyone, and have not talked about it since. I was once in love, and that was my first true love. She moved in with me, but we were not married. We stayed together for three years, then one day I came back from a trip only to find this woman on our bed with another man. I was so hurt, and felt betrayed. I thought the world was going to end for me. She said I was not in town most of the times and she needed someone around all the time. I felt like taking my life. I did everything to make this woman happy. I sometime took her with me on my trips, and took her to wherever she had always wanted to go. I never thought she could do this to me till that day when I saw her with my eyes. Since then I had no feelings again. I couldn't love and didn't want to come near a woman. Within the first two years I always felt the pain when I saw women, but with time I got healed and moved on. I made up my mind never again to fall in love or come close to a woman. But with time I learned to forgive, but before I could, I had to forgive myself first. Then I had to love myself, so I stopped hurting myself and learned to love and care for myself again, to care and be the kind man I used to be. This took me years, but thank God I am here today and happy again. I decided to join eharmony to see if I could find someone, all I prayed for was to find someone who knows how it feels to go through pain, someone who knows how it feels being betrayed and so on.

I finally have this confidence that I could give my heart, soul and mind to someone who deserves it, I just hope you are the one. I feel I can trust you. There are just somethings that words couldn't describe. I have always since wanted to live in a place where I find my quiet, somewhere I could find much happiness. The first time I came to Whitehorse, I really found much peace and everything I have ever wanted there. I decided to move there and I moved in two months later. I am now in Orlando because I have a contract and will be leaving to London soon. That will be my last deal, after, I will start my NGO, and make much time for my family. I have to go now, I will mail you later and tell you much more about my work. Take care and have a nice day.

Davis

On 8/13/08, Tess wrote:

Hello Davis,

I want to say thank you for sharing that part of you that obviously was a very painful part of your life. It sounds that you have made peace with yourself. It sounds as if this happened quite a few years ago. It's something that we always carry with us, our past, even having moved on, and the past is still with us; I know for myself, I had a hard time trusting. When I first met my friend and he would tell me he was busy, the first thing that would pop into my head was, he's with someone else. I would have to talk myself through it, the feelings, the fear, because I had it happen to me—the lies, the unfaithfulness; it took   a lot to believe in myself again. My friend also helped me with this because he wasn't with anyone, and he would reinforce that because he would tell me if he was going to see anyone else he promised he would tell me before the fact. It took a couple of years but I was able to begin to trust. And I feel that I'm ready to trust again, so like you I need honesty for the trust to be there, and I believe that you are being honest with me as well, so once again I thank you. I also believe that what has happened to us in our past can strengthen our character, hopefully for the positive and we need to carry that with us so we can enhance our other relationships.

So on that note, I'm not too sure how I feel, ( I'm just going to ramble here about my feelings) When I think of meeting you, I feel excited and at the same time not scared but, well maybe scared is the word. There is always this expectation of how a person is and then when you meet do we live up to those expectations? When you mention your sports cars, I've never sat in a sports car, I've lived a very somewhat sheltered life, and you have travelled the world. As I said you have done things, just by what you've told me so far that I could only dream about. I guess my question to you is what do you expect from our meeting? Myself, you sound wonderful, I hope that when we do meet there is a connection between us, however if there isn't, would you please be honest with me in that, and I will be honest with you. If our first meeting each other goes well then can we agree to go on a date However if it doesn't then lets be honest with each other.

One of the things I am looking for in a relationship is romance. Romance to me comes in many forms, in many different ways; even a simple message saying 'I'm thinking about you', can mean so much. I am a very romantic person, I have so much inside of me to give, romantically, caring, just wanting to love someone who will share with me their love, and share with me their life and be willing to share themselves not only with me but with my daughter, because she is a part of my life. It's been a long time since I've been given the opportunity to be in a relationship that is open, respectful, affectionate, romantic, and filled with love, everything, When you talk about being ready to love, I want that, I guess that's what scares me, I'm afraid of hoping that it might happen and then to lose it would hurt so much, I think you may understand what I'm trying to say. Saying that, I also say to myself, that to never try, I will never gain; I've also said that with love there is pain, but to never feel the pain means you've never really loved. Again I ramble.

One thing about me is that, Whitehorse is my home. I want to live here, my daughter loves her school, and she will be going into grade two this year, so it's important for me that she continues with her schooling here.

I love to travel, I love the cities, the excitement of the city, the lights, the theatres, the restaurants, the variety, and seeing everything that there is to see that is possible within the time limits; it's fascinating. I enjoy what the different places have to offer and everywhere I've been, there is a beauty to that place that is it's own, and I have often thought how wonderful it would be to be able to stay a month or two on Vancouver Island (my daughter and I just got back from there two weeks ago) and then I really enjoy coming back home. Driving to Skagway this weekend I looked out at the mountains, the lake, and just had this warm feeling inside of me, and I was in complete wonder of how beautiful and how lucky we are to be here, no major city just raw simple beauty. Going out has made me appreciate my lifestyle that I have here.

Davis, have you spent any time in Atlin? I would like to write more, but it is now 11:00 and I need to go to bed, I look forward to hearing from you again, I enjoy your e-mails and your honesty.

Have a wonderful day. Tess

From:Davis Barienda

Sent: August 14, 2008 9:46:25 AM

Hello Tess,

I am very glad to be communicating with you. You are the kind of woman I have been looking for all this while, and really look forward to having a very good and healthy relationship with you. I am not scared of meeting you, I know and feel deep inside me that when we meet, we will be able to meet our expectations. I will be very honest with you about everything Ok. I want the best relationship, one that is filled with much happiness. I am also looking for romance in relationships, I am also a very romantic person, and have so much inside of me to give.

Just wanting to love someone who will share with me their love, and share with me their life and be willing to share themselves not only themselves, but everything that makes them. I want a relationship that is open, respectful, affectionate, romantic, and filled with love, everything.

I love to take a walk to the park after dinner, but love it much more holding hands with someone special. As I told you before, I like to take trips to somewhere cozy on my of—days, and to other places. Love to be on the mountains, see the lakes, cities and so on. Once again, I would love to go with someone really special to me, and hope we can do that someday. I like to drive-inn, with my partner and surprise her with a picnic. We, sitting outside, under the stars, on a rug next to the car. With candles to add that special touch, and watched the movie in each other's arms . . . it sure is a moment to cherish. I like to take my partner to the lake, have a nice picnic supper table, set candles everything. After we eat, take a walk to the shore area. Take a blanket with her and hold each other and watch the stars. You never know it might just be the night of your life.

I like to go to some kind of water side without my partner and set everything up. Place a picnic table out and set up so she can have a candle light dinner. Go pick up the food and my partner and go watch a sunset. After that enjoy a candle-light dinner under the stars. I know once in a while there may be too much to do at work, and my partner would be tired, so I would like on the spur of the moment to pick her up in a limo and to spend the night paying attention to each other and just enjoying doing whatever we wanted with no interruptions from kids, work, friends etc. I called a limo co. I would walk across the street to a local florist, pick up flowers, and stop at a local tavern to make sure that her favorite drink would be in the limo. I would call my partner at work and tell her I would pick her up. I would change into dress clothes and wait for her at the side entrance to her building. The look on her face when I put the window down and called her name makes it all worthwhile.

There are much more romantic side of me that you would know as we get along. I finally have this confidence that I could give my heart, soul and mind to someone who deserves it, I just hope you are the one. I know I can trust. There are just somethings that words couldn't describe as I always say. I have a meeting with the bank manager. There is this project I am working on and will be leaving to London soon. I like to take over business, but this time around, I am havinga little problem, which I am going to resolve when I get to London. I will make sometime this afternoon and send you a mail to let you know more about my work. Take care, have the best of the day and let me hear from you soon. I will be thinking of you.

Davis

From:Davis

Sent: August 14, 2008 3:16:58 PM

Dear Tess,

I hope your day is going well. Mine went well and is almost about to end. I just want you to know a little about my work. I really want to meet you and spend some time with you. I just ended my conference call meeting to London some minutes ago. I might be leaving for London sooner than expected. I will want us to plan on our meeting soon as I get back. I will love to spend time with you. I will give you the details of my coming back. I want to get much closer and know each other much better if that is ok with you. I seek contracts to mine and sell oil all over the world. There are people and companies that reward contractors with the right certificate to miners, the contractors own elegant to these companies and individuals who reward the contract, and account to them with everything that happens with the contract. But mine is different. I pay this so called contract rewarders off, so I can have full ownership of the project that is to be done. I don't like to work under someone and have never. The most is being into partnership. But I had a bad experience with that before, and have made my mind up since never to go into partnership. But I will go into partnership with you if you want us to . . . lol?

There is a lot of money in mining, but very stressful and tiring. You also realize you never have much time for yourself. I have decided this is going to be my last deal, after I resign and start with something else. Something that can give me the much time I need to be with my partner. I have come to realize money is not all. You can get everything you want when you have it, but true happiness is to find in one special person. I feel true happiness and warmness just reading and thinking about you, and can't imagine how it will be like spending special time with you. I am so excited to know you and will be very truthful to you in all my ways. I hope your daughter is going good, I'd love to meet her too. I sure can bet that she is as pretty and nice as her mom. My number here is 104-555-8464. Call me when you feel like talking. I will be thinking about you. Mi permetta di sentire da lei al più presto, meaning let me hear from you soon.

Davis

On 8/14/08, Tess wrote:

Hello Davis,

I've been re-reading your e-mail over and over, I close my eyes and I feel like you've walked into my dream. Your words, you have taken my breath away, and started my heart racing . . . I can only hope for such a dream to come true. You shouldn't be setting me up like this, but WOW. I was thinking you make it sound like you can give me so much enjoyment and pleasure and I will do the same for you, I can't appear at your work in a limo, but there are other things I would like to do for you, one thing that came to my mind, I would write a poem, it's been a long time since I've written any poetry but you have inspired me, with the emotions and excitement that you instilled in me today, is this real . . . and yes I am looking forward to meeting you.

Please forgive me, but I won't phone you right now, I've thought about it . . . a lot . . . but I have hesitation, I still feel that meeting first is important, you mentioned you would let me know when you will be getting back, I look forward to that day, again I close my eyes, and smile. Thank you, see you don't even have to do anything you can just tell me what you would like to do and I'll smile.

Now, there have been a couple of questions that I still have. First how long have you been in Whitehorse, you mentioned that you moved here after a couple of months after seeing Whitehorse. When was that and where did you live before moving here? And have you been to Atlin BC at all?

There is something else I would like to know about you, how are you at dealing with situations that don't always go the way they should? Myself, I can feel disappointed, but I usually can go with it and I don't get huffy or stomp around or slam things, I don't like yelling at my partner or being yelled at; on that note, I must confess that I do raise my voice to my daughter at times. I think it's the single mom syndrome, when it's just me telling her what to do or she can't do that, she tends to tune me out sometimes and the voice needs to be raised in order for her to hear, and saying that, we are working on that, because I don't like having to get upset with my daughter. She is seven, she is beautiful, she has a face like an angel and she can  be stubborn, sometimes in a good way, she is independent and she is assertive, I once got a phone call from her grade 1 teacher and in the conversation he told me that he had to inform her that he was the teacher of the class, not her. She likes to guide people so to say, she has a wonderful sense of humor, and she's a girl, what more can I say. She does make me laugh.

How are you with kids? That's the one thing about me, I'm a packaged deal, I do believe that is what they call it, whoever they may be.

Davis, I have to get going, I'll try and write again later if I can, one thing I would be very interested in, is what it is that you are thinking of doing when you finish with the mining contracts.

Looking forward to hearing from you Tess

❀Here's a flower for you, from me . . . just to say I've been thinking of you . . . a lot

From: Tess

Sent: August 15, 2008 5:06:37 AM

Good Morning Davis,

It's just after 4:00am, I'm awake because I had to pick my son up at the bus station, he's just arrived back from Penticton last week from a wedding, and now I can't sleep, so I thought I would write to you. I want to share with you one of my life—long dreams and that is to write a novel, a love story. The story I want to tell is the story of my great grandparents. I'll start at the beginning and introduce you into how this story came about to begin with. My mother and step—father were going on vacation to Australia in 1994 I believe it was, and my Mom took with her my great grandmother's birth certificate to see if she could find any information about her, being that she was born in Australia. I can't remember the name of the town, anyhow my great grandmother's name was Mary Stewart before she married my great grandfather whose name was Frank Henry. Now before I go on, I should tell you that when my mom was growing up, her father, whose parents it is we're talking about, never mentioned anything about any relatives, as far as my mom's dad knew, there were no living relatives on his side. (my grandfather passed away about ten to twelve years prior to this ; his sister Rita, still lived in Atlin but she too knew of no living relatives).

When my mom and stepdad reached the town where my great grandmother Mary Stewart was born, my mom opened the phone book to the name Stewart and started at the top of the list and began to make phone calls. The first Stewart she called turned out to be a relative, who had no idea there were living relatives in Canada, she knew that Mary had gone to Canada, she in fact had letters still from Mary, saying that she was in Canada and was married. Well the following year, these new-found relatives came to Whitehorse and to Atlin and stayed a month with us visiting and a week before they were to leave, Margaret, mom's relative, sat my mom and her sister, my Aunt Georgia, down and told them that before she left Australia to come to Canada she received a letter in the mail, a letter from a gentleman by the name of Greg Henry. Greg had sent out letters to families with the last name of Stewart throughout Australia to see if anyone had any information of a lady named Mary Stewart who worked as a maid for a family by the last name of Henry. Now Margaret, after meeting my mom or it may have been from a letter Mary had written, knew that Mary had married a gentleman by the name of Frank Henry, so she phoned this Greg Henry and told him that she may have information for him. She also told him that she was going to Canada and she would find out for sure if there was any connection. So when she sat my mom and aunt down, she knew that whom Greg sought was indeed my great grandmother and grandfather. As soon as Margaret told my mom and aunt this story, they immediately phoned Greg and introduced themselves. Now here is where the story starts. It seems that Mary Stewart was the maid for a minister, Frank Henry and his wife Isabelle, for a couple of years. Frank and Isabelle had five kids together. Mary, I guess loved to gamble and it seems that Frank did as well.

Well one day Frank leaves by train on a trip and a few days later his wife Isabelle receives a letter from a gentleman that Frank apparently met while on the train. This letter stated that this gentleman had met Isabelle's husband and they had got along quite well, that this gentleman invited Frank to go fishing for a day before continuing with his trip, and during this fishing trip Frank lost his footing in the boat, fell into the lake or river and drowned. This gentleman was not able to save him or to retrieve the body. After receiving the letter and having the police look into it, it was decided that Frank had staged his own death based on the fact that there was a discrepancy between the post mark on the envelope and the date on the actual letter and it was discovered that a couple matching the description of Frank Henry and Mary Stewart were seen boarding a boat to Vancouver. Greg was able to trace Frank and Mary as far as Winnipeg and then there was nothing. Unfortunately for Isabelle, not only was she left alone with the five kids, but the insurance money that Frank thought she would get because of his so called accidental death, she never received. I don't know if he ever knew that or not. Once Mary and Frank were in Canada they went to Winnipeg and my Uncle Marty was born there and then they went north and settled in Atlin, there was a gold rush happening in Atlin at that time, and my mom's dad and Aunt Rita were born, in Atlin. My great-grandfather became a minor in Atlin and no word was ever mentioned about their lives in Australia.

This was exciting for my mom and Aunt Georgia, for now there are half brothers and sisters to my grandfather who had kids; an extension to our family. The only hard part was to tell my Aunt Rita. She wouldn't believe it at first, and then she felt as if her whole life had been a lie and then after she thought about it for a while, and she was told that these new found relatives a son of one of her half brothers was coming over to Canada to meet this other side of the family, she started to accept it, and it was about a year later that my aunt passed away, but at least she knew the truth.

So I want to go back to the beginning in my story and tell the love story that happened between Frank and Mary. From what I can understand, Frank was a wonderful person, a man who gave to his friends and to his family, so I want to find out what happened, and write about the tragedy and the love story that happened between Frank, Mary and Isabelle.

Well now that you know that scandal runs in my family, I should see if I can fall asleep for a couple of hours before having to get up and go to work. Have a great day, and please do let me know when you will be back . . .

Take care Tess

From:Davis

Sent: August 16, 2008 11:05:18 AM

Dear Tess,

Please pardon me for not being able to mail you for a while, I had a little problem with my connectivity, and have been very busy. But I have been thinking about you so much in everything I do. I was living in Pentiction before I moved to Yukon. I have lived in other places before, but for now I like Yukon very much and have no plans to leave there. I love my house and everything around me. I have been to Atlin once, I was there for three days. I have lived at Yukon for over five years now. I get very disappointed when there is a situation that doesn't go the way they should, but I usually go with it because I understand things don't always go the way we wish it goes. I like kids so much and love it when they are around me. I will like to know much more about your daughter, and will love to be close to her when I get the chance to meet her. You have not yet told me her name. It feels good to open my mail find your e-mail there. When I think of you, I see you smiling at me, I also see you serious at work, I see you and me taking trips to some nice places in the world, having dinner and holding arms while we talk. I see us all the time having good time together and wish that really happen between us.

Some of the most superb feelings and tingling emotions come from what love an Angel, such as yourself, and I make. Our world, as we have come to see it, has no bearing and an infinite boundary when people in love are locked lips to lips. No one person can sever that bond of nothing but pure affection and intimate passion. We are the Angels of Our Heaven and with merely our names to live with. A name, which consists of nothing more than symbols of a language taken for granted as I read in a book some years ago. I would soon rather speak nothing.

A true test of love of which we hope to accomplish soon merely by the elucidation in one's eyes. Earth moves with such apathy that only Our Heaven can keep the pace of our devotion for one another. As slow as the heartbeat of a Goliath at rest. Why would the world seem so passive? I believe it is a chance for us to make our own time to spend finding true love. It is what binds the thoughts of all beings trying to

understand it. I have to leave it here now, I will e-mail you again later. I am dying to talk with you soon and to meet you. I hope you can sometime soon give a chance for us to talk on phone before we meet. Tell me what you will be doing today. Take care, have a nice day. I think of you a lot and will be thinking of you in everything I do.

Davis

From: Tess

Sent: August 16, 2008 11:18:37 AM

Hello Davis,

I've been sitting here thinking about you, wondering as to where you may be. How are things going for you? Are you in London or still in Orlando? As I have said earlier I have been thinking about you, I've been thinking of phoning you, I won't call, I would hate to interrupt a meeting or call at an inconvenient time. This is a big step for me, and I do want to get to know you some more, so I will give you my phone number if you would like to call me. I will be home today (Saturday and most of Sunday) but I will be driving my son to Atlin Sunday evening, no cell phone coverage in Atlin. My home number is 311-555-2121. My cellphone is 311-555-0101. I do get nervous thinking about talking to you for the first time.

Take care of yourself, Tess

From: Tess

Sent: August 16, 2008 1:03:36 PM

Davis,

You give me much warmth as well reading your e-mails. When I think of you I feel the warmth and the closeness that we can share, I get the feeling that our wants and needs are quite similar. You are a beautiful writer; I would like to let you know a couple of things about me, because I have not been in a relationship so to speak for a long time. One, that I feel might develop hopefully between us, and I do know that I want to find the happiness that comes with a good relationship. When I first meet someone, I tend to get very, oh what is the word, closed in, maybe, if it feels like things are too much too fast, and I get uncomfortable. I would like to take things one step at a time to get to know each other, then I guess it's up to us as to how fast our steps will move once we do meet, and feel about each other. I'm telling you this because I would like for things to go well between us, and I know this about myself. My Daughter's name is Zoey, my sons are Chad and Zack. They're twenty. I'm hoping that I will get a chance to build my shed today. I bought one from Sears and now it needs to be put together piece by piece. My sons and one of their friends are supposed to help me later this afternoon.It's starting to cloud over so I hope that it doesn't rain. I just finished building my deck the weekend before last with the help of my daughter's other brother, whose name is Johnathan. (He's twenty three or twenty four, we just met him last year and he's from Germany.) I'm hoping that I will be able to get my back yard organized by the end of August.

Yesterday I spent the day with my daughter; she had been in Atlin with

my mom for the last week and arrived home Friday morning. I took the day off because I had no one to look after her; she was originally going to come home in the evening. Well we went for lunch to the deli, and then we went for a tour on the SS Klondike, I do know the SS Klondike as I use to be a tour guide on the boat when it first opened to the public in 1982. After our tour we went for a trolley ride from Rotary Park to Walmart where I had to make a couple of picture CDs for a couple that we met in Vancouver. We went out on a boat with this couple to watch the fireworks; they forgot their camera so I offered to send some pictures to them. I'm sending them a CD with about 200 pictures, I like to take photos. It was the second time ever that my daughter saw fireworks, the first time was a couple of days prior to this, when we were in Butchard Gardens When you talk about having to go to London, do you mean London England or London Ontario? I am looking forward to hearing from you.

Have a great day

Tess

From: Davis

Sent: Aug 16, 2008 7:28:21

Tess

I hope your day went well, I was thinking of calling now, but on another thought, I will rather call tomorrow. It may sound crazy, but I miss you from thinking about you all day. I can almost feel you beside me as I write this letter. I feel sometimes as if the greatest part of who I am is slowly coming back. I am trying to hold on, though.

I took a nap this afternoon, and dream about you, in my dreams, I saw you on the pier. The wind was blowing through your hair, and your eyes held the fading sunlight. I was speechless as I watched you leaning against the rail. You are beautiful, I thought as I saw you, a vision that I could never find in anyone else. I slowly began to walk toward you, and when you finally turned to me, I noticed that others had been watching you as well. "Do you know her?" they asked me in jealous whispers, and as you smiled at me I simply answered with the truth, "Better than I know myself"

I stop when I reach you and I take you in my arms. I long for this moment more than any other. It is what I live for, and when you return my embrace, I give myself over to this moment, at peace once again. I raise my hand and gently touch your cheek and you tilt your head and close your eyes. My hands are hard and your skin is soft, and I wonder for a moment if you'll pull back, but of course, you don't. I know that this is the moment I have been waiting for, and I pray that the moment will come when we meet and never ends. I will get some sleep now, its 22:27 and I am very tired and sleepy. I will mail you in the morning and will also call later in the day. Good Night, You are in my thought and will be in my dreams again as I go to bed.

Davis

From: Tess

Sent: August 16, 2008 11:25:29 PM

My Darling Davis,

I close my eyes and I can feel your touch, as your hand cups my cheek and as I lean into your warmth, I can feel your strength as your arms encircle me and take me into your embrace, and you're right, I don't turn away, I lean towards you for I feel my destiny within you.

The feelings that you show me and entice in me, I haven't even met you and here already you have walked into my dreams, you have made me feel beautiful without even seeing me, just a picture of me is all that you have, I have always felt attractive, but never beautiful and yet when I close my eyes and see us, I feel that you can see the beauty inside of me the beauty that I feel that I have. You make me want this, these feelings, the romance, but more than that, the love that I feel is possible that we, one day, may share. That is what I want. You could bring tears to my eyes, when I close my eyes I see us walking together my hands are wrapped around your arm and as I'm leaning into you, and resting my head on your shoulder, I can feel your eyes looking at me, and I feel the peace in both of us. How is it possible to have these feelings and to only have written words between us, this is what scares me.Are our wants so great that we create these illusions, or are we feeling what we want to feel because we need to feel and we need to love? Is this where we are meant to be, together? I have looked at your picture a lot today, I find myself very much attracted to you, I wish you could send me another picture—one that is a little bigger, I still feel that I have seen you somewhere before, I feel as if I know you. Yet I am sure we have never met.

I had this saying on my wall years ago, it read, Success is getting what

you want, Happiness is wanting what you get. I think it's time we were both HAPPY, I am looking forward to talking with you, to hearing your voice, which will let us get to know each other even more.

I will go now, it is now 23:15, I need to go to sleep. I look forward to reading your e-mail, you have the ability to make a girl swoon with your written word. Is it possible to fall in love with the thoughts that the words bring forth . . . ? I will be dreaming of piers, and turning and seeing you . . .

Tess

From:Davis

Sent:August 17, 2008 7:40:22am Good Morning My Dear

Hello, Darling,

I hope you had a good rest, I had one and have not had this good sleep in so many years. I felt your warmth and touch. As I read your mail, I was thinking of what must have made you think we have met before, then the thought came to me that we might have not met in person, but our souls have met. It's time we know we are meant for each other and need to start doing things that will give us the joy and happiness we have always wanted and have been looking for. I am ready to do anything and everything just to be with you and have you forever, because I find much happiness in you. No one has ever made me feel this way ; you are the perfect one for me, and I really want to get closer to you. I hated to leave but I want you to know, I left a big part of me with you. It is yours now so, take care and tread lightly. I wish that I could be with you now as you, but know that I am there in spirit. Soon, we will be together and happy forever. I promise. No matter where this life takes us, together or not, know that you and Zoey will always be in my heart and "my favorite" even though I have not met her yet, but I turn to like everything that makes you and I want to be a part of her life. I will give you a call later in the day, and will send you a mail again. Take care and know I will be thinking about you in everything I do.

Yours . . . Davis

From Davis

Sent:August 18, 2008 8:47:56 AM

Hi Tess,

I have not heard from you since yesterday, and that is making me kind of worried. Did I say something you didn't like; if I did, I am sorry. I wanted to call yesterday and even now, but don't know if you have changed your mind about me and don't want to communicate anymore. Please let me hear from you. Take care and know you are always in my thought.

Davis

From: Tess

Date: Mon, 18 Aug 2008 09:18:55

Oh Davis,

You have not said anything wrong, just everything right, I got your e-mails both of them in the morning, and I looked at your pictures, and I anticipated you calling, I was going to write, but I thought no, I'll wait to talk to you, that was the only reason I didn't write, and then my sons were here and we started to build the shed, hopefully we will finish today. I forgot that today was a holiday, so I don't have to work. I have been thinking a lot about you, and I definitely have not changed my mind about you, I do want to meet you, to get to know you, I want to see, if when we meet, we feel the connection that we feel now. So please don't apologise, and please don't worry, know that you are on my mind every minute it seems. When I do something, I wonder what it would be like if you were there with me, doing whatever with me, how that would feel, and what that would be like.

Would you be a part of the things I do? And would I be a part in the things you do? I'm curious as to what are some of the things you do here in Whitehorse, just on an average day, what is it like for you? . . . I've been thinking a lot . . . Thank you for the pictures, I'm hoping you will tell me about them, where they were taken, whose boat you were on . . . Take care, Davis.

You do scare me, but it's in a good way . . . Thinking about you Tess

I accidently sent this email to my son.

I could just imagine what he was thinking. his thoughts would be something like. what the heck, who am I kidding with my son it would be ' what the f. what is Mom doing now. ?'

From: Tess

Sent: August 18, 2008 1:53:45 PM

Hello, again,

I just wanted to let you know that I told you to call me and that I will be home, however plans have changed and I may not be home, so can we possibly set a time where I will be home, I don't know if that is possible with your schedule, but the best time to catch me is around 7PM my time, during the week. I believe there is a three—hour difference between us. Davis, I do know what it feels like that feeling of uncertainty, you question yourself, as well as the other person. Davis, right now we are just beginning to get to know each other, and please understand that I do want to get to know you.

Thinking about you Tess

On 8/18/08, Tess wrote:

Davis, the e-mail I just sent you, I don't know how it happened, but you may notice that it went not only to you but to someone else, my son. I have no idea as to how his email address got attached because I basically replied back to you, so I will be telling my sons about you, I hope you are ok with that. I can just hear it now, "ahh mom . . ., I got this e-mail . . . from you . . ."

I just wanted to let you know, because I figured you'd be wondering as my son's last name is not the same as mine.

Again I'm thinking about you . . . Tess

From: Davis

Sent: August 18, 2008 6:16:01 PM

Dear Tess,

Hey Beautiful, I am so excited to hear from you and want you to know I don't have any problem with you telling the boys about me. As I said before, I want to be a very part of your life and everything that makes you. I just hope they don't have problems with me coming into your life. I just wanted to do something simple to say I need you and to put that smile I will always love so much to see on your face. I want everyone to know how much you mean to me. Ever since you have entered my life, I've been flying on Cloud Nine and I have not come down yet, and I don't ever want to come down. You are the most beautiful person I know, inside and out and I see that more clearly with each passing day. I love everything about you, about us. You do something to me that no other has, you have made me so happy, the happiest I've ever been. You give me the most amazing feelings inside, the feeling of being in love with you. I still don't know what I did to be so lucky to have you in my life, my dream come true . . . I am so thankful though. In this short time that we've been communicating, we have grown so much and I can't wait to see what the future holds for us. I need you in my life, Tess, with all my heart and soul, always and forever. I will talk to you sooner, enjoy the evening.

Davis

From: Davis

Sent: August 18, 2008 6:34:44 PM

Hello,

I was just about to call you, but guess I have to wait for a while. I know and understand the uncertainty, and all the thoughts that comes into mind. I will want us to talk about it when I call later. Thinking so deeply about you.

Davis

From: Tess

Sent: August 19, 2008 7:11:36 AM

Good Morning Davis,

You are so generous with your words, you do make me smile. You talk of being in love already, please be careful of the illusion, the feelings that are brought on by the words we share, I speak with experience. It scares me that you build me up so much, a little is good, but too much, high expectations that I'm scared I won't meet. There are things about me that aren't perfect, I'm not perfect. For one I'm not the best at housekeeping; my place is clean, yes, but it can look like ten kids have been through my place at times. It may look chaotic, but I know pretty much where everything is.

Please before you speak of being in love, let us meet. How long have you been on e-harmony, and have you done any internet dating before? I don't know how things have gone for you in the past, but my experience, I've had a few in the last six years, a couple of men that I did meet we talked for a short time and then met, just for a date and it was a really nice experience and I made a couple of good friends, but nothing more than that, and then I have met a couple of men who we e-mailed and talked on the phone. Expectations were there and then when we met, it was a different feeling; what they told me about themselves wasn't the way they were. I'm sorry to be telling you this, I just want to be sure and for you to know that when we do get the chance to meet, I have no expectation of you right now. I like the feelings that you create, they're feelings that I have not had in a long time, remember when you see me, I may not be the way you have envisioned me, I ask again to please let

34

us move slowly, tread lightly, and go from when we meet. I am a very patient person. I hope that we can talk soon, take care and know that I am thinking about you.

Tess

# 3

# I THINK I'M FALLING

On 8/19/08, Tess wrote:

Hello Davis,

Now it's my turn to sit here and wonder if I have said something wrong, I don't want to turn you away from me. I hope that you can understand my cautious approach (I think that is what I want to say) to what we share and the feelings that are brought about by this. I would very much like for things to work between us, I was thinking the other day, what you talk about, sounds so much like a fairy tale, I've always wanted the fairy tale and I'm scared to hope too much. I will leave the ball in your court so to say; I'm hoping that I will hear from you again soon,

Thinking about you

Tess

From: Davis

Sent: August 20, 2008 4:17:41 AM

Hello Tess,

Pardon me for not getting back to you on time, I was not feeling too well and was admitted in the hospital yesterday. I am doing ok today.

I understand we need to take things slowly. I will send you a mail later. Ok. I miss you and thinking about you.

Davis

*Davis called me; we spoke with each other for about 30 minutes. His voice sounded deep, a manly Italian voice, it reminded me of that commercial on TV when the statue of David speaks to the lady with the shopping bags. very sensual, very Italian. Davis's phone was very garbled during our conversation so it was difficult to hear him or understand him at times.*

From: Davis

Sent: August 21, 2008 7:55:38 PM

Tess,

It's just less than 45 minutes I spoke with you and I am missing you already. It was so nice talking with you, and look forward to talking with you mostly. I think about you as usual. I want you to know how much sincerely I appreciate and love the time we spend talking. It means so much to me. It truly seems like I've known you forever. There will be no looking back, no second thoughts and no regrets, because I am ready and willing to make everything perfect with us if only you are too ready for that. This feeling will only grow stronger.

I think about you most of the time, I want to build my walls around you. Our souls are connected, our mind is focused It's left for our bodies to meet and accept each other. I know deeply that we have the connection, but it's left for you and me to learn to accept each other when we meet. We are humans and can never be perfect, but we can learn perfection, to accept, understand, care, love and be there for each other every time. I am ready to accept you and learn to live with you the way you are, to learn your ways, understand you, and to always be there for you. I want you to start thinking about how wonderful it will be if we can learn to accept each other, point our mistake, accept it when we go wrong. I promise you if we start understanding these things and walk on this path, everything will be very fine with us and we will be very happy together forever. I know we might sometimes have different ideas, but we need to understand each other's thought and become one in everything we do. I am ready to do that with you and hope you are too. I will give you my heart and everything I am, and hoping in return you do the same. I really want to be with you forever, to be the best man you have always wanted to be with, to understand you and always be there for you. I want to be that special person you will come to when you need someone to cry to, that special person when you need someone to share your joy and happiness with. Let me be that one. When you need someone to walk to, laugh with, play with, sing and dance with, or do anything with, let me be the one. I want to protect you, fight for you. I swear I want to be that angel in your life. Please hold my hands and let's take this step one after the other to this paradise. Let's build it with all our strength and might. I hope to catch you on MSN?. Take care, enjoy the evening. You are always in my thoughts and I want to be with you forever.

PS: I hope I didn't scare you with this mail Davis

On 8/21/08, Tess wrote:

Hello, Davis,

I hope you are doing ok, after you being sick and having to go to the hospital, and then not hearing from you, I've been a little bit concerned. Please let me know how you are doing. I'm hoping all is well. I wanted to tell you about my walk with my daughter last night. I walked and she rode her scooter, which fell apart piece by piece as we went. We walked over to the millennium trail and then over the bridge to Robert Service Campground and right at the bridge there was a white water rafting race and demonstration going on, so we watched for a little bit. I would love to learn how to kayak, that is one of my goals for next summer, to get a kayak, but I think I would prefer to just do the lakes and calm rivers; I don't know if I'm into the white-water kayaking at all.

After a few minutes we continued on our way and headed to the office at the campground, got our ice cream, sat down on the couch that's outside, relaxed for a bit and then headed back. I had to walk briskly to keep up with my daughter. Throughout this walk I thought about what it would be like if you were there joining us. It was a feeling that I want to experience. Waiting to hear from you

Tess

On 8/21/08, Davis wrote:

Hi Tess,

I guess you are home by now and will call you soon. Pardon me for not being able to call again last night, I fell asleep while waiting to call in an hour. I hope your day went well. I have been thinking deeply about you.

Davis

From: Tess

Sent: August 22, 2008 6:56:05 PM

Hello Davis,

I didn't get home from work until 6:30 this evening, needless to say Zoey and I are staying home, I'm going to leave my MSN on and hopefully I can catch you on line.

I couldn't get on line last night and this morning my computer would not stay connected, I wanted to tell you that what you wrote last night does scare me. It scares me because it is what I have hoped for, and I'm so afraid of having it taken away from me if I hope too much. What you have talked about, supporting each other, giving each other strength, accepting one another for our faults and for who we are, it is so much how I've longed to have in my partner that I can go through life with, I know you understand this because, it seems that you feel and want exactly what I want. You make me feel wonderful, I am looking forward to the time that we will physically meet, and then we can hopefully start the rest of our lives as one. I close my eyes and I can see you, us doing things together, I keep this vision strong inside of me. I do hope that I will hear from you tonight. I will be leaving first thing in the morning and I won't be back until Sunday afternoon, I will keep checking to hopefully catch you online thinking about you Tess

From: Davis

Sent: August 23, 2008 2:50:49 AM

Hello Tess,

It's 5:51am here and I am awake and thinking deeply about you. I didn't get your mail yesterday, I hope you are doing well with Zoey.

This is my way of showing you how much I truly care for you. I can't really find the words to explain the way I feel when I heard your voice. All I can say is that I like the feeling that I feel. I am online now, and will call you before you leave this morning. I want you to know I want you so much in my life, you are the perfect one for me, and I for you. I promise never to disappoint you if you give your heart and love to me. I want to share with you all that I am. My love, my whole being, and everything that makes me, and I want you to share with me your love, your whole being, Zoey, and everything that makes you. I have never felt this way about anything in my life, and willing to do anything to make things work between us. Take care and hope to talk with you before you leave.

Your . . . Davis

On 8/23/08, Tess wrote:

Davis,

It was wonderful to hear your voice, I wish we had a better connection so that I could really hear you. I hope that we can talk tomorrow; I will try to be here at my house by 5:00pm. I do have to go now, take care and know that I'm thinking of you always

Tess

From: Davis

Sent: August 23, 2008 11:59:24 AM

Tess,

It was really nice hearing your voice too, you make me so excited and I hope I also give you the same feeling you give me.I truly want you forever and will do anything just to have you forever. Take care and drive safe. I will be thinking about you in everything I do as usual. Yours . . . Davis

*I spent the weekend with Steve, it would be our last weekend together, and I wanted to tell him about Davis, but I just couldn't, not during the weekend. We spent a really good time together. I told him I would miss him, his humor, and I will. Deep down, I Love Steve, it's just he didn't want to admit how he felt. He did it again, on our last night together, he turned and looked at me and said " I do love you", how I have longed to hear those words from him, he again said them while he was drunk, will he remember? The next morning I never mentioned it, I gave Steve a hug, he hugged me, I said Good-bye as he walked out my front door. I whispered, "Goodbye Steve, I will miss you"*

From: Davis

Sent: August 24, 2008 4:10:35 AM

Hi Tess,

I hope your trip went well and you and Zoey are doing pretty well. Not hearing from you for a day has made me really miss you. You are my queen and my princess. You are my knight in shining armor. We have so much in common. I am so glad we like most common things and look forward to going out to eat at romantic restaurants and watching movies. I know you have been hurt in the past and I will never hurt you like that. I am yours and you are mine forever and always. I want to die loving you. I want you to be the last woman I ever kiss. I cherish each and every day reading from you and thinking about you, you give me the warm feeling inside, and everybody who knows me will bear witness to that. You are the first thing I think of in the morning and the last thing at night. I love to hear you laugh, it makes me so happy, and can't wait to see you smile and watch you eat. You have a way about you. You are irresistible to me and I don't know how anyone could let you go. I know I never will.

I have come to learn much about you and I admire your strength. I will love to go to places with you like weddings, the beach and walking, taking a trip, as a matter of fact, I will love to do everything with you.

I am yours for as long as you will have me, that is a promise. I will call you later tonight.

Davis

From: Tess

Sent: August 24, 2008 7:07:10 PM

Hello Davis,

I just read your e-mail, I tried to call you and I couldn't get through, and it was all garbled again when the message came on, I could just barely make it out, we may have to chat through MSN. Your e-mail starts my heart racing, you don't really know me and yet you touch me, I have never heard words written/spoken as sincerely as yours. You too sound like a pretty spectacular man, you must have women wanting to be with you? I know what you told me about what happened to you in the past and why you haven't gotten into another relationship, but you speak with such passion, how is it possible that you have not shared that passion. Don't get me wrong, the passion that you talk about, I close my eyes and I can feel it, but we really need to meet first and take each other from there. I want you to know a little bit more about me before we meet, the one thing that I do eventually want, and this is something that I've wanted for along time.I've just never found the right person, is that I want a total commitment and the security that comes with that commitment in the way of marriage. There I said it, I do want to eventually get married to the one person who will love me forever and I will love them forever, as I said I want the fairy tale, the happy ever after and I'll stand by you no matter what. Most important for my daughter, she keeps asking me when will I, meaning me, ever get married, I keep telling her that when that person and I find each other, that's when. I feel that you need to know this up front so that if that isn't what you want, please be honest with me, right away, even if everything goes well, when we meet, I have this strong feeling that it will. You speak of everything that I've ever wanted. And that scares me as well. Now you have said that we have a lot in common, well Davis I love to go out on the water, I enjoy going out in a canoe, and I want to learn how to kayak, but my biggest dream is to go on a sailboat and learn how to sail. Do you, have you ever done any of these things? I know one picture that you sent me; you seem to be sitting on or in a boat? Do you enjoy boating?

I also would like to have one day, a cabin on the edge of a lake, with a dock. That is another one of my dreams is to be sitting on the deck of the cabin listening to the water as it laps against the shore and painting the mountain scene in front of me. I don't know if I told you or if it's in my profile, but every now and then I paint watercolour pictures. What types of things do you like to do, for pleasure, as a hobby, or to relax? I had better get going; Zoey needs me to go through her clothes with her, we need to weed out the clothes she won't wear anymore. Davis, thank you for making me feel so special I hope I haven't' scared you away with my honesty but I do feel that you should know this up—front. We do need to meet before we can make any decisions, such as if we will have a first date. You make everything sound so perfect, I'm afraid to hope, but I'm not afraid to dream, and when I dream I dream of you . . . Thank you Davis . . .

Thinking of you Tess

I'm going to try and call you again.

From: Davis

Sent: August 25, 2008 4:57:28 PM

Dear Tess,

I am sorry again that I couldn't call, I fell asleep again, and didn't hear the phone ring. I couldn't make it on MSN this morning because I had a meeting very early this morning. I am glad to know this much about you, we both seem to want the same thing. I also want a total commitment and the security that comes with that commitment in the way of marriage. I do want to be with the one person who will love me forever and I will love her forever. I also like fairy tale. I love to go out on the water, like kayaking, go on a sailboat as you saw in one of my pictures as my pleasure. Never in my wildest dreams did I think I would meet a woman that could captivate and win my heart at "Hello".

Every moment from when I wake up till deep in the night, there is no place on earth I would rather be than holding and kissing you tenderly, which I really look forward to. You are a special woman with unique and intriguing qualities that drive my desire for you far beyond any imagination. I want to share everything, offer all my love unconditionally, and grow old with someone to one day reminisce of the years we shared together. Just the thought of offering my total heart and spending my life cherishing every moment with you, brings these incredible emotions to me I have never experienced before. The worse day of my life would be letting you slip out of my life. I will not go on another day without giving us a true chance at a life with love and happiness I know we could embrace together. A wise man once told me, "When it is real, you will know, " . . . I know. I am very tired now, but will try to call soon. Thinking deeply about you, Love, hugs & kisses.

Davis

From: Davis

Sent: August 26, 2008 1:06:18 PM

Hi Dear,

I hope your day is going well. Just miss you and wan you to know I am thinking of you. I will call later. Take care.

Davis

On 8/27/08, Tess wrote:

Just wanting to let you know that I'm thinking about you . . .

From: Davis

Sent: August 27, 2008 1:47:58 PM

Dear Tess,

I just can't seem to do anything without thinking about you, you have taken over my thought and my soul. My heart belongs to you now, and I hope you will take good care of it as I will take very good care of yours if you decide to give it to me. I hope your day is going well.

I wanted to tell you today how good I feel about us and our future. I enjoyed talking with you. It seems that everything we say is even more meaningful because it isn't just for today . . . it's for always. You make me feel really happy, and I'll always love making you feel special too.

I'm glad that I can count on you to be there when I need someone to understand, to encourage, to reassure me and I hope you realize you can always count on me too. We share so much of our lives, but it's nice to know that we can still go our own ways now and then and somehow, the more we grow as individuals, the closer we become. I'm sure that this feelings I have for you will last forever . . . that I'll cherish you through a lifetime of beautiful tomorrows. I want you to know how pleased I am to be a part of your life, how much it means to me to know I'll always be yours and only you! I will call you later this evening. Take care and know I have been thinking about you all day.

Yours . . . Davis

From: Davis

Sent: August 27, 2008 4:45:03 PM

Dear Tess,

Just want you to know I am deeply thinking about you. Davis

On 8/27/08, Tess wrote:

Hello Davis,

You do make me feel special, Thank you . . . you make everything sound so easy and wonderful, if everything is there between us, it will be wonderful, however I doubt it will be easy. I don't have any idea how you are with kids, but myself being a parent and being around others who don't necessarily have kids or around kids that much, having a relationship with kids involved, and I want Zoey to be involved with things that we do, can be a challenge at times. Spontaneity is not always an option; plans have to be made sometimes if a quiet evening alone is what we want and thoughts of where to go and what to do take on a different light as well. I tend to be at home during the week or home early because of school. There are family get—togethers and school assemblies and concerts. There are also times when Zoey can be difficult, when she gets stubborn and doesn't want to do what she needs to do and needs direction. I just thought I would run this by you, preparation so to say. I have to go, I have to get some groceries downtown and I should be home by 8:00. I'll check to see if you're on line when I get home and maybe we can chat again.

I think about you alot Davis, you are in my thoughts always Hope to talk to you soon . . .

Tess

From: Davis

Sent: August 28, 2008 9:42:46 AM

Dear Tess,

Its was really great talking with you late night and this morning. I am sorry we lost communicating at the end, I guess it had to do with my connection. I will mail you again later, and will call you. Take care and know I will be thinking about you in everything I do. Yours . . . Davis

*I called Steve today and told him that I had met someone online and that I wanted to meet this person.*

*Steve's response to me was "you know how I feel about that"*

*"Given what you said to me the other night, I wasn't too sure how you really felt" I replied.*

*"What?" Steve Said*

*I could feel the emotion building, my throat constricting, "you told me you loved me"*

*"I did?" was his reply.*

*"There you go, that is exactly what I thought" I said my final goodbye to Steve. I took a deep breath, I didn't cry. but I did feel a sadness.*

*Steve did wish me well. he will always have a place in my heart for everything we had been through; he was a friend to me.*

On 8/28/08, Tess wrote:

Hello Davis,

I want you to know that . . . remember I told you about my friend that we would spend time together once in a while, no commitment between us . . . well I would like to let you know that I phoned and talked with my friend and told him that I was going to be meeting you and that we've been talking, he wished me well and said that "this guy had better treat you right". So basically I won't be spending anymore time with my friend such as we had in the past. I want to focus on you and us . . . I wanted to share that with you . . . I have to get back to work right now . . . I look forward to talking with you and even more so to seeing you . . .

Tess

From: Davis

Sent: August 28, 2008 5:26:07 PM

Hi darling,

It feels good to know you will not be communicating with this friend as you used to. That alone has really made my day. I promise to treat you right and always make you and Zoey very happy. You people are now the most important thing in my life and I will do anything just to make it up to you forever. I really want you in my life forever. I tried calling earlier, guess you were working. I will get some rest now and will communicate with you later. Take care and know you are always in my thought and I am thinking about you in everything I do. Talk to you later.

Yours . . . Davis

From: Tess

Sent: August 28, 2008 5:52:55 PM

Hello Davis, it was so good to finally get a chance to talk to you. It was a shame that we got cut off. I think that it was my phone that cut out and we had such a good connection to begin with. I will be here this evening. I plan on doing some chores this evening so I will wait for your call and I'll also keep my MSN on just in case you can't get through on the phone. It feels so good thinking about you, and talking to you . . .

Tess

From: Davis

Sent: August 28, 2008 5:47:56 PM

My cell just went off, I am charging it and will call you soon. I am so excited talking with you and look forward in talking again soon.

Davis

From: Tess

Sent: August 28, 2008 10:22:58 PM

Hello Davis,

My sweet Davis, the things you say to me make me feel wonderful, you are so real to me Davis, I look at your picture and it's as if I can reach out and touch you, I want so bad for this to be real, I'm taking everything that you've said to me and holding it dearly inside of me, I want to know everything about you, what your favourite food is, your favourite colour, your birthday when is your birthday? I want to find out what you are most passionate about, I want to look into your eyes and see into your soul for that is where I will meet you.

It means a lot to me that you are willing to get to know my daughter, that is so important to me, Davis you fill my heart with just your words, and I will love to have you make me one of your special Italian dinners, in fact I would love to cook with you forever . . . I look at you and I see forever . . .

Goodnight Davis you are in my dreams Tess

From: Davis

Sent: August 29, 2008 2:29:04 PM

Hi Darling,

I am sitting here somewhere in the world thinking about you, thinking about all the things we've spoken about, all the things we've said to each other. I know you are somewhere at work thinking about me too. Wherever you are and go, you go with me. I walk by your side. When you go to bed, I am stepping in it at the same time you are. When you sit down to eat, I am next to you to eat too. When you are combing your hair, I am there kissing and stroking it, smelling the smell of the shampoo you use. I am so into you—and I can even feel you here . . . behind me, touching me, saying, "darling, come with me." I would come with you without hesitation.

My Winter Moon, all I am saying now is that I am so happy to have found you. You mean everything to me now. You are my earth, my water, my sun. You are everything that maintains life, everything that gives life. Having you with me is like being reborn. Before you, I was dead.

I was a zombie wandering around with no destination, or a robot that people commanded. I didn't have a life. Now I have you, and all I want to do is be with you and feel ALL of you. Know that you are wanted . . . how much? That is not something I can describe in words – eternally much, horribly, awfully much? I can't wait until I can embrace you, kiss you, to melt with you, to show you HOW much you are wanted. We will be together soon . . . I know, a look in your beautiful eyes . . . Oh God! I just need You! I will call you later, Take care and know you are so dear to me.

Your . . . Davis

On 8/31/08, Tess wrote:

Hello Davis,

I'm thinking that you may have fallen asleep it would be close to 10:00 PM your time. When you wake up, no matter what time it is, if you're able to call me, please call me otherwise I will wait to hear from you when you can get hold of me. I have to go to work for a short time tomorrow; I may go in the morning around 10:00, the same time you have to be at the airport. I've been waking up at around 4:00 in the morning these past couple of mornings. If that happens again tomorrow morning being Monday morning, I'll check on line and maybe, catch you on line for a short time, just to talk to you before your day gets underway. Zoey and I are right now going to go for a walk to Robert Service campground we go along the millennium trail, she gets an ice cream cone once we get there, I'm going to have water . . . I will be thinking of the day when you will be walking with us . . .

Tess

From: Davis

Sent: August 31, 2008 10:00:32 PM

Hi Tess,

I am here lying on my bed thinking deeply about you. I got back from town and tried doing some cleaning around. I later decided to relax while the new phone charges, so I can call you, but fell asleep. I will like to call you now, but I think you need some rest. I will call you early in the morning. When I think or look at your picture, I know there is a bond between us that no one can break, the feeling you give me. When I think about you, I see the love that abides deep within your soul; they tell me you need me in so many ways than just one. When two people love each other, they don't look at each other; they look in the same direction.

I will go back to bed and call you in the morning. Davis

On 9/1/08, Tess wrote:

Hello Davis,

Thank you, I will be waiting for your call, looking forward to hearing you, hearing your voice. You make me feel so alive and so happy Davis just knowing you're there makes me feel complete.

I was so frustrated today with trying to do my shed. I needed help with doing what I needed to do and I couldn't get a hold of anyone to help. I'm hoping tomorrow will work. If I had just bought wood and built it, it would be done by now. Sometimes it's hard being alone . . .

I have to get going, I'm really tired, and so I'm going to bed, I've been thinking about you so much . . . you're inside of me . . .

Thinking of you Tess

From: Davis

Sent: September 1, 2008 9:53:30 AM Dearest Tess,

I hope you are doing well this morning, and Zoey is also doing great. I want you to know soon you will not feel alone and will not need to ask for help because I will always be there to keep you company and give a helping hand without you needing to ask. I just hope you can understand me, I will not be able to call till I get to London, I have been very busy this morning trying to get things done before I leave. Don't think I am putting other things ahead of you, it's just that I don't have anybody living here, and have to make sure everything is right before I leave. I need to get ready to leave to the airport for check in. It's sometimes very hard to do everything alone. I have decided to employ about two or more people who will take care of some part of my business and other stuff, since I have made my mind to have much time for you when I return. I have to go. I will mail you when I get the chance. Take care and know you are in my thought in everything I do, and will forever be. I cherish you so much.

Davis

On 9/2/08, Tess wrote:

Hello Davis,

I've been thinking about you all day, you fill my thoughts and body with a warmth that completely covers me; I feel you are with me and know that I am with you. I understand you are busy, I hope that things are working out for you, I just wanted to write to you to tell you that you are in me, in my heart and in my soul . . . you have completely taken me over . . .

Thinking about you and missing you Tess

From: Davis

Sent: September 2, 2008 5:16:05 PM Hello Tess,

I arrived here in London safe and sound, I hope you are doing well. I am glad to know Zoey now knows about us and very willing to meet everyone person in your family. The only persons in my life when it comes to family is my mum and aunt, and I have already told them about you. You have been in my throght all day and while I was in the flight. You give me much warmth, and I am so happy to have met you and have you in my life. It's almost 1AM here, and very tried, so I will get some rest now and will get in touch tomorrow morning. Good night and know I want to also love you with all that I am.

Davis

On 9/2/08, Tess wrote:

Hello Davis,

I'm glad you're safe and sound, can you tell me where you're staying. I'll google—earth it so I can get an idea as to where you are, and maybe you could tell me what your street address in Orlando was and I'll have an idea as to where you've been.

My son and I worked some more on this shed that should be used for scrap metal, the roof is two steps away from being completed. Tomorrow if all goes well, I may see the final finishing of this thing. If anyone were to ever ask me about ordering these sheds from the catalogue, I would tell them to go with the wood, this may have been cheaper but the headache it has caused me has been a bigger price. A lesson learnt, at least. It's able to be fixed as we go . . . and it'll have character!

I made penne pasta this evening with thinly sliced steak, peppers, tomatoes and Italian spice, and olive oil, and I thought about you, wondered what would you have done. I also put a bit of garlic in it as well. I had no onions, if I did, I would have put some in and then the crème de la crème, the taste de la resistance . . . I grated real parmesan cheese on top. Voila! Smack my two first fingers with my lips, it wasn't bad, but with you, it would have been better, I just know it . . . and we would have had a glass of red wine . . . I look forward to cooking with you . . . and doing a lot of other things with you as well . . .

Zoey has finally fallen asleep, she has been going all evening and it has taken her awhile to settle down, so now I'm going to go and have a shower and go to bed myself. Take care, have a great day today, and know that I'm thinking of you and you're in my heart. I'm dreaming about you always . . . You make my heart melt.

Tess

From: Davis

Sent: September 2, 2008 11:23:17 PM Good Morning Darling,

I just woke up and as usual, you were the first thing that came in mind. I know you are sleeping as I write, and what you know I am with you. I am getting ready for a meeting this morning, I would get in touch soon after the meeting. I am doing fine, only missing you so much. I think about you in everything I do, you give me the strength to move on, I am so excited about everything, and so glad to have you in my life. I want to love you forever, be the best man you will forever love to be with, care, protect and be your strenghth when you are weak. I have fallen in love with you, I don't know how it happened so soon, but I feel it deep inside me. You are so perfect for me, so special to me, and the best thing to ever happen to me. I cherish you and will, forever, adore you. I have to go, will get in touch again soon.

Davis

From: Davis

Sent: September 3, 2008 3:49:00 PM Darling,

Had a very long day and a long meeting, I may have to leave to the mine sometime this week. Don't really like the place, the mine, and trying to make sure it a right deal. It's very late here and I am very tired. I need some rest now. I will get in touch later, and hope to meet you on MSN if I am not able to call. Just know you are always in my thought, and my heart, soul and mind belong to you forever. forever . . . Davis ciao ciao (bye bye)

On 9/3/08, Tess wrote:

Davis my Darling,

My messenger is not working, so do call me if you get the chance I will have my cell phone with me, I keep asking myself is it possible to fall in love with someone I've never met, because I feel myself falling, I look forward to hearing from you and seeing you . . .

Tess

From: Davis

Sent: September 3, 2008 7:05:59 AM Darling,

Its sad I can't chat with you now, I miss you and want to feel you close. It's 3:07 PM here and I just ended a meeting. I have another one some few minutes later, and will be done. I just want you to know you are in my thought and in everything I do. Your face is in my mind and helps me and keeps me smiling. you are so pretty. I have finally found what I have always wanted, and that is you. We are falling, yes it is happening soon . . . these feelings that we are developing for each other without even meeting. I suppose that is what soul mates feel no matter where they are. Have to go now, I will get in touch later. Take care and know I care, cherish and adore you.

Yours Truly . . . Davis

On 9/4/08, Tess wrote:

Good afternoon Davis,

I fall in love with you more each day. I can't get onto my MSN, I've tried, I'm online right now. I just want you to know how close I feel to you, I close my eyes and imagine that you're standing with me, your arms embrace me, and I can feel your warmth, it feels so real—I feel so alive, and it feels like we belong. It's the strangest feeling I've ever experienced, but it is there . . . Thank You, Davis for making me feel like this, for loving me . . . you have filled me with so much warmth and love I feel I'm going to explode . . . I promise you that I will love you everyday of forever . . . for you are my destiny . . . I feel this . . . . I know you don't have much time, good luck with everything. I'm glad that your meeting went well and I want to hear about all of your experiences . . . Can you tell me where you're at, then I can google—earth it and see or at least get an idea, as to where you are . . .I Love you Davis and I send you all of my love . . .

Tess

From: Davis

Sent: September 4, 2008 6:11:17 AM Good Morning/Afternoon my Love,

First of all, pardon me for going off while we were talk/chatting. I don't know what happened, I just got disconnected and tried so many times to get back. I later realized my time was up and had to leave, so I got ready and left. I hope you slept well and are doing fine. I am doing well, and feel so warm inside. Thanks to you, I feel much alive again and have much strenghth.

My meeting went well, they agreed to my terms but asked for 10% of my offer. I agreed to give them what they want because I know what I will gain later. We are meeting in the next forty—five minutes to start the transcation, I hope to complet everything by the end of the day tomorrow, and will leave for Ghana on Sunday to visit the mine. I am also going to order for machines for the mine, I want to get everything in place so I don't ave to rush when I get back and spending time with you. I want to have all the time in this world for you, and nothing should ever become between me having good time with you. I will be here for a while, hope to chat with you before    I leave. I love you and cherish you so much. Tell Zoey I send my greetings, and that she will see me soon and we will spend much time togther doing so many things. And she shouldn't worry or feel disappointed not being around on our first date. On the onther hand, if you want her to be there, I want you to know I will not have any problem with it. Take care, have a wonderful day and know I am so much in love with you.

Love always . . .

Davis

On 9/4/08, Tess wrote:

My Darling Davis,

If I were with you right now, when your meeting was over, you would come back to the room and find the room lit with candles and I would be standing there, waiting for you to walk towards me. I would reach up and caress the side of your face. I would take your hand in mine and kiss your fingers one by one, I would then raise my head and look into your eyes wanting your kiss, I would then lead you into the bathroom where I would have a bath drawn for you. I would then remove your clothing slowly, piece by piece, caressing you, touching you, feeling you, feeling your strength.    I then would guide you to the bath and you would climb in and      I would give you a glass of wine and sit beside you—letting you relax in the bubbles, you would tell me about your day, how you felt, what you did, and then I would let you relax, close your eyes and bask in the warmth of the water. And then when you are done, I would bring the towel to you, you would climb out and I would slowly dry your body, caressing lovingly. And then I would lead you back out to the room lit with candles, and on the floor there would be a rug. I would lay the towel down and ask you to lie down on your stomach and I would sit next to you and massage you slowly, deeply, lovingly . . . If I were there with you right now, that's what I would do for you . . .

When you say, you may have to go to the mine, you don't sound very happy about this. Let yourself be your guide. I worry when you say you don't like where the mine is . . . please be safe and come home to me, no matter what you do, just come home . . . promise me that we will meet, because you are my dream . . . and I don't ever want to wake up from this one . . . I know you will let me know what you're going to do, but is there anyway you can let me know of a way I can get a hold of you, just in case I don't hear from you for a couple of days.? . . . I long for you Davis . . . I really do. My computer has been acting up, it took three hours this evening to defragment., I hope that it has fixed the problem. If you get a chance to call, call me anytime and I mean anytime. If I'm sleeping and it's 3:00 in the morning I don't care. To hear your voice, would be wonderful, to talk to you would be beyond wonderful. I hope everything goes the way you would like it to . . . I'll be thinking of you. You are always on my mind and a part of me . . . and the massage is very real, it is what I will do for you, many times . . . there is so much I would like to do for you, to you, with you . . . I do hope you're able to call and I hope that we have a good connection. My MSN has not been working very well. I can't believe how close I feel to you. When I do something, like tonight I was shopping at Super A and I thought about what it would be like to have you there with me, and it felt wonderful, it felt so right, and it felt so real . . .

I'm falling Davis, you have done something to me . . . so you had better be there to catch me, because no one else can . . . only you . . .

Falling fast . . . Tess

Date: Thu, 4 Sep 2008 17:46:00

From: Davis Hello Darling,

My day has ended and I am just about leaving for the hotel. I will come back to town for dinner with, should I now say my contract rewarders ?. I hope your day is going well. I will be going to a place in West Africa called Ghana to see the mines and start something. I am at the airport city now. You are with me in everything I do, I have fallen so much in love with you, and can't imagine how it will be like spending special time with you forever. I am so excited to have you and will be very truthful to you in all my ways. I think about you in everything I do. You are everything I have ever wanted. I cherish you so dearly, and love you with all my heart, soul, mind and body. I want you to know I am yours now and forever. I will try to get a calling card and will call you later tonight. Take care and know I am with you in everything you do.

Love always . . . Davis

On 9/5/08, Tess wrote:

Goodmorning My Darling Davis,

I have spent my whole day thinking of you, I do hope that we can talk soon, and that we may have a good connection. I looked in google— earth at Ghana ; there are a few cities/ townships in the area, otherwise it looks pretty remote. Do you have any idea which city/town or lake the mine is near? I know you will have to do whatever you need to do and then you'll come home to us, so that we can finally touch each other. I don't think now it's a matter of you and I meeting. I feel, in a way that we have met and now it's a matter of being able to see one another and touch one another. Does that make sense to you . . . ?

I was standing in my office looking out the window, I closed my eyes and put my head back, and I thought of you standing behind me, my head would rest against your chest, I could feel your arms wrap around me, I embraced your arms with mine: I could feel you kissing my neck, slowly, tenderly, I reached up with my arm and caressed your head as it bent towards my neck, I could feel you, I can feel myself turning to you, facing you, looking deep into your eyes, looking into you and seeing me, where I belong. I have such beautiful thoughts about you, all I want and need is to feel the caress of your lips on mine . . . this was one of my thoughts with you today . . . I'm falling deeply in love with you Davis . . .

Do you know when you will be leaving for Ghana? I hope all goes well, totally for my own selfish reasons of course, the better it goes for you, the faster you can come home, and I can finally touch you . . . and I do hope it goes well for you too . . . I'm hoping that you do get a chance to call me, I came home late this evening, I had to go to my storage shed. I have a storage shed, there is a story to that, anyhow I had to get Zoey's birth certificate that shows that her father is not stated because I am getting our passport application sent away for tomorrow. I've never had a reason to push to get our passports done, other than the fact that in January we will need them to go to Skagway, but now since meeting you, I am hoping that we will be able to travel together. So I'm getting them done immediately, I should have them back by the middle of October.

And then once I got home, I was tired after today, I made us a quick supper and then I had a couple of ladies come over and talk to me about financial planning. I have a life insurance policy that I got when Zoey was first born, and I haven't talked to anyone about it since, and with the boys not living at home anymore, my premium could possibly go down, and they also talked to me about a program they have for dept consolidation which I may take a look at depending on the interest rate. Anyhow they just left about forty-five minutes ago. They'll get back to me with a plan once they plug everything into their computer program. I had to get Zoey into bed, she was playing a computer game and I told her that you liked computer games and she said, "my kinda guy". I have to tell you this as well, I went for lunch today to the New Asia restaurant with my mom and my stepfather, and as we were leaving I read my fortune from my cookie and it said, You will soon experience a change in your life for the better. You are my change Davis . . .

I'm stalling a little in saying goodnight to you as I was hoping that I would catch you waking up and coming on line, I'm going to be puttering, straightening up a little before I go to bed, so if you are up within the next half hour, that would be 6:00-6:30 your time, just give me a nudge and I should hear it, and if I'm not on line and you are able to call me, I'll have the phone beside my bed.

I Love You

Yours forever . . . Tess

From: Davis

Sent: September 5, 2008 6:43:18 AM Dearest Tess,

I have been very busy, but all the time have you on my mind and having wonderful thoughts of you. I hope you slept well and Zoey and you are doing pretty fine. I don't know yet when I will be returning till I get to Ghana. I will keep you informed when I decide on my plans. As you said, I don't think now it's a matter of you and I meeting, I think now it's a matter of being able to see one another and touch one another, because we have already met and that makes sense to me. We are still on the papper work and transaction, I hope to complete everything by the end of the day. I have already odered for the machines for the mine. I hope to get the software I will need to install the machines before I leave on Sunday. I use imac, so I ordered for the imac software. I have to get going, I wish you all the best in everything you do, and know you are in my thought, in everything I do and close to my heart. I love you so much and keep falling deeper and deeper. I am yours forever.

take care, and in everything you do, just know someone here called Davis is so madly in love with you. I Love You!

Love always . . . Davis

On 9/6/08, Tess wrote:

My Darling Davis,

I wanted to let you know that I've downloaded Yahoo Messenger, so we should be able to chat, it works with my contacts that have MSN messenger, so hopefully I can catch you on line soon. I will check when I get home this evening; you're eight hours ahead/behind so it should be 5AM. Maybe I'll just leave it on for awhile, hoping of course that you will have time to chat. The funeral was a good one, people talked about my friend's father's life and the type of person he was, about fifty people were there. My heart goes out to the family and the loss that they will feel from their dad being gone; he was the pillar of the family.

Zoey and I are off to the birthday party now. I saw my friends Gina and Pierre. They're our age, I was in my vehicle outside of the deli, and we went in to check out the ice—cream cone selection. As I'm getting into my vehicle, these two people on motorbikes pull up behind me, as if they're going to park, I start my vehicle and they start honking at me and waving their hands, gesturing in what I thought was for me to hurry—up. I'm thinking, give me a chance people, and then they honked again. I rolled down my window to see if there was a problem and here it was my friends. Gina was on a Majesty bike, Pierre says its motor is a 400cc, and she was wearing a black leather jacket and black leather pants with black and bright pink stiletto—heeled boots. I took a picture, she looked great. They have a daughter the same age as Zoey and are just about to hopefully adopt a little boy that has been living with them for the last three years.

Anyhow I told them about you and they have extended an invitation to us when you get back to go out and see them and their new house. They're very nice people . . . I'm sure that they will like you and you them. I miss you

. . . I Love you . . . Know that I am with you . . . and I'm hoping we get a chance to chat before you leave to Ghana . . . Everyday I'm so amazed as to how I feel about you, and how you feel about me . . . It just fills me up knowing that you feel the same way I do . . . I await your arrival patiently . . . And I keep telling myself the best things in life are worth waiting for . . . We have to go . . . I love you . . . Tess

From: Davis

Sent: September 7, 2008 2:46:40 AM Hi Love,

I miss you so much and want you to know I have you on my mind all the time even if you don't hear from me. I hope you are doing well, and Zoey is doing fine. Thanks so much for the picture, you look so beautiful and pretty to me. I like Zoey's smile, it's just like yours. She is a very pretty, sweet girl and seems to be a very nice kid to be with. No wonder she is your child, just like her mom . . . lol. I am very fine and always feel this warmth inside me whenever I think about you, read from you or talking/chatting with you. What is so wonderful is that I find myself thinking about you all the time. My day yesterday went well, couldn't get in touch because of bad connection. I had so many things to take care of and paper work to complete. Glad I was able to finish and get ready for my trip to Ghana this evening. I love you, Tess, I want you to know I want to be with you forever and I keep loving you the more every moment. I don't know what to say. Nothing can change my feeling for you and I will always be the love of your life . . . forever. I will always have a special spot for you in my heart. No matter where I go, I carry you in me. I'm hoping that you, Tess, feel the same way as I do. Remember, I Love you so dearly and will always and forever love and cherish you. I think about you in everything, I do. I adore you my queen. Take care, I will call you before I leave for Ghana.

Love always . . . Davis

# 4

# THE COMPUTER

From: Davis

Sent: September 8, 2008 11:17:03 AM Hello My Dearest Tess,

I hope you had the rest you needed last night, and your day is going well. I arrived in Ghana 3:28am London time, which was 7:28 home time and 2:28 Ghana time. My first time here and the first experience are so bad. I had a crisis when I arrived. I was picked up by one Mr Warleh, who was supposed to be my tour guide. The next thing was that I lost my luggage at the hotel to the taxi driver who took us from the Airport. The hotel manager is helping me with the police to get my stuff back, I only thank God I had a place to sleep when I arrived at the hotel. I have lost my imac, my suitcase and also some important documents. The taxi driver was so kind to us at first, he was helping us locate a suitable hotel for me since all the hotels around were booked out, He just drove away when we got off from his taxi to book for the room. But we are lucky the hotel manager is assisting and helping us. I am going to contact my bank due to my credit cards and Traveler's Cheques, they were all in my suitcase and are gone. I have been really worried, but I am now feeling much better. I think there are somethings we just can't understand and have to let go. I am using the internet cafe at the hotel now since I don't have my computer with me. I will get a new one this week, because I need it to install the software on the machines when these arrive. I just want you to know you are always in my thought and i care so much about you. I miss you so much and look forward in talking to you soon, and to feel your touch.

I need you so much and will forever be there for you. I love you the more every moment, I know without you in my life, there is no life, because you coming into my life has changed so many things, and have brought so much joy and happiness to me. You are the part of me I can never do without. I was not able to do anything today, because of what happened. Mr Warleh will be picking me up soon for dinner. I will be back to e-mail you and hope to talk to you soon. Another thing, please send me your home and cell numbers again, I have lost them all too. Take care and know you are always in my thought. I love you so much.

Love always . . . Davis

From: Tess

Sent: September 8, 2008 12:22:14 PM My Darling Davis,

I'm so sorry to hear that this has happened, just keep persevering on getting your stuff back, positive thinking and it will come back to you somehow . . . I hope you were able to deal with everything without difficulty, are you able to get copies of your papers? No, you will get back what you lost, positive thinking, . . . and like you said sometimes, things happen you can't explain. I do believe that things do happen for a reason, whatever that reason is, it is sometimes shown to us very clearly and sometimes we just have to go with the situation to find out what it is we have to do.

I did get some rest, thank you, but funny enough, I was awake at 3:00 this morning, I woke up with thoughts of you . . . I read for awhile and then went back to bed until 0600. I do feel rested today. When will you get to go out to the mine? And one more question, which city are you in?

My cell phone number is 311-555-0101 My home number is 311-555-2121

I Love you Davis, my thoughts are with you . . . I am looking forward to hearing from you, I need to hear your voice, feel your laughter, I need to feel you close . . . I know that things will work out for you. It is a good thing that you have people there to help, sometimes it's the people that we need to turn to for help in cases such as this, that turn out to be important people in our lives.

I feel you are already a part of my life, and you will become more so, so much more, I want to be a part of your life as well . . . I want you to know that when things happen, I am here for you. Even if it's just to listen to you, to listen to your worry. To console you, to comfort you, to give you strength to carry on; to love you in everything you do. I look forward to your e-mail. Let me know how things are going for you. I have such strong feelings for you, they make my whole body feel so warm. I have to tell you, like I said earlier, you've turned me into feeling like a teenager. I have put your picture onto my phone so I can look at you during my day, and I sigh and I melt. I love your smile . . . see what you've done to me . . . It's terrible . . . but I love it. I love the feelings that you give me and have given to me . . .

I had better go being that I'm at work, and my break is almost over, if you get a chance to call me, I will be busy during the day from 1:30 to 3:30PM after that I will have my cell phone with me at all times, and I will be home this evening from 6:00 onwards. I hope everything works out for you, you get your briefcase back and if not that you are able to cancel and replace everything in the time that you need it. I love you and know that you are in my thoughts always . . .

Tess . . .

I miss you Davis . . .

From: Davis

Sent: September 9, 2008 5:34:24 AM Darling Tess,

I am doing well and hope you are fine too. I have still not gotten my stuffs yet, and pardon me for not being able to e-mail you before I went to bed last night. I got back to the hotel only to find out that the cafe was closed. I am so lucky my passport and ticket were with me. It would have been a big blow to lose my passport. Anyway things are ok. I was at the police station this morning, and I asked Mr Warleh to get me a connected phone. It's funny here, I was told to check in for a connected cell at 5PM. So I will not be able to call you till then. I will be going to the mines tomorrow. I have to see the place and know what I will need or if there is some renovations to be done. I am in the capital town of Ghana, which is called Accra. The mines are a four hours' drive from here. I will have to call my bankers and credit card company to cancel the other traveler check and block my credit card, and see how best I can access my money here. I was again lucky I had enough money with me. I use a business passport, so I am allow to carry enough money on me.

You are always lighting up my heart with the things you say. I feel so happy just being with you this way. You're my baby, and will forever be my baby. You will always be the love of my life, and please never give up, always have faith in yourself and you will gain the greatest gift of all, the gift of hope and the love you righteously deserve. I like your mails so much; when I read them, I feel warm. I feel so, so good and very happy. Now when I look at your picture, I miss you lots—all day and all night. I wonder what you are doing now and how things are going at work. Are you okay? Darling, if I was around you, we would be having our meals together or going out together. I want to intelock your fingers with mine, when I think about this. I feel very happy. I want to tell you more and more . . . I love you so, so much. Take care and have a wonderful day. Don't worry about me, cause your darling is doing pretty fine, and everything is going to work out well Okay. Love always . . . Davis

On 9/9/08, Tess wrote:

You've touched my inner soul with only your words, Your words have spoken to me in so many ways,

Your words are your heart, your words are your love . . .

Your words are you . . . I fell in Love with your words, I'm falling in Love with you . . .

On 9/9/08, Tess wrote:

My Darling Davis,

I'm glad things are going well for you, and thank you for relieving my concern and the fact that you had your passport and wallet on you, was extremely lucky and a smart move. I have faith in you and in me, and I will keep hope for both of us as well. I know that things will work out for you and that everything will be fine . . . I don't give up very easily, that is one thing that you will learn about me, I persevere, always . . . and one thing I know for sure, is that I will never give up on you . . . Never . . . It is a relief though knowing that you're ok, and that you have such a positive attitude towards your situation. I like that about you. Actually I love that about you.

You asked me how I was doing, I'm doing ok as well, as I mentioned earlier, you've put a bounce in my step, a smile on my face and laughter in my heart. I feel alive, just like you do I imagine, and it is a wonderful feeling. I again thank you for making me feel this way, I'm still in awe when I think that you are actually real and in my life and feel the same way I do . . . actually I Love You MORE . . .

Zoey is doing pretty good, she has been not wanting to go to bed at her bedtime between 8:30 and 9:00 PM, so she has been pushing it to the limit, Mom I want this, can I have that, I'm not tired. that sort of thing. Finally I read her a story and that did it, she fell asleep. My electrical plug got put in outside, hopefully it will work. Joe said it may trip the breaker as it seems the whole living room is on the one plug; however the hot tub only draws the same as a 75—watt light bulb. It's an inflatable tub.

The roof of my shed will be done tonight, I'm keeping my fingers crossed on that one, and then the gazebo goes up and the hot tub gets inflated, even if it's just for a month until the end of October, at least I can enjoy it a little bit. Now correct me if I'm wrong: did you say when we talked on the phone at one time that you had a hot tub as well? I get so many visions of you and I doing things together, one is sitting in a hot tub, relaxing, touching each other, and if I go on, I will just get myself all bothered and possibly bother you up as well, because there is alot more going on than just touching, but I can tell you in my thoughts you do know how to please me . . . I hope that I can please you as well.

When I look at your picture I feel your warmth and I feel close to you as well. I am hoping that you will be able to phone me, however I do understand if you're not able to. I will carry my cell with me all day, and even if I'm at work I will stop and talk with you, however there will be a time from 1:00 to 2:00 when I will be in a meeting again today where I won't be able to have my cell phone with me, after that It's on me.

My son Chad is still in Edmonton visiting, he will be back on the 23 of this month and my son Zach, who quit his regular school and went to what they call the individual learning center in his 12th year, ( I shake my head at him), anyhow he completed a couple of courses at this other school and he had a couple more to do in order to graduate, so finally after taking a year off, he has gone back to school. The Individual

Learning Center ILC for short . . . is great for kids that don't fit in with the regular hours of school, they either live on their own and have to work or just can't get up at 8:00, funny how teenagers do that, anyhow. The ILC works on a drop—in basis and they have to put in 8 hours a week and complete their assignments. So I'm hoping my son can do this and graduate this year. He is one that needs direction my son Zach—I have been pushing him to go back to school and to get a trade. He works at the bar on the weekends so he is in a perfect position, oh lord I'm sorry I didn't mean to go on, but I do worry about my son. My sons are good boys. I think you'll like them, they'll definitely like you, you play playstation . . . I'm a little worried . . . between shopping with my daughter and playing playstation with my sons, I may have to set times with you . . . ok, now you play with me . . . lol I do hope you're ready for a family, my family—because joining me, you join my family . . . we're a pretty good family, I must admit and we have a lot of love to give . . . I have a lot of love to give to you . . . for the rest of forever . . .That's a promise . . . I have to get going and get ready for my day . . . I love you and I miss you . . . even though you've only been in my life for this last month I feel as if I know you, as if you've become a part of me, and not being able to touch you, talk with you I am missing you . . . you have become so much a part of my life.

I Love you Davis . . . you're always in my thoughts . . . Tess

From: Davis

Sent: September 9, 2008 8:58:11 AM Dearest Tess,

I miss you so much and can't wait to have a cell so we can get to hear each other's voice again. I just got back to the hotel, thought I would catch you online before you leave, but I got late. I will be most happy to be a part of your family, as I told you before, I want to be part of everything that makes you. I am very ready for a family, a family with you is all I want. I love you so much, Tess. I never thought that I could ever love this much, but you came into my life and showed me that I can. I have never been as in love with anyone before as I am with you. I now feel without your love I would probably die. I promise you this, from this day forth: I will love you forever—don't' ever doubt that. I will never want anyone else's touch but yours; you make me feel like I am the only man in the world. You are the only woman in the world as far as I am concerned. You are my heart and soul. I feel as though we are meant to be together, that we have been brought together by God.

I have always believed that I had a soul—mate out there and I am sure that is you. I see it every time I look into your eyes in your picture, and I feel it when I close my eyes and imagine your touch, and I have hottub when we talk. I hope your shed is completed tday, and want you to know you can talk to me able everything/anything. I will get in touch later and hope we can talk on phone. I love You.

Love always . . . Davis

From: Davis

Sent: September 9, 2008 11:46:53 AM Hi Tess,

I hope work is treating you well. I spoke with my bankers, and the credit card companies a few minutes ago. They all seem to say the same thing, they can't do anything to help me till I come there in person, the reason being security. They said I didn't inform them I will be coming to Ghana, and from past experience, they can not offer help till I am at their office in person. I understand them in a way, it's great to know my money is secured, and no one can have access to it that easily. I will have to just deal with what I have on me till I get back. I am telling you this because I think you need to know everything that goes on with me. But please don't get worried about me because I am doing fine and have much experience with this kind of issues. It's just that things here are very different, I haven't been to a place like this. But I need not complain much because I expect staffs like this when coming to a third world country. I will be going to the shop tomorrow to get a new computer. I just hope I can get it here. Oops, I have to get going, Mr Warleh is here, he is picking me up for dinner. I will not stay long, and will e-mail you if the cafe is not closed by the time I get back. I have a cell now, and will call when I get back. Take care, you are always in my thought and in everything I do. I love you the more every passing minute, and can't wait to have you close to me and see you lying next to me. Talk to you later . . . love you love always . . . Davis

On 9/10/08, Tess wrote:

Hello my Darling Davis,

I Love You, I want you to know that everyday I will tell you many times that I love you and how much I love you, for the rest of your life, which will be forever     I hope you never tire of hearing it, for

I will never tire of saying it, and that is a promise you can hold me to. I was standing outside today, looking around at the trees and the mountains, the leaves are turning yellow, orange and red, fall is one of my favourite seasons for all of the colours it brings. There was a little bit of snow on the outlining mountain tops these last couple of days, none on grey mountain yet, usually when that happens, the snow is getting close . . . the days haven't been very sunny lately, I hope that next week we will start to see blue sky and bright sunshine. I'm hoping to get to Skagway for the last weekend in September, I hope you will be home by then and we can then go together, even if it's just for the day. It's the last weekend for the tour boats and there are sales galore, it's a great time to get stocking stuffers and last year I got some really nice tops, jackets and rain pants for $5.00, gifts for the boys and Zoey. I would like to take Zoey to Skagway and let her get a few knickknacks for fun. It would be great if you were here. I'm hoping you'll have an idea soon as to how long you will have to be in Ghana.

I imagine today you will see the mine site if you haven't been there already, let me know how it is. And thank you for letting me know what goes on and how things are going with you, it does make me feel closer to you. I'm still in awe over you and I long for the day when we will stand looking at each other face to face, knowing that this will be the rest of our lives . . . and then we will touch . . . that thought completes me . . . You will complete me. I can just feel it . . . I feel like you are my destiny. I can hardly wait for the day when I can reach my arms around your neck, raise my lips to yours and feel your lips caress mine, I long to feel your kiss . . . I need you Davis, I want you . . . I Love You . . . Before I say goodnight, my friend sent me this questionnaire to see what kind of sports car you would like. As you can see, I am being compared to a Ford Mustang, the picture that I get is of a Red sleek Ford Mustang. It gives a little blurb of what the meaning is and I have attached that below, now I'm wondering what kind of sports car would you like . . . let me know I Love you so much and I'm thinking about you every minute of my day . . .

Love always . . . Tess

From: Davis

Sent: September 10, 2008 4:32:33 AM Darling Tess,

I hope you had a good sleep and dream about us, as I always do. I am doing really fine, and hope you and Zoey are good. Sometimes, I can't express to you the way I really feel inside. There are times I want to write poetry, or sing a song but they just say some of what my heart wants to tell you.

It saddens my heart and sometimes I feel like crying because I want to be with you, but work has brought me this far and I don't know what to say or how to tell you how much I need you so much in my life. I am so proud of you and for who you are. I believe in you, and know that our love will conquer all. I write you this letter to tell you how much I care, and love you, and if you ever needed me, baby— please know I will be there. I may not be the most handsome man in the world but my heart is filled with gold. I know our friendship will continue to grow strong and we will conquer all obstacles placed between us. You make me feel so special and it overwhelms my heart to know there is a special you who thinks highly of me. Let's grow in love, unity and respect forever. Miles separate us and our culture is not alike, but we are connected and share similar interests. Everything that makes you happy is what I will also want. I want to wake up to see the sun rise in your eye, I want to have you forever and love you forever. All I want is the best for us, I want all of your love as I have given all of mine to you. It's yours forever, and you don't need to worry about a thing, because I will always be there to hold you when you need someone to lift you, to guide you when you need someone to protect you, and to love you with all that I am. Sweetheart I will try harder and never give up because I pray our love overcomes all other thing. I love you. I tried calling last night, but was having difficultly. I will try again before you leave for work. You seem to know about me so much—my kind of sportscar is Ford Mustang, a sleek Red. I Love to drive top of the line exotics like Ferrari and Lamborghini too. I have to leave now. Mr Warleh is here, we will check some shops around to get a new imac, I really need it for my work here, and for the installation. We are supposed to go see the mine, I will let you know when we are going. I love you so much and more.

Love always . . . Davis

From: Tess

Date: Wed, 10 Sep 2008 22:55:03—0700

My Darling Davis,

I have felt so . . . my god what can I say, I felt so saddened not being here when you called. I can imagine how you must feel sometimes not being able to get through. I felt the same myself when I couldn't reach you, sad . . . you can make me feel such emotions and I also feel your strength. I'm going to try and call you at 11:30 I was misdialing, I've never made an international call before, so calling was a learning experience. I discovered that along with the country code you have to also dial the city code. I'm glad you let me know that you were in the city of Accra, and then I have caller id on my phone so I was able to get the phone number. I'm hoping that this will work; I hope I was able to wake you up this morning, I want so much to be the one to wake you.

If by chance I couldn't get through, would you be able to try again to call me. My schedule for today will be, home until 8:30am and then I drop Zoey off at school, I have to do an interview at work at 9:00am so I won't be able to answer my phone until 9:45 and then I will keep my phone next to me and make sure that I leave work at 5:00 PM, so if you should call me at the same time that you did today, 5:15 I will be here. Or please call me and wake me, If you read this and it's 600AM or 7AM (your time), call me, wake me . . . if you can get through . . . Davis you know how this is feeling, almost a desperation to talk to you, a want and a desire so strong to hear you, to be close to you . . . and yet I know and understand your position, you being there and me being here, promise me that we will keep each other going until we can be in each other's arms.

I have fallen so deeply in love with you Davis . . . and I don't ever want to lose this, what we have, so I will keep myself strong for you, for us. Zoey, when she told me that you called, she was so excited and then she told me that you asked her if she was alone and she said yes, and then she told me you asked her if she was ok. Thank you for your concern, my son was here, he actually was leaving when I came home, so he wasn't inside the house. Zach watches Zoey for me after school until I can get home.

There are so many questions I want to ask you about how things are going, what is the city like, the people, the food, the mine, I'm going to

70

save it until I can talk to you . . . I will get going right now, I'm going to do my workout and then I'm going to try calling at 11:30. I do hope I've talked with you by the time you read this, if not. I hope I will hear from you soon.

I Love You I send you all my Love Tess

On 9/11/08, Tess wrote:

My Darling Davis,

I have tried calling you so many times, and I have had no luck what so ever, I have the number that you called me from on my caller id and when I call it I get the message saying that this number does not exist. I have tried so many different ways, dialing different combinations with and without the prefixes, to try and get it to work and every thing I do I get number does not exist, the only thing I can think of is that maybe your phone is registered in a different city code, caller id does not show me the country code or city code and when I call the number directly it is no longer in service and it is out of Kentucky. I have to admit defeat in trying to call you   I'm sorry, it is completely up to you now to be

able to get a hold of me . . . or here's an idea: if you can, e-mail me your number, please, one that will work or even your hotel number. I have a calling card that I got in order to call you. I can't even give you the number because it's from Canada to Ghana, so I have to call you to use up this calling card anyhow, Davis I have to go to bed now and

dream of you   I hope you are able to call me when you get up this

morning please call me anytime and wake me, as I said, I would love to wake hearing your voice . . . and if you can't I cherish your e-mails . . .

I love you Davis. Have a great day and know that I go with you All my love     Tess

From: Davis

Sent: September 11, 2008 4:39:56 AM Good Morning My Love,

You always make my day when I wake up to see a mail from you. I hope you slept well. I have been also trying to call, and will keep trying. It's a cell phone I am using here, you don't need to add the city code. Everything is very differenet here. The country code is 00233, and the number is 0271234567. But to dial, just dial it this way, 00233271234567. This is how Mr Warleh said it should be done. I am happy to know Zoey was excited talking to me. Send my love to her for me, and the boys. I have still not been able to get myself a new computer from the shops here. They don't have imac or mac products here. I can't believe what I am seeing here, I bet you will never want to be here. Anyway I am here for business and just have to do what I have to do and get the hell out of here. All I want now in this world is to have you in my arms where you belong forever. I was awake very early today, I kept thinking about you and missing you so badly I couldn't sleep well. If I had a computer, I would have met you online so we could chat/talk before you went to bed. I walked to the cafe in the morning hoping they would be open by then, but they weren't here. I have already been to some shops this morning with Mr Warleh to get the computer, but have still not been able to get one. We will keep trying other shops before I leave to the mines. I have not been able to see the mines since I arrived because of what happened, and me spending most of my days looking for a new computer. But come what may, I will have to see the mines today and will be leaving in the next two hours. We will not start work today, I just want to see the place and know what level of renovation I will be needing. I miss you so much and want you with everything that I am. I have been looking for you all my life, you are so perfect to me. As much as I have accepted you the way you are, know you have also to accept me the way I am. Never think for a second that I will use someone's photo in search of true love. It's me on the picture, it had to be me because I was looking for someone to accept me the way I am, and love me for who I am. Thank God I found that person, you. I find all I have ever wanted in you, and I am never going to let you go. I will love you with all my heart, love your family, your dog, I mean   I will love everything about you. You are always in my thoughts, I see you when I close my eyes, and feel your touch and tender kiss all the time. I hear you telling me never to give up on anything. You give me the strength to face anything. Your love has covered me, and keeps me safe and warm. Thank you so very much for the love and new life you have given me. I will keep calling till I get the chance to hear that sweet and clam voice of yours. I will never let you down, I promise. Ti amo.

Amore(Love) . . . Davis

On 9/11/08, Tess wrote:

My Love,

I have tried calling again this morning and the way Mr. Warleh said to dial it, just doesn't want to work from here, so I've been getting help from the operators and I finally get a phone that I get a ring on and then it goes into technical difficulties please try again . . .

You will have to tell me how things are there. I can imagine they must be, should I say difficult to see, just by your statement. I can sense your frustration. I was thinking, if you're having such a hard time finding an imac, how about if I bought one here for you and couriered it to you. I have a Visa I can put it on and you can just pay me back. Give me the description of what you need and I'll just go online or pick one up here and literally I could fed-ex it out to you tommorrow and you could have it next week sometime. Let me know because it would be something I can do for you. It's totally for selfish reasons, the sooner you get an imac the sooner you can come home . . . lol

I Love you Davis, when you say you're willing to accept everything about me, I want you to know as well I accept everything about you—quirks, quarks, whatever you have about you, you have made me so happy and have given me your love, never have I felt so much love, caring and respect and just with your words, you have made me so happy, how can I not accept . . . you do realize that you probably have more to accept of me, than I do of you . . . if that makes sense. I'm not only asking you to accept me, but my kids, and my dog, my ways, which really aren't that bad. I'm not set in any sort of way that I have to have things certain ways, I kind of tend to go with the flow, so to say. I have been alone for quite a while, you've been alone longer, you probably have some set ways about you, your routines, and I have mine, and we'll work together to get around them and with them. I mean so far we've done pretty good, I'm definitely attracted to you, I keep flipping my phone open just to look at you . . . and I melt . . . and I get a strong feeling that you're attracted to me . . . we have a lot in common, I also get a feeling that we feel the same way, our emotions . . . I have this feeling that if we were to disagree on something; we're just going to do it, just so we can make up. The passion between us is learning the little things about each other, and I think that is how we will grow, we will learn to accept and we will love, and each day I am going to be thankful for having you in my life. That I do know. I Love

You Davis . . .

It's supposed to snow on Wednesday, slight flurries, or maybe freezing rain. I shouldn't be telling you this, you're probably in nice warm weather in Ghana right now. I had better go . . . it's getting late . . . and work calls as I said in my earlier letter.I will be home by 5:00 tonight if you can call me, this time change makes it late for you, I know . . . I want to know how it went at the mine. And let me know about the computer, I have lots of room on my visa so you don't have to wonder about that if you're wondering. Amore . . . That's the language of love. Italian.yummm . . . I can't believe I just wrote that, yes yummmmm. I'm so in love with you Davis . . . and I'm looking forward to hearing your voice . . .

Amore . . . Tess by the way, what did I say to you in Italian? I thought I said I Love You . . . That's what I meant to say.

From: Davis

Sent: September 11, 2008 10:37:12 AM My Love,

You are so wonderful, and the best woman a man can ever have. I love you so much and will forever love you with all that I am. Ti amo, as you got it right is I love you. I love you so much. I am at the mine and will be leaving soon. Mr Warleh said he hopes we can get the imac at another shop, so we will check it out when we arrive at Accra. If I am not able to get it, then I think I will have to count on you to buy it and send it to me here, and I can pay you back. You are so sweet, and am so glad to have you in my life. You will forever be cherished deep in my heart and I will forever adore you. I love you Tess, I swear I truly love you with all my heart, soul and mind. I used to be a dead—living man before I found you. I never knew I could madly be in love.

As soon as you came into my life, my fingers met joy and my heart felt at peace. I was like a land without water, where every plant witnesses drought, a sea without oxygen where every organisms met with God and like the rose without nectar, which was deserted by every insect. When I found you, a new me was made. Sometime in a life time, we meet people we have no expectation of meeting. Sometimes you meet people and your whole world experience reforms. I meet you and started realizing the reason why I have to stay longer. There are times I search for who cares and loves me but I never see, until a day I want to fail in faith and hope but going down I meet your soft, tender hands waiting to lift me up, which shows love and care.

My heart accelerates at the speed of light, every time I breathe, I hear the rhythms of your sweet name, Tess, Tess, Tess, so melodious and charming. Every time I breathe I notice the inclination in the level of love I have for you. Maybe it's because I keep you in the most integral part of my heart. Without your love, I realize, "I can stop breathing, because even if I do, my brain will never cease in passing the impulse of you to my soul because my love for you is burning out of control. Ti amo, Ti amo Ti amo, I will keep trying to call and hope to hear your sweet voice soon. Ti amo.Amore sempre . . . Davis

(Love always) . . . Davis

*Davis called me, he had such a romantic, Italian accent in his voice, that I just loved hearing from him.He told me that he was having no luck in finding an imac computer so he told me to go ahead and get him one. He reminded me to make sure that it was an imac computer as that is what the program he had for the machines needed to be used on. I asked Davis if he could tell me where he suggested I should go to get an imac, and just after asking that question the phone cut out and I couldn't reach him again. I immediately started looking around Whitehorse and discovered that an imac was not an easy machine to come across. Being the determined person that I am, I contacted a computer store in Vancouver that dealt with imacs and ordered the best that they had.*

*When I told Elliott, the store manager the address where I wanted the computer sent to, he started to ask me questions as to why I was sending a computer to Africa, and me, the person that I am, I told him. He told me that he wished for me that everything would work out, he did asked me if I wanted to get the insurance that would cover me if the computer was stolen, this I agreed to.*

From: Tess

Date: Fri, 12 Sep 2008 10:39:53—0700

Hello Elliott,

Could you please contact me and let me know when the imac gets picked up and is on it's way. I still haven't received the Visa information; I would feel a lot better once I have paid for this. Thank you

Thanks again the fax number in case you need it is 311-555-3232 Please put Attn Tess

From: Tess

Date: Fri, 12 Sep 2008 10:06:02—0700

Hello Elliott

Again Thank You, This is for the imac computer. The name and address is

Davis Barienda c/o Mr. Earl Warleh Totoei Tayamer #1 Front Street 00233

Accra-Ghana, West Africa. phone number 0271234567

It has been told to me that it is important for the address to be written like this in order for the package to make it there. My account number at FedEx is 000000000 It was set up this morning so it is a new account. Again my phone number is 311-555-0101 if there are any problems please call me.

Thank you Tess

On 9/13/08, Tess wrote:

My Darling Davis,

Here is a copy of the invoice, I have the tracking number for the fed ex package if you need it.

I Love you . . . Tess

*When I told my friend about the computer that I was having sent to Davis, her immediate reaction was "No", she told me that I was being scammed. She even went online and googled Earl Warleh, his full name, and listing after listing of scammers going by that name came up. My response to her was, No, I believe Davis, I want to believe Davis. I told her, even if I am being scammed, he has made me feel so wonderful, so alive, so loved for the last month that I'm willing to take the risk and take that chance. I got that gripping tight feeling around my heart, that feeling that something wonderful was going to be taken away from me, and I felt scared, scared of not losing my money, but of losing the love that I was feeling.*

*I e-mailed Davis, (again, that e-mail is missing) and basically asked him about Mr Warleh, and what the scammers list had stated. I told Davis about my friend's fear of me being scammed.I had such an empty feeling in my heart; I didn't want this to be happening.*

From: Davis

Sent: September 13, 2008 4:03:42 AM Hi Tess,

I know you are sleeping as I write this mail, so I will not worry you by calling. I think we need to talk, I don't like the way people around you seem worried about you and me. You have been the most wonderful thing to ever happen to me, and I have never been the same since you came into my life, but I feel insecure after reading all those mails about your friend and other people around you thinking otherwise about me. All I have ever wanted is to have someone I can truly love with all my heart and the person loving me the same way. I found all I have ever wanted in you. If you think your friend and others around you are right, I think it would be better if we stop communicating till I come home. We will decide if we truly want this relationship or not. I have never brought a third party into my relationship, I do what I feel is the best and what my heart wants. My heart wants you and I have so much falling in love with you and keep falling. I already have some problems settling down with business since I came here. Things have not been good at all, but with the strength you give me, and knowing you love me has had me being able to manage. Just as I thought everything was moving perfectly well, your friend comes in. I spoke with Mr Warleh, and his name being googled, and he drove me within ten miles and introduced me to over ten people having the same name here. He said the name is a family name, and every male of that family holds that name. That is their culture, and they are known by their name wherever they go. He was introduced to me by those I took over the mines from, and they have been working with him for a very long time now. I think about you so much all the time, and in everything I do. It hurts my heart to know I am being seen as someone different.

Things are going well with the mines. We were able to get a contractor to estimate the renovation at the mines, we are going to get the materials that we can get today, and start work as soon as we can. I am rushing things to be done very fast because I just want to come home to see you, kiss you, feel your touch, look into your eyes and tell you how much I love you, but if you think otherwise to, please let me know. I am getting late and have to go now, I will call soon so we talk about this. Send my love to Zoey, tell her I look forward to our first shopping. Take care, enjoy the weekend and know you are always in my thoughts. Ti amo.

Love always . . . Davis

On 9/13/08, Tess wrote:

My Darling Davis,

I love you so much. I wish I could put my feelings into words that would make sense to you. I have told you that I believe in you, and I have told a friend of mine about sending you the computer and she has become quite worried about me getting hurt, she has been the only one that has, doubted the world of online dating in regards to people saying they're not who they say they are, she is worried that, that is what you are doing to me . . . she doesn't want to see me get hurt. Davis, I want to be honest with you about everything, I feel so bad about this though, because seriously, with everything you're dealing with you don't need this. Please forgive me . . . I LOVE YOU so much. Since you've come into my life, you have sent me soaring, and again I hope you realise that if I did have any doubt about you I wouldn't have offered and I wouldn't have sent you the computer, nor would I have given you all of my Visa info either . . . That's how much I trust you and believe in you. I unfortunately sat and listened to my friend reading these internet scammers to me, it's terrible what people do . . . All I can say is that I want you in my life in Zoey's life more than anything that I have ever wanted, if nothing else, what this has done is brought forth the feeling of how I Love You and how much I need your Love and how deep your love goes into me, because just the thought about you not being in our lives has been tearing my heart apart, the thought of not being able to touch you, kiss you, talk with you, be with you leaves me feeling so empty. I don't ever want to lose you, Davis, and please, no, I do not want to stop communicating with you, I need to hear from you. Seeing your e-mails, chatting with you, talking with you on the phone, keeps me close to you . . . Please believe me I never doubted you, I knew you would e-mail me, and reassure me, if that makes sense. I had to tell you, what I was dealing with, which I'm sorry about. Can you forgive me . . . and please don't feel insecure about me, about us . . . my feeling for you is very real, very alive, I need you Davis, I Love

78

You, you have made my life wonderful, I don't want to ever let go of you and these feelings that you have given me . . . they're beautiful, and please, I apologize to Mr Warleh for the questioning, again it's a terrible thing that these scammers do . . . call me when you can. Zoey everyday talks about you taking her shopping, you've become a part of our lives already Davis,

I hope you as well have a great weekend, and know that this . . . stops now . . . I will let my heart guide me, I promise you. I was awake when you sent me the e-mail, you could phone me anytime you know that . . .

Ti amo . . . amore . . . I will love you forever . . . Tess

From: Davis

Sent: September 13, 2008 9:30:55 AM My Love,

It was so wonderful hearing your voice this morning. I am always dying to hear from you all the time. Once again I am sorry for the disconnection. I tried calling back again, but you didn't pick up. I hope everything is ok. After sending you my last mail, I was starting to wonder if I could live without communicating with you, you have been the reason why I live since you came into my life. I just can't stop thinking about you for a minute and all the wonderful things you do to me. I took a break from the mines to look for a place to send you this mail just to let you know I am thinking about you and love you so much. I have been walking for thirty minutes looking for a cafe to send you this mail. I hope you can understand how important you are to me and how much you are cherished and adored by me. Nothing comes before you, you and Zoey are and will forever be the most imortant part of my life. Without you, there is no me. I trust and believe in you, and know you also do trust and believe in me. What you have done alone speaks for itself, it shows how much you believe in me, I am very thankful for that. I think it will be best if you don't talk to your friend about what goes on with us till I get back. I will like to meet her when I get back, she needs to learn a lot. To be able to find what you truly want, one needs to open up, trust, be very honest and believe. That is what I think, and she needs to learn about that.

Thanks a lot for the computer, you are so sweet. I just saw the invoice, and will pay you when I get home. I think I will need the fed-ex tracking, so please try and send it to me.

We were forever meant to be together, of that there is no doubt. You are truly the woman, the partner and the wife I have only dreamed of until now. I love you, Tess. You are my heart and soul; I am so wonderfully blessed to have you in my life. I LOVE YOU, always and forever. I have to get back to the mines, wrap off and get back to Accra. I will try calling again. Ti amo.

Amore . . . Davis

On 9/13/08, Tess wrote:

My Darling Davis,

I Love you, I have been tired all day, I didn't get a very good sleep last night, I can only imagine how you are feeling. I'm sorry things have not been going all that smoothly for you, I hope once you get the computer, you will be able to do everything that you need to do and then you will be able to come home. I hope that the computer that I ordered for you is what you need, I went for the best one they had, only the best for my guy . . . I wanted to share with you a little bit about my family; my family is a very important part of my life. My mother and father were divorced when I was fifteen and since then both have been remarried. Both sets of my parents live here in Whitehorse, my dad and step-mother, live out of town a ways. My Dad is retired. He is a man who has done a lot throughout the years. Before he retired he worked as a consultant for the government, and my step-mom she too worked for the government as a manager for one of their divisions. She now owns her own business here in town. They have a hydroponics greenhouse, in which my step—mother grows beautiful tomatoes, cucumbers and basil, lots of basil. In fact tomorrow Zoey and I, are going to go out to their place around 11:00 ( it would be today for you, Sunday) and we are going to harvest the basil and make pesto., The leaves on these basil plants are huge, I hope you like pesto. Zoey prefers pesto, Grandma's pesto to be exact, on her pasta, except she calls it pepto. Anyhow, my dad is a very gentle man; he is what I consider a spiritual person. I know you will like him, I told him about you, he is hoping the best for us.

My mom and step-father, live close to us in town, which is nice for Zoey and me. I am very close to my mom; she is like my best friend. She is retired, she used to work for the government for years. She was the secretary to one of the big honchos there, I forget exactly the title. My step-father is a retired RCMP officer and he now works on a casual basis for the government as well. My mom and stepfather are very busy, as they have a house in Atlin, which was my grandmother's house and my mom inherited it when my grandmother passed away two years ago. I'll tell you about my grandmother sometime, she was an amazing woman, anyhow my mom and stepfather are always creating projects of some kind that keep them busy in Atlin. When you get back I would love for us to go in to Atlin so I can introduce you to my family there and to my town. In Whitehorse, my mom and stepfather are building an addition onto their house here. My mom is a very beautiful woman and she has a sense of humour, she also is a very strong woman, she too wishes the best for me, and is looking forward to meeting you.

Both sets of my parents remain friends with each other, in fact when we have a family dinner, both sets of my parents are usually there, which for me, is wonderful, and for my kids as well.

My brother who is a year older than me, lives on Vancouver Island with his wife.

My brother used to be a production manager for a very popular musician who is from here, and is very popular in Taiwan. My brother went to Taiwan several times producing concerts. He is also a musician and song writer, and he is now playing in a band called Anjopa. I will tell you more about him later as well. I also have a step—brother and a step—sister who live in lower BC. I see my step brother and his wife more than my step—sister. That pretty much is the rundown on my immediate family here in Whitehorse and my brother. As I said earlier my family is a very important part of my life and I know that they will love you, when they see how you make me feel and how good you are to me and Zoey. They will be very happy for us.

I think about you so much Davis, and how complete I feel, knowing that you will be a part of my life, everyday you will be there. I look forward to planning our lives with you. I want you to know that you are my life . . . I Love you . . . How are the renovations going, and is there a lot of renovations that need to be done? Is the mine actually a working mine right now or is it just in the starting phase? I guess I should get going, I want to have a bath and go to bed early tonight, I'm hoping you will be able to call me in the morning and please if you're reading this and it's 2, 3, or 4 AM here in Whitehorse, and you can call me, please do and wake me, it was wonderful being woken by you this morning. I look forward to the day when you're lying down next to me in bed and you lean over me and kiss my forehead, my eyelids, the tip of my nose, my lips, and I wake, and reach up and stare deep into your eyes reflecting my love, I patiently wait for the day when you will make love to me . . . Davis, I LOVE YOU . . . ti amo

Amore . . . Tess

From: Davis

Sent: September 14, 2008 6:22:10 AM Good morning My Darling Tess,

I hope you are able to sleep well, because my love is supposed to keep

you warm and safe. I am doing well here, only for the fact that I have a little cold. I guess it's from the dust here. Thank you for sharing this much about your family to me. I know they are a very important part of you, and I am going respect them and make them very important in my life too. As I always tell you, whatever makes you will always be very important to me, what you cherish will also be cherished by me forever. The only important thing in my life is my mom, it's so sad at times to know she is going older everyday. I know and believe deeply that you will cherish her and make her important in your life too. I told her about you and she was so excited for me. She could feel the new life in me, and told me I should hurry and get back home to meet you. She said she wants to meet us right away, and reminded me the most important thing in life is family, so if I have to even forgo this contract to meet you, I should. But I told her you understand that I should finish soon, then come to you. It's been a very long time I felt my mom so excited about something, when I asked her why she seems so much excited, she told me she could feel deep inside her I have found what I have been looking for, for a very long time. My mom has been my everything, and I am so thankful to her for everything. It wasn't easy growing up with her, we had our very hard times, but she always made sure I was okay and had everything I needed. I remember sometimes she had to sell her jewellery just to get me what I wanted. Life in Italy those days were hard, and not having a dad around to support made things more difficult. She was my mom, my dad, my brother, and my sister, and we did everything together. You are the only one who has been able to share the love I have for her. I told her and she laughed and said give Tess the love you had for me, she deserve it for keeping you alive again. My mom is a wonderful person to be with, and I know you will like her so much. I am at the mines, I had to force the workers to come because I want to get things done soon, so I can get back home and be with you forever. I hope to be done with the renovation by the end of this week, and hope the machines will arrive by then. Once I get the machines here(the mines), you should know I will be on the next flight back home to kiss you, feel your touch and hold you so close. I will have to install the software on the machines, show Mr Warleh how to operate it, and see them mine the first oil. Once that is done, I can leave everything in the hands of Mr Warleh and come to you. All I will need is he keeping me updated on what goes on, and I directing him as to what he should do next. Tess, I just want you to know that I feel like I am the luckiest man in the world to be with you. I have never been happier in my life than I am when I have the thought of me having you in my life and going to love you forever. You mean the whole world to me and I can't wait for the day when the world knows the love I have for you. I want nothing more then to be a wonderful husband and perfect father for Zoey. I love you so much Tess, and I will always do. I will call you. Ti amo.

Amore . . . Davis

On 9/15/08, Tess wrote:

My Darling Davis, my Love,

I know I don't have to explain to you as to how it felt to talk with you, I know that you have the exact same feelings as I do. When you tell me how you feel, it's as if you can read my thoughts, as if you can look inside of me, and you're seeing my feelings, my love, and taking them as your own. For my feelings are your feelings. My love for you equates your love for me . . . It's the most beautiful, warmest, wonderful sensation and feeling I have ever experienced, or had. Davis, I am so happy, so utterly happy that you are in my life and will be in my life for the rest of my life and beyond.

A friend of mine called tonight and when I answered the phone, she said "man, you sure sound happy" She wants to meet you, the man who has done this to me, she is happy for me, for us, I have very special friends that are all supportive and want the best for me and are thrilled that I have found someone who makes me so happy, so complete. My step-mom, today, after I talked with you, said to me that she felt a very positive feeling about you, about us being together. She saw my joy after we talked, it's been a long time since I've had that type of joy come out from inside of me . . . Thank you, Davis, and I will thank you everyday. I want to make you happy, I want you to feel special, as you make me feel special, I would like to do something for you, other than give you a massage, cook you meals, pleasure you, what can I do for you Davis, to make you feel special, you've offered to give me everything that I could possibly want, I want to do the same for you, I want to give you everything, and I want you to let me know your wants, your desires, what it is that pleases you, for I want to provide those things for you. And I will meet you at the airport when you come home, I will be standing there waiting for you to walk through those doors and into my arms, Davis I told you I wasn't going to get excited just yet that I was going to remain cool, calm and collected, that's all going out the window. I'm feeling quite excited thinking about you coming home. I know that once we touch each other we will be complete and our lives, both of our lives are going to change and change for the best. Davis, there are so many things that I can see us doing together, each day will be an adventure for us, for all of us, hopefully some adventures will consist of quiet evenings snuggled together watching a movie, drinking a little wine and just holding each other close. I feel like I want to do everything with you, like right now, and I keep telling myself we have a lifetime in which we can do everything and anything, so I don't need to rush everything all at once, You just fill me Davis, you are a wonderful person, and I thank you for coming into my life. I was thinking today, of everything I've been through. It has led me here to you, I needed to go through the things that I did so I would go on eharmony and then, I was so discouraged with this online—dating thing, because I had a couple of bad experiences, that I was just deleting any match notifications and I would get like ten a day. However, your request came up saying fast track communication requested so I looked and there you were from Whitehorse and the rest is a wonderful love story of how two people who needed love in their lives, to give love and to be loved, discovered each other.

I Love You Davis, and on that thought I'm going to go to bed and dream of you, I love your laugh, it fills me, I want to see your smile, you are my light . . . I hope you have a wonderful day today. You are in my thoughts . . . Zoey and I made a lot of pesto, and I hope you like garlic because it is loaded with garlic. I will say goodnight from my end . . . I need to get some sleep.

I Love You . . . ti amo. Amore . . . Tess

From: Davis

Sent: September 15, 2008 4:00:14 AM Good Morning My Love,

I wake up to a lovely day because I felt your love while sleeping. It's always with me, and I can feel it in anything I do. I don't know what I will want you to do for me to make me feel that special, as a matter of fact, I find all I have ever wanted in you. You make me feel so special in so many ways. All I want you to do for me is to always love me the way I love you and always be there for me as much as I will always be there for you. I want us to understand each other in everything we do, and have a happy home forever. I will not do anything to hurt you, and will want you to talk to me about anything, and point to me when I go awry. You have done what I will ever want you to do for me, and that is the feeling you bring to me. I love you so much and will always do. It will be my pleasure to take you and the kids to Disney World, as I said before anything for you. I know you may not be used to someone paying for all expense, but for once, let me take care of this trip. I make enough money, and we are going to make much more with this new mines. Everything I have is yours, because I am yours forever.

Please let's not talk of who is going to pay for the trip to Disney World, because I am. I don't need you supporting. I want to do it for my new family PLEASE. Which is first, Disney World or the romantic getaway ?. Let me know. It will be so nice to see the white sandy beaches with you, sunshine and beautiful blue wate., I want to feel the sand caress my feet as we walk hand in hand along the edge of the water, the waves lapping against our legs, you and I will just be one, and we will be able to feel our hearts as one. I came with Mr Warleh to get some more materials for the renovation, and we are just about to leave to the mines. The contractor working on the renovation on the mines just called that we will need some other things to complete the renovation, and some more worker so we can get things done soon. I told him I didn't know much about the right materials, so I will have to come with him tomorrow so he can get them. I also told him to get some more hands if he thinks that will make things fast with effective work done. I always want things to be done very well and right, it's the best way to get much trust with people you work with or people you supply. I just want to tell you how much I love you, you have brought so much happiness to my life and you do so much for me that no one can ever do to fill my heart. I will continue to love you for the rest of my life . . . and forever. I have to go now, I will try calling and will e-mail you when I get to the mines. If you don't hear from me again before you leave home, just know you are in my thought in everything I do, and I am with you in everything you do. Take care, have a nice day and send my love to Zoey. Ti amo

Amore. Davis

On 9/15/08, Tess wrote:

My Darling Davis,

I don't know what to say, just believe me that I believe you. I just feel sick about this, and I don't know what to do. I've told you I will be honest about everything. The Fed—Ex office called me and they are stopping all shipments over to West Africa that have these type of circumstances until payment or at least half of the payment for these computers is made to the women sending the computers overseas. Davis, the scam of internet-online dating, is huge I guess, and I'm not saying this is what you are doing by any means, anyhow Fed—Ex has seen too many women and men get burnt. They're told that they will get paid back, the computer is bought, sent over and then they are never heard from again and the person who sent the computer is out of a lot of money. So they have this man who is involved in security with Fed—Ex who questions these computer packages. He asked me to ask you, he said if he's legit, he won't have a problem with this, if you would e-mail to me half of the money 1500.00 so they can be assured that I'm not getting ripped off and they will get their money as well. I am so sorry Davis, but if you can go into your bank account online and then you just do an e-mail money transfer to my e-mail address, once I get that they will send the computer over. I am so sorry about this Davis, I love you more than anything and I don't want you to think that I'm questioning you, unfortunately others have caused this to happen and I know you will be able to do this. If you would like his name to talk with him so you can verify, he also wanted me to ask you questions about Whitehorse to verify that you actually lived here. Davis, we can get beyond this; Davis, you said you would do anything for me, would you do this without being upset with me—this just tears me apart that I'm being asked to do this. But they say they are doing this for my own protection and I understand where they are coming from. Davis will you tell me the house number that you live at, so I can say to this guy that yes, he verified. Tell me the business at the end of your street on 4th and Jarvis, but please do this quickly so that the computer can get shipped out and get to you by Wednesday or Thursday now. I want you to come home as soon as possible. Know that I love you so much, I want you in our lives, I'm so sorry about this . . . but there will be no problem, I know that, I just don't want you thinking that I doubt you, because I don't. This security guy is in Vancouver He said that Ghana—Accra to be exact is a haven for this type of scam and unfortunately we fell into it. I Love you Davis . . . with all of my heart . . . I will wait to hear from you . . . ti amo

Amore. Tess

From: Davis

Sent: September 15, 2008 11:10:14 AM Hello My Love,

I hope Zoey is getting better, and you are taking good care of her. I love you so much and will forever love you. I had a letter at the mine this after, it came from the ministry of mines and enegy here. I am to meet with the minister of mines and enegy for a small meeting. I hope to get back to Accra early. If I do not, then I will have to meet him tomorrow. I will call you when I get back to Accra. I love you, you are so sweet and wonderful. Tell Zoey I said she should get well soon. Ti amo.

Amore . . . Davis

From: Davis

Sent: September 16, 2008 3:44:17 AM Good Morning My Darling Tess,

I guess you are sleeping deep by now and dreaming of us having a wonderful time which will happen soon. Just came from the office of Fed-Ex. I was told there was an improper or missing paperwork, and that you needed to contact Customer Service. Please do that first thing this morning by calling them. I am off to the meet with the minister of mines and energy. I am not sure I will be able to go to the mines today because of the timing. I will be online 7 AM your time if I am not able to get you on the phone. I tried this morning, it went through though you didn't pick up. Guess you were asleep. I love you so much and miss you. I am getting late, I will talk with you at 7 AM your time. I am crazily in love with you, and this love only grows stronger. Ti amo.

Amore . . . Davis

From: Davis

Sent: September 16, 2008 3:49:00 AM Love,

This is the address they are supposed to ship to, Davis Barienda

C/O Mr. Earl Warleh Totoei Tayamer #1 Front St 00233

Accra-Ghana W AFRICA, Phone:(027)123-4567

You had it right, but I thought you should have it again. I love you. Ti amo . . .

Amore . . . Davis

On 9/16/08, Tess wrote:

My Love,

I am so crazily in love with you . . . Amore . . . Tess

From: Davis

Sent: September 16, 2008 8:33:19 AM Hi Love,

I have been trying to call, but having problems with the connection. I tried calling Fed-Ex, also not being able to get them. I want you to call or go there and tell them to get the computer to me as soon as they can. They have no right to hold on to it. You ordered it to be sent to me, and that is what they are there for. Insist on them sending it now. They can send it to me through the hotel's address or the other address:

Davis Barienda Arahan Hotel 5th street, 00233

Accra-Ghana W AFRICA, Phone:(027)123-4567

I count on you to get this resolved, and let me have it soon so I can finish with what I have to do here and get back home to you soon. I love you so much. Ti amo

Amore. Davis

From: Davis

Sent: September 16, 2008 1:39:14 PM Dear Tess,

I am so sorry for what is going on. I didn't know such a thing was going on around this world, and in Africa till this whole issue started coming up, and I had to start asking more. Mr Warleh told me a lot more'n I needed to know. All I can say now is that I have trusted you with my whole heart and willing to do anything to make you happy. I love you so much and have been honest with you about everything. One good reason why we are connected is because we had been though the same hurt and pain in the past and have been looking for this joy, happiness and love we found in each other. I feel very bad when you I feel you doubt me about something, i have never doubted you of anything, I believe you so much and will do anything to make you happy forever. Thanks for the trust you have had in me to call Fed-Ex to send the computer to me. I know it must have been hard on you, but you took that step just because of the love you have for me, and I promise you this day that I will never let you down. I think it will be best if you tell the Fed-ex security guy that I am your husband and he should send the computer to me. That is, if he tries to hesitate.

I love you so much and will always make you happy.. All I want is to get home sooner so we can begin our new lives together forever. Sitting here and thinking back as to how you have made my life so much better, I could never begin to tell you what your love means to me. You have shown me countless times how you care and how you believe in me, how you have given me the strength to give up something that has had a hold on my life for a very long time, without you I don't think I could be following my dreams, much less having someone like you standing beside me.

I know I tell you all the time how amazing you are, You're an incredible woman; there is nothing I believe you can't do. The way you make me feel is like nothing I've ever felt before. I know I'm a very impatient person coming back to see you and to spend time with you. I want you to know I am trying like hell to do the right thing, but the more time time we talk makes me realize that this is our life's plan, this is how our path of forever is suppose to happen, and sometimes I know it's hard for us to deal with but in the end, we'll be stronger and able to handle just about anything that comes our way . . . we got thru' the hard part, babe, now all we have is the downhill side.

You have brought out a part in me that I put away a long time ago and thought I'd never be able to find again. You make everything so simple and easy for me to let go and with you in my life I don't need to hide that part of me anymore. What you make me feel for you is nothing short of the ultimate happiness. You are in my thoughts, my dreams, my desires, but most of all in my heart. You are my baby girl, my sweetheart, my Tess, and most of all my future wife. I love you now and always, today, tomorrow, and forever. I LOVE YOU SO MUCH and will forever love you. I will try calling you right now, and hope to get though. I am sorry I couldn't hear you when you called. I LOVE YOU SO MUCH and will forever love you. I will try calling you right now, and hope to get though. I am sorry i couldn't hear you when you called.

Amore. Davis

On 9/16/08, Tess wrote:

My Darling Davis, Goodmorning,

My love for you grows stronger each and every day; I want you so much in our lives. I think of the day when you will be home and we can begin . . . Davis I will pray everyday for you, for us, . . . I Love You, I want every night to be able to tell you just how much I love you before I go to sleep, and dream of you . . . Goodnight my darling . . . I Love You . . . ti amo.

Amore . . . Tess

*I felt so torn here, I was in complete conflict with myself, and I had this tightness in my belly and around my heart. If I send the computer I would be taking a chance that this whole thing was a scam and that I may not get the money back and if that was the case, then Davis wouldn't be real and that thought alone made the band tighter around my heart. I kept telling myself, that I had to trust, I had to believe, isn't that what true love is supposed to be, trust and honesty?. I had to believe Davis otherwise he would disappear. I had to take that chance. I didn't want to lose the feelings*

On 9/16/08, Tess wrote:

I love You Davis,

I phoned the security guy who is stopping the packaged from going on and left a message saying to him that, you have made me happier than I have been in my life and that it didn't matter if this was a scam or not. I told him to send the computer, I love you, I wish more than anything that you will be coming home; I ask more than anything no matter what. Please be honest with me. As I said you have given me more love in this last little bit than I have felt in a very long time and I thank you . . . I Love You Davis Barienda . . . ti amo . . . Amore . . . Tess

On 9/17/08, Tess wrote:

My Darling Davis,

I must say that today has felt like an emotional roller coaster. Davis, I will be so glad when you are physically here. I would like you to please keep me informed as to how things are progressing and let me know the day that you will be coming home and when you get to Vancouver I want to know when you get there so I know you're safe and then you will let me know when you are going to arrive here so I can be standing, waiting for you as you walk through the doors at the airport. I keep picturing you walking through those doors and imagining what you will look like. What it is going to feel like to see you, to go to you and have you wrap your arms around me, I imagine what it would be like to look into your eyes and feel for the first time when your lips meet mine, when your tongue caresses mine, for the first time, I imagine this everyday. Then I will leave it up to you to tell me where we will go and I know I will just want to spend every minute with you and hold you. I know you will keep me up to date.

It's almost 9:00 PM, I'm so tired, I'm going to go to bed and read for a while. Do you know one thing that I would love to do with you? I would love to sit with you on the floor, my body leaning against yours, as you sit with your back against the couch—.my head resting against your chest and you sitting with your head touching mine, your eyes closed, and I'm reading you a chapter of a book—a book that you've picked out, that you enjoy. I've always wanted to do that, read with someone. I see these images of you and I all the time . . . they're always so peaceful, so relaxed, and so special. I have kept you special. I Love you so much. What would you like us to do Davis, what do you see you and I doing, will you tell me what you would like us to do?

I do have to go to bed, please Davis, if you get a chance and can get through, please call me, If it rings at all I will hear it, I'm not a heavy sleeper, I wake easily, so if you call and it rings but there is no answer, please try again right away. I have been keeping my cell phone next to my bed so I will hear it. You have a wonderful day today; I love you more each day it seems.

I am so glad today is over . . . each day ending brings us closer to our beginning. I want to share with you what the man from Fed—Ex said to me today. I left him a message to begin with and then I called his pager to make sure he got my message. He did and he said it would be on the plane this evening for London, he said he didn't know what transpired between you and I but he hoped that it worked out for me, and asked me to call him and let him know how things go. Davis, I want to be able to call him and tell him once you get back here that I will be your wife that is what I would really love to tell him. Please make it happen for us . . . I Love You with all my heart . . . ti amo

Amore . . . Tess

From: Davis

Sent: September 17, 2008 3:27:58 AM My dearest Tess,

I Love You so much. I hope you are sleeping calmly and dreamming about us sitting on the floor, your body leaning against mine, as I sit with your back against the couch. Your head resting against your chest, and your eyes closed. I will really love to do that with you and any other thing you have always wanted to do. I am here for you and will always be there when you need to do anything with me. I am going to the ministry again today. There was some paper work to be done to show I am the rightful owner to mine oil at the mines. Yesterday was kind of a bad day for me, I couldn't really do anything right, with a whole lot going on my mind. I am so glad you asked them to ship the computer to me, I know you don't doubt me, and will do everything I can to prove you I am who I am and the perfect man to love you. I love you so much Tess, I love you deep in my heart. I need to go now, I will keep you informed about everything that happens and when I will be coming back home to kiss you, feel your touch and look into your eye and say to you I Love You. Thank you for everything, you have really brought much joy, love and happiness to me. Send my love to my sweet Zoey, tell her she will see me soon. I love you two so much. Ti amo

Amore. Davis

On 9/17/08, Tess wrote:

My Darling Davis,

Every time I read your letters I want to wrap my arms around you and hold you so close to me. You make me feel wonderful, Thank You. How did everything go at the Ministry of Mines? It seems like your day yesterday reflected my day, emotions and feelings have such a strong role in how things happen around us. I was just thinking, I told you I wanted the fairytale, and in every fairytale there seems to be a time when love has to be fought for, this is what I feel is happening to us, we need to fight for and stand up and say to these people love is real, will you rescue me, we will be able to show everyone how strong love, true love, really is . . . You are my true love and what I feel for you is so strong, it takes my breath away at times. I told you that I had to get another power pack for my hot tub sent to me. Well it has to be sent to Juneau as it's too expensive to ship to Whse. So we may have to go to Juneau when you get back to get this. In the five years that you've lived in Whitehorse, have you ever been to Juneau? Myself, I have lived in Whitehorse most of my life and I have never been. Anyhow, I said the hell with it, the one I have right now, even though it's leaking I'm going to use it.It'll heat the water it runs the jets, and I have to throw this one away when the other one gets here, (I'll keep it for spare parts, just in case) anyhow I put the water in last night at 6:00 PM temp was 60 and now this morning it's up to 81 degrees, so maybe tonight, however, I need to put more cold water into it before leaving for work so who knows, if its up to 90 degrees tonight I'm going in . . . I had better go and start my day . . . I hope your day has gone well for you . . . I Love You Davis, I Love You with all of my heart. Zoey asked me to tell you HI from her, she asks me everyday, did you talk to Davis, mom, will he be here soon? . . . She is really looking forward to meeting you and to having a family, she said to her friend the other day that you are going to be her new step-dad . . . I have never mentioned to her anything about the fact that you and I have talked about this, . . . it's the shopping thing, a guy who loves to shop well, he's the one . . . lol I have to get going, I love you . . . I will be thinking about you . . . and I'll let you know how my inflatable hot tub feels.    I give to you a great big hug and lingering, sensual, tongue caressing kiss, one that lasts for more than

two minutes, yumm. ti amo. Amore Tess

From: Davis

Sent: September 17, 2008 10:00:19 AM My Love,

It feels so wonderful to have someone like you in my life, I am so grateful and so excited to have you and will forever love you. I love you so much Tess. My day at the ministry was good, we still couldn't finish getting all the paper work in place, but hope to complete it tomorrow, then I will continue with the mining at the mine. I was at the port this afternoon, and was told the machines will be in mid-next week. I just hope it doesn't delay. I have never been to Juneau, and will love to go with you. I think we will have to go the first weekend I arrive.

Thanks for being there when I needed you to be, for patiently listening to my personal problems. I just want you to know how happy I am to have you in my life. Thank you for the love and the joy you bring. You've changed my life. You have given my heart so much excitement and thrills. When I think about you I feel like I'm out of love control. I know that when you say you love me, it's truly from your heart. I love you too so much and it also comes from my heart. I love you and that's what I want you to bear in your mind, and it's for keeps. I will try calling later, you can always try calling it you have the chance. I am happy Zoey will love me to be her step-dad, I promise to do anything to be the best she will ever want. Tell her I am doing fine and will be back home soon. I love you. Ti amo

Amore. Davis

On 9/18/08, Tess wrote:

Hello My Darling Davis,

I Love You. How has your day been going? I can imagine that you are extremely busy. I hope all is going well for you; I have complete faith in you. I get this feeling that you are an incredible man, a strong man, one with a good sense of what needs to be done and you do it right. I love that about you. A man with conviction. That's the feeling that I pick up from you.

I thought that these two other pictures I sent you last night you would have this morning, but it seems they didn't attach to my e-mail so I'm sending them to you now. I tried again to call this morning when I woke up and I'm still not able to get through. I'll keep trying, I will never give up, I promise you that. I had better get going and jump into the shower. I also have to get Zoey up which on some days can be a challenge, she likes her sleep. I keep thinking just wait until she's a teenager. I need to steer her in the right direction before puberty hits, or else we are in trouble. I have a feeling that you will help me in that area. Maybe she can get a job of being a personal shopper for someone . . . lol I have to go, and get naked and rub soap all over my body, see I'm thinking of what it would feel like  if you were washing my body, caressing me with soap suds . . .  and then I would take the soap and caress your body, all over . . . oh my . . . I could go on but I'm afraid that you wouldn't be able  to handle it, you'll just have to be here, in person to see how that one plays out . . . lol I love you so much . . .my thoughts are with you . . . ti amo.

Amore . . . Tess

From: Davis

Sent: September 18, 2008 11:20:21 AM Hello My Love,

I hope your day is going well. I am doing good here, but really miss you. I haven't been able to mail you till now because I have been very busy today. I am glad you have finally been able to set the hottub. It surely is wonderful. I left the hotel at 7 AM this morning, went to the ministry of mines and thought I could leave there soon so I can meet the contractor then buy the other things he said we will need for the renovation, but things didn't go that way. After the meeting this morning, I realized I will need a barrister to help me go though the process. Mr Warleh got me one and we had to go though the thing. I am told to continue with work, I need to have a Certificate of Incorporation. I will be working that one out with the barrister. This brings me to another important point. I have been doing a lot of thinking about you, Zoey and my business. I thought the love you have shown me and for your willingness to be there for me all the time as much I will be always there for you, then a thought came to my mind. I thought it will be perfectly good if I use my name and yours as the owners of the mining company. I feel whatever I own belongs to you and Zoey, so why don't I involve your name. What do you think about it.? I told the barrister this mine was for my wife, my kid and me, and I wanted your name in everything, and he said it was permitted. So I will do it that way. Let me have your fax machine number, so I can send you a copy of all the documens. You will need to have one for safekeeping, just in case . . . I have decided to let Mr Warleh go with the contractor to get the materials tomorrow, so I can get the paper works done soon and get back to business. I am leaving the ministry now for dinner, I have not eaten all day. I am having problems getting through with the phone, but I will keep trying and will mail you before going to bed. if the cafe is still open at the time I get back to the hotel. I love you so much and think about you in everything I do. You are now the part of me that I just can't do without. I adore you. Take care.

Ti amo.

I . . . Love You . . .

Amore. Davis

# 5

# I OWN AN OIL MINE. WOW

On 9/19/08, Tess wrote:

My Darling Davis,

I've been thinking all day about what you said you're going to do, put my name with yours, and I'm still in awe of you. I have never been given such a gift of trust as you have given to me, you bring tears to my eyes, and fill my heart, all the time, I still don't know what to say, other than I LOVE YOU, and if this is your way of trying to prove that you love me more, well you're doing a pretty damn good job. However, I'm not done yet, I will make sure that you know how much I love you . . . more . . . know that my whole being is within you and you are within me.

I just finished reading Zoey a chapter from her book we're reading when she goes to bed, it's the high school musical series, if you don't know about high school musical, you will soon enough, I have a feeling that I am going to learn a lot from you, and about you, just as you are going to learn a few things from us, and about us. I'm looking so forward to discovering you.

I miss you . . . I miss talking with you. When we talk I feel so close to you, I can only imagine what holding you is going to do . . . I sit here sometimes and close my eyes and feel you . . .

I imagine that today will be another busy day for you, I checked the Fed-Ex tracking info and it's showing that the computer is in Accra so you should have it today. Let me know. I'm hoping that with you having it, we may actually be able to chat once in a while. I love talking to you, hearing your voice, your laugh, you have won my heart over so many times, when I hear your laugh, I hope I can make you laugh everyday.

Today I signed up to take pottery lessons. I've taken two courses already; I haven't been able to do pottery for about two years now, so I figured that taking another course would be a good thing, also learning from someone else I think is important, gives me a chance to pick up other tips and practices. I love doing pottery, and this gives me a chance to make Christmas gifts. I have a rule, that I have followed forever, and that is, that I make my family, such as my parents, aunt's, uncles etc . . . and friends, Christmas gifts. I have made a lot of different things over the years. I do buy gifts for my kids and that special someone, YOU, in my life, (wow, I was just thinking that I haven't been able to buy a gift for someone special in my life because I've not had that opportunity for years. It's going to be so wonderful to do things for you, give you things and know that you will cherish them, appreciate them and accept them. I know this. (I can feel that you would do that.) Again I'm going to enjoy you, enjoy us. See, there I go again, off topic, just thinking of you. Anyhow this course starts Oct 9th and goes until Nov 22 I think, Thursday evenings. Davis, do you feel there is a chance you will be here by your birthday? I'm going to keep the faith . . . and believe that you will be . . . and maybe throw in a prayer or two as well.

I'm now going to get into my robe and climb into my hottub, completely naked, it's dark outside, my neighbors shouldn't be able to see. I want to sit and feel the warmth around me. While I'm sitting, I'm going to think of you, sitting next to me, your hand brushing against me lightly, teasing me, slowly, my hand caressing your chest, slowly, lightly touching you . . . yes . . . there is so much I want to do with you and to you. I look forward to the experiences we're going to share. I had better get going, before it gets too late, I will check again in the morning, it seems I wake around 4 AM these days and I check to see if you're online. And if not then I check again at 7AM. Maybe by then you'll have the computer, will you have the computer at the mine or will you have it in your hotel room for a while?

I Love you, I LOVE YOU DAVIS, with all my heart . . . Have a wonderful day,

I will dream of you, I will dream of us. ti amo. Amore . . . Tess

From: Davis

Sent: September 19, 2008 3:30:37 AM Good Morning My Sweetheart,

I guess you are sleeping warm with the thought of you and me having a wonderful time soon and with my love keeping you warm as you sleep. It has been raining this early morning here today, good for me because I will not have to breathe much dust. Today is going to be another busy day for me as you can see. I was with the contractor and Mr W. earlier on. We went to get the materials we will be needing. I couldn't get all, because I have run out of money. I supplied a company in Japan oil before I started this contract, they have not yet paid me, so I will call them so they can write me a check and send it to me here. I was called from Fed-Ex office this morning that my package was in, I will go with Mr W to pick it up when he returns from the mines later in the afternoon. Thanks you much, I LOVE YOU.

I am meeting with the barrister soon, we will need to first have the Certificate of Incorporation, while we work on the others. I truly hope I can finish with what I am doing here before my birthday. I want to be with you by now and spend it with you and Zoey. I will do all that I can to make sure I am home by then. I will fax you every document that comes to me, and will fax you the Certificate of Incorporation soon as I have it, so I guess you need to info your mom, and please keep it safe. It's yours, it's mine and its Zoey's. We are now a family, and I want you to know I cherish you two. I want us to do everything together. I love you so much, and can't live a minute without thinking about you. I feel you in everything I do. Only you can stop me from breathing, because you hold my heart. I have to go now, I will mail you when I get the chance again. Another thing, the barrister said I needed to get a different communication network, one that will be much easy to get to me, so he said he will get it and will let me have it by the end of today. With that, I don't think we will be having hard time talking on phone. I love you so much Tess,

I adore you. Ti amo . . . I LOVE YOU . . .

Amore . . . Davis

From: Tess

Sent: September 19, 2008 4:46:42 AM My Darling Davis,

It looks like I missed you again, I woke at 3:45, my computer takes forever to start up and then to sign on to the internet, then by the time I got online it was after 4:00. I'm so glad the computer is there. YESSSSS. Everything will work out, just keep the faith, and all will go well. I will hope and pray that you will have me in your arms for your birthday.

When I went to arts underground yesterday, at Hougens, what used to be Zola's is now Board Stiff except for the very front of the place, it is a food specialty store, the proprietor is going to bring in all different types of specialty ethnic foods, spices, sauces, etc . . . it's called the Bent Spoon, he is just opening, oh and he also has an expresso/latte machine, anyhow, right now he has all Italian foods there and all I could see was you . . . lol. I kept thinking, now that's Italian . . . lol . . . Its not a big store, but it'll definitely be interesting, I smiled as I looked at everything, and I wondered, what could I make for you . . . better yet, what would you make for me? I can just imagine what we will make together. I LOVE YOU DAVIS with all my heart and soul. You have me. I sat last night for the first time . . . IN MY HOTTUB, ok it wasn't' that hot, 96-97 degrees, but that was ok, it was nice, relaxing, and peaceful and for the whole time I laid out in the tub, I just thought of you, of us being together, and how beautiful that feels. I told one of my best friends about you yesterday, I told you about her father passing away a couple of weekends ago, I have known her since we were 14, we are very special to each other, I don't know if you know her, she goes by Katherine McMoore, I'm the only one that calls her Candy. She's a wonderful, beautiful artist, she's a sculptress, she does animals, ravens, caribous, bears, wolves, mythical beings, she spent a lot of her time overseas and has come back to Canada just a couple of years ago and now is working here. Anyhow she is very happy for us and would like to meet you. Her partner is also an artist. She asked me yesterday if I was scared, thinking about meeting you for the first time, I looked at her and said no, I'm not scared at all. It's incredible, but this is so right, I'm excited, I'll probably be a little bit nervous, and ask myself the big question as I stand there waiting for you, do I look ok . . . that always goes through a woman's mind . . . lol but I'm not scared one bit, because, I told her, that you have become a part of me, and we are together, it's a wonderful, whole feeling. I had better get back to bed, I hope that you do get a better phone, one that will work, I have called you so many times, and all I get is a type of busy signal, I still think it was a miracle that I got through to you that day and was able to tell you to check your e-mails regarding the computer. I felt such sadness coming from you, I needed to talk to you that day, and I did and since then I haven't been able to get you . . . I will check online again at 7:00 to see if you're online, that's just after lunch for you, so hopefully . . .

I should get back to bed and dream of you. Take care of yourself my Darling, and know that things will work out . . . I LOVE YOU DAVIS with all of my being . . . ti amo

Amore. Tess

I'm feeling frisky this morning . . . mind you that happens every morning about this time . . . lol

From: Tess

Sent: September 19, 2008 7:14:02 AM My Darling Davis,

I Love You . . . I just can't and won't stop saying it or thinking it. I love you. I will look forward to this evening when hopefully we can either

talk on the phone or chat online and if not this evening hopefully tomorrow morning. I miss talking with you; at least we have this, e-mail as it is.

I hope things have gone well for you, at the barrister's and with getting your money that you need. My Mom and stepdad are away in Atlin for the next few days, but I have a key to their place so when you do fax anything over just let me know and I will get it. I also have a safety deposit box that I will put these papers into, and Davis if there are other documents that you would like me to keep a copy of for you, for any reason what so ever, feel free to use my mom's fax number and I will let her know. Again you have left me speechless, I know it doesn't show with all the writing I'm doing but you know what I mean, you have no idea what you have done and what you are doing to me, it's amazing, I'm sending out a hug to you, an embrace, that has me wrapping my arms around your neck, your arms go around my waist and we pull ourselves into each other, we can feel each other's heartbeats as they become our own, and then I look into your eyes and you bend your head to mine and you caress my lips with yours, I gently part my lips and invite your tongue to caress mine, and we can feel each other so deep inside, it's as if I can feel you now. You complete me . . . I had better get going and start my day, again I look forward to hearing from you . . . Take care of yourself . . . and hold me close to you . . . I Love you . . . ti amo.

Amore . . . Tess

From: Davis

Sent: September 19, 2008 11:23:16 AM My Love,

I hope your day is going well, mine went well here. I got the document, and faxed it to you. You will need to sign your part and fax it back to me as soon as you can. I will need to present it for approval to continue work. Anyway, work this by far going on well. I was able to get in touch with the company in Japan, they said they will write me the check and send it to me here. But the barrister just told me I wouldn't be able to withdraw the money here, because of bad networking. This is a third world country, so what else will you expect . . . That is what he told me. lol. These people here are way back behind development, and very corrupt. I am extra careful about whatever I do here. Mr W. and the barrister have been really good and are directing me in everything I do. I may call the Japanese company again and stop them from writing me the check. I will want you to do another thing for me, I will want the company to write the check to you, so you can withdraw the money and send me what I want whenever I need some more money. Let me know if you can do that for me. I love you so much, I want to do everything with you, I want to share my life and everything I have, with you. You are so special to me, I have grown to love you so much and cherish you. You are my heart, my joy, my everything. I was not able to get the new cell today, we got there late, but I hope to get it tomorrow. We also got to Fed Ex late, and were told to pick it up tomorrow morning. We were told it has been cleaned and ready for pick up, so we will do that tomorrow. I will also have to meet the barrister tomorrow for a little talk about business. I am now going to get dinner, then will get to the hotel, have my shower and try calling you. I get the chance to talk with you. I will try sending you another mail before falling asleep. Have to get going now, take care and enjoy the rest of your day. Know I am crazily in love with you, and will do anything to prove I love you more. Ti amo . . .

Amore. Davis

From: Tess

Sent: September 19, 2008 11:46:34 AM My Darling Davis,

Just let me know what you want me to do, and how I can do it for you. I don't know what your banking situation is there, sounds like it's not good, If you have them send me the cheque or I do have internet banking which is fast, they can e-mail me a transfer and I will get it that same day. I can then wire you the money via Western Union, if that will work. They just e-mail to my e-mail address, otherwise, they can send it to me at my home address.

Of course I gave Davis my home address.

Because I'm working, if I know how the money is going to be sent, if it is through FedEx? Then I can call the office here and have them notify me as soon as it comes in.

I will fax the document back to you, I thought about it when I was there, and I wasn't too sure how to dial in the fax number or which fax number to use, please let me know, I don't want to send it somewhere, where it shouldn't be. Do I need to put in the country code 233 before the number or can I dial that number directly? Do the 011 for international and then the 614 and then the number? I will attempt to send it, I may try and run down to Mom's before I finish work, and I hope that receiving the fax tomorrow is not going to be a problem. Davis, thank you for your trust, for your belief in me, Thank You, I will do whatever I can for you. I Love You . . . in fact I'm going to run out now, I will write later, and hope that we get a chance to talk later as well . . . I Love you so much my dear. ti amo. Amore . . . Tess

From: Tess

Sent: September 19, 2008 11:03:28 AM My Darling Davis,

I'm at my mother's right now and I have received the certificate, . . . I'm still in shock that you have done this, I'm just going WOW, do you need me to sign this and fax it back to the barrister? There is a number here 614-555-1986. I will keep this safe. I Love you . . . you have taken my breath away. I have to get going I'm at work. I will write again soon, I love you with all my heart, you have me, you have me real good I hope you don't mind but I'm going to stay with you forever. You'll just have to learn to put up with me, but I'll make sure you enjoy it . . . gotta run Love You . . . ti amo. Amore . . . Tess

*Davis faxed me a copy of the Certificate of Incorporation. It had a government looking logo at the top center of the page and it statedthat it was a Registration of Business Act, dated 1962.m The certificate had the Business Act number., The title of the mining company and it was dated and signed by the Registrar of Business, a witness which was Davis's lawyer and the company's owners which was Davis's signature and myself listed as co-owner, T.G. Diamond.*

*When I received the certificate I couldn't believe what Davis was offering, what he was doing. Everything looked so official. I never heard of an "oil mine" before so I went online and googled oil mines in West Aftrica and discovered that mining for oil was just starting up in West Africa and that there had been a lot of exploration and oil found in the Ghana region, these mines were called oil mines.*

*I wanted to believe in what Davis had told me, I felt that he was sharing a part of his life with me and making me a part of his life. He was including me in what he did. I had wanted to have that feeling, I longed for that feeling, I wanted to be a part of something and be able to share the experience with my partner, and Davis was handing that to me. It was very surreal for me. But it was a feeling I wanted to feel.*

From: Davis

Sent: September 19, 2008 11:33:21 AM My Love,

I just saw your mail when I send mine, I guess we were writing to each other at the same time . . . lol? I Love You. Please sign it and send it back. You keep the one you have signed. I am not sure of the number, I will call the barrister and get you the number in my next mail, or if I am able to talk with you on phone tonight.

I love you . . . Ti. Amo Amore . . . Davis

From: Tess

Sent: September 19, 2008 1:32:52 PM My Love,

I will wait for you to send me the correct number to fax the certificate back to you, I see that you will be meeting with the lawyer first thing in the morning so even if you get me the number and it's midnight here, or later I will run over and fax it. Let me know about the e-mail money transfer as well if that will work for you? I Love you, you have completely consumed me and my thoughts. I love you . . . I have to go as I'm busy at work right now . . . I Love you . . . ti amo Amore . . . Tess

From: Davis

Sent: September 19, 2008 4:29:23 PM My love,

I hope you are doing well. I have been trying to call over an hour now, still having dificulty getting to you. I will want you to sign and send it to me as soon as you can. I will be meeting the barrister first thing in the morning. The fax number is 00233212345678, please let me know when you send it if you can't still get me on the phone. I will keep trying till I fall asleep. I miss you so much and miss hearing your sweet voice. I just wished I could even hear you talk to me for a minute. I know soon, we will not need to worry about this, because I will always be there when you need me. You are my everything. Thank you for loving me the way no one can. You understand me and you know just how to make things right. You will never know just how much I love you, but I will spend the rest of my days trying to show you. You saved me from the worst, and you are always there for me. Fighting is never an option and making love to you will always be as sweet as the first time. No matter what, there will never be another for me and I will always keep you safe. I love you . . . for all eternity. Thank you, Tess. I will go to bed now, and hope to be able to get to talk with you on the phone. Take care and say hi to Zoey for me. I Love You . . . Ti amo . . .

Amore . . . Davis

From: Tess

Sent: September 19, 2008 6:33:30 PM My Darling Davis,

To talk to you, as you said for even a minute, would be priceless. I just missed you online. I've tried calling you all day long myself and I haven't been able to get through at all. I'm at my mother's right now and I can't get through on the fax, so what I've done is, my mom has a scanner so I've scanned the document into the computer and I'm e-mailing it to you, I hope this will work, you should be able to print it out and Voila!. Do let me know if this is okay. I've tried the number you gave me several times and it does not go through at all. I get a beeping sound and the fax shuts off, so then I did 011 and the number country code etc . . . and it rings but does not connect to the fax. I will have my computer on, and I'll be up around midnight 1:00 which will be 6:00-7:00 your time and I'll stay up until I either talk to you online, phone or get an e-mail from you, if the e-mail certificate does not work I will come back to my moms and try again, maybe the office has to be open in order for them to receive the fax. This should work though. Are you okay with me telling my boys what you've done for us? I still find this hard to take in right now Davis, the only thing that I know for sure as to what this means is that we will be together, there is no doubt. I love you. I had better get going I promised a friend of mine that I would go to her candle party tonight, her daughter is in Zoey's class, so I will get a candle with thoughts of you and I. I will write later tonight, I love you with all my heart and soul. ti amo, . . . Amore. Tess

From: Tess

Sent: September 19, 2008 11:44:50 PM My Darling Davis, my Love,

I'm not too sure what order you will open your e-mails in, but in case you open this one first, I just wanted to let you know that I tried to open the certificate document that I e-mailed you and I wanted to let you know that it took quite a while for it to come up, in fact I went out of it a few times and kept trying and it finally opened, I sure hope that this will work because I have my doubts about the fax working. I'm going to remain online until I hear from you, I promise, we will talk somehow someway, today, even if I have to stay up all night long. Zoey and I had another hot tub tonight, and it was hotter this evening than last, it was up to 101 degrees, it was nice. Zoey really enjoys this one; she can swim around in circles in it, and bounce along the bottom. The candle party was pretty good, I did buy a couple of things, and I did get a couple of ideas that I can incorporate into my pottery. I feel so wonderful with you in my life, I believe you when you tell me that you will keep us safe, that feels so unbelievable, so real, and so wonderful.

Thank you Davis, you are going to save me. I'm right here next to the computer so please just buzz me, I will try to phone as well and I hope that one of us will get through. I Love you so much, I will love you completely, wholly, and there will only be you. You are the one, the only one for me; I love you, so much . . . I had better get this out to you . . . ti amo

Amore . . . Tess.

From: Tess

Sent: September 20, 2008 9:44:42 AM Hello My Darling,

The sky for the first time in a month, does not have a cloud, the yellow, orange and red leaves are brilliant against the sky—blue background, it is so beautiful here this morning Davis. Even if the sky was grey with clouds, it would still be beautiful because I got to chat with you, even though it was only for just over an hour, it was still wonderful. There is so much more I want to ask you that I didn't get a chance to, I do hope that when you read this letter, you are using your own computer and you will have the ability to tell me, that you will be online at such and such a time. I realize that you are very busy and tired, so make sure that you tell me when we can chat as to when it will work for you, I don't mind staying up later, or getting up in the wee hours of the morning, if I have a time, I can do it. I must confess that I just got up about twenty minutes ago, mind you I was dozing off and on until 4:00 AM, then I went straight to bed after talking with you and I slept like a baby, I fell asleep with the image of you and I at the airport. I'm keeping that image in my mind and close to my heart, because on that day, our lives will change wonderfully.

I had better sign off now and get a few things done. Zoey has dance lessons in an hour, less than an hour, so I will check my e-mail again once I drop her off, and I'll keep checking throughout the day, and with any luck we may be able to talk on the phone. I Love you Davis, so completely.I Love You will talk to you later . . . no matter what . . . ti amo

Amore. Tess

From: Davis

Sent: September 20, 2008 11:23:41 AM Hello My Darling,

I am glad to know you slept like a baby after talking, I will always want to see you sleep comfortably and warm all the time, and know you will have that kind of sleep all the time when I find myself lying next to you on bed. Mmmmm . . . I can imagine how wonderful it will be to always wake up to find you lying next to me. I will want to see your first smile in the morning, kiss you and tell you how much I love you the more every time I wake.

My day was okay, nothing much done, but it sure was wonderful after talking with you before starting my activities. The barrister and I presented the certificate to the register general, then Mr W and I went to pick up the package from Fed—Ex. I am so happy to have a computer again, it is the most perfect one I ever wanted. Thanks a lot. I have not yet gotten to the hotel, I will need a technician to configure it to the Internet, and will get one at the hotel. I couldn't go to the mine nor the port, we spend almost all of our day at the register general. I have a new cell, and pretty sure we can talk this evening. The number is 00233244567899. You may not get me now if you call, because I have not activated it yet. I will need to change the cell first before activating it. I will try calling you first thing when I get it active. I could not get in touch with the Chinese company today, I will just have to hold on till Monday. I have told you many times and I will still want to tell you again, Tess, I really thank God for you in my life. Maybe in this lifetime, you will never know how much I love, I care and cherish you. You mean so much to me, even more precious than my own life. I can never afford to lose you, dear. Your actions speak it all, that you also care and love me that much, but I love you more . . . lol? Those little things that you have done for me will always be kept in my heart, where you'll always be. Your patience is always the alternative for us. Thanks for all these, Tess. In the past I had always yearned for a relationship that is genuine and lasting, as for all these, I've found them in you. I will make sure that the hand I will be holding will forever be yours. Whether we're living in a fairy tale or a non-fairy tale world, I still believe there is such a thing as "Live happily ever after", and even if you do believe it, then let's make it happen in our relationship. I really look forward to the day when the both of us will be walking down the red carpet hand in hand and in the name of love, we exchange marriage rings looking into each other's eyes saying, "I do not regret for choosing you in my life. I Love You Tess. It has started raining again here this evening, I am with Mr W, and barrister. We are going to get dinner, then I will head to the hotel, change the cell while I get the computer connected. Whatever happens, you will hear from me. There are some other things I will have to sort out with the barrister. I am not sure we can do it today, but if we do, I will let you know. He seems to be a very good man, and I will need his help and advice in almost everything. okay darling, I have to go now, it's always hard for me to leave. I love you with all my heart, and will talk to you soon.

Ti amo.

Amore . . . Davis

From: Tess

Sent: September 20, 2008 1:46:43 PM My Love, My Darling Davis,

I love your letters, your words, your love. I want to find out in this lifetime how much you love me, I don't want to wait for another lifetime to discover you, I'm greedy and I want you now in this one. Everyday Davis, your love comes through in your words and in your actions, that's pretty powerful given the distance between us, if we have this much power and strength now, we are going to have an incredible relationship when we finally connect physically and see each other. Our beliefs in how we will treat each other are so much connected, I too don't believe in fighting, arguing but rather in listening and working out a solution if we do disagree. However I don't know what we may disagree on, as I'm the type of person that, if you want to do something then I feel you should do it, and if there is something that bothers me about what is being done I will tell you but I will tell you that this is how I feel and why. In a relationship I believe in working with you, supporting you, helping you, and the beautiful thing about you is that I feel you will do the same for me, that is such a wonderful feeling, I have not had that in such a long time, Davis, thank you so much for giving me this, for giving me you.

I would be honoured to walk beside down the red carpet and exchange rings, to know and say that I will always be by your side, and I will never regret having you in my life, in our lives, because I know that you are meant to be a part of me. When we make love it will be beautiful because making love with you will be real, and true. MMMMMmmmmmmmmmmmmmmmmm . . . the thought of you warms me.

I tried calling your other number before I read your e-mail and the number is no longer in service so I'm looking forward to hearing your voice. I will be in and out all afternoon, I have to go to the recycling center and then do a little bit of shopping, so I will check my e-mail again, I hope that you are able to get the computer up and running, it's like our lifeline to each other. I'm glad you like the computer. I hope it is what you need. As I said earlier, I went for the best, that one has apparently what you need for good gaming quality, see I thought about you when I asked about it. I Love you . . . and I was thinking I am going to have to show you how much more everyday. I promise you.

Davis, I will respect you, trust you, believe in you, and I will be your friend, your confident, your sounding board, your lover, and I will be your wife. I don't want to be your mistress or your girlfriend; I want the honour of being your wife. I should ask have you asked me yet? again don't answer that until we physically see each other and I can kiss you and touch you, okay ? I Love you so much. I had better get going, I want to ask you the next time we talk, being that I am involved now if you would tell me about the mine, an idea of what it looks like, what type of renovations you have to do and how the oil is mined? all that . . . please . . . I look forward to hearing your voice. I will have my cell phone with me at all times and I will make sure it is fully charged. I love you with all my heart Davis Barienda. I am thinking about you every minute. ti amo

Amore. Tess

From: Tess

Sent: September 20, 2008 5:12:12 PM My Darling Davis,

It was so good to hear you, your voice, I love the sound of your voice and your laugh, I can hear the smile in your voice as well. I've been trying to call for the last fifteen minutes, it's 5:00 PM now, and I can't get through, I hope that you have been able to, and we've talked since you first reached me, if not, know that hearing your voice will carry me forward and I promise I will be patient. I know that you have a lot to do, but a girl can dream, and what a dream.

And if you haven't been able to get through this will be the last time that you will say to me, I'll call you back, next time I'm not letting you go. I love hearing you saying to me that you love me, that is so special to me, you saying those three little words, means so much and is so encompassing, it's infinite my love for you, I will patiently wait to hear from you once more, and if you should wake and it's in the early hours of the morning for me, do call me, I will willingly wake up for you, and to hear your voice as I've been dreaming about you, sometimes it's almost too much to bear, this feeling of love that I feel that surrounds us, it's overwhelming at times, it's wonderful, Davis. I will keep trying to call you as well. I love you. ti amo

Amore . . . Tess

From: Tess

Sent: September 20, 2008 10:04:18 PM My Love,

I got your call but I could not hear you, and then it just cut out, I tried to call again several times but the circuits are busy, we will get this figured out. The funny thing is, that the call display that comes up when you call me is your old number the 233 027 123-4567, when I couldn't get through on the number you gave me, I tried the old number and it says again it's no longer in service, but when you called this afternoon that was the number on the call display and again tonight. I'm going to keep trying, and I will be up at 4:00 checking to see if you're online.

And Thank you for keeping your promise, you must have woken up around 3:00, I was wondering if you called my home number at 9:00 my time, I had an unknown caller on my phone; I had just stepped outside for a short time. I hate missing your calls. I want to talk with you so much, I Love You my Dear, with all my heart. I will see you online at 4:00 my time. I'm hoping and praying. I will try again several times to call you, hopefully by the time you get this e-mail we would have talked . . . I Love You . . . ti amo

Amore. Tess

From: Tess

Sent: September 21, 2008 9:10:23 AM Hello My My Darling Davis,

It is absolutely wonderful being able to talk to you. And when you say that it could be another week, I must admit, there was uncontrollable excitement inside of me and my heart started to race.

I'm just going to make this quick, I have to have a shower and get ready so I'm ready before you call me back as well. I just really wanted to let you know that I was very surprised that Zoey asked me if she could say hi to you. I have a very strong feeling that she is going to take to you in a very strong way, I trust you and I trust you with her. I just hope that you are a patient man. Actually it's me that has to have the patience as she is great with everyone else, it's her mom that needs to not let her test me. It's the single mom syndrome I call it. You are going to be so important and good for the both of us. I am looking so forward to getting to know you, getting to know everything about you as well. I had better get busy right now, I'm going to do my 1/2 hour workout, before having a shower and then you should be calling me. I Love You so much . . . I can feel the excitement but I will keep it contained . . . for now . . . ti amo

Amore. Tess

From: Davis

Sent: September 21, 2008 12:55:51 PM My Darling Tess,

It was so nice talking with you, I got sad when I couldn't say to you I love you. I tried again so many times, but couldn't get though. I am going to say what I wanted to say before the line cut. All I wanted to say is that I love you so much with my heart any with every breath I take. You are so special to me and forever you and Zoey will be. It feels so great to know Zoey is ready to accept me in her life, and it was wonderful talking to her. I look forward in having much fun with her and you. I hope you understand that I like kids a lot and will want to make time for her to, and do most of the things she will want to do with me, like going for shopping, taking a walk playing together and so on. Don't get jealous, I am going to get much time for you, we are going to do everything together. I love you Tess, I cherish you so much. You are like the air I breathe. I feel, without you there is no life for me. I am so excited about everything and so glad to have you in my life. Have a safe drive, oops, you can only read this mail when you get back . . . lol. okay, I hope you had a good time, it would have been much better if I were around, but I am assuring you that will happen soon. I am going to take a walk, then will come back to rest myself for tomorrow. I will try calling after 6 PM your time, and you can also try calling me. I hope to talk to you soon. I love you more, and will spend the rest of my life proving that. Ti amo. Ti amo. Ti amo Amore. Davis

From: Tess

Sent: September 21, 2008 11:18:35 PM My Love,

It is so wonderful to come home and have an e-mail from you, better yet was talking with you just before we left this morning and then the phone call that came just as I walked through the door when we returned to Whitehorse, that would have been around 8 PM my time 2 AM your time, your actions say so much, I answered the phone and that was when it went beep beep. I knew it was you because your number comes up, but it is always the 233 027 123-4567 that appears in my call display, and when I dial it, I get no longer in service or circuits are busy and when I dialled the other number you gave me, which I did as soon as I missed your call tonight, the message said that the mobile phone was either turned off or out of the service area. I tried calling about six more times and always the same thing, so I'm not too sure as to what number I am suppose to call, so I'll just keep calling both. I am so glad though that you are able to get me once in a while, at least I know that I will be able to talk with you. Oh Davis, I wish so much that I could get through, please know that I try at least ten times each time I call. I thought of you all day today, throughout our whole trip I wondered what it would be like if you were with us, Zoey even mentioned that you would enjoy being with us, it had something to do with all the shopping you could have done, and by the way it's settled, you have to be home for your birthday, even if you have to come here and then go back, ( yeah right) . . . (not without me) . . . Zoey and I have your birthday gift so you have to be here . . . again . . . no pressure. I'm sorry if I may seem impatient, and I do understand that you have a lot to do, and you are doing the best that you can, I do understand that, but you have to understand that I will let you know how I'm feeling and how much and how desperate I am to touch you, to kiss you to feel you, I want to look into your eyes, and I want to melt into you, so badly do I want this . . . I want you . . . and I know that you want this too, so please forgive me if I do seem to put the pressure on you, it's just that I do want you as soon as you're done . . . I love you. Now let me tell you about our day, and then I will go to bed, again I will probably wake around 4 AM and if I do, I will check to see if you're online, first off, what I didn't tell you is that our dog is not doing very well, she is thirteen – years—old, and is overweight ; she has slowed down quite a bit in these last two years and has put on a lot of excess wt which I know is not healthy at all for her. She hasn't been with me for a year and a half; she has just started staying with me these last six months so she can be comfortable. Anyhow, she slipped yesterday upstairs and both of her back legs went out from underneath her as if she were doing the splits. I knew this really hurt her, she never yelped but her mouth was parted and the gums of her mouth were white and the look in her eyes was nothing but pain. She couldn't get up, I finally was able to adjust her legs into the proper position and she slowly managed to stand up. She was quite wobbly. When we go to bed at night, she has to lie next to me, so she has to climb two set of stairs, she is too heavy for me to carry her. Tonight I'm sleeping on the couch so she won't feel any need to go up the stairs, and so she knows

I'm close, I've been giving her aspirin twice, three times a day. She gets up slowly and it's hard for her to walk on any slippery surface, her legs give out as soon as she does, I had to get my son to help me carry her into the house this morning as she slipped on the deck. Fortunately I was right there and caught her before she went down.

I know what I need to do, I know that I'm going to see how she is doing tomorrow and then I will have to decide. Shawna, our dog has been with us since the boys were six—seven—years old—she's been through a lot with me, she is a part of our lives, and now I have to make the decision to let her live or let her go. I had to do that with her daughter, who was also with us for six years, she was like my baby, and she suffered from epilepsy. She had such a bad seizure for three hours that I didn't want her going through that any longer.So I made the decision to put her down and I stayed with her as she left us, funny thing is, that it was Thanksgiving day when this happened and it soon will be Thanksgiving. Shawna keeps looking at me with the look of knowing that she needs to go. I think she is trying to tell me in her own way that I have to let her go . . . it's very hard, Davis but I do know it is for the best . . . Anyhow let me tell you about our trip to Skagway, the drive was beautiful, the fall colours were magnificent the yellow, oranges and reds, and then green still in there and as we got closer to the summit, the mountains had just a little skiff of fresh snow, the kind that looks as if someone took icing sugar and sifted just a little over the top. As we were on our way to Skagway, I hate to admit this, because I thought about it. I just didn't do it when I thought about it in Carcross. In between Carcross and Skagway my check engine light came on, I don't know if you're familiar with the Skagway road, anyhow it's about an hour drive to Skagway from Carcross and half way there, is the suspension bridge rest stop. So I stopped there to check my oil and it's halfway between the add and the end of the dipstick, this is where I'm thinking to myself, I knew I should have checked before leaving Carcross. I thought about it. Anyhow, no one at the suspension bridge had any oil, so we stopped at Fraser the Canadian customs and I asked there if they had any oil by chance. And the one customs officer who lives right there, he had some at his home and he was just about to go for lunch. So he said he would give me a litre. I told him I would repay him on my way through, so we got the oil into the vehicle and we made it to Skagway. We went right away to one of the outlet stores and there were shirts for five dollars, sweatshirts, fleece tops three-ten dollars, so Zoey and I bought shirts for Zach and Chad, herself and my son's girlfriend. I bought myself pj's. We went and had lunch, went to a couple of other stores and then everything started to shut down at 4:00 so then we decided that we should be heading home as well it would have been 4:30 Alaska time, 5:30 our time. I didn't drive too fast on the way home between 90-100km/hr so it was a nice leisurely drive and we got home just before 8. In fact I had been home maybe five minutes if that, when you called. So it was a good day for a drive. I thought of you the whole time, every song that played on the CD, I danced with you, some songs told our story, our feelings; you were with us the whole trip, Davis. I guess I had better get going I'm looking at the time and realizing that I'm pretty tired, now, know this, I may be tired but I will wake up if you call . . .I Love You Davis, so much . . . I Miss you, and yet I feel so close to you . . . ti amo. ti amo

Amore . . . Tess

# 6

# THE CHIEF KING MAKERS

From: Davis

Sent: September 22, 2008 7:43:02 AM Hi Darling,

I hope you were able to have a little rest after we talked. I was on my way to the mines when I had a call from the mine that there is something going on wrong there, so I am going back to see the lawyer and talk things over with her. They they explain what was going on, but I did understand them well and hope the lawyer will be able to explain it to me much better. They said the chief of the community where we are mining came around to stop them from working. The reason was that I still need to come and perform some traditional rites before I can continue with whatever I want to do on their land. And that the government might have sold the land to me, but it's their community and they still have right over it and will not permit me to work on it till I do what their tradition requires. I will let you know whatever the outcome, soon as I am able to resolve things. I hope the lawyer can get things worked out soon. I have to go now, I love you so much and want you to know everything will be fine, and you don't need to worry about anything. I will be fine. Send my love to my sweet Zoey, and you take care and have a wonderful day and week. I love you so much,

Date: Mon, 22 Sep 2008 07:48:59—0700

From: Davis

Pardon me, I do not know what I pressed to send the mail. I guess this

116

land issue with the chief and the people in the community is getting to me, but I want you to know I will be fine okay, and you need not worry about anything. I Love you, you give me the strength to face everything. I love you, talk to you soon. Ti amo

Amore. Davis

From: Tess

Sent: September 22, 2008 9:26:48 AM Hello My Love,

As long as you're not dancing around a fire with hallucinogens in your body I won't worry, but I think that it is important and good that you do that, and maybe quite possibly the mine being there could help the community. Is there any possibility to that?. I was reading some articles online about how the gold mines have ruined some communities and these communities are scared and don't want the mines. Now these are gold mines that the article was talking about, because the community did not gain anything. Davis, is there something that we can support, once the mine is producing and there is a profit, is there something that the community may need? I don't know what this community is like, but do they have a good well? Is there a school with books, medical needs, that type of thing, if there was something that the mine could help with even farming we could assist them with, then the community would be more supportive towards the mine . . . I hope all went well with you.I'm curious for you to tell me what type of traditional ceremony you had to be part of. I know you will be safe, and I won't worry. I love you and I await your phone call, and or your e-mail to tell me all. I did have a rest. Our dog is not doing well, so I'm phoning the vet this morning to see what I can do, if they'll give me the drug to put her to sleep so I can do it or if I have to take her to the vet. That will be difficult as she is too heavy for me and I'll have to wait until tomorrow, when Zach and Chad are off and they can carry her out to the vehicle. I have to run right now. I love you, and I am sending you my strength today, I have a feeling you may need it. I love you so much. You are in my thoughts, and it's a good thing that these things are coming up now, when you are there rather than after you leave, because some things are not so easy to take care of over the phone or online . . . Know that I am with you . . . I Love you with all my heart . . . ti amo

Amore. Tess

From: Tess

Sent: September 22, 2008 6:11:58 PM My Darling, My Love,

Thank you for what you did today, letting me talk with the lawyer, I can sense from you a weariness, when you asked me today if I thought you should continue, I've been thinking about that, and again, only you can decide that because I don't have any of the information in front of me, you know what you researched, does it look profitable? I know that the oil found in the Ghana area is a new discovery as of last year and that there is an estimated six—hundred billion barrels of oil in the region to be mined, do you know what the estimated barrel amount is for our mine? Also Davis, what is the risk to us regarding the mine, I know on the certificate it states as an incorporated company that the liabilities are limited, so what does that mean? Also, you've invested already a lot of money into this, as well as your time, and is it worth it to you to continue, if it is, and you can see within a five—year business plan, good production, profit margin as well as a support to the community, then I think it would be a good thing, that's my opinion based on what you know and what you feel, and if you feel that it is going to be a risk and that it is a dangerous liability then maybe you should rethink what it is that you want out of the mine. Personally, now this is me being selfish but also it could be a good thing, based on what happens today for you at the traditional ceremony/ritual/hearing, an amount of money will be determined as to what you will have to pay to the community, I'm interested to know if this is a percentage of your profit on a yearly basis or is it a one—time thing? Anyhow, if things go like this, here is one scenario to think about: if the Chinese company has already sent a cheque to you, you will have to send it back in order for it to be redirected to me, unless of course they can cancel the cheque and do an e-mail transfer. Anyhow, what we talked about, about you possibly coming home and then going back if you have to; I was thinking if you did this then we could set up an account here, that would allow me to access your business funds to send to you, you could come home for a couple of weeks, we could finally see each other, then I would be okay. If you had to go back, to get things done, and then you wouldn't have to feel so rushed and you and I would both know where we were and we could continue to give each other strength, because right now, there is so much happening with you and with your Visa's being gone and not being able to access funds. You need to get that fixed, and then if you were gone for another month I would at least be able to help you from my end. Then we would be able to be together, and you wouldn't be so rushed. I don't know if it's possible for that to happen or not. It is a thought. I do know that what we have between us is bigger than I have ever experienced and no matter what you decide, I will support your decision even if it's to stay and complete everything. My only concern is for you, how you are holding up and for your money situation, because on my own, I can't help you. I have no money. I wish at this moment I could win the lottery and I could send that to you right now. I Love you so much Davis, I tried to call you a couple of times and the phone rang and rang. Twice I called and then I thought that you must be exhausted after being up all night trying to get me, and then this to happen when all we want is to get things done so you can come home. You do what you feel you need to do, I am here beside you no matter what, and here is where I will remain. I love you with all of my heart, I will try and wake up in time to chat with you, or if you have to go to the hearing. I forgot to ask what time it was, please call me, wake me before you go, if it's possible. Today was amazing being able to chat with you for a whole hour and then getting you on the phone when you needed me. That was the second time that I was able to reach you and every time I called the phone rang. There is hope, I love you Davis, if for some reason we don't' get to talk before you go to the hearing, I'm with you in spirit, my strength is your strength, my energy I will send to you, it is yours and my hope is your hope . . . I love you with all my heart. ti amo

Amore . . . Tess

From: Tess

Sent: September 22, 2008 7:41:56 PM My Love,

You know how much I love you, how much you have become to mean to me, how much you have become a part of our lives, I've been thinking about this a lot, and I know what I said in my first e-mail and I meant what I said about standing by you no matter what and I will, but thinking about things, if you have the company, send me a cheque. I have no idea how much money we're talking about here but I imagine it's more than just your average five—thousand dollar cheque, anyhow, any cheque that I put into my bank gets held for at least five—seven business days, and if the company has already sent you the cheque, then it's another wait.If the company e-mails, then there is no problem but Davis, if they send a cheque given everything that has happened, and what is going on, you said you would do anything for me, would you come home, so we can take care of the money issue together, and then you could go back to finish what you need to do, please would you consider this. This would be something that I feel is important for us right now, as well as important for you so you can continue. If this is not a good idea to you, I will understand as well . . . I love you with all my heart and soul and right now, I need you . . . and I think that you need me . . . we need each other. See, you come home, get refuelled and then you're good to go for another month and then we'll have forever. But I need you, I need to feel you and I need to touch you, can the mine survive without you for two weeks, that's the question? . . . I will go, and I will write again later . . . I Love you so much, I hope that we get a chance to talk . . . ti amo

Amore. Tess

From: Tess

Sent: September 23, 2008 6:48:45 AM My Darling Davis,

By the time you read this, the hearing should be over, I'm wondering how things went, and I know you will let me know. There are a lot of things that are different there. Have you ever run into this before. I'm wondering about here in the Yukon, thinking about similarities with the first nations, if there is a mining company on traditional land, and then I'm wondering if the mine has to pay royalties to the band, and I think they do, which is similar to what is happening with our mine. They just go about it a different way. You'll have to tell me what it was like, the hearing, how were people arranged, was there a round table, did you sit in a circle formation or was it the chief at the front and you sat facing him with other people behind you. In some cultures a circle stands for equality, in a setting where there is the person at the front and the others facing, that's authoritive, and could be considered intimidating to some degree. So I'm curious how they arranged the seating. And of course the outcome, I'm very interested in that.

I'm glad you are thinking about coming home, Davis, being that the company has already sent you the cheque can you suggest to them to cancel the check and email me the funds. If they can I will get it immediately. However, if they can't, it will be two weeks or more before you get the money probably more, so that is why I'm thinking it would be good to come home during that time. If there are things that can happen while you're gone, great, hopefully you are able to continue to work now that the hearing is over. Anyhow, if you bring the cheque here and we set up an account, how long does it take to get here two days, you put the cheque into the bank and you can take the money out immediately, and that my dear will be faster and you could even send the money to the lawyer or Mr. W to take care of the immediate necessities that have to be taken care of for the mines renovations to be completed. I sound like I'm trying to convince you. I am . . . and more than anything, I want to see you, I want to touch you, I want to kiss you, I want to have us make love, the way love should be made . . .I want you . . . I will admit it will be hard to let you go, but it will be easier as well because I will be a part of you, and closer to you than what I am now and I will be able to help you. and then I'll be able to make love to you in my letters every night that I write to you . . . I will leave the decision up to you, as you know better what needs to be done . . . I love you so much.

Today is going to be a very hard day for all of us, I have decided to have Shawna put to sleep today at 4 PM I was hoping the vet could do a house call, but he is unable to until Friday. It would be cruel to keep her alive until then, we will take her to the vets, and to my dad's and bury her next to her daughter. She has been a part of our family for fourteen years, I will miss her, and she is like my confidante. When I needed to talk to someone I would often talk to her, she would look at me sometimes like I was crazy but at times she knew what I was talking about, and she would lean her nose into mine and give it a little lick. She is a very gentle dog, with gentle eyes, I love her, my Shawna, I'm going to hold things together, I do a good job doing that as the kids are going to need my strength today then when I'm alone. I will have a good cry and let the sadness fill me. I do know she is better off; right now she is in pain every time she stands and sometimes she can't even walk. We had to carry her out this morning and then finally she stood up and went over and had a pee, we carried her on a sheet, I think she stood, because I was going to carry her back into the house with the sheet and she decided she didn't want to have anymore of that so she was going to stand and walk no matter what . . . I had better get going, I want to do a little bit of a workout before having a shower, my calling card has about 15 minutes left on it so I'm going to see if I can reload it this morning and then I will try calling as well. I love you so much . . . What have you done to me, and I hope you keep doing it to me. I love you . . . ti amo

Amore. Tess

Date: Tue, 23 Sep 2008 10:43:08

From: Davis

Good Morning My Love,

I am sorry I didn't hear the phone ring last night, I fell deeply asleep after trying to call so many times. I will not be able to chat with you this morning, because the hearing is just in fifteen minutes I have been trying to call all morning, I just realised I will not be able to talk with you on the phone before the hearing, so I send you this mail to let you know I love you so much and know you are with me in everything I do. I will let you know so after the hearing whatever went on there. I was able to get the the director of Japanese company after trying so many times, he said they had already sent the check to me here. I told them to cancel it and send it to you, and they said I will have to send them back the cheque they wrote to me before they can send you any other cheques. I also talked to them about the net transfer, and he said he was going to call me back today. I will let you know when I hear from him. Finally, I am giving it a big thought about me coming home for sometime, then get back here to finish what I have to do. I will have to go now, till get in touch soon as the hearing is over. I love you. Ti amo

Amore. Davis

From: Tess

Sent: September 23, 2008 11:36:08 AM My Darling Davis, Hello My Love,

I have been calling for the last hour, and all I get is the busy signal, I did get your message, I think I got it while trying to call you, anyhow, I stopped at home real quick to check Shawna and to e-mail you. I'm hoping you will have luck sending the e-mail transfer. If you have any problems I can walk you through it, that is the only way that I will be able to get you the cash, and then once I get your e-mail transfer, what is the best to get it to you, I think it is Western Union, and as a password use our dog's name, for both. The e-mail transfer and western union if they want more numbers with the letters use your house number. Add that after our dog's name (that should make the password long enough, sometimes they require 8-9 letters/numbers) If you can do the email transfer today, I can get the cash this afternoon and send it to you as soon as I get it. I'm leaving work at 3:00 so I can stop at the bank then and pull out the money as there is no holds on e-mail transfers. Again send it to Tess, as the e-mail transfer/payee.

I have to go right now, I'm still having a hard time taking everything in Davis, I'm still not too sure what it means, owning a mine, etc . . . if you can send me pictures so I know what it is that we own. I love you and I hope this will work. I have to go ti amo

Amore . . . Tess

From: Tess

Sent: September 23, 2008 12:35:39 PM Hello My Darling Davis,

I also thought that you could do an e-mail money transfer to your lawyer and he could deposit into his acct:: and give you the money that way—that would be the quickest. Have to go I'm at work not supposed to be here . . . I love you. ti amo. Amore . . . Tess

From: Tess

Sent: September 23, 2008 1:28:45 PM Hello My Darling Davis,

I have been trying to call you back, so many times, and each time it's a busy signal, or just a beeping, anyhow I'm leaving work at 3:00 this afternoon. I have no idea where you're at with the money transfer but if I can't get things done today, I will do it tomorrow. It will be after 9:00 my time. That is, if you're able to e-mail me, I still think the best for this is to e-mail your lawyer or Mr. W. I have to go and get to work. I love you so much and I would really like to talk to you about everything. Take it easy okay. I love you lots ti amo. Amore. Tess

From: Davis

Sent: September 23, 2008 1:53:35 PM Hello My Love,

I am sorry we have not been able to talk to each other on the phone. I have also been trying to call you for over two hours now, it's very difficult to get through, and when I do, I only get the voice mail to leave a message. I tried doing the e-mail transfer, only to have a feed back that my acct::is restricted, so I can't do e-mail transfer. The reason being that sometime back I took my bank to court of losing some money from my acct:. I was out of town on my usual business trip, when I came back, I realized someone had accessed my acct: and taken some money out. Since I was not around and never gave anybody any means to access my acct:, I sued the bank and won. Hence, I was advised to restrict my acct:, which I did. We will have to get another means of making things work. Another thing you should know is that, I am in a third world country, things are not like home. There are so many things that do not work here and can not be accessed. I talked with the lawyer to see if there was another way we could resolve this issue since I am not having the money now, and he said he will try to talk with them to see if they will understand and that work continues so we get the money to them later. I really want to come home to see you, spend time with you and make passionate love to you; it will be the best moment of my life forever seeing you, but I also need to make sure work is going on while I am away. I have invested so much money and time into this, and the least thing I do will have us lose. The best thing I can do now is to settle this chief and community issue, then I will come home to spend that special time I am really looking forward in spending with you. Then I can come back later and continue work. I need to see that things have been resolved with the chief and his people in the community, and work can start before I can come. I will want to come this weekend, and will have to make sure work in the mines is going on. I don't know if I am making sense, this whole thing is eating me up, but I can assure you I am and will be fine. This is my first time I am having these problems, but I know we will overcome. I will keep trying the phone, and hope we can talk before I go to bed, if I am even be able to sleep. I hope the lawyer will have a good impact on them and they will allow us to start working so I can come home to see you and relax while we spend special time doing what we have always wanted to do. I am going to the hotel now, I love you so much and am so grateful for your care and concern. You give me the strength, you are with me in everything I do. I can feel you so close. I will never disappoint you. I Love You with all that I am, I love you with all my heart, soul, and mind. Ti Amo.

Amore. Davis

From: Davis

Sent: September 23, 2008 1:57:53 PM Oh Darling,

I just saw your e _ mail, I guess we were writing each other at the same time. I am going to have dinner then, to the hotel. I will keep trying the phone. I love you so much, you are my everything. I love you for the strength and energy you give me. I love you . . . Ti Amo.

Amore. Davis

From: Tess

Sent: September 23, 2008 2:12:16 PM Oh Davis my Darling,

My heart started to pound when I saw what you wrote about coming home this weekend. Personally, and I'm not saying this because I desperately with all my heart and soul and body, and mind need to see you, touch you, make love to you kiss you and do everything and anything to you and you do to me. I'm not saying this just for all that, but I do think that given the circumstance with the money situation coming home is the best solution. You can access your funds and send the lawyer the money immediately when you get here or Mr.W so even if work can't start until you pay the chief you can have payment to them by the beginning of next week. I love you so much Davis, talking with you gives me the strength to hold on every single time. Things will work out, they will, this is just a slight delay but it may be happening for a reason and we have to sometimes go with that reason, and I think it is coming home for you, even if you're here only for a week before you have to go back, we can hold onto that week. Then you will be able to come home after that and you will also know what and who you're coming home to. Have to run. I love you . . . so much . . . ti amo. Amore. Tess

Date: Tue, 23 Sep 2008 20:57:52

From: Davis Oh Darling,

I just saw your e-mail, I guess we were writing each other at the sametime. I am going to have dinner, then to the hote. I will keep trying the phone. I love you so much, you are my everything. I love you for the strength and energy you give me. I love You . . . Ti Amo.

Amore . . . Davis

# 7

# GOODBYE OL' FRIEND

From: Tess

Sent: September 23, 2008 2:49:09 PM My Darling Davis,

I am leaving work soon, in about fifteen minutes and I will be putting Shawna to sleep. There is a lump in my throat just thinking about it, but I'm holding everything together. I know I will need to be strong for the kids; the process of life and death is not always a bad thing. At my place of work, people passing away is a normal occurance that happens, it seems lately, every other month. I feel that it is a privilege for me to be with someone when they pass, and in this case Shawna. I will hold her and be with her as she goes to sleep so she will not be scared, . I will be there for her, as I said earlier, I will grieve for her afterwards. We will take her out to my dad's to bury her. My mom and stepdad will come out as well. They'll bring pizza and we will have a wake for Shawna. I have to go before the tears start. I Love you and wish you were here so I could get a support hug from you . . . knowing you will be soon, is enough, thank you so much my dear . . . I love you . . . ti amo Amore. Tess

From: Tess

Sent: September 23, 2008 10:44:33 PM My Darling Davis,

I've cried, my tears have dried and the sadness has left and I hold my thoughts of Shawna close to my heart. We took her to the vet. The boys carried her in to the room and put her onto the table. She was on a sheet the whole time. I snuggled her nose in my hands and put my nose next to hers, and whispered to her, that I would be with her. I held her face so that she could look into my eyes as the vet shaved her leg and inserted the catheter and then the needle with the sleeping drug. And just before he released the plunger I said goodbye to my friend, and then she went, peaceful, and no more pain. Zoey cried her heart out, and then I bought her an ice cream before going out to Grandma's and Grandpa's, that's where we buried her, just a little ways out of town, just off the road that goes to Dawson. When we arrived at the vet's it was pouring rain outside, and it continued to rain until we got to the top of the hill, just past the hotsprings turnoff, there is that hill just before the straight stretch. We call it that as the road is straight for five kms. Just as we came to the top of the hill, there was a rainbow at the end of the road, and the clouds, just where my dad and stepmom live, the clouds parted and there were sunbeams shining down. I told Zoey that the angels were telling us that Shawna was okay and she was happy. I just felt peace and a sense of relief and I smiled and felt warm inside for my puppy dog. When we got to dads the sky was grey all around us except for the part of the valley where we were and we dug the grave for Shawna next to her daughter Tandra. I told Zoey that Shawna and Tandra were running together once more. We found some nice rocks and interesting pieces of wood to lay on top of the grave site. Just as we finished the rain started to drizzle. It was a good, peaceful experience. The boys, Chad's girlfriend and myself said our good byes to Shawna. Zoey was in the house playing on grandma's wii, She said goodbye to Shawna several times and I don't think she wanted to see her buried, she's not ready for that part yet. She did give Shawna a kiss on her head after she passed while we were at the vets, she did really good. It was when we got into the car that she really cried, and her crying helped me to cry. And then seeing that rainbow, and the sunbeam, it was peaceful, and all was well. My mom and step—dad came out with four pizzas to my dad and step—mom's place, so we all had pizza, wine, and apple pie for supper. It was a good family dinner, and I could see you with us, it will be good when you are with us, we will have a complete family dinner. Be prepared.

We got home just after 9: PM. I'm going to try and be online tomorrow morning, or I'm hoping you get a chance to get through. Today was frustrating, and I could sense your frustration. Every time I called, the phone was busy and I know the two times that you left voice mails, I was on the phone trying to call you. Using a calling card takes time, and I'm supposed to have call waiting so it notifies me when there is another call coming in but that feature wasn't working. I miss you, I miss talking with you. When you say you want to come home this weekend, I keep thinking I'm dreaming again, The most incredible amazing, thing that could happen, would be for you to come home, and for us to finally touch each other. You will have to let me know how things go and if it will happen for sure because I will notify my supervisor and take next week off of work, so we can spend it together getting to know each other and to get some business taken care of. You have a lot of filling me in to do not to mention filling me up . . . lol. I had better get going; I have this sense of exhaustion coming over me. I hope you were able to sleep. Rest assured that no matter what, if work is unable to happen until the chief gets paid and you have to come home in order to make it happen, then it will happen next week. We'll send Mr.W or the lawyer the money for the chief and then work will resume. Hopefully it will work, that the Chief will allow the workers to go back knowing that the money will be sent to them within the week of your return to Whitehorse. I think I'm repeating myself, I'm tired my dear, I have to go to bed, I wish you were here so I could lie in your arms, feel safe and secure, close my eyes and drift off to sleep knowing that you were watching over me, protecting me, keeping me warm—it's a beautiful feeling. One I have not had for a very long time. I love you with all of my heart and soul . . . I hope you have a great day and I look forward to talking with you soon . . . I will try and be online at 4 AM It seems that no matter what, I tend to wake at that time. If I'm not on, it's because I am so tired that my internal clock just didn't click in, otherwise I will talk with you real soon . . . I love you, see I just have to keep telling you, I love saying to you I Love You . . . till we meet online or on the phone . . . I will sleep now with you in my dreams . . . ti amo

Amore. Tess

Date: Wed, 24 Sep 2008 09:56:20

From: Davis

Good Morning My Love,

I hope you are sleeping well, I couldn't have a good sleep, kept waking and rotating on the bed. I have to meet the lawyer this morning and not sure I will be around at 4 AM so we can chat. Before I can come this weekend, I have to make sure work is going on. The lawyer and I are going to meet with the chief and talk things over. If he understands that we can continue work and get him the money later, that will be fine. Then I will direct them as to what they have to do and get ready to come back home. But if he does not agree, then I will have to find a way to get the money before I come. The one reason why I can't leave things the way they are and get home is because the machines are supposed to be in today, if not, by the end of the week, and they will have to be transported to the mines. Once machines will be kept and that alone will not give me the peace of mind I will want when I am back home. I need to see the machines and make sure they are safe, work is going on, I know the machines are safe in the mines. But if they don't allow us access to the mines, then I will not know where the machines will be kept and that alone will not give me the peace of mind I will want when I am back home. I need to see the machines and make sure they are safe, and not Mr W, or the lawyer can make me feel safe till I know it myself. As I said before, things are really very different here. The lawyer tells me a whole lot of things that happens here and it scares me. But at the end of the day, I came to do business and will get out of here afterwards. I will have to get going, wish me luck, wish our business luck. I hope the chief will be understanding. It saddens me to know Shawna is gone, sometimes, somethings we cherish so much will have to go, but when they go, we always find another thing taking their place. May her thought be with with us forever, and may she rest in peace. I will try to be online at 7 AM, if I don't get the chance, I will try calling you. I love you so much, you are my everything and always in my thought. I love you now and forever. Ti amo

Amore. Davis

From: Tess

Sent: September 24, 2008 5:33:12 AM My Love, My Darling Davis,

I wish I could wrap my arms around you right about now, just think of me in that position, standing right in front of you, my arms are wrapped around your waist and my head is on your chest. If I close my eyes I can hear your heart beat. I'm praying that the chief has said yes, you can continue work knowing that he will receive his money soon. I'm praying, so please tell me this is what he said. Davis, I wish I had the power to make everything just go the way it's supposed to go. All I have is my hope and my faith, and the faith that you and I will be together and that everything will work out the way it is supposed to. I have a lot of faith in us.

You are right about making sure the machines are safe. And I don't know what it is like. It's easy to take for granted what we have here and the luxuries that we now take as necessities and forget that other places such as Africa have no systems in place or have different systems. You are there, you know what has to be done and I trust you to do whatever you need to do. I do wish, Davis, that I did have money to send to you, but I don't have that type of cash. I don't even have that on my Visa card. I'm sorry that I can't help you in this matter. When you're home, maybe we could set up an account that I would be able to access to send you funds when you need them, in case something like this happens again. Did I tell you that I was a bookkeeper for seven years, I'm not an accountant, I was a bookkeeper, so I do have an idea as to how to keep track of funds and what needs to be kept track of for the accountant. Just thought I would throw that in, a little tidbit about myself that may come in handy one day. Davis, I woke at 5AM, I slept out of pure exhaustion, I was afraid that I missed you, and I can see that I didn't so I will look for you at 7AM, however, my yahoo messenger I've been trying to open and it's not working, so I will shut down my computer and restart and hopefully that will do the job. If it doesn't work, I will send you an e-mail to let you know and hopefully we can get through on the phone. I did try calling you as soon as I woke at 5, before checking my e-mail and it said that the mobile device was out of the service area or turned off. I imagine that you were talking with the chief at this time. Anyhow I will wait for your call, so we're not calling each other at the same time like what happened yesterday. I love you so much Davis, I am praying that you are able to convince the chief to allow you to continue or at least have access to put the machines at the mine. I am praying that this has happened. I will talk to you soon, I Love You with all my heart . . . ti amo

Amore . . . Tess

# 8

# DAVIS NEEDS MONEY

From: Davis

Sent: September 24, 2008 8:03:29 AM Hi Love,

I am sorry again I can't meet you online so we talk. I hope to call you soon. We had to fly here because of the timing I hope I told you before it was a four hours' drive, and looking at the time, we are sure we would not have made it. Things didn't not go right, the chief said they have rituals they needed to do before work can continue, and that can only happen when payment is made. I will have to find a way to raise this money so work at the mines can continue. We are flying back to Accra, I have to get to the port before they close. I will keep in touch. Take care and have a nice day. I LOVE YOU. Ti amo

Amore. Davis

From: Tess

Sent: September 24, 2008 10:34:27 AM My Darling Davis,

I am so sorry I'm not in any position to help you, I hope you realize that if I had the money I would send it to you. I wish we were in a different position. I still think that coming home, and sending the funds as soon as you get here is the only thing that may possibly work, however there is the safety and security of the machines. Can you hire a security guy to watch them until you get the funds over there? I'm just throwing thoughts and ideas out. I know that you probably have decided what you need to do. I feel so helpless here. All I can think of is that you coming home will solve a lot of things right now. I don't think I'm suggesting this just because I desperately want to see you, I honestly think that it will solve a lot of your frustrations. This is where the money can be obtained. I love you Davis, if you want to call me and throw ideas out at me, or share your frustrations with me, I am here, and I will listen. I don't know what else I can do, other than be here, and let you know that I love you. Keep strong for us, and know that one closed door always leads to another open one; we just have to find it. I love you with all my heart. ti amo.

Amore . . . Tess

Date: Wed, 24 Sep 2008 19:30:57 +0000

From: Davis My Love,

I just missed talking to you, I picked up and did not hear anything. Then the line got cut. I hope you are doing well. I want to be very frank with you about something, I have not asked you to send me any money. I know your friend and Fed—Ex said a lot about to stop you from sending me the computer, and all I wanted to do afterward was to prove them wrong. It hurt me that things have to go this way, I know you can send me the money if you want to, because you were willing to let me use $5000 and more to buy the computer, and I never even tried using your credit card because I did not wanted to try it. I have not asked you for the money, I realized there is a whole lot going on around the world that I never knew till I got there. I know you can get me the money if you really want to, but I want you to know I don't need your money, all I have ever wanted is to have someone who truly loves me and will always be there for me, so stop telling me you don't have that kind of money. I know you truly love me, and I love you with all that I am. But please stop telling me you don't have that kind of money and so on. You never will have any idea of the amonut of money involved in this and how much I have invested into it. I have been into this business for years, and know what is involveld. I want to come home to see you, I want to come home to touch you and show you how much I truly love you with all my heart, but at the same time, I have to make sure the right thing is being done here while I am away. I am going to try to raise the money by any means possible, soon as work continues, I will come home to see you and prove to you I am truly who I am. I LOVE YOU SO MUCH, you have really showed me what it is like to truly love, and I know deep inside me that I can and will never get someone like you. All I want you to know is that I am coming home to you. I LOVE YOU. Ti amo, and send my love to my sweet Zoey.

Amore . . . Davis

From: Tess

Sent: September 24, 2008 12:48:51 PM My Darling Davis, I Love You,

I don't know what to say to you other than I love you so much, but I am serious about what I tell you, I would not lie to you, I know you are who you are and I have complete faith in you, and I do know that you have never asked me for anything, and I don't have any idea what is involved. I believe you when you tell me you love me and believe me, I le you with all of my heart. I will wait for you to do what you need to do, I love you Davis, with all my heart and soul . . . ti amo Amore. Tess

From: Tess

Sent: September 24, 2008 6:43:06 PM My Darling Davis,

I have re—read your e-mail a few times now and it's my turn to be frank with you, and clear something up with you. Reading your e-mail I got a sense of frustration from you, I want you to know that I love you so much and you have become a part of me that I don't want to do without, I am dreaming of the day when we will actually be able to look into each other's eyes and touch. One of the biggest qualities that I found or find so admirable about you, is how adamant you were and are about honesty. I too am adamant about honesty, I will not lie to you or to anyone else, Davis, and you need to know that I'm doing this because I don't want you to think that I'm telling you something that is not true. Honesty is so important to me, so this is important that you know this; Davis, my credit limit on my Visa is 10, 000.00, my balance right now is 7, 173.46—this includes the 2500.00 for the computer, you see. Before I got the computer I did have 5, 000.00 on my Visa. That's why I authorised for 5, 000.00. The Fed—ex amount for some reason has not appeared on my visa account as of yet and that could possibly be 1000.00, that is what I was told by fed—ex. Davis, this is all I have. I felt that I wanted or needed you to know this, I love you so much. You are my dream, my fantasy, I don't ever want to lose

133

you, sometimes this scares me, but I talk with you, or I read an e-mail that you've sent me and you make everything right.

When I talked with you on the phone last night, I woke you, I'm sorry, you sounded so exhausted, I wanted so badly to reach through the phone and hold you, hold you so close. My heart is with you, and I want so badly to touch you, to look into your eyes and hear you echo my" I Love You", I can close my eyes and feel your caress against my cheek. I do that a lot, close my eyes and imagine I can feel you touching me. Davis, I will wait to hear from you, and you can let me know how you are doing. I am concerned about you. I know that you've put a lot of yourself into this and for this hold up to happen must be extremely stressful to you. I promise you when you come home, I will give you a full body massage. I'll start with your temples, your eyes are closed and I will rub in a circular motion, gently then I will massage your back, deeply and slowly so I can release the tension from each muscle. I will massage your arms, your hands, your fingers, and then I will kiss each finger, and every once in a while I will caress your finger with my tongue, and then I will go back up your arm, and continue down your back, rubbing deeply in an upward motion, deep and hard at first and then softly, gently and every once in a while I will, bend over and kiss your back where my hands have just caressed you. And then I will massage each of your legs and rub your feet and your toes, and continue up the insides of your legs, slowly and then I will reach with both hands to one side of your body and ask you to roll over, and then massage your chest, with gentle strokes, and tender kisses, and I will continue to caress and kiss you from your chest to your abdomen. my tongue tasting the saltiness of your skin, and then I continue to what I've been wanting to caress for so long . . . I love you Davis, I really hope you like massages because I want to give you one so badly. I want to release all the tension that you've been building up, just close your eyes and think of me touching you, imagine you can feel it . . . I had better get going, I hope you were able to sleep a little better last night, I'm hoping that I will wake and find you online . . . if for some reason I miss you, I Love you and I wish for you to have a great day . . . my thoughts are with you. ti amo.

Amore . . . Tess

From: Davis

Sent: September 25, 2008 2:37:14 AM Good Morning My Love,

I also do love you so much with all my heart. I took some bottles of drink last night and got drunk . . . lol? I had to take out the frustration and stress out. I don't do drink or get drunk often, and most importantly, when I am working, but I had to yesterday, and I guess it helped me have the rest I needed in a way. I am going to the lawyer's place, so we can go to the port. I spoke with the lawyer on phone this morning, I want him to try and get me a loan, so work can continue while I come back home to organize myself and get back here to continue what I have to do here, and he said he will try his best for me. He will want me to go with him to meet some people to see if they can help.

I hope something good comes up. I am looking forward in coming home once work continues at the mines. I think it really important that I come home to relax myself with you beside me, and put things in place so I don't have to go though this stress and frustration I have gone though so far here.

You are the love of my life. We have been so close, yet so far apart. No matter where my life takes me, my heart is set on you. Like a blossom growing, our friendship gets stronger everyday. I feel safe and close to you every moment. All the laughs we have on the phone together have become a part of my life and you will always remain in my heart forever. I LOVED YOU TESS, and I will always love you deep in my heart. I am again not sure if I will be able to meet you online at 4am, but I will try to meet you at 7am. If not, I will let you know. Ti amo, you are in my thought in everything I do.

Amore. Davis

From: Tess

Sent: September 25, 2008 3:42:47 AM My Darling Davis,

I just love you, I hope everything goes well for you, and that that the lawyer was able to help you secure the loan . . . I too think, and you know this, that this is the best thing and it's the best thing for us, you need to get your frustrations and stress out of your system. This could be a slogan: use me, not booze . . . to release . . . lol? My heart goes out to you, because I can sense your emotions when I talk with you and read your e-mails. Know that I am with you, my heart beats as yours. I woke at 3 AM, thinking you may be on earlier, and I just woke thinking of you, and again I just missed you, which is probably a good thing. Otherwise our talk would have had to of been really short as you had to meet with your lawyer. He sounds like a good man and he has been helping you a lot. I'm sure things will work out Davis. I will meet you here at 7 AM, and hopefully you will be able to meet me, you are wonderful. It means so much to me, the consideration that you give to me, just something small as telling me about when you may or may not make it online, and telling me what you're doing, that means so much to me and touches my heart. Thank you Davis, Thank you for being you and for loving me . . . I want and I will be in your arms soon, I can feel it . . . and then all will be put right . . . I'm going to go back to bed now, I Love you so much . . . I dream of you . . . ti amo

Amore . . . Tess

From: Tess

Sent: September 25, 2008 7:50:59 AM My Darling Davis,

I am hoping and praying that everything is working out as it should for you. I'm thinking, if you didn't meet me online, then this may possibly be a good sign and you are busy getting things taken care of. I know you will fill me in on how your day was as soon as you get a chance. I have to get another phone card or try and reload the one that I have, if that is possible I will try to call you. It's amazing how much one phone call costs. What's more amazing is how much time I used up when I couldn't get through. Anyhow soon we won't have to worry about that. I will keep praying and keep the faith for us and that all will be working out for you and that you will be coming home soon. Then all will be as it should be.

Zoey has today and tomorrow off from school. A teachers' convention I think. Everyday she asks me about you, and I tell her that you have asked about her and send your love; she too is looking forward to seeing you. She includes you in things that we talk about doing. Just as an example, I have these cute little plastic turtles that I have on the sides of my plant pots as a decoration, I think there are four altogether, anyhow she was playing with three of these turtles and she said see mommy one is you, one is me and one is Davis. We're a herd of turtles Davis. Anyhow, I just saw you come online and then you went off again, bad connection?    I know you will contact me when you can.

I love you so much; you are a part of me that I don't ever want to do without. I love you. ti amo

Amore Tess

From: Davis

Sent: September 25, 2008 8:12:12 AM Darling,

I hope all is going well with you, I have been trying to get online, but having problems. at the end, I was able to sign in only to find out that you were gone. I tried to buzz you. We were at the port this morning, the machines are arriving tomorrow evening, and will have to be transported to the mines. Not excited about it arriving, I guess you know why??? We went to some banks to seek for loan, but I was told there was no way they could help me with loan because I am not a citizen. The only way is to keep trying, and I know we will have someone to give me the loan. All I want is to make sure work is going on at the mines, and the machines are safe at the mines when we clear it from the port. The lawyer and I have some other places we have to go, wish me luck.

I just missed your call again, I am trying to call back and please try at your end to. I love you so very much sweetheart. You are the love of my life. I have a hard time explaining how I feel. I have never felt anything like this before. You are always there for me no matter what. I do not know what I would have done this week without your love and support. You are the most loving, caring, compassionate and absolutely most awesome person that I have ever met. You hold the most special place in my heart, you have gone way above and beyond. I never thought that was possible. I want to marry you now, I want to be your husband. You are a dream come true and I want to spend the rest of my life with you as my wife, lover, and best friend. I feel much love in me for you. I have to catch up with the lawyer, please try my phone again, I will keep trying yours. I love you so much. Ti amo

Amore. Davis

Date: Thu, 25 Sep 2008 15:17:53

From: Davis My Love,

Can you please try calling me again, I will also keep trying. I have to catch the lawyer, hope to talk with you soon. I Love you. Ti amo Amore . . . Davis

From: Tess

Sent: September 25, 2008 8:40:45 AM My Darling Davis,

I have been trying to call you, so many times, it gets through and then nothing, I will keep trying, I have to go to work now, I know something will work Davis, and with the machines being there, it will work. Hopefully the lawyer may be able to secure something for you, and once you get here my god you can transfers the money immediately via Western Union to the lawyer so he has the money to repay the loan. I just hope that he will do that, or that someone will do that for you. You make my heart throb. I love you so much Davis, I will always be here for you. I have to go. I love you with all my heart and soul and being . . . ti amo . . .

And Good Luck, may God go with you . . . so you can come home to me, to us

Amore . . . Tess

From: Tess

Sent: September 25, 2008 12:12:58 PM My Darling Davis,

You are the love of my life,

Talking with you, being able to talk to you and hear your voice just fills me and gives me so much joy and happiness. My god, to actually see you and be able to touch you, I don't' know how I'm ever going to be able to contain myself. There is so much feeling and emotion inside of me and the love that I have for you is so overwhelming,   it takes my breath away and causes my heart to pound. Davis, the thought that you might actually be able to be here next week, that we may actually be able to touch and that I may actually feel your lips on mine and taste your kiss, makes my head feel light, and fills me with these sensations that I have not experienced since I don't know when. Davis, I have complete faith in you, that you will be able to do what needs to be done, and that you will be here. You are a man who can make things happen. I Love talking to you, I love hearing your voice so much. These feelings that you give to me, that you create inside of me, I don't ever want to lose these feelings, you have given me so much Davis, I had better get going, You are my life, my love . . . I love you . . . ti amo

Amore. Tess

From: Tess

Sent: September 25, 2008 8:44:18 PM My Darling Davis,

I just got back from going out to dinner with a friend of mine. I told you about her, she is one of my best friends, the artist. It was her father that passed away two weeks ago, she is doing really well. We had a good talk her and I about how things were going. She has been with her partner for about seven months now and she was telling me about him and how wonderful he is to her, and with her. I told her about you, and how wonderful you are, and how you make me feel. The happiness that you make me feel and most importantly the love that you give to me. She said she will keep a candle burning for us, so it will send you good energy so that you can come home. She sees my happiness and is happy for me, for us. And I'm happy for her, she deserves to have someone in her life that will treat her the way she deserves to be treated, special. Anyhow we went to the new Japanese, sushi place in town, (do you like sushi?), it's the one on Wood St., where the Tung Locke use to be, it was wonderful, the food was great and we got to sit in the Tamari room ( I think that is how it is pronounced) it's like these little booths with a bench that goes all the way around the table and you have to take off your shoes and climb over the bench. The table looks to be sunken down a little bit, anyhow, I thought, that it would be a wonderful place for us to go to when you get home, that is if you like Japanese food. They have more than just sushi there. I would love to go to so many different places with you. I would love to be able to get dressed up, to look good for you, so that when you see me the only thing that you want to do is take my clothes off instead of going out . . . lol . . . seriously, I want to look good for you. I want to look beautiful in your eyes, and I would love to wear sexy, seductive clothes, but with class and taste, just for you . . . I find dressing to please you, would be in itself erotic and would turn me on just thinking about it . . . oh, Davis you do need to come home, I'm going to be quite upfront with you.

As I was driving home tonight I was thinking about what you wrote, about wanting to make passionate love to me and that was all I could think about, and I felt you, I felt you making love to me, passionately. I felt everything, it was so strong, and so intense. I think I orgasimed just thinking about it . . . as I said earlier you do need to come home as soon as you can. Oh wow here I go again thinking about it . . . thinking about you . . . oohhhhhhh.

I hope today finds you successful in what you need to do and what you need to get done. I know that you will be busy, if and when you get online, and I'm not there, will you try to call me and wake me? I keep my phone next to me, with the hopes that you will wake me one morning. Anyhow, if you call me, and even if we can't talk on the phone, if I see it's you, I will go online right away. My computer sometimes takes about ten minutes to start up and get the programs running so you will have to allow me a little bit of time to come online. I want to talk with you so much and find out how you are doing. Right now it's 8:30pm and I'm feeling exhausted, I'm thinking I should just go to bed, it has been a very emotional week for me, between dealing with Shawna and wanting you and wishing I could be there for you. I think I am ready to sleep now, I pray everyday, every evening, for you, for us. I hope that my prayers will be answered real soon. I LOVE YOU DAVIS BARIENDA, and I want to marry you, I loved the way it sounded when the lawyer said to me, he was talking to my husband, I loved that, it felt as it should, like it was meant to be that—you just have to get home so you can ask me . . . you are my world now, and no matter where you are in this world I will love you and I will love you forever . . .

I love you Davis . . . you have a great day, and I hope to be able to talk with you sometime today, talking with you just makes my day so right . . . ti amo . . .

Amore . . . Tess

Date: Fri, 26 Sep 2008 10:48:22

From: Davis My Love,

We just came from a meeting we had with one bank manager. I guess I told you about it yesterday. We met at 8 AM this morning, and had a lengthy talk. He said he will have a meeting with the board of management and get back to us tomorrow at 4 PM. So we will be meeting with him again tomorrow. I hope and pray something good comes out of it. I am now going to the port with Mr W, and will meet with the lawyer in the afternoon. I want you to be my wife, and I promise we will be happy together forever. I really look forward in making passionate love to you as I said before, and hopeful, it may be on my birthday. I LOVE YOU TESS. You are so beautiful to me and very pretty, and forever you will be. I love you. I love every little thing about you. I love your laughter, and can feel your smile in it, I love your magical eyes, and the sound of your voice. I love the warmth I feel when I think of you. I can't stop thinking about you, I need you by my side. You complete me. You mean the world to me. You are the best thing that has ever happened to me. You are the one I've always wished for. I never thought that I would ever meet someone as special as you. I love you the more each and every moment I breathe. I will call you before you leave for work, and know I am always with you in everything you do. I can also feel you beside me in everything I do. I love you, I love you now more then I did last night. Ti amo

Amore . . . Davis

From: Tess

Sent: September 26, 2008 7:25:02 AM My Darling Davis,

I Love you, I wish you Luck and send you all of my Energy, Hope, Faith and Prayers, that all will work tomorrow. Believe me I will be praying for the bank to agree to loan you the money. You think they would, with the mine being registered and located near Accra. As you said earlier, things are very different there, and I'm sure the banks too have to be cautious. But for you . . . I am hoping that they listen to you and realise that you are an honest man and a business man, and they will say, alright, we agree to this . . . Mr Barienda . . .

WE WILL make passionate love on your birthday, many times. I keep imagining what it will feel like to see you for the first time, my body gets hot just thinking about it. The thought takes my breath away. Davis, please make my dreams come true and I too will make yours come true everyday of our lives. I want to grow old with you, to watch Zoey grow up with you and see her grow up with the laughter that we can share. I told Zoey that one of the things you wanted was to have a happy household. I asked Zoey if she figured we could give you that, she said "Oh Yes" she has lots of jokes she can share with you, and we can play games, she has lots of games, and she asked me if you liked games, and we can go for walks, and we can go . . . the best ever . . . SHOPPING . . . Yes we can give you a happy household. You just have to have a really good sense of humour around here. And know that Zoey can be a very emotional child every once in a while, but we will work through it . . . I have been told I am a very patient person, sometimes I need to be.

Davis I see you with us, in everything that I think of doing, you are with us, you are beside us, I love you so much, you are incredible, and I am amazed by you. I want to get to know you, all of you, I want to know more of what you like and what you dislike, what little intricate thing is there about you that will intrigue me—that is what I want to find out. I know in your picture, the way your hand rests against your face, that's a very masculine pose, and that excites me about you—your look—your eyes—your eyes look very gentle and kind; your nose, I want to kiss the tip of your nose. Your smile—your smile draws me into you. Your lips, I want to take my finger and touch your lips, and then reach up and kiss your lips where my finger just touched, ever so gently. I want to fall into you and have you catch me . . . I love you Davis, again I send you all of my prayers and energy to get you home . . . You are a part of me now, and I need to feel that part of me, to survive . . . to be whole . . . I love you . . . ti amo

Amore. Tess

From: Tess

Sent: September 26, 2008 10:49:41 AM My Darling Davis,

I just can't seem to tell you enough, just how much I love you, I want to tell you every minute of the day that I think it, I feel it, I LOVE YOU Davis Barienda, and I just wrote to tell you that . . . I have to get going, you are in my thoughts, every minute, I can't stop thinking about you. Good Luck with everything let me know how things go today with the machines and with the Lawyer . . . again . . . I LOVE YOU . . . ti amo.

Amore. Tess

From: Davis

Sent: September 26, 2008 11:39:31 AM My Love,

I hope your day is going well, mine was okay, and just about to go for dinner. The machines arrived this evening, but I can only have access to it on Monday and that is good for me. I hope everything goes well tomorrow, and sure it will. I want to start by saying that I miss you, and you have no idea how much I love you. I know you don't need another reminder because I tell you mostly how much I love you. I really do and that is one way to show you. I love the hundred ways you show me how much you love me, and I know my simple words can never compare.

From day one, I knew there was something in you that no one had. You are the most AMAZING woman I have ever known. You have shown me the meaning of true love, it makes me smile and fall all over for you again.

Baby, you make my heart beat faster each time I thnik about you, and you give me butterflies. You are the one I want to hold for the rest of my life. In my arms is where you belong. I love you so much and will forever love you with my whole heart. I will try calling you soon. I love you Tess . . . Ti amo

Amore. Davis

From: Tess

Sent: September 26, 2008 1:10:40 PM My Darling Davis,

Your words are never simple, your words speak volumes to me. Your words, what you say to me Davis, I fell in love with you, through your words. You are so wonderful, you make me feel so special. I thank you so much for that. I have had a permanent smile on my face since I met you. People have commented on how much I just glow lately, my god Davis, you have done this to me with your simple words that have been spoken with so much love. I do feel your love and it is the best feeling ever to have someone say to me that they love me as you do. You love me as much as I love you and you feel what I feel. It's incredible, there are no games, there is no guessing, there is no wondering. I Just love you more. I'm sure of this . . . lol. It's wonderful to share the feelings with you and know that you love me, and I can't say it enough, I love you, and thank you so much for what you've done and what you will do to me.

I'm glad the machines will be there, and tomorrow I will pray for everything to work out for you, and then you can call me and tell me what you think will happen and when. I figure you may need three days to get home at least two depending on flights. Your birthday is Sunday . . . so it has to go well tomorrow and it will. And if for some reason it doesn't work, then we will find another solution. There is always a solution to the problem we just have to find it.

Just finished talking with you, my god, I love hearing you, hearing your voice, your laughter. I too want to feel your touch, your kiss. Oh Davis, I feel excitement building. I had better get going, Thank you for calling me. You fill me and just make me beam. I want to shout out to everybody, I Love This Man mind you that's what I tell them, I just don't shout it loudly, I Love you Davis so much, I'm sending all my strength and faith your way, you need to come home . . . and hopefully that will help send you to me. I Love you, see I just can't say it enough . . . I love you, I gotta go . . .you are my everything . . . ti amo.

Amore . . . Tess

From: Tess

Sent: September 26, 2008 2:54:16 PM My Darling Davis,

I'm taking another opportunity to tell you I LOVE YOU . . . I just wanted to let you know that I just talked to my supervisor and I'm taking the week of Oct 6 to the 13th off, I will return to work on the 14th Just so we can spend time together, I figure you will be here by Oct 3 (if I'm really lucky) or Oct 4th, so I want to spend as much time with you as possible. So it is done. Have to go. I Love you. ti amo

Amore. Tess

From: Tess

Sent: September 26, 2008 9:49:52 PM My Darling Davis,

Did you sleep well? It's funny, I miss you, I only got to talk to you once today, and one e-mail and I feel like I'm missing you so much. I just heard something that sounds so right, there's a word that's used when everything feels right, you don't have to worry about today, or what's going to happen tomorrow you feel safe. It's a word that's called Love. L O V E, everything is just right. The way it should be. That's how I feel with you, that everything is right.

How did it go with the machines? Have you been at least allowed to go and inspect them or do you have to wait until Monday to even check them out? I would love to see pictures of everything, I want to see what the mine looks like, Mr W, and if possible the lawyer who has been helping you, and the people who are working at the mine? What does the community that the mine is close to, what is that like? After all, this is the community that will benefit from the mine being in their area, right? There is a lot I would like to know . . . and you, a picture of you, as you are in your element Davis. I'm praying that all will work out today for you, for us . . . I imagine that today will be  a busy day for you, and one that will be mentally exhausting I think, no matter what happens, please let me know, I love you Davis, I will be with you, my hand will be resting on top of yours, my fingers will squeeze your hand every time I want to say to you, I believe in you Davis, we will get through this, and then my arms will go around you and I will hold you close to me, your head resting against mine, our cheeks touching, feel my strength Davis, I'm with you. I Love you Davis. I will be home tomorrow all day, I may have to run downtown a bit, but I will always have my cell phone with me, and I will wait for your call. I will also keep the computer on, and I will keep checking it. Good luck today . . .

I volunteered for our Volunteer Appreciation Dinner held at the Firehall at the end of Main St I manned the coffee and punch bar. It was to say

`thank you' to the volunteers who help out at my work place. It was a pretty good time. Again, if you were here I thought, I bet you would be willing to come with me and I was wondering if you would have helped me, I felt that you would have been right beside me and then afterwards we could have walked along the riverfront to the SS Klondike and maybe did the millennium trail. I would love to go walking side by side with you, our hands holding onto one another; we wouldn't have to say much, we would just be content being together. Smiles we would share; every once in a while I would rest my head against your arm and hold your hand tighter and every once in a while, I would get the urge to laugh. Laugh because of the sheer pleasure of being with you makes me feel so happy, and the feeling of pure pleasure just bubbles up and out of me . . . That is how I feel when I think of you walking next to me . . . I love you Davis . . . I'm going to go online as usual, to see if you're online at all. I will check at the usual times, four and seven . . . if I miss you . . . know that I am with you today . . . you are my love . . . Davis, I want to be with you . . . completely with you. and only with you . . .I love you Davis . . . ti amo.

Amore . . . Tess

Sent: September 27, 2008 4:34:46 AM Good morning my Love,

I hope you sleeping well, and slept well and doing fine. I hope everything will go well today. My hopes are very high. I have a dream about what you wrote in the e-mail, we taking a walk and stuff, and I am wondering if I read the mail already, which I didn't, or I was dreaming about it while you were writing, or better still, is it because we both want this so badly ? Whatever it may be, I am so happy we both are looking forward for the same thing. I want to feel your touch, kiss you, and look into your eyes and tell you how much I truly love you with all my heart. I love you. Hopefully, everything is going to work out perfectly well, so I can be home next week to have you in my arm. I am going to the lawyer's place with Mr W; we will be going to the port. The machines will be moved to the clearing park today, but I will not have access to it till Monday. I want to be there to make sure everything is done well and the machines are just as it should be. It was the lawyer's advice, he said the people here are corrupt and will try to get the container open just to take something, so it will be better if we are there to see every step on the way. This is one of the reasons why I need to have the machines at the mines before I leave for home. Once it's there and the workers are working, Mr W can keep his eyes on it and the lawyer will also be coming there once in a while to make sure everything is perfect. We will also be meeting the manager at 4 PM, and I will let you know whatever the out come will be. I love you.

I read something in a book sometime ago, it said "Valuing a relationship is not merely done by seeing each other everyday. What counts is how much in our busy lives we remember each other." I feel this relationship is more valuable to me than anything because as busy as I get to be here, you are always remembered with every step I take, and I am so happy about that because I love you so much and more. I want you to know that you mean so much to me. From the first day I knew you were that special person I have been looking for, and so glad you are in my life and are the most important part of me. I want you to know that every moment we've spent together communication holds a special place in my heart. I trust you, and I know you'll be there for me no matter what. I trust that you'll be faithful to me and that you won't hurt my heart. You are so beautiful to me. I love everything about you. You just make me feel extra special, you make me feel a sense of warmth inside. I want you to know that I love you for this! I love you for being so caring and genuine. I love you for everything you've done to me. I love you for the happiness and joy you bring to my life. I love you for you. I know we will not even need to talk to communicate with each other. By just being together, holding hands, or cuddling, we can sense each other's thoughts and inner feelings. I want you to know that I want the best for you, for us. I want all our dreams and fantasies to come true. I hope that in me you see a man full of kindness, understanding, and compassion. A man with an open heart. A man who puts a smile on your face everyday. I will be that man who's there for you just as you're there for me, the one who encourages you through life's ups and downs. But ultimately, I want to be the man who is your everything. Not a minute goes by that I don't think about you. You have brought so much joy to my life and you give me so much to look forward to when I wake up every morning. I want you to know that I sincerely appreciate you and I can never tell you enough that "I LOVE YOU. I will get in touch soon as I can again and will call you. Take care, enjoy the weekend, send my love to Zoey and know I love you. Ti amo Amore . . . Davis

From: Tess

Sent: September 27, 2008 8:15:04 AM My Darling Davis,

You are my everything, Oh Davis, You sweep me off of my feet. I know we belong together; I have been waiting for you, for all of my life. What you quoted about being valued in a relationship, that no matter how busy you get, you think of me, know that, that is the same for me with you; I think of you, in fact my thoughts of you are so much a part of me, I love you so much . . . and I do see you as a man with compassion, with understanding and with an open heart—all ready we've been through a couple of issues, that both of us, through the frustrations that I knew you were feeling, the helplessness that I've felt, we've supported each other and have been there for one another. You never shut me out, you talked to me about how you felt, as I did with you, we were honest with each other and we trusted our love for each other and when I talked with you on the phone, hearing your voice, I knew, I just knew, everything would be okay. But the biggest thing, during all of this, I believed in our love and I loved you more each day and I love you more everyday. You just keep filling me up with love. Never again will a day go by where we will have to wonder about being loved. From when I first met you, I started falling in love with you . . . and I will fall in love with you for the rest of my life and beyond.

I know you are a man with an open heart. You ask me about how Zoey is doing, all the time and the fact that you are willing to accept my child and make her a part of your life as well, without question, that means so much to me Davis. You are a wonderful man, one that I feel that the word wonderful is not adequate enough. You are so much more than that. I also think of you as an impressive man, and an intelligent man. I am looking forward to lying in your arms and have you tell me about your adventures, places you've been to, things you've done. I want to know everything about you; I want you to tell me, what you were like growing up, how you felt, people that you met in your life that gave you direction and were important to you. I want to know everything Davis. I keep thinking we don't have much time together. We only have, with luck and love on our side, and hopefully science, fifty years to find out about each other, that is almost the age we're at now. You're closer than me, but do you know what I mean . . . I don't want to waste anymore time, I want you in my life, in our lives, and I want to love you, only you for the rest of our lives . . . So yes, I am hoping everything works out . . . because I want to start the rest of our lives with you right away. No matter what, even if we can't be touching each other everyday, even if you have to go away to work for a while, I will be with you, even if it's in spirit, mind and soul. I will be with you. I promise and vow to you, I will never hurt you, I will never say anything hurtful to you. I will always share with you my feelings without anger, I will respect you, and treat you as such; I will always be faithful to you, and I know that you will be faithful to me, there will be no need to question. I trust you, you are honest, I believe you and I believe in you . . . I give to you all that you have offered to give to me, and I give you these with my heart open and my love wrapped around you . . . I love you Davis Barienda . . . WOW . . . Never have I felt so consumed and so loved as I feel with you . . . thank you, thank you for coming into my life, our lives. Thank you for loving me . . .

I had better get going, I have promised Zoey that I will make her and her friend that stayed over last night chocolate chip banana muffins for breakfast this morning. May all go well for you today, my thoughts and hopes are with you, know and feel me with you . . . I love you so much Davis . . . Please come home to me as soon as you can, so we can complete each other the way we need to . . . so that we can become whole. You are my life . . . I love you . . . remember we don't have much time, fifty years . . . ti amo . . .

Amore. Tess

I'm so sorry I missed you this morning, I must confess I slept right up to 7:00 AM It's been an exhausting week I was holding up pretty good regarding Shawna, and then one of the girls at work who we used to be my neighbor, she knew Shawna and she gave me a hug. I had a good cry with her . . . I love you Davis, I hope to talk with you soon . . . ti amo

Amore . . . Tess

From: Tess

Sent: September 27, 2008 1:55:19 PM My Darling Davis,

I've been sitting here, well not really sitting, I have been puttering around the house. Getting things done and I even went for a run, a short run. I need to work up to where I may be able to keep up with you; I did this while Zoey was at dance. I did try to call you but it said you were out of the calling area or your phone was off. I'm praying that all is well. I know that you will let me know when you can as to how everything went and be able to tell me what will happen next. I just wanted to talk with you, so I thought I would write to you, I have to run downtown right now to do some mailing. Zoey received a special letter notification in the mail yesterday so we have to go to Shoppers on Main to pick it up. I'm wondering what it is. I also have to go and get propane for my barbeque as it ran out yesterday when my son was cooking burgers for himself and Zoey. I'm also picking up a steam cleaner from one of the rental places so I can clean my rugs. Shawna had a couple of accidents when she couldn't move. So that is my day. Not as exciting as yours I'm sure. You probably would like the mundane, day to day home activity right about now, and myself, I would love the excitement. We will just have to live vicariously through each other. How does that sound? . . . lol . . . Oh, and Zoey and I are going shopping for shoes . . . I know you wish you could be with us on that one . . . lol I would love you to be with us . . . Soon, no matter what . . . soon . . . I had better get going . . . I love you . . . I love you so much . . .

You are everything to me. Zoey asked me to say hello to you from her. I am looking forward to hearing from you my dear. Maybe we can get a chance to sit and chat and have a glass of wine together. Actually it will be nice to sit with your body entwined around mine, sharing one glass of wine between us, and talking . . . softly, while we caress each other, and kiss the places we've just caressed . . . and on that note I have to get going . . . again I love you . . . ti amo.

Amore. Tess

From: Tess

Sent: September 27, 2008 7:51:11 PM My Darling Davis,

I'm sitting here hoping that everything went well with the bankers, and that you have been extremely busy. However, I'm not going to speculate. I will wait for you to tell me how it went. I just want to tell you that I love you and that you are so special to both Zoey and I. Davis, I think so much about being with you. Sometimes I feel that I know you. I close my eyes and I know your smile, the warmth in your eyes; I feel that I know what you would say and do in certain situations. It's incredible these feelings that I have, and when you tell me how you feel about me, I know that both of us are experiencing the same kind of feelings if that makes any sense? Davis I want to talk with you so much. So badly do I want to talk with you that when you read this e-mail and I'm not online could you please try calling me so I can get online. That way if we get cut off on the phone I can still talk to you online. If you're checking this e-mail and it's 8:00 AM your time that will make it 1 AM, 2 AM my time, please call me, and I will also try, no I will get up at 0330-0400, and check to see if you're online . . . I miss you Davis, I know that you weren't able to get a hold of me yesterday, so today, I will wait to hear from you. I also want to know how you are doing. Are you okay? I care so much about you and yes I will be concerned for you. I want everything to work out for you with the mine and for us, however possible; I want you in my life to be a part of my life and me to be a part of yours. I should get going, I enlarged a couple of my photographs that I took of some butterflies, now I'm going to frame them and hang them in my bedroom. I enlarged one of a pink flamingo for Zoey and her room. Oh Davis, I want so badly to be in your arms right about now. I ache to feel you. You have become to mean so much to me . . . I love you my dear . . . You are my everything . . . ti amo Amore . . . Tess

Date: Sun, 28 Sep 2008 13:04:35

From: Davis

My Dearest Tess, My Love,

I guess you are up by now and was hoping to talk to me online or on the phone. I am sorry that has not happened yet. The network has been down since yesterday, both Internet and phone lines, and I have been here for over three hours trying to get online and calling so we could talk. I will try again after sending this mail. I love you, Tess. The meeting with the bankers went well yesterday, but was not what I was hoping for. They said they will get me the loan, but not until two weeks, because they have their own system of doing things here and it's a favor they are offering me because I need to stay here for at least six months before I qualify for loan, and that is the way the banking system works here. I just can't wait for that two weeks, and the lawyer knows as much, so we have decided to go see one of the chief's king-makers, and talk to him to let the chief allow us to start work or be able to get the machines to the mines. Then I can come home soon and will send the money to the lawyer and Mr W so they can do the payment of whatever and control things till I get back. We will be going to his place at 2 PM this afternoon, which will be 7 AM your time. I am wondering if it will be possible to talk with you before I leave. I miss you so much and wish you were lying in my arms right now.

You are very right about us not having any more time to waste, and need to get together and start our new happy and loving lives together. I want you to know I am coming home so we start just that, and then will come back to finish what I came here to do and get back to spend the rest of my life with you forever. I love you: loving you comes so easy to me. You are the wind beneath my wings, the cream in my coffee and the flowers in my garden of life. You make my heart flutter.

Sweetheart, I want you to lay our sorrows in my hands and I will guard them with tenderness. Trust your grief to me, and I will protect it with gentleness, like delicate breeze touching the water. You can cry in my arms and I will hold you until the tears subsided. With unbending confidence even through the worst pain, I will give you the strength beyond compare, and we will hang on together in the toughest of times. We will stand together in the best of times and continue to share a love, devotion and care that will span far more than our lifetime. Holding each other through darkness of night and waking to the brightness of day—knowing that God is where we are—we will know peace again forever. I love you so much and so excited to have you in my life. I want to be yours forever, to hold you and love everything that you care so much for. You are the best part of me, that part I will never be able to do without, and I am forever going to cherish and adore you for the warm feelings and much excitement you bring to me. I love you, I love you so much and will forever love you. I will try to sign in again, and will try calling too. But if I am not able to, then you will hear from me when we get back, and will let you know the out come. I love you . . . Ti amo

Amore. Davis

From: Tess

Sent: September 28, 2008 7:40:28 AM My Darling Davis,

I'm glad things went well at the bank and I'm sorry about the timing. Two weeks, that doesn't work. You're right with what you are doing. I hope that this will at least allow the machines to get to the mine to be safe and then once you're here and get the money to Mr, W that will be less than two weeks. My god Davis, this must be so frustrating for you—all this for five thousand. When you deal with such large sums of money all the time. But no matter, I know you will see that everything is safe and then you'll come home and we will make sure that this will never happen again. Okay, et's set something up, where if and when you need funds, I can get them to you.

We just finished chatting online; my heart skipped a beat when I saw you come online, just something as little as that excites me about you. I keep thinking that seeing you, in person, being able to touch you, being able to feel your kiss against my lips, deep into my soul, will be so overwhelming that you had better hang on tight to me, as I just may fall. God, I love you Davis. One week, one week will be your birthday and I want to give you the biggest birthday gift, me. I want to give myself to you Davis, on your birthday. I want to feel what it feels like to have you make passionate love to me and I want you to feel me make passionate love to you. I know it's been a long time for you, so I want for us to take our time and spend hours making love. Feeling each other, learning about each other, accepting each other . . . Oh Davis, I'm looking forward to not only seeing you, making love to you, but I'm looking forward to YOU . . . to being with YOU. I am so looking forward and ready to be with you. I love you so much, you just complete me. I want now to meet the man behind the words, so to speak, and I know it will happen real soon. Davis, do you feel nervous about meeting me? I can't say I'm nervous meeting you. I feel I am more excited; not really nervous about seeing you, as I said a long time ago, I feel as if we've already met; now we just need to meet physically, to be complete. Sometimes I wonder if I'll recognise you, then I think, I know I'll know you. Do you still have the goatee? It's your eyes and your smile I'll know. I look at your picture everyday and you will hopefully see me, in fact, I'll be the first person you'll see when you walk through the doors of the airport.

Davis, you have done so much for me, you have lifted me up, and have given me the feeling that I do matter to you. You have made me realise and remember how wonderful and beautiful falling in love is, and how love is, and how it can be with the right person. You next to me, it is so fulfilling and so powerful, you have given me your love, and I have given you mine, and it's the best feeling I have ever experienced this feeling of ours. What we share, it's incredible and I know that once we meet it will just keep getting better, and bigger. I love you Davis Barienda, again I hope all went well, and what needs to be accomplished can be accomplished. I will wait to hear from you. Thank you so much for trying so hard this morning to get online, you do make me feel special . . . I Love You . . . ti amo

Amore. Tess

From: Davis

Sent: September 28, 2008 1:48:31 PM My Love,

I hope your day is doing well, mine was okay. First of all, I want you to know I am not nervous and have never felt nervous in seeing you. I feel you are a part of me and we have met already. I feel like I have known you forever. We just got back from the chief's king-maker's place. I tried to get online, but still having problems. So I decided to send you a mail and try getting online afterwords. We were not able to talk with the king-maker today. We are told he was in a meeting. The lawyer told them to let him know our presence and that it was very important and we will wait if his meeting was done. After waiting for over an hour, he sent a message to be brought to us that he will not be able to see us today, but if we could come very early tomorrow morning, he was going to have the best of time for us. I felt from this message that everything will be fine tomorrow and he knew why we came to see him. The lawyer, I and Mr W have decided to see him as early as 7 AM in the morning. If he is still not awake by then, we will wait till we get the chance to talk with him. I will send you an e-mail and try to talk to you on phone before we leave to meet him. I have this strong belief that everything is going to work out well.

I thank god every night since I found you, you provided the light to find my way. I have never been so certain of anything in my life like I am of us. I know that everything is going to be perfectly wonderful between us, and we will be happy together forever. We are meant for each other, everything proves it right that we were meant to be from Genesis. You have totally changed my outlook in life and I thank you for that. I never thought that someone could love me like you do, but guess what? I love you that much too. I feel as if I'm walking over clouds just thinking about you. You make my life complete. Know that with you, I wouldn't mind being a fool for the rest of my life. I love you so much and I know you love me too. I know that others looking at our relationship might think that we're saying too many foolish things too soon but they just don't know how we feel about each other. There's nothing foolish about falling deeply in love with someone as special as you, I mean every word I said to you, I love you and for you and Zoey. I would do anything, I love you both so much. Today I promise you that I would do anything in my power to make you a great person, outstanding father and loving husband. I LOVE YOU. I hope I can talk with you before I fall asleep. Tell Zoey I say hi, and hopefully, she will see me before the end of the week. I LOVE YOU. Ti amo.

Amore. Davis

From: Tess

Sent: September 28, 2008 4:12:04 PM My Darling Davis,

I love you so much, you speak volumes to me. When I read your letters I picture you standing or sitting or lying next to me, whispering these words into my ear. I'm in your arms, and the warmth that covers me gives me the feeling of being completely safe and protected in your arms. Your warmth flows over and around me, your love keeps me . . . and Davis, you say that people may think us foolish with our feelings, they think I'm crazy, until I tell them how I feel, how you make me feel and how I feel about you and how you feel about me, and by the time I'm finished telling them my feelings, they wish nothing but the best for us, and a wish that they could love or have such love as we do.

I speak with such conviction when I talk of you, and how we feel, that no body dares say anything about being foolish or crazy, because they can see my happiness and they can see me glow. Davis, this is incredible what has happened to us and what continues to happen to us. I know at the beginning I was saying to you to beware of illusions created by words, but we have gone beyond that, there are no illusions, you are so real to me. Like you said, I feel as if I have known you forever. Please forgive me, but when you talk of Genesis, what do you mean? I think I have an idea, but I would like you to explain it to me . . .

I'm so sorry I missed you online, I have been busy getting my house organized. Zoey was out raking leaves with her friend and I promised her an allowance of five dollars so now we are going to walk to the store so she can enjoy her five dollars. I will write again this evening, I find I want to talk to you all the time, and even if it's writing to you, it's a way that I can talk with you. I had better get going the young one is chopping at the bit . . . I love you so much. ti amo

Amore. Tess

From: Tess

Sent: September 28, 2008 11:53:44 PM My Darling Davis,

It's late right now, 11:30 almost, I'm thinking that it's around 630 AM your time, you should be awake about now. I would love to be able to wake next to you; When I wake, I would find myself wrapped in your arms. I can feel myself snuggle into you closer, feeling your body against mine, so content does it feel that moving is debated. I would turn around in your arms so that my breasts would touch your chest, I would watch you as you sleep, taking in every detail of your face, the lines on your forehead, your eyebrows, your eyelashes how they lie against your skin, your nose, your moustache, your lips, your chin, your goatee, your cheeks. I wouldn't be able to help myself, I would lean into you and kiss your cheek, softly and then I would kiss the tip of your nose, you would wrinkle your nose up and scratch it with your hand, and then I would laugh softly, your eyes would open and you would pull me to you, kissing me deeply, as I lay across you, my body falling into yours. That is how I see myself waking you up some mornings, you fill me Davis . . . ohhhhhh. I just finished about an hour ago, washing my rug in the living room, I rented a machine and now it's done. I had to clean it after Shawna had been so sick. The deed is now done, and I will feel much better for it. I'm going to try

155

and catch you online in the morning if possible, I'm pretty tired right now so I may not wake till 4:AM but you may still be in the meeting at that time. I'm hoping that you were able to get hold of me before your meeting, and we have an idea when we'll meet online, if not, I will check at 7 AM, that should be 2 PM your time, but you may be really busy then. So if you're not on line, I will know that you're busy but also that you're thinking of me. I know that you do, I feel it, just as you know that I think of you, every second, with my whole being. In fact this evening I was grocery shopping at Superstore and the line was incredible, anyhow it gave me a chance to just stand there and think of you. I closed my eyes and I thought of you standing behind me, in fact when I put my head back I could feel my head resting against your chest, your arm would come around me, your hand would be holding onto the cart and I would rest my side against your arm, this is how we're going to stand waiting in line you and I. So close we will be and so comfortable, that it'll almost be a shame that we have to move. This is what I think of Davis, all day, how we will be together, what you and I will be like, and it just fits, everything just fits. I love you with all of my heart, into the depths of my soul, you have taken me . . . you are amazing Davis. Good luck with everything today. May you be able to get the machines safe and if all else fails, maybe you can hire a security guard. Mr W can pay him as soon as you can send him some money, and then the machines can get to the mine, if the chief's king-maker can't help, but as you said, it looks and sounds promising. So I'm praying for you Davis that all will work and you again are a very impressive man. I like the fact that you don't give up and that you look for the solution, even if it's not exactly what you wanted, you will work with it, I like that about you. You impress me Davis, with your words and with your actions. I had better get going my eyes are getting heavy, and when I'm this tired, you never know what will come out of my mouth, or fingers I should say, in fact, one thing that you should know about me, is when I get tired like this, I get, oh what's the word, frisky . . . ? See you should be here to put me to bed . . . lol . . . See I had better go before my fingers get the best of me . . . I love you . . . you have a wonderful day . . . I am thinking about you every step of the way . . . I'm looking forward to hearing from you . . . I love you . . . ti amo

Amore. Tess

Date: Mon, 29 Sep 2008 07:44:37

From: Davis

Good Morning My Love,

I guess I missed you with some minutes. I will not call to wake you; you are tired and need much rest. I love you so much. We just got to the king-maker's place, we were told he is still sleeping and we will have to wait for more than an hour or go and come back later. I told them we will wait, even if we have to wait for five hours. I have high hopes that this will work. The only way that I will feel safe when I come home is knowing that the machines are at the mines, so I am going to do anything possible to get them to the mines, and will come home to you. Once things are settled down and the machines can be transported to the mines, I will then let Mr W book a flight for me, and I will let you know my flight information soon as I know. As you can see, this week will be a very busy one for me. In Italy, they say there is always someone who has been with you in the bringing, and will be with you till the end. The Italian word is Genesi, (Genesis meaning bringing), and that is what I meant. There are no words to express the gratitude I feel in my heart that our hearts have come to dwell together, as one. You are my life, my heart, my soul. You are my best friend. You are my one true love. You are my destiny. I love you more today than I did yesterday, and I'll love you more tomorrow than I do today. Love is the only thing that makes life worth living. Your love. With all my heart I am forever yours. I will have to go now, sleep well, sweet dreams and know I love you so much. I will let you know how the meeting goes as soon as we are done. You are my true love, and I will forever be there anytime you call on me.

I love you. Ti amo

AMore . . . Davis.

From: Tess

Sent: September 29, 2008 7:07:33 AM My Darling Davis, My Love,

You have wrapped your love and warmth around me, and you make me feel so alive, so loved, and so complete. That is a beautiful saying, Genesis, I will remember that. You are going to introduce me to so many different, interesting, wonderful things, I'm hoping that there are things that I can introduce you to as well. I think there is, and there definitely will be. You are the part of me that has been missing throughout all these years. I feel in fact, I know, that you are who, I've been waiting for. The person you are, your kindness, your thoughtfulness, your consideration, your gentleness, your compassion, your strength, your intelligence, your sense of humour, your wants and your needs, your love, these are all things that I admire about you. I sense about you, just through our letters, our phone conversations I know that you are all of these and more, so much more. I know that you will accept me for who I am and accept my faults, but I also feel that I want to be the best for you, and with you in my life I can be the best with you. I too will accept you for the person that you are, for you are a part of me.

I'm hoping that you have been able to talk to the chief's king maker—and that he has been able to help, and that you are extremely busy right now. I look forward to hearing from you so you can let me know how things are. I know that when you get home to Whitehorse you will tell me everything. I think we'll not be getting much sleep the first couple of nights, we'll be talking too much . . . lol

I'm going to make myself a coffee, and then get myself ready for the day, I will be busy at work this week as I'm doing all of my assessments for next week as well, so I can take the week off and not have to worry about my work at all while I'm with you. I want to be able to spend all of our time together while you are here. I love you Davis, with all of my heart, and soul You make me smile everyday. Thank you for that, I also thank God everyday for bringing you into our lives, I prayed for you, I prayed for someone who would love me as I love them, fully, completely, honestly and whole—heartedly, someone who would be a father to my daughter, and someone who would want to marry me. My prayers have been answered. I had better get going, again the best of luck to you, I hope your day is going well, I am with you, every step you take, I am beside you. I love you so much. ti amo

Amore. Tess

*Davis called me and told me that the Chief King-maker agreed to half of the royalty fee which was 2, 500.00. That would be enough to cover the traditional ceremony that once performed would enable the workers to continue working at the mine. Davis asked me if I could get him that amount of money and send it to him through Western Union. I remember when he asked me this; I got that gut wrenching tightness deep inside of my belly. I thought about what Davis was asking me I did have enough money to cover the 2500.00, I could do it. And if I did do it and Davis was real, he would be able to come home. I wanted to take that chance, so thinking about what I had available to me, I withdrew the money and went over to Western Union. However sending 2500.00 has a fee of 40.00 attached to it, so it cost me 2, 540.00. I sent it, in anticipation that Davis would be paying me back once he was back home. I also knew I couldn't tell anyone, I didn't dare. I was in this on my own.*

From: Tess

Sent: September 29, 2008 10:26:46 AM My Darling Davis,

My Love, I don't have long, I'm late for work and I have to do an assessment ASAP, the control # which you'll need is 705 112 8921 and I've put a test question of which you'll know the answer so only you can get it, and I've asked them to call so you should have had a call by now hopefully, being that it is instant. So Davis, please do something for me, please book your flight tomorrow . . . Would you do that for me? I have to run I love you. ti amo

Amore. Tess

On 9/29/08, Davis wrote:

My Love,

I was just sending you an e-mail, but I lost it all. I am going to Western Union right away, and will let you know when soon as I get it. Thanks so much, you have always been there for me, and I will always be there for you too. I LOVE YOU TESS so much, and I will forever love you. I will get in touch soon as I get the money. I love you . . . Ti amo.

Amore. Davis

Date: Mon, 29 Sep 2008 17:49:31

From: Davis

I will book my flight tomorrow, I will do anything for you. I love you.

ti amo

Amore . . . Davis

From: Tess

Sent: September 29, 2008 10:50:10 AM Davis I love you

Date: Mon, 29 Sep 2008 19:56:32

From: Davis

Tess I love you more.

I hope your day is going well. I could not get the money today, I don't know if they will be opening tomorrow. If they do, that will be fine. If they don't, I will have to wait till Wednesday. Whatever the case, I will book my flight tomorrow and will let you know and have the details soon after I am done. I love you so much and so thankful for everything you have done for me. You are and will forever be the most important part of me. I love you for what you do to me inside.

We will be going to see the king-maker first thing tomorrow morning to let him know the money was ready and if they don't get it by the end of day tomorrow, they will get it on Wednesday. I want them   to give us the permission to start transporting the machines to the mines.

You are my everything. Thank you for loving me the way no one can. You understand me and you know just how to make things right. You will never know just how much I love you, but I will spend the rest of my days trying to show you. You saved me from the worst, and you are always there for me. I will always keep you safe. I love you . . . for all eternity. Thank you, Tess. I will try calling again, and hope to be able to talk with you. I love you so much, have the best of the day, and know you are always in my thought. Ti amo.

Amore. Davis

From: Tess

Sent: September 29, 2008 1:11:45 PM My Darling Davis,

My Love, I Love you more, If it will make it easier for you, tomorrow I can scan the piece of paper(the receipt), so you have it as proof   to show the chief, it may help. I hope this works, and thank you for booking your flight tomorrow. I would like to have an idea as to how soon you can be here, so I can make arrangements for Zoey. I get to see you and spend time with you, and then you can meet Zoey and she can meet you. She wanted to know this morning if we could go back to Africa with you when you go. I told her not this time, but maybe sometime, she is also wondering if there are tame jaguars in Africa? Davis, I love you so much, to have you in my arms, to be in your arms in hopefully four days. This will be the longest week of my life, you realise this. Please let me know how things go, I have to run . . . I love you . . . ti amo

Amore . . . I wish I had Yahoo on here or even MSN so we could chat. You just send me this e-mail so I know you're online, or were online . . . . I want to talk with you so badly . . . I love you . . . ti amo

Amore . . . Tess

From: Tess

Sent: September 29, 2008 10:04:44 PM My Darling Davis,

I love you, I am hoping all goes well today, and I'm also hoping that you are able to get a flight that will get you home before the weekend. I have to confess I did look up some flights and the only flight that you can take that will get you home for Thursday is Wednesday at 1140 PM, from Accra to London, London to Vancouver and then Air Canada from Van to Whitehorse. Otherwise it's Friday and you'll get here Saturday after midnight, which means you will still be here for your birthday . . . However, me being curious as to flights available to see how soon you could be here, I have no idea how you were planning on going or coming so to say . . . so the rest my dear is up to you . . . I love you and I'm looking forward, really looking forward to seeing you. I want to hold you and be held by you, so bad. It was wonderful talking to you today, hearing your voice, we finally get a good connection and I run out of time on my calling card. You really need to come home so we can talk undisturbed and without interruptions. You did sound tired, I hope I didn't wake you, mind you I think I enjoy waking you, you sounded so . . . inviting . . . so to say . . . I wanted to reach through the phone and hold you, and I would have loved helping you fall asleep . . . I promise you, that I will make sure that you get a good night's sleep every night, it may get interrupted, but it will be good . . . lol. I love you so much Davis . . .

I have attached a copy of the Western Union receipt. I had one hell of a time getting it to scan properly, and it kept scanning it in and putting the dollar amount in pounds. I have no idea why this was happening, anyhow I figured it out, changed what I was doing and hopefully it will e-mail to you properly. Again if you can't get the money until Wednesday, this may help today when you go and talk with the chief, good luck with everything.

Davis, I will hopefully be able to wake and check online first thing this morning, I am hoping that I will wake between 3 and 4 AM and please, if you are online and you can get through to me on the phone, please call me . . . anytime, wake me. I want to be woken up by you . . . . I had better get going right now, and get to bed myself . . . you are everything to me Davis . . . and I know you will come home as soon as you can, I love you . . . ti amo

Amore . . . Tess

From: Davis

Sent: September 30, 2008 8:48:36 AM My Love,

It was so nice talking with you, I love you so much. I love you with every part of my being. If I could marry your soul I would. I dream of nobody else. Everyday is a true struggle when I'm not with you. If I could conjure up all the power in the world to translate my love to every form of living: physical and spiritual, I would. You are my everything, and I love you more than life itself. I love you truly, take care and have the best of day. Ti amo

Amore. Davis

From: Davis

Date: Tue, 30 Sep 2008 19:35:30

Hello Love,

I hope your day is going well. Mine has ended and I will be going to my hotel room after sending this mail. I miss you, it was so wonderful talking with you, it made my day. I love you so much and think about you all the time. I will pick the money first thing tomorrow, then will go to the king-maker's place so he can talk things out with the chief. Aftewards I will go to the mines, then to the port to see how things are going. Then I will go to the travel agent's place to get my flight info and will let you have it as soon as I get my flight ticket and the info. I will mail you in the morning before I leave and will keep you updated about whatever goes on. I truly love you Tess, with all my heart and everything I am. I now can be myself when I am with you. Your idea of romance is dim lights. Because you make me feel like I have never felt before, I can tell you anything. Your undying faith is what keeps the flame of our love alive. You and me together, we can make magic. We're the perfect one for me. Thinking of you fills me with a wonderful feeling. Your love gives me the feeling that the best is still ahead. You never give up on me, and that's what keeps me going. You are simply irresistible.

I love you because you bring the best out of me. I love your terrific sense of humor. Every time I look at your picture, my heart misses a beat. You're the one who holds the key to my heart. You always say what I need to hear. You have taught me the true meaning of love. Love is, what you mean to me—and you mean everything. You are my theme for a dream. I have had the time of my life and I owe it all to you. And, of course, I love your intelligence, because you were smart enough to fall in love with me. I will try calling you before I go to sleep. Take care and know you are always in my thoughts. I love you so much and more. Ti amo.

Amore. Davis

From: Tess

Sent: September 30, 2008 1:14:10 PM My Darling Davis, My Love,

I'm sorry I haven't had a chance to write to you sooner, I feel so wonderful whenever I talk with you, or read an e-mail from you. I feel so close to you, and I am a very intelligent woman for I am very much in love with you and you sir, are extremely intelligent for choosing me to fall in love with . . . I don't think I will ever be able to thank you enough or be able to show you. I will try though, as to how grateful, and thankful and just completely overjoyed that you have come into my life, our lives. Davis, I am counting the days, until we can actually touch and I just feel so comfortable with you, I want to do so much with you, I know we won't have a lot of time to do things when you get here, but I would like to do a couple of things. The rest will have to wait until you come back and what you said about when I see you, I'm not going to want you to go back alone. I don't have to see you to know that, I know that the hardest thing for me to do, is going to be seeing you off, but I'm not going to think about that. I'm going to concentrate on seeing you come towards me. I love you Davis, so much . . . you have become a part of my life that I'm not going to do without. I had better get back to work. I wasn't in my office this morning so I couldn't access the e-mail, but I'm here this afternoon, if you do get a chance to call me, I love to hear your voice . . . I don't have a calling card right now, so I can't call you. I have to go, I love you . . . ti amo . . . oh and you definitely have made my day, you just lifted me up this morning . . . I love you

Amore. Tess

From: Tess

Sent: September 30, 2008 10:30:06 PM My Darling Davis,

Good morning, my dear, I hope you slept well . . . I have been thinking about you all night long, and I haven't even been to bed yet. That's when I drift away with you in my dreams . . . First things first . . . I love you . . . now, how are you going to do all this in one day, go to Western Union, then the chief king-maker, then to the mine, which is four hours out, then back to the port, then to the travel agent; how many hours do you have to do all this in? As I said you are amazing. Good luck with everything. I am hoping as well that you will be able to tell me that you can be home Saturday night or Sunday . . . I'm praying for this . . . please let my prayers be answered. You're the only one that can do this. I wanted to ask you this morning when we were chatting, and I never got the chance to—I wanted to ask you, what do you normally have for breakfast? I'm full of curiosity once more. I love talking and chatting with you, I look forward to being able to see you while we talk.

Davis, you still seem so far away, a dream almost. A dream that I want to be real. I have fallen so deeply in love with you; I feel as you do, there are no words that can describe how deeply I feel.

Right now, it's just after 10 PM. I'm going to take off all of my clothes and then I'm going to sit in my hot tub, I wish that I could be with you, sitting in the hot tub, I can just imagine the feel of my body gently gliding over yours, as I move on top of you, my breasts would rub against the hair on your chest, exciting them, as I leaned into you, to kiss your lips, slowly, sensually, oh yes, I think I'm definitely going to enjoy having a hot tub with you . . . I was thinking today about music. Every song that I listen to reminds me of you, of our situation, of our love, and of how I feel about you. I enjoy lots of different types of music. Unfortunately my collection of CD's has been diminished due to me moving so many times. I have most of my stuff in storage still. I will tell you the story around that when I see you. I want to have a lot of music in our lives. I want to dance, I want to dance with you. I want to make our own beautiful music together, and I want to have a wonderful versatile CD collection that has all types of music . . . I had better get going so I can still enjoy my hot tub tonight, oh and just so you know the snow melted and it was actually 17 C today. I love you my Dear Davis, you are my everything, my dream, I want my dream to come true . . . ti amo

Amore . . . Tess

From: Davis

Sent: October 1, 2008 2:38:52 AM Good Morning My Love,

I hope you slept well and are doing fine. It's going to be a very busy day for me, but I really need to make sure I do all these things before the end of day. I am going to keep up the money now, then we will go see the king-maker. Afterwards, I will have to see the travel agent to get my flight details, then will go to the port to see to it that the machines are getting ready to be loaded and transported to the mines. I want you to know how much I love you. You mean so much to me and I want so much to make you as happy as you make me. Each passing day has me falling more in love with you. You can do the slightest thing and it warms me. You are always in my thoughts and in my heart. I never knew that love could be so wonderful until I met you. You have given me a new perspective on so many things. I will always treasure our love and keep it safe. I love you, Tess. I will keep you updated about whatever goes on. Ti amo

Amore . . . Davis

From: Tess

Sent: October 1, 2008 7:36:13 AM My Darling Davis,

Hello My Love,

I've been wondering how things have been going for you today. I'm guessing that you have been very busy and have accomplished a lot today, and if you're sitting down reading this, then your day may almost be over? I love you Davis . . . I had a good sleep thank you, and all through the night I dreamt of you holding me. I think that is why I can sleep, I'm with you. My day is not going to be as busy as yours. I have to be downtown for work this morning, and then back up the hill this afternoon. Davis I have to get going, Zoey needs to get up and I have to finish getting ready for work and get Zoey ready for school, you still need to let me know what you normally do for breakfast . . . I Love you so much Davis Barienda . . . you are my dream. ti amo Amore. Tess

From: Davis

Sent: October 1, 2008 8:44:26 AM Hello My Love,

I have been trying to call you, I am glad you had a good sleep. I LOVE YOU SO MUCH. My day is going well. The chief has allowed us to continue with work. I am still at the mines, the traditional rite was preformed at the mines today and I had to be there. I am leaving here for the port right after sending you this mail. I spoke with the travel agent, he said he has booked me for Friday flight, and I should pass by the office for my ticket. He also said the flight is $4, 880 USD, and I will have to do the payment when I come for the ticket. I told him the reason why I am going is because I have run out of money and was going to organize myself and will be back in two weeks, so he should let me have the ticket and I will pay on my return. He said it was going to be difficult because he had to account by the end of day everyday. I tried to make him understand, but he said the only thing he can do for me is to allow me to pay half, then pay the rest on my return. Now, what I want you to do is to send me half of the money which will be $2400USD today, I will have it first thing tomorrow morning so I can pick up the ticket. I am not sure you can do it this morning, so do it anytime today. I must have it tomorrow morning. I have to get going, we will arrive at Accra late, but I will still pass the port. I want to make sure everything is being loaded. We will be transporting it to the mines tomorrow morning, after I have picked up the ticket. I LOVE YOU SO MUCH, and really looking forward to you picking me up. I will let you know the flight details soon as I pick up the ticket. Take care, have the best of the day, and know you are always in my thought and I Love You with all my heart, soul and mind. Ti amo

Amore. Davis

From: Tess

Sent: October 1, 2008 12:04:08 PM My Darling Davis,

I am sitting here with tears in my eyes and my heart breaking . . . I Love you so much . . . You have given me a fantasy, a dream, I don't want to lose. I hope and pray that will not happen, do you know that just this morning Zoey said there are only four more days mom until the 5th. I asked her what she meant by that and she said it was Davis's birthday and we needed to plan his party. She also mentioned how much she is looking forward to meeting you, her words exactly were, "I wish Davis would be here soon".

I am looking forward to seeing you, to being able to love you openly. Davis, when I told you that I didn't have $5000.00 I was very serious. The 2500.00 that I sent you I went into the hole on that, just to get it to you, because you needed it. If I don't get that back, I will be in trouble, I have no more money left, I am so sorry, I wish I did, but I have no more, please don't tell me you can't come because then this would all be just a fantasy, and I don't want to lose you . . . to lose the love that you have given me, please think of something to come here, give him the computer, if you have to and you can bring another one back with you when you return . . . Please Davis . . . don't go away from me . . . There has to be a way . . . I am just not able to make it so, I am sorry again. I love you with all my heart and soul . . . but I have no money. I don't know what more I can say other than I Love you . . . ti amo

Amore . . . Tess . . .

From: Tess

Sent: October 1, 2008 12:42:30 PM My Darling Davis,

My first e-mail that I sent to you, started with a band of steel gripping my heart. This one, if you haven't read the first e-mail I sent you, maybe you should before reading this. Anyhow, I Love you with all my heart and soul, and I believe everything that you have told me, and I believe in you, and I trust you and I know that you will do everything in your power to get home, not just to see me, but in order for you to continue working, you need to take care of your money situation. There is always a way, whether Mr W can loan you the money or the lawyer, because they know that you will be able to send money to them first thing Monday morning, and maybe both could help you out. Oh what the hell, for that matter give the travel agent my visa number to hold just in case. Mind you it won't do him any good, there is not much on there, but he could put it through on Monday once we put money on my visa for the computer. I feel sick to my stomach that I can't do this. I wish to god that I could, but please find a way to come home, and as I said in my first e-mail, the computer may be given or sold, that should be worth a little bit of money, Davis . . . Please tell me you are coming home . . . I need you . . . I want you . . . I love you with every being of my soul . . . I love you . . .

Amore. Tess

From: Davis

Sent: October 1, 2008 2:14:58 PM My Love,

I hope your day is going well. We just got back from the mines, there was a little traffic on the way. I could not make it to the port, I will do that first thing tomorrow morning. I will try to talk things out with the agent in the morning, and will let you know the outcome. I am really looking forward to coming home and spending my birthday with you, and will try my possible best to make that happen. I asked the lawyer and Mr W if they could get me the money when the agent brought up this issue, but they told me they don't have that kind of money. They make less then $100 dollars or a little above in a month, they have kids to look after and living here is very high. At the end of the day, they have nothing to write home about. I have seen the hardship here and I truly believe they would have given me if they had it. Let's see what happens tomorrow, I will try my possible best to get the agent understand thing, and if possible give them the computer as you said. I love you so much, and will do my best to make it home as planned. I will be at the agent's place first thing tomorrow morning. There are no words to express how I feel about you. I constantly search for the words, and they all seem less than I truly feel. You are my life, my heart, and my soul. You are my one true love. I think of you every day, and dream of you each night. I hear the sound of your voice in my mind, it's the sweetest sound I would ever hear. I have to be near you, have you lying on my chest. I need to show you, that you are the best. I have made the decision to tell you how I feel everything. When you say you feel the same as I feel, I feel it's a dream come true. I am on a cloud, living in a dream, and a few days from now, it will feel real. I have said it before and I'll say it again, words cannot express how you make me feel. I make this promise to you my darling, to love you the way that you love me and more. I now look to the future and see you in everything I do. Your life is mine and we will make it last. I love you with all my heart, I am forever yours. I will let you know what happened when I get to the agent's place tomorrow morning. Take care, enjoy the rest of the day and know you are always in my thought. I Love You . . . Ti amo Davis

From: Tess

Sent: October 1, 2008 2:27:08 PM I Love You . . .

From: Tess

Sent: October 1, 2008 3:05:41 PM My Darling Davis,

I love you so much, you know just what to say and do to make everything alright. I will be okay as long as I have your love, your strength, I will be okay. You mean so much to me. I know you will do whatever you can and something will work, we need to come together, we both need this. You are my life Davis, I have complete faith in you. I can't write for long right now, I need to get going so I can finish my assessments. I just want to say I love you with all my heart, you fill me completely . . . I will pray that all will work out for you, for us, I am so glad that things are going ahead at the mine, don't forget to get pictures. I'm looking forward to seeing them. I have to go . . . I love you.ti amo

Amore. Tess

From: Tess

Sent: October 1, 2008 7:13:52 PM My Love . . .

Here we are, across the world . . . Here we are, across the seas, Here we are, you and me . . .

Please bring your love home to me . . . Only you, can change my life,

Only you can make me your wife . . .

I give you love, I give you my all, for you are my everything, you are the part of me that I have now found . . .

Here we are, across the world . . . Here we are, across the seas

Here we are, you and me . . . Please bring your love home to me . . . I have found in you, the love I need.

I have found in you, the man of my dreams. you have shown me what love should be like, you have shown me what love should feel like, Here we are, across the world . . .

Here we are, across the seas . . . Here we are you and me . . .

Please bring your love home to me . . . I Love you Davis . . . Amore . . . Tess

From: Tess

Sent: October 1, 2008 10:15:42 PM My Darling Davis,

I have been sitting here looking at your picture, you make my heart melt, just looking at you, I want to disappear into you. I want to feel the caress of your lips, the touch of your hands; I want to feel the look in your eyes. I want to know what it feels like to have you look at me

and see the love in your eyes and I know you will see the love that I have for you in mine . . .

Davis, no matter what happens, I love you like I have loved or felt for no other . . . You have done something to me, that has taken me by surprise, and has turned me completely upside down. Never have I felt so deeply this love that we share, and with you, the man I love with whom I have never touched, with whom I have never seen in the flesh and with whom I have only seen in my dreams. I've heard the caress of your voice, and I have read your words. I want more than anything to be standing, waiting at the airport, to watch you walk through the doors and walk towards me. I want to be able to wrap my arms around you and have you wrap your arms around me as we hold each other like we will never let each other go . . . I want to be able to look into your eyes, just before you lower your mouth to mine and take in my lips, and caress your tongue with mine as you completely take me with your kiss . . . I want to know how you feel . . .I don't want to imagine anymore. I pray that we will feel each other soon, I pray that I will wake with you next to me. I pray that I will wake and be able to bring you coffee in bed, and lay next to you as we drink our coffee and have you tell me everything about the mine, about your experiences. I want to plan the day with you. I want to plan the week with you. I want to plan my life with you . . . Oh Davis, I pray that this will happen . . . even if it can't happen now, you should have that cheque from the Chinese company and we could revert back to the plan of having them send me a cheque which I can then deposit and send you the money that way. However, it will mean more waiting. I want to be with you now, greedy of me and somewhat selfish I know. I will wait if it means that you will come home to me. I will wait for you forever . . . but please god, I pray that you will be able to tell me you will be on your way Friday . . . I Love you Davis . . . I Love you more than what you could possibly imagine, I find it hard to take in sometimes the magnitude that our love has grown to. It has taken me by surprise, and it's a wonderful beautiful surprise . . . I will wait for your e – mail . . . I know you will do your best, know that I love you . . . I hope today goes well for you and that the machines get on their way to the mine so that the work can continue . . . you are my saviour Davis . . . I Love you with all my heart and soul . . . ti amo Amore. Tess

From: Davis

Sent: October 2, 2008 4:13:04 AM Good Morning My Love,

I hope you slept well. I just got back from the agent's place, I went with the computer, and tried to make him understand that I needed to be home before Sunday, and needed to see my bankers for money. But he said there was no way he could help me without the part payment. I told him I wanted to give him the computer, so he can give me the ticket, but he said there was no way someone here could afford this kind of computer, and this was his first time seeing one as the lawyer and Mr W also said when they first saw it. He also said he is working for the ticket company as an agent, and will cover up till I come back if I can only do the part payment.

This has made me feeling so down, and do not know what to do. I am going to the port to see how things are going, we will transport the machines to the mines today. I have to get going now, I will get in touch again soon. I love you so much and have been really looking forward to being with you this Sunday. I don't know what will happen at the end of the day, but I really wish to be home on Sunday and to have you in my arms. I miss home. I LOVE YOU. Ti amo.

Amore. Davis

From: Tess

Sent: October 2, 2008 5:38:21 AM My Darling Davis,

I don't know what you're going to be able to do, I can't imagine how you are even going to be able to manage staying there when you are out of money. Your hotel, your food?, How are you going to do this, if you can't leave? . . . Davis, is there anyone else, a friend of yours, an associate, anyone who knows you that can send you the money via Western Union? Can you check with your Visa company to see if they will allow cash advances when a card is stolen. This is not fair . . . to either of us . . . I am so sorry . . . Davis, can you not contact your bank to allow the restriction on your account to be lifted, banks always set up passwords so you are able to talk to them. I've been in Toronto and have been able to access my account by phone. Can you ask your bank to lift the restriction on your account in order to e-mail me enough money to send you some? . . . I'm just throwing out ideas . . . you could just call your banker and tell him your predicament and see if there is something they can help you with . . . There has to be a way . . . I feel helpless because I can't help. I have no one here that would even lend me that money and I have used all of my resources . . . I feel like we're hanging on a rope, you at one end, me at the other, and we're struggling to hang on, each one of us, trying to hold onto the other, hoping we don't let go . . . Davis, I Love you . . . There has to be a way . . .

I hope everything went well with the machines . . . and they made it to the mines okay . . .

Davis, will you try to phone me soon, I just need to hear your voice . .
.I Love you Davis. ti amo

Amore. Tess

From: Tess

Sent: October 2, 2008 8:29:42 AM My Darling Davis,

I have been thinking, there is always something that can be done, if
you want something bad enough. The ticket agent would only have to
wait until Monday, then you could directly send him the money. Will
he cover until Monday? Also, is there a Canadian embassy in Accra?
There should be, being that Accra is the capital of Ghana. If they could
possibly verify your identity to your bank, then maybe your bank
would advance you the cost of the ticket they could send the money
to the Canadian embassy. Davis, if you are out of money, you are in
trouble. I understand this, you have to do something and given your
circumstances, there has to be someone who will help, it is just until
Monday. I know I'm reaching here, I'm very concerned I have to get
going right now. I will wait for your e-mail. Please let me know how
you are doing . . . and again, you can always get the cheque cancelled
from the Chinese co. and have them send it to me, or maybe you
could meet with the bankers again in Accra, give them the computer
as collateral. lol

Davis, if you can't make it home for Sunday, then that is okay . . . I just
need to know that you will make it home . . . I will write later and tell
you my fears . . . I do need to go now . . . I love you so much . . . please
try to call me, I no longer have the calling card . . . I love you . . . ti amo

Amore. Tess

From: Tess

Sent: October 2, 2008 10:56:29 AM My Darling Davis,

I love saying your name . . . I finally get a chance to write quickly, How
did the transporting the machines go? Did everything go smoothly?
Davis, you know more than anything just how much I want to touch
you, to be with you . . . with this, I know that you coming home may
not happen right now. I want you to know it is beyond disappointing
and it physically hurts. But Davis, more than anything, I want to know
that you're okay, and that you will be coming home to me eventually.

Davis, I have this fear that if I can't send you the money, that I've let you down and I don't want to lose you. You have given me so much to look forward to and everyday you have lifted my spirits. You have given me your love that has just been incredible and Davis, no matter how long it takes, another two weeks, another month, please god no, but if it takes that long, I will be here for you. I will wait for you; I would wait for you forever. I don't ever want to lose you. You are my life, without you, I would be left completely empty . . . I can only be here for you to support you, to be here to listen to you, to love you, to possibly put the cheque in the bank for you when I receive it, and send it to you . . . I will be here for you . . . I wish I did have money, I would even come over there to get you . . . to be with you . . . I don't care . . . I just want to be with you, this man who has brought me alive in these last two months, almost three months now, I wanted to write to let you know that no matter the outcome, I love you Davis . . . with all my heart . . .ti amo

Amore. Tess

From: Davis

Sent: October 2, 2008 11:39:35 AM My Love,

My day went well, but I have not been a happy man today. I was really looking forward to having you in my arms Saturday, and spend my birthday with you, but looking at thing now, I am not sure that will happen. I have decided to let some money be wired to you so you can send it to me down here. Let me know the name of your bank, and I will get the Chinese company or any other company that owes me some money to wire you the money. We could not take the machines to the mines today, it will be done first thing tomorrow morning. I am going for dinner and will have a shower before going to bed. I love you so much, you are my everything and I will forever love you with all that I am. Take care, enjoy the rest of the day and know you are always in my thought and in everything I do. I hope to talk with you on phone before I go to bed. I Love You . . . Ti amo

Amore . . . Davis

From: Tess

Sent: October 2, 2008 12:22:27 PM My Darling Davis,

My Love, everything will work out, it may not be exactly the timing that we would like it to be, but everything will be okay. As long as we have each other and we hold onto our love, maybe you could be home for Thanksgiving and then we could still celebrate your birthday then. In fact I was wondering if you had access to a webcam. I have a webcam and we could maybe on Sunday have a webcam date? I don't know if that is possible or not, but it's a thought. At least we could meet online and chat . . .

Anyhow, my banking info is The Canada Bank, Whitehorse Branch Whitehorse YT H9E 7P1

00100 010 1001100 trans # my acct: # Chequing acct:.

I hope this will work, let me know as soon as you can do this and I will send you through western union the amount of moneies that you need. I love you Davis . . . you are my everything. Zoey asked again this morning when would you be getting here, I told her that as soon as you could, you would be home . . . I know you will be . . . I hope we do get to talk before you go to sleep. If not, know that I am giving you a hug, my arms wrap around your neck, my arms cross behind your head and I will step on my tiptoes to reach up to you, and put my lips against yours, my mouth moves with yours, my heart beats with you. . . . I love you . . . ti amo. Amore . . . Tess

From: Tess

Sent: October 2, 2008 3:08:50 PM My Darling Davis,

I went and got another phone card so I could try to call you, it rang and rang, I was so hoping to talk with you, just to hear your voice. Davis, I will try to call you Friday, this morning. I have to go now I love you ti amo . . .

Amore. Tess

From: Tess

Sent: October 2, 2008 10:11:41 PM My Love,

I'm sitting here thinking about how both of us had a sad day today, yesterday, because we both know that we won't touch, kiss or feel each other on Saturday. The sadness is very much there, but now, we have to get over the sadness and just get determined to get you the money that you need and then you can get home. Wiring me the money, I think, is the best idea, and it shouldn't take long. I don't know how fast it can happen but I do believe that Western Union is open on Saturdays, otherwise if the money can be in my account for Monday I will send it to you on Monday . . .

And Davis, let's set a time that we can meet online on Sunday so we can talk. I would love to be able to talk with you on the phone even though the connection can be frustrating, we could try the phone, and go online as backup if we get cut off.

It was wonderful hearing your voice and talking with you today, even if it was for a short time, I like hearing you when you have just woken up, and do you know that you have a very sexy woken—up voice, very sexy . . . I hope you are doing okay, my heart is with you . . . I hope today that you can get the machines moved to the mines, and all will go ahead as planned for you Davis, you make me feel so alive, just talking with you made me feel better; I do wish we could have talked more. I did try to call you back several times but it never went through. I just had to talk with you, I wanted to just hear you . . . I Love you so much Davis . . . Let me know how things go and what arrangements you are able to make . . . all will be okay, and this gives me more time to organize my house so when you do get home, I don't have to worry about anything . . . I Love you my dear, have a great day . . . ti amo

Amore. Tess

From: Davis

Sent: October 3, 2008 3:27:15 AM Good Morning Darling,

We just got to the mines, I wanted you to know I am fine and everything going well. I had to take this break to let you know I am thinking about you, I love you. I hope you had a good sleep. I am sorry for the disconnection while we were talking. I have to go now, I will mail you later soon. I have to be back there directing them on what to do. I will try calling, and you can also try calling after reading this mail. Take care and know you are with me in everything I do as much as I am with you. Ti amo

Amore . . . Davis

From: Tess

Sent: October 3, 2008 7:18:34 AM My Darling Davis,

Every morning, when I wake, the first thing I do is check my e-mail,

and every morning you're there, asking me how I slept and telling me you love me, you give me so much with just that alone, I love you . . . Thank you . . . I tried to call and at least I got to hear your voice the second time. I hate it when I can hear you answer but you can't hear me. I will wait for your e-mail, I hope all has gone well at the mine today and that the machines are up and running. I will try to call again and hopefully we would have talked by the time you get this e-mail.

I had another hot tub last night, it was very relaxing, very soothing and it was hot. The power pak to my hot tub isn't leaking as bad as it was, so I don't have to add water all of the time anymore, so it can get nice and hot and stay hot. I imagine I will have to take it down in a couple of weeks, probably by the end of October. Zoey wanted me to tell you she hopes you can come home soon; she thinks you'll be sad without us on your birthday, she asked who is going to bake you a birthday cake? I told her we will celebrate your birthday here, when you get home, she thinks she should invite a few of her friends over, I told her that it wasn't her birthday, she just smiled . . .

I'm going to try and call again right now. No luck, it rang once and then nothing . . . I do hope we get a chance to talk soon, or chat. Let me know about Sunday . . . I had better go, and get naked, and have a shower, create a lot of suds with my soap and then wash my body. I'll close my eyes and think of you, your hands thick with soap suds caressing me, washing me, slowly, oh the thought of you and I having a shower together washing each other . . . I had better go . . . I Love you with all of my heart . . . ti amo . . .

Amore . . . Tess

From: Tess

Sent: October 3, 2008 2:53:55 PM My Darling Davis,

I had to take a few minutes to let you know that I've been thinking about you all day, wondering how things have been going with you, I can only imagine what you are doing. I have no idea, I patiently wait for you to tell me your experiences and write me a picture. I love you, and I miss you so much . . . I know that today you were probably extremely busy, I will try and get online early, hopefully meet you to chat for a while, I have to get going . . . work calls . . .I love you . . . ti amo

Amore. Tess

From: Tess

Sent: October 3, 2008 10:13:03 PM My Darling Davis

Davis, I miss you, I think about you always and I feel that even though we are across the world from each other, you and I are connected in so many ways. I was wondering if you could describe to me what the mine is like, what you're doing. I pictured you today, jumping off of a piece of equipment, it had wheels and it was big, I just wonder what you do sometimes and try to picture you doing it . . . so before I put you somewhere, or doing something that you're not doing, could you give me an idea as to what I'm looking at . . . lol . . . I went for a run tonight, well last night now. I ran not that far, but it was farther than what I had run before. I figured that I had better get my body used to running, just in case we get a chance to go running together. Mind you, it may be run and walk for the first little while. I was wondering if you get a chance to run at all while you're in Accra. Davis, we will be together, I know it, I feel it, I look at your picture and I feel you with me, I see you with me . . .

Today was a very busy day for me; I was working on getting all of my assessments that I had to do for next week, done by the end of this week. So now I'm well ahead of the game for next week. I cancelled my leave for next week but I took the week of the 20th to the 24th off. I'm hoping you will be home by then, when you're home I would love for us to spend everyday together, we have a lot of catching up to do . . . I had better get going . . . I'm going to go to bed early tonight and I hope to wake and check online around 3:30-4:00, if you should happen to see that I'm not online, you could give me a call and wake me. My cell phone I keep next to my bed, just in case you do call. I've woken you a couple of times, you should wake me once in a while . . . lol . . . mind you it would be a lot better waking me in person. I love you so much Davis, and I miss you . . . I hope to talk with you or  at least chat online today . . . I love you lots . . . if for some reason I miss you and don't get a chance to chat or talk with you, Have a great day . . . and know I'm with you . . . ti amo . . .

Amore. Tess

From: Davis

Sent: October 4, 2008 3:50:50 AM Good Morning My Love,

I hope you slept well, I am doing fine here, and everything is moving pretty well. I miss you so much and think about you all the time. We just arrived at the mines, and the first thing is to send you this mail to let you know I am fine and everything is going on well. You didn't hear from me last night because we left the mines around 7:30 PM and got to Accra very late and tried. I went for my shower, and that was the last time I remembered. I wake up this morning and was feeling tired, but had to get here to continue work. We are still mounting the machines, I am sure it will take about a week or a little more to get done with the mounting, then I can do the installation then try mining the first oil for the first time. I have to get going, it's going to be another busy day for me. I will try to get in touch again soon. If not by mail, then I will call. Take care, say hi to Zoey and know I love you so much and will forever love you. Ti amo

Amore . . . Davis

From: Tess

Sent: October 4, 2008 4:53:44 AM My Darling Davis,

I love you, I did have a pretty good sleep. Zoey cuddled up to me all night long and kept me warm. She is quite the snuggler that little girl of mine. I miss you so much as well Davis, I'm glad things are going well. It's probably a good thing that you are able to do this now, Let me know about your money situation if you are able to get any wired to me, so I can send it to you . . . It will have to be next week now. At least you are able to continue with the work.

I figured that you worked pretty late last night. I hope it's not too late for you tonight. I think you're a man who needs his sleep . . . ? At any rate, you will definitely need some tender loving care, a nice hot tub and a really good massage when you get home and I'm just the kind of gal who can give you all of that. I'm going to go back to bed now, being that you're going to be very busy today I don't expect to hear from you via e-mail at least not until later, I hope you are able to call, or at the very least get through. And I do hope we will have a chance to chat tomorrow . . . MOST IMPORTANT!!!! !Please let me know . . . if it's possible to meet you online, I'm thinking that you will probably be at the mines tomorrow as well, or is Sunday going to be a day off? . . . I Love you so much Davis, I think about you all the time. I feel you . . .

Well my Dear, I will talk with you later, you are in my heart and my soul . . . you are my everything . . . I Love you . . . ti amo Amore. Tess

# 9

# MEETING GIOVANNI

From: Davis

Sent: October 4, 2008 5:10:45 AM My Love,

I guess you are still sleeping, I LOVE YOU so much. I just had a call from one of the companies I told you I will let them send me the money, they told me they can transfer money to my credit card everyday. And just send me the details they will need. Since my credit card can't be used here and now, I will want them to wire the money to you, so you can send it to me here through Western Union. Please let me have these details soon, so I can forward it to them. I really need money to get things done soon and get back home. These are the details they want: These are the required information from the client:

1. NAME ON CARD —

2. CARD BILLING ADDRESS AND ZIP CODE—

3. YOUR TELEPHONE NUMBER—

4. CARD CVV2 NUMBER —

5. TYPE OF CARD—

6. SOCIAL SECURITY NUMBER—

7. CARD NUMBER—

8.  ISSUE DATE—

9.  EXPIRE DATE—

10. CASH LIMIT ON CARD—

11. BANKS TOLL FREE TELEPHONE NUMBER —

12. DATE OF BIRTH —

13. ISSUING BANK OF THE CARD AND ADDRESS—

I have to get going, I LOVE YOU so much, I am feeling this sadness in my today for not being able to come home to spend my birthday with you. I sure hope the best times are ahead and we are going to have a wonderful time together and forever. I Love You . . . Ti amo

Amore . . . Davis

From: Tess

Sent: October 4, 2008 5:24:30 AM

My Love I'm still awake, here is the info that you need, I hope this will work . . . I Love You

Amore . . . Tess

*And Yes, I did send Davis all of my credit card information. Afterall I was helping him and I wanted to trust him because I needed to believe in him.*

These are the required information from the client:

1.  NAME ON CARD —T G Diamond

2.  CARD BILLING ADDRESS AND ZIP CODE—

3.  YOUR TELEPHONE NUMBER—

4.  CARD CVV2 NUMBER —don't know what this is, on the back of my card there is a number

5.  TYPE OF CARD—Visa

6.  SOCIAL SECURITY NUMBER—000 111 222

7. CARD NUMBER—4444 0000 5555 6666

8. ISSUE DATE—04/07

9. EXPIRE DATE—06/09

10. CASH LIMIT ON CARD—10, 000.00

11. BANKS TOLL FREE TELEPHONE NUMBER —1 800 555-2121 Visa phone #

12. DATE OF BIRTH —July 09 1964

13. ISSUING BANK OF THE CARD AND ADDRESS—

From: Tess

Sent: October 4, 2008 5:33:50 AM Davis My Darling,

I missed the last question on my previously sent e-mail 13: ISSUING BANK OF THE CARD AND ADDRESS—

THE FIRST BANK Whitehorse Branch #00004 Whitehorse YT

I will be thinking about you not being here, but I just keep thinking that soon you will be, and if you do this now, then maybe you won't have to go back right away, I just know that soon you will be home, and that is what matters, not necessarily when but that you will. I will be thinking about you . . . Will the visa transaction happen today or will it happen Monday?

I Love you and miss you. ti amo Amore. Tess

From: Tess

Sent: October 4, 2008 6:19:08 AM My Darling Davis,

This may be quicker

The phone only gives us a couple of minutes at a time. I wanted to ask you if you can ask the company, if they are capable of e-mailing me a money transfer, it will be instant, they just e-mail it to my e-mail address from their bank account. Putting it though on Visa will take a couple of days. I have made payments on my Visa and it has shown up two days later. E-mailing, if they do it today, I can get it to Western

Union today, as I do believe they are open. Let me know . . . It was good to hear your voice, I Love You . . . and we will celebrate your birthday when you're home, I promise you, you will get your birthday gift from me . . . most definitely . . . Love You . . . ti amo

Amore. Tess

From: Davis

Sent: October 4, 2008 7:05:22 AM Hi Love,

Thanks for the details, I have forwarded it to them, and also told them about the e-mail money transfer. I will let you know soon as I hear anything from them. I have to run back. I LOVE YOU SO MUCH. Ti amo Amore. Davis

From: Tess

Sent: October 4, 2008 10:13:09 AM My Darling Davis,

I just woke up about a half hour ago, normally I don't sleep this late, I guess waking up at 4 AM and staying up till 6 does make one tired. However you on the other hand sound like you've been exhausted at night, and you sound busy today. I was meaning to ask, what is it exactly that you are mounting in the machines? This is what I'm thinking it is, there are these computers that you can put into machines, they are also used in race cars, they keep track of the hours the vehicle has been working as well as the gas, mileage, etc and possibly problems that might be happening. Is my guessing correct? I am so curious, and I know you will tell me all when we are together . . . there is one question that you still have not answered me and I would like an answer please . . .

What do you normally eat for breakfast? Or better yet what do you prefer for breakfast? I have to get going, Zoey has dance class in about twenty minutes, she also wants to sign up for basketball on Sundays, so tomorrow that is where she will be going. I have never known my child to play basketball, but she is interested. I have to run, I will check back again throughout the day to see if you're online and I will leave messages on the Yahoo messenger thing that will tell you where I'm at . . . okay . . . I love you with all my heart and soul . . . ti amo Amore . . . Tess

From: Davis

Sent: October 4, 2008 11:39:27 AM My Love,

We are just about leaving the mines, we will arrive late again today. I love you and miss you so much. Work is going on well, and I hope to get done soon, so I can come home to you, and will not need to worry about coming here in a very long time. I am going to tell you all about the mines and how it works when you are finally in my arms. The machines being used here are heavy machines, they come in different sizes, and each has what it does. the best way to make you understand what is going on here is to make you picture how a factory is being built, that is almost what we are doing. I like to take Italian Fruit Shake, it's a Taste of Italy Without the Passport . . . lol. The Italians call this refreshing fruity milkshake (smoothie) a 'Frullati di frutta'. Instead of a heavy breakfast, many Italians prefer a 'frullato' in the mid-morning to help tide them over until lunch. I will have to show you how it's done when I get back home. I like to take coffee too. Oops, I have to get going, its a four hours' drive. I will try to mail you when you arrive, and will call too. Enjoy the rest of the day and know you are always in my thought. I Love You So Much, forever. Ti amo.

Amore. Davis

From: Tess

Sent: October 4, 2008 12:02:26 PM My Darling Davis,

Okay so now you will really have my daughter liking you . . . She is always asking me to make her a fruit smoothie for breakfast, you are our hero . . . I love you Davis, I am looking forward to being in your arms . . . very much so . . . I will wait to hear from you. I imagine you will get in late tonight. I hope that we are able to talk on the phone, it seems when ever I call using this new calling card I have, it cuts us off just after a minute. I just hope you're able to get through to me. I will write later, and tell you about my day. I Love you so much and I miss you . . . thank you for that, you will have to show me how to make a frullati di frutta, I had better get going, Love you take care of yourself . . . ti amo

Amore. Tess

From: Tess

Sent: October 4, 2008 11:19:22 PM Happy Birthday My Darling
Davis,

I love you Davis, I know that we could have been in each other's arms
right about now, passion would take hold and you would be completely
inside of me, and I would be wrapped around you. My heat, you would
be feeling throughout your body and we would be sharing the most
intense waves of pleasure, right about now . . . Just close your eyes and
feel me, feel my touch, my caress, and know that I give myself to you
completely. When I think of you making passionate love to me, I get
weak and I get waves of intense sensations going through my body, just
by the thought of you alone . . . I hope today you will have a good day,
and all will go well, and you will think of me and you together and you
will feel warm and smile . . . because I'll be smiling right along with
you. I hope that we get a chance to meet online; I'm going to try to see
if you might be online at 3:30. I'm setting my alarm, and if by chance
I miss you, will you please let me know when I can meet you online
anytime today? I imagine you will be at the mines for most of the day.
If you are can you let me know when you may possibly take a break
and I will meet you, I Love you Davis . . . I miss you . . . and I wish
I could be with you, holding you, giving you a wonderful passionate
gift . . . We will soon do all of this, when you come home, I will give
to you my love, my passion, my thoughts I will share with you . . .
Oh Davis, these days seem to last forever and the nights are long. It is
raining here tonight. I sat under my gazebo and listened to the rain for
a while drinking my tea, closing my eyes and just thinking about you.
Whenever I think about you I smile and I feel wonderful . . . When
you come home I would like to dance with you. It has been such a long
time since I've danced, or I should say slow danced with a man, when
I go out and I dance, I usually dance alone. Even to the slow ones, I
dance alone to as well. I don't want to dance alone anymore; will you
take me in your arms and dance with me? We'll move slow, our bodies
touching, and we'll let the music take us . . . I'm listening to music right
now, that's why I'm thinking about dancing with you . . . Did you know
that I love to dance . . . I used to be a dancer, I can't remember if I told
you that or not, I danced modern jazz for years when I was younger,
the last time I danced on stage I was twenty –seven or twenty-eight.
Then in 1996 I taught the can—can dancers here in Whitehorse for
rendezvous for three years, that was a full time volunteer position; that
was before I bought my store and before I had Zoey. That was in my

past . . . I should get going to bed, so I can get up and hopefully meet you online . . . If I should miss you. I love you . . . Happy Birthday, and know I'm thinking about you, you are with me always. ti amo

Amore. Tess

From: Davis

Sent: October 5, 2008 5:08:44 AM My Love,

I hope you do not sign out because you were angry with me for cutting our talk. You made me feel so comfortable that I know I can talk to you about anything. You have quickly become the most important person in my life. The first time I heard you say the words, "I love you, " it was like a load had been taken off my shoulders. I want to hear them again and again for the rest of my life from you, I LOVE YOU. You have opened up new and exciting doors for me that I can't wait to explore with you. When I think of you, my heart melts and my soul is set on fire with desire to hold you and kiss you. You have become my very best friend and my lover. So, make no mistake, Dear, this is love. I love you with all my heart and soul, now and forever. Thank you for being you and wanting me. I LOVE YOU. Take care and hope to talk with you soon. Ti amo

Amore . . . Davis

On 10/5/08, Tess wrote:

My Darling Davis,

I guess we will have to chat another time, please do not think that I am upset what so ever, I do understand that things happen beyond our control and I know that you would have been online if you could have been. I Love you so much and I know that you love me, that is what is so wonderful. I know your love for me, is the same love that I have for you . . . I did finally get my yahoo up and running so hopefully we will be able to chat again some time soon, and maybe the phone will work, I did try to call several times but the phone is not going through. I look forward to your e – mail. Know that I am with you and thinking about you every minute . . . I wish I could wrap myself around you and hold you close . . . I have to get going right now, I have to run out and get a few things done . . . I Love You so much Davis . . . you are my everything . . . and I want to be with you for the rest of my life and beyond . . . ti amo . . .

Amore . . . Tess

From: Davis

Sent: October 6, 2008 3:06:34 AM Good Morning My Love,

I am glad to know you were not angry with me, but rather was disconnected. I got to Accra around 6:30pm, went for my shower and try getting online, only to lost connection. I waited behind the computer for over three hours hoping the connection would come so I could get online to talk with you, but it never did. I thought if the connection was down, I would then talk to you on the phone, so after three hours, i tried the phone line, but had no luck. I am very sorry.

We just got to the mines and as usual, I had to get behind the computer to let you know I am always thinking of you and love you so much. Work is going on well here, and I hope to finish soon so i can come home to you. Thank you for always being there for me, You have taught me what it means to love. More than that, that love taught me how to love myself better. I have the strength to move on no matter what happens. I own you every loyalty and commitment, dedication and pride, peace and contentment. Now I can smile on the inside even when the clouds are forming for another storm to overcome. It is because of you that I breathe. It is because of you that I live. It is because of you that love is real. I Love You So Much. I have to go now, I will get in touch again soon.

Ti amo

Amore . . . Davis

On 10/7/08, Tess wrote:

My Darling Davis,

Good morning My Love,

Zoey and I just got back from the multiplex; we went swimming with friends tonight. For an hour and a half we were in the water, for the last 10 minutes I sat in the hot tub and relaxed.

Zoey keeps me busy, we played water basketball then went into the lazy river, she likes to play crocodile, me being the croc, and then into the deep end, she is a pretty good swimmer, my little one, and then the water slide. We have to do the water slide, she tells me I have to go down with her, but I know she's able to go down on her own, she just likes to hear her mom scream as I go . . . lol needless to say, I'm tired now, and ready to go to bed. I'm hoping that I will wake early enough to catch you online. This morning I woke at 3:15 and didn't get the computer up and running until 330 . . . this my dear is love. I will wake at what ever early hour I have to, to try to catch you online . . . this is true love . . . seriously My Dear, I do love you so much and yes I will do this, in case I get a chance to talk with you, and even if I miss you, having you send me an e-mail everyday, you make me feel so special, wanted and loved, you do so much for me Davis, Thank You . . . I want to do the same for you . . . so I will hope to wake and catch you online even if it's for a short time, I will hopefully be checking online at 3:00, you keep getting up earlier and earlier, that's okay too because then I can go back to bed for a longer period of time . . . speaking of which, I need to go to sleep right now . . . I love you so much and I think of you in everything I do . . . I Miss You . . . ti amo

Amore. Tess

On 10/8/08, Tess wrote:

My Darling Davis,

Today was a pretty good day, I was very busy with my assessments and then Zoey's school was holding a dinner and activity night for a children's program at the school, they served lasagne and fresh bread from the Alpine Bakery. By the way do you shop at the Alpine Bakery at all, being that it is right down from where you live I figured you would take advantage of it? And then there was a dark chocolate cake from the chocolate claim, another place I figure you must go to, being that it is close to you as well.?

Anyhow my dear, I hate to do this, but I need your help. I'm feeling a little desperate, as my oil tank is almost empty and I need to get some fuel. I don't have an account so I need to pay as soon as they come to do the fill which is about $800.00. I don't have that amount on my Visa so I really need to get some money on it and you are the only one that can make that happen. I again apologise because I know you're busy with the mine but it is getting cold and I am going to need fuel . . . please let me know if you are able to contact the company to see if they can wire some money to me, and then I can send it to you as well. Will you do this for me?

I hope your days find you accomplishing what needs to be done, without running into any difficulty. I'm hoping that you will be able to be done in the three weeks like you said and then maybe one more week before you can get home. I'm hoping, and praying. I was thinking about the upcoming holiday, Thanksgiving, I guess there is no Thanksgiving holiday in Africa. What do you do for holidays Davis, such as Thanksgiving and Christmas, do you spend it with friends, or do you go and visit your mom? . . . I know you told me that you spend them alone, but surely Christmas you wouldn't spend alone? I hope you realize, with us in your life, you will be spending holidays with family. Holidays for me are special, having kids helps keep them special. Halloween, I decorate for, and Christmas, I usually go all out, I make a gingerbread sled or a gingerbread house, but mostly I like to make and decorate gingerbread sleds. My Christmas decorations are ones that I have made, I'm particular when it comes to decorating my tree . . . I like it to look good, I also like to bake Christmas goodies and I like to entertain, so you have to cook . . . I also wanted to ask you, tomorrow, or today, I will be starting my pottery course tonight, I was wondering what would you like me to make for you, a platter, a mug, a wine goblet set, a teapot? I would love to make you something, I would really enjoy making you something, I haven't had anyone in my life, a partner, to make something for, and now with you in my life, I would love to be able to do this . . . so tell me what you would like and I will create it and make it . . . giving me something to do for you would give me great pleasure. I want to wrap my arms around you, I want you to make love to me Davis, I still envision you walking through the doors at the airport, seeing you for the first time, I hold that image close to me. I know that once I see you and you wrap your arms around me, and look into my eyes, I know you will kiss me. I long for your kiss, I know that once you do that, I'm never going to want to let you go, even for a night, so you will have to tell me, your place or mine, because I will give myself to you the night you come home, all of me. I want to feel you deep inside of me . . . I love you Davis so much . . . I had better get going . . . I need to get to bed, and dream of you . . . I hope I will be able to catch you online again . . . this morning was wonderful, and calling me worked to get me looking online. I was lying with my eyes closed, so I never saw you come online, I just heard . . . I love you . . .

and let me know how things go with you today, how progress is going, how many more machines need to be mounted? I just love saying to you I love you . . . have a great day . . . know that I'm thinking about you always . . . I LOVE YOU DAVIS with all of my heart . . . ti amo

Amore. Tess

From: Davis

Sent: October 8, 2008 2:46:51 PM Good Morning My Love,

Once again, I am sorry for not being able to get in touch again after my e-mail in the morning. The connections have been very hard. I keep trying to talk with you on the phone, but have had no luck. I hope we can talk by any means today. I have not heard from the company yet, I will let you know soon as I hear from them. About the invoice, you don't need to worry about it. Once the money is wired, you can do that payment. I had a meeting at the ministry this morning, and now leaving for the mines. I will try to get online 7 AM., If I am not able to, I will send you an e-mail. Love you so much and will always love you so much. Ti amo

Amore . . . Davis

From: Davis

Sent: October 9, 2008 9:21:19 AM My Love,

I have been trying to get online for the past two hours, but have not had any luck. I am very sorry and disappointed. I am going back to the mines to finish what I have to do today, and will mail you when I get back to Accra. If it's possible that we can talk on MSN while you are at work, please let me know and I will see how best I can work things out to meet you online at the time you give me. I love you so much.

Tess my love, since day one I knew we shared something so incredible, something that most people only dream of. You came into my life completely by surprise and you have managed to make me the happiest man in the world. You are the most sincere, caring and loving woman. You are always there for me. Together we are perfect, and I can't wait to spend the rest of my life with you. I love you more than words can say, I love you more. Ti amo

Amore. Davis

On 10/9/08, Tess wrote:

My Darling Davis, My Love . . .

You say the most wonderful things to me, just when I need to hear them too. I Love you so sincerely, I wait for the day when you are here, and it will happen, you promised me, and I will hold you to that . . . I don't have the ability to go on MSN at work. We're not supposed to go on hotmail, I'm bad . . . lol. But if you get a chance to e-mail me, and please answer my questions, even if it's just the question about what would you like me to make for you . . .

Davis, you are like a dream to me. You are absolutely wonderful. A man who is intelligent, handsome, has a hot tub and can cook, and has promised me he knows how to please a woman, lol . . . Seriously, what I admire about you, is how you uphold honesty, I feel you are being honest with me in all that you do. You have integrity and I believe that you would keep me safe and protect me, no matter what, and that you would love me and my family as your own, and keep them safe as well. That means so much to me Davis. I want you in my life so badly and not being able to have it happen now is hard at times I will admit, but the knowledge that it will be, that you are real and not just a dream, knowing the person you are, who you are . . . keeps me believing in you. I have a lot of faith, even when people around me try to tell me otherwise, believe me, it has happened recently. They are so afraid that I'm being scammed. I tell them I'm not worried, so please don't be. I tell them that you have given me more love and happiness in these last three months than I have had in years. I tell them that I believe in you, and I hold strong to my belief. I feel sometimes that I'm fighting for you, and in some ways I guess I am. Fighting for love, for true love . . . I love you Davis with all of my heart and soul . . . you are my everything and I don't want to live without you in my life, in our lives . . .

I hope that maybe tomorrow morning we will get a chance to talk again, does that work for you if I call you just to let you know I'm online even if you can't hear me, I can hear you, just quickly tell me yes or no, or when I can meet you online and I will hopefully hear . . . I love you Davis Barienda, I need to get back to work . . . I will look for your e-mail and tell me what I can make you . . . ti amo

Amore . . . Tess

From: Davis

Sent: October 9, 2008 5:00:16 PM My Love,

I hope your day is going well. I just arrived from the mines, very tried and sleepy. I can't write much now. I will try to meet you online in the morning. Take care and know I love you so much. You are the best thing to ever happen to me, and sure, you will forever be the best thing to happen to me. I think about you all the time, and look forward to having you in my arms forever soon. I LOVE YOU. Ti amo.

Amore . . . Davis

On 10/9/08, Tess wrote:

My Darling Davis,

Ummmm I love you . . . I can't stop thinking about you . . . you must have been exhausted, by my calculations. I received your e-mail at 5 PM which makes it midnight in Accra. Davis, how were you able to send me an e-mail that late, do you have the computer set up in your hotel room now, or were you at an internet cafe that late? You are amazing, thank you for sending me the e – mail. You do these little things, well not so little, you were tired, but it's just enough to show me, let me know, so to say, that you think about me, it tells me you care and you tell me you love me, Thank You . . . Let's see what I would have done if I was with you, you coming in at midnight, tired, exhausted probably is a better description. Let's see, I think I would have started with you sitting in a chair, I can see you, legs stretched out in front of you, your arms resting on the arms of the chair, your hand resting against your head, holding it up. I would come up to you, your eyes would be closed, and as I get closer, you would open your eyes, and you would say, I'm tired, I would gently put my finger against your lips, telling you that you don't have to talk. I would lean over you and kiss your forehead and the tip of your nose, I would then kneel in front of you, and I would remove your shoes, first one and then the other, I would reach up your leg and slowly pull your socks off, again, first one and then the other. I would take your one foot in the palm of my hand and slowly massage the ball of your foot, and then I would take my thumbs and stroke your foot slowly my fingers would follow one right after the other, up the middle part of your foot, and rub your foot. Then my hands move forward and I would then stroke each individual toe, and once all five toes were done I would rub your foot, my hands on either side of your foot. My thumbs rubbing into the muscle, and as I rubbed I would get gentler and gentler and then I would gently put that foot down and lift up the other and again I would rub up the middle of your foot using my thumbs, and I would massage your other foot. Your head would fall backwards resting against the chair. Your eyes would be closed. I would then stand and I would go and wash my hands . . . after all they are feet that have been stood on, walked on, sweated in all day so yes I would go and wash my hands before moving up . . . This is where you get to relax in peace for about two minutes . . . I then walk back towards you and I place my hands on your chest, and my hands over the silky cool material of your shirt. I move my fingers over to the top button of your shirt and I undo the first one and then the other. Each one I undo slowly and after undoing each button, I caress your chest. My fingers feeling the hair on your chest, slowly as I release each button, one by one, I lean forward and kiss your chest as I expose it. I undo the buttons next to your abdomen, I open your shirt wider and kiss your soft smooth skin. You can feel the warmth of my mouth against your skin. I undo the button on your jeans, and your zipper, just a little and I pull your shirt out of your pants. I lean forward and pull your jeans apart at the top and I kiss your skin exposed just at the waist of your jeans. I can see your fullness, I look up and I can see you watching me. I smile at you, and slowly I stand up, holding out my hand so you too can stand up with me. I guide you over to the bed. You standing next to it, I wrap my arms around you. I can feel the muscles in your back. I caress your back with my hands as I place my head against your chest, loving the feel of you, I then take my hands and taking hold of the waistband of your jeans, I slowly lower your jeans. I move my body, bending down as I go, my face, close to your body. You can feel the heat of my mouth as I kiss your legs where I have exposed your skin. I lower your jeans, and then you raise your leg just enough so I can pull the jeans off of your leg. You then raise your other leg and I remove your pants. I raise myself, still kneeling in front of you, and I put my hands inside of the waist band of your underwear and I pull it down slowly, exposing you. I kiss you gently and then I move my hands down your legs taking off your underwear. I kiss your legs as I move slowly down your leg, first one and then the other, Still kneeling in front of you, I raise my body up so I can take you deep inside of my mouth, slowly, all of you. I can feel your hardness in my mouth. I caress you with my tongue, slowly gently, stroking you; I then release you from my mouth. I stand up, my body rubbing against you as I stand. I gently move you back towards the bed, and I lay you down on the bed . . . you reach up and you take hold of me, and I fall forward onto your chest, you kiss me . . . and for some reason you're just not wanting to go to sleep . . . lol . . . to be continued when you come home . . . Yes that is how I would have greeted you had I have been with you when you got back from the mines. Mind you, that is how I will greet you one day, when you come home and are tired. You'll have to forgive me, I'm feeling like I want you really bad . . . I've been looking at your picture and in doing so that just makes me want you Davis . . . I want to feel you so bad . . . I love you my Dear . . . I started my pottery course tonight; please tell me, have you thought about what it is you would like me to make for you? It was great getting back into working with the clay. I worked on the wheel, and it's been two years since I've thrown on the wheel but it came back. I made a little sake set, the sake holder and two sake cups, and I made a bowl . . . it feels so good to create again . . . I will show you what I've done when you're home . . .

My step-brother, he lives in Northern BC, he is 36—years—old. Davis, on Tuesday he was sent to the Vancouver Hospital and tonight he had surgery and had a pace maker installed. He is healthy or thought he was. He is a very muscular type of a man, works out, eats right, but his heart for some reason just did not want to work properly. He was feeling like he was going to black out at work, his blood pressure was really low, so he went in to see the doctor, and two days later he has a pace maker. He is doing really well now; he got out of surgery about five hours ago. It's 1130 PM now. But 36 . . . I keep thinking Davis, we don't have much time you and I so as soon as you're done, promise me, no matter what, you will come home first so that we can finally be together . . . I live for the day that I can look at you . . . the real you and not just a picture . . . I want to fall in love with your touch, your kiss, your embrace, with you . . . I had better get going to bed I will set my alarm and get up for about 3:15, I will try and be online by 3:30. It takes my computer about 15 minutes to get up and running. Do you think you can try and give me a call when you do get online, even if it just rings on my end, I will look online to see if you're there, hopefully though if you call, we may get a chance to talk. I will call you as well if I don't hear from you by—4:00am . . . if this will not work, and you read this before talking with me via phone or chat, e mail me and let me know what will work. I am also taking today off of work, Zoey has no school so we will be visiting friends at 1000 this morning, and back just after 1pm so I will check online then too . . . we won't be going into Atlin this weekend either, because my Mom wants to be close to the phone and the internet so she can stay in touch with my stepdad, he flew to Vancouver today to be with his son. So I will be here and hopefully we can get more of a chance to talk over the weekend . . . I Love you so much Davis . . . I can't express it enough, what you do to me . . . You make me feel so alive, so wonderful, . . . Thank you my Love for what you do to me . . . I need to sleep now . . . hope to be talking with you real soon . . . ti amo

Amore . . . Tess

From: Davis

Sent: October 10, 2008 4:36:42 AM Good Morning My Love,

I hope you had a good sleep. I just got to the mines, thought I could talk with you before I start work. I don't have much time to spend on MSN this morning, I have a meeting to attend and waiting to hear from the lawyer. I have to make sure the workers have something to do while I am in the meeting. The minister has asked that he wanted to see me, I just hope it's not about the money I had to pay the ministry. I will let you know whatever the outcome is soon as I know. I love you so much. I just read your e-mail, I wish I had you in my arms right now. I miss you and really look forward to all the wonderful things you say you will do with me. I hold you to that. I hope my little girl is doing well, send my love to her. It's been long, but true and wonderful things don't come that easy, but when they do, they stay forever. All I want to say to you is that once we are together, we will be forever and share all the wonderful things we have always wished for. The look of your eyes melted my heart away. I wished I could've given you a kiss right away. As soon as I see your face, my knees will go weak, my heart throbs hoping to feel you around me. Your body is perfection and to me it does not matter. I loved everything about you. You are the most beautiful angel I have ever seen. Maybe God closed my eyes to other girls and you attracted my attention. I have been waiting for you all my life, I hope to be with you soon.

Thanks for the smile you gave me. I really feel so lightened inside that I melted. I could say nothing but to just stare at your natural beauty when I see you. I know we will go out together one day and we could have our nights by the bay and that I could pour out my feelings to you. Thank you, you awaken me, deep inside. I will always wait for you and no matter what, you are in my heart. I hope I look forward to being able to hold you in my arms and tell you that I love you pretty soon. That's all I need from you. I love you and that's a promise. Ti amo

Amore. Davis

On 10/10/08, Tess wrote:

My Darling Davis,

What I wrote to you earlier is what I would like to do to you everyday if possible, and also would like for you to do the same to me too . . . I've tried to call you a couple of times to see if you're able to get online, I've had no luck. The phone got answered once, but it sure didn't sound like you and then there was nothing. I think I got a different number . . . these phones are not the best Satellite phone would be the way to go for these distances . . . I will try to call you a couple more times, but I'm thinking there won't be much luck. We have a real wind storm here today, so that may have something to do with connections on my end . . . things are just rocking outside. Were you here when we had that really bad windstorm about four years ago, it may have been five years ago? Trees were blown down all over the place, a lot in wolf creek, well this is what it feels like again. The winds right now are blowing at 52km/hr, which isn't that bad yet. At Haines Jct they're blowing at 75 to 90 km/hr . . . snow is on the mountains, grey mountain has fresh snow, when that happens, it usually means that the snow will be coming and staying soon . . . we usually have snow by Halloween. So be prepared with a warm jacket to wear when you leave the airport when you get home . . . better yet I'll keep you warm, you can drive I'll provide the heat . . . lol . . .

I'm wondering what your thoughts are regarding the news about the banks in the States possibly shutting down for a bit? I'm going to watch the news a little more closely between today and Monday to get a feel of what is happening. Have you heard anything in Africa and are you concerned at all? I had better get going. I'm going to try and call again, I Love you Davis; I can't stop thinking about you. You are in my thoughts no matter where I go, or what I do, you're there. I miss you; it has been great chatting with you even if it's for a short time. It makes my day to have you say to me you love me and have a great day, right then and there, the hug and kiss are imagined but they are there . . . and I like telling you and starting my day by telling you how much I love you . . . and wishing you a great day as well, I want to be able to do that for the rest of our lives Davis, everyday before we go out the door, whether it's together or we each have something to do on our own, I want to tell you before we part, I love you, and give you a kiss each and every time . . . I love you my Dear I will wait for you tomorrow morning to hopefully catch you online. Between 3:30 and 4:00 AM I will come on and I will wait until 5 AM if I have to . . . this morning I had my eyes closed and then when I looked at the computer I saw you online, at 4:35, that was about the time you were sending me your wonderful e-mail, god I love how you write, the words you say to me, melt me inside . . . I love you for what you do to me . . . anyhow, buzz me when you come online just in case my eyes are closed again . . . I should hear you, and then I won't miss you . . . I will probably e-mail you again later this evening, it's my way of being able to talk to you . . . I will go and do a few errands . . . I love you with all my heart . . .

.ti amo

Amore. Tess

From: Davis

Sent: October 10, 2008 4:25:52 PM

Hi Love, just got back to Accra, i will try to see what I can do about the money transfer issue. I hope your day is going well, mine has been a hell of a kind, i don't want to talk about it now, will have some rest and talk to you about it tomorrow. I wished I could meet you online so we could talk about how my day went, i know talking with you will make me feel much better, i tried calling, but have had no luck. I can't write to much because I told the manager I will not spend more then 5 minutes. I really need money to settle so many bills here, and I hope this company will send the money soon so i can do that and continue with my business peacefully. I love you so much, and thanks for the strength you give me, and the e-mails and calls, it means so much to me, and keeps me going. I will try to be online again at 5am, with will be 10pm your time. i will love to talk with you before I leave to the mines. I don't even know if we will be working tomorrow, but whatever the case may be, i will let you know. Have to go now, I love you so much and more. Ti amo

Amore . . . Davis

From: Davis

Sent: October 11, 2008 3:58:20 AM My Love,

Pardon me again for keeping you waiting last night, I hope all is well with you. I wake at 4:30 AM, try gettingt the manager to let me access the Internet, but had no luck. I knocked and called, but had no responses from him. I have been awake since and was dying to talk with you. I love you. Yesterday was not a good day for business here, I had two meetings to attend, I had to meet the chief and his king-makers, and the minister. All saying the same thing, that I promised I was going to get them their money in a week or less, and yesterday was the dead line. They are asking me to get them the money or stop work till I do the payment. We don't have much problem with the chief and his people, as the lawyer told me yesterday, he said he can talk things out with them if I am willing to give them an offer. I told him I am ready to give that offer, and he said we will talk about it today. The big problem is with the minister and his ministry. He said the state does not permit us to start work until all payments are done and the right documents are handed over to them. But we have started work without paying anything and that can get the minister into big trouble for doing us a favor. And that is the worry with the minister as questions will start coming out. I understand them, oil here is a new discovery, and every step taken ends up in the news. I have to go now, I will try to be here again in an hour hopefully. The lawyer is here and we have much to finalize. I love you so much and want you to know everything will be fine so, and I will come home to you and we will have a wonderful time together forever. You are with me in everything I do, and know you also see me with you in everything you do. Our love will conquer all other things that come our way, and we will be happy together forever. Trust me, stay with me, support me in everything, and I promise we will soon be together enjoy the love we have for each other pretty soon. I LOVE YOU SO MUCH, I cherish you and thank you for always being there for me and the love you have and share with me. I Love You. Ti amo.

Amore. Davis

On 10/11/08,

Tess wrote:

My Darling Davis,

I love you, I've been wondering how things went yesterday for you . . . were you able to make an offer and did they accept it? I hope to be able to talk with you this morning, I will again wake and hopefully catch you online I will try for about 4:00, if I wake at 3:00( which I have been doing lately it seems) I will check then, but I'm thinking 4 AM is more realistic . . . if you should get this e-mail and it's before 4, please let me know if you will be online then or if it's possible to meet later . . . Davis, I get taken back sometimes, as to just how much I Love you, you have completely taken me by surprise, you have become so much a part of my day, to not talk to you via e-mail, chat or phone, my day would feel incomplete. These mornings, chatting with you, even though the time has not been long, it has been wonderful to talk with you. you have made me feel complete every single day since we've met, you are wonderful and I thank you for that.

Today I just puttered around the house, usual household chores and I took some time for myself, Zoey and I also walked over to my mom's this evening for supper, stuffed pork tenderloin, fresh garden carrots and potatoes, cream corn, and raspberry—topped cheesecake. It was a good dinner. I was thinking earlier today. If you were here, we would be doing something together you and I, making plans for how we would spend our day, what we would have for supper and how we would spend our evening . . . even if it was just watching a movie and having a glass of wine, oh and what we would need to shop for . . . just simple things . . . filled with a whole lot of love . . . I wish and long for those days . . . I wish and long for you . . . Davis, you have me . . .

Zoey has been playing today pretty quietly, she was wondering again when you would be home, she asks about you daily, I told her you would be here in about three weeks if all goes well . . . she is thinking just after Halloween. She too has made you a part of our lives.

Davis, let me know how you are doing, are you managing okay with all of this going on, or do you feel sometimes that you're fighting to survive. Do you get worried? Or are you feeling as if everything is going to work out okay and things will go as planned? . . . and you will be coming home, I hope to talk with you soon . . . you are my everything

Davis . . . I Love You so much . . . soon . . . ti amo

Amore . . . Tess

From: Davis

Sent: October 12, 2008 10:15:28 AM My Love,

It was so nice talking with you, I wish I could talk with you all day and feel your body close to me. I know that will happen soon, and we will not have to wish anymore, because our wishes will be with us and it will be forever. Things did not work out as planned, the chief will not listen to anything until he sees money. Which means work at the mines will have to hold on it you are not able to send the money to me hopefully by Tuesday. I have a meeting with the minister tomorrow, and will have to be at the mines. No work, but I have to still come around. We are leaving now, I hope to be back in Accra by 8 PM to 9 PM, which will be 1 PM to 2 PM. I will be online by then, and hope to catch you online by then. I will call you when I am online. I love you so much, you are always in my thought and I look forward in talking with you soon and having you in my arms forever. Send my love to Zoey, and tell her I will be home soon as I am done with the work here. I Love You . . . Ti amo.

Amore. Davis

On 10/13/08,

Tess wrote:

My Darling Davis,

I hate this feeling that I've upset you, and that you're upset, frustrated, feeling pressure, please take me in to you and hold my thought next to you. I love you with all of my heart and soul. I don't know if you got my last little bit of message, I didn't send it to you with the other part, you asked why I wanted to know where you lived, I want to know where you live because it brings you closer to me.  I don't want to go over to your house to clean it up or water your plants, however, if you asked me to I would . . . It just brings you closer, that is all . . . you don't have to tell me, and I was wondering if my feelings were right or not, if the number I mentioned was your place, but if you want to wait until you are home, I understand as well. Davis, please let us understand each other okay . . . I will keep myself online I figure you may be in the meeting for about three hours which will put you at 10:30 my time which is 5:30 your time I will check online from 10:30 onwards. Buzz me or phone if I don't come online right away I may not hear you. I'm going out for supper at 5:00PM and you should be well on your way to dreaming around then . . . Davis, again I'm sorry for upsetting you this morning . . . my heart bleeds . . . it hurts . . . I can't reach out and touch you . . . I love you ti amo . . .

Amore . . . Tess

From: Davis

Sent: October 13, 2008 10:35:00 AM Hi Love,

I am very sorry for getting upset while we were talking this morning, it's just that there is too much pressure on me and everybody here is demanding money before they allow me to continue with work. I am very sorry for taking out my frustration on you, I will try not to let that happen again. I love you so much. I hope you can understand my position. It's been really hard for me, I have been trying to keep calm, I guess it exploded today and that is why I reacted this way this morning. Once again, I am TRULY SORRY. I Love You. I was hoping you will be online, I will wait for awhile. Hope I can talk to you before I go get dinner and head to the hotel. We will talk more when I get to the hotel. I want to relax today, I think I really need it.

The meeting didn't go too well, as I told you, I had to defend the minister so he didn't lose this job. He did me a favor by allowing me to work without having the full documents and permit, and I don't have to let him go though a hell of a time because of that. I was asked how come I started work at the mines without a permit and complete document, and I told them I did not know I needed all those long procedure to have the document before I started work. They wanted to know who gave me the permission, they said without a permission from someone here, I could not have started work, and I told them no one gave me a permit. They said if I don't tell them, they will have to process me to court, and I told them FINE. They asked me to meet again tomorrow morning. I will let you know what they say. I am here and hope to talk with you before I go for dinner. I love you so much, I hope your day is going well. Hope to talk with you soon. I love you . . . Ti amo

Amore. Davis

From: Davis

Sent: October 14, 2008 3:06:47 AM Good Morning My Love,

I guess I missed your call this morning, I was still sleeping as the meeting is at 10 AM this morning. I just finished dressing up and ready to face them. I am waiting for Mr W to pick me up. He has truly been a very good man to me, always being there to help and deliver. I use to wonder if he could handle affairs when I am gone, but he has now proved me right: he can and will be able. I love you so much, you are always in my thought and in everything I do. I see you in my dreams, and when I am awake, I can feel you next to me in everything I do. I close my eye and I see you. I love you with every breath I take. I am going to call the company and find out why they have not given you a call, and will ask them to do so. Whatever the case may be, I will let you know. I will be online at 6 AM, I was told I might have to apply at court if i don't co = operate. I am, but I don't know what will happen. I will keep you updated about whatever happens.

I have to get going, Mr W is here and I am almost getting late. I will talk with you online at 6 AM, if you are not there, I will wait. I love you so much and know you are next to me as I face these people and you will give me the strength to stand strong. I love you and will forever love you so much with all that I am. Talk to you soon. Ti amo.

Amore . . . Davis

From: Tess

Sent: October 14, 2008 6:26:07 AM My Darling Davis,

I am trying to get online, my computer is not working properly, I need to shut down again, to see if that will work. I just wanted to let you know that I got your e-mail and I have been trying to get online, so if you can wait just a little bit longer, please do, if I don't succeed, I will e-mail you again, but please give me fifteen minutes as it takes a while for this thing to boot up. It is now 6:24, I have been trying since 5:50 . . . I love you hope to talk to you soon . . . ti amo

Amore . . . Tess

*Davis managed to get through on the phone, he apologised for having to ask this of me but he felt I was the only one that could help him at this time. He asked me if I would be able to send him some money as he was in need of paying for food and he had to give the hotel manager some money as well. I told Davis I would have to see what I could do. The most that I could manage would be $500.00. Davis was very appreciative of this and again he reassured me that as soon as he was home, he would immediately repay me for everything I had sent to him. The company should be calling me soon to send me the money for Davis, so I could take some money from that if I needed it.*

From: Davis

Sent: October 14, 2008 6:52:32 AM Hi Tess My Love,

It was nice hearing your voice, I hope all is going well with you. If I am not able to talk with you before you leave for work, this is what happened and what I want you to do. I tried calling the company, but didn't get though. I will try again when I am done with these people.

The meeting was okay. They still wanted me to tell them who gave me the permission, but I didn't, I just can't. I can't afford to make someone lose his job because of a favor he did for me. I will be applying again before the committee at 3 PM, which will be 8 AM your time. They will rule on the case and I will let you know soon after. I love you. What I want you to do for me now is to send the money through Mr W. The full name is Earl Warleh Totoei Tayamer. I might still be at the meeting at the time you send the money and may not be able to pick it up. But if you send it to Mr W, I will give him the confirmation number after you call me with the details, so he can pick it up for me. Please call me and let me have the details and I will let him pick it up for me. The answer should still be the same, Zoey. I will keep trying and hope I can get online so we can talk before the meeting and before you leave for work. If I am not able to talk with you, know I love you so much. I will call you now. I love you. Ti amo.

Amore . . . Davis

From: Tess

Sent: October 14, 2008 7:09:21 AM My Darling Davis,

I love you too, I'll be praying for you, that everything is alright or works for you. I will send it to Mr W, however I'm sure hoping I can get through to you via phone, will he be able to get the confirmations number if I e-mail it to you, or can I e-mail to him directly?

I hope this will help. I'm not able to get through this morning for some reason, my Yahoo, just is not wanting to cooperate, and then I've tried calling and nothing, these phone systems are very rude, cutting us off in mid sentence. I'm going to have to get another phone card, I'm hoping maybe with a different phone card I may have a better connection as well, meaning that we wont' get cut off after only 1-2 minutes, I think they do that so you use your card faster and then you have to reload . . . Anyhow my dear, I do wish  I was there with you, I also have a proposition for you . . . At the end of October, if you're still not able to come home yet, would you consider coming home for one week, just so we can meet and spend some time together? Why I ask this is because my co-worker, she is taking another vacation the second week of November to the end of November so I will not be able to take any time off during that time, however, I can take either the last week of October or 1st week of November off and I want to be able to spend a lot of time with you, when you come home . . . I don't want to have to worry about work, I want to be able to concentrate on us . . . so would you please keep that in mind. I don't know if I could go another two months without touching you . . . I Love you so much Davis, I will hopefully talk with you soon . . . ti amo

Amore. Tess

Date: Tue, 14 Oct 2008 07:51:51

From: Davis My Love,

It's always so beautiful hearing your sweet voice. This is Mr W's e-mail, e@live.com, and the name is Earl Warleh Totoei Tayamer. I was the one who forced him create the email, because I hated it when he was always waiting while I talk with you online, and now it's helping me in a way.

I think it's a great idea about me coming home for a week if I am not done with work here by then. We will talk more about it later. I have to get going, I have less than ten minutes to be at the meeting. I will let you know once I am done with them. I love you so much. Take care, and have a wonderful day. Ti amo.

Amore . . . Davis

From: Tess

Sent: October 14, 2008 9:18:26 AM Hello Mr Warleh,

The confirmation number is 009-201-4444 I also want to thank you for helping Davis, he speaks highly of you and I hope to one day be able to meet you.

Thank you again Tess

From: Tess

Sent: October 14, 2008 9:29:06 AM My Darling Davis,

You should have the transfer by now . . . at least I hope you do. I did try to call with no luck . . . I'm waiting for you to tell me what happened; I have been concerned for you. Now all we need to do is to get some more money over to you and I will need the company to send more money so as I can cover some of my bills. I used my bill money to send to you this morning, so I will need to take some when the company sends you some more money, oh I hope they are able to Davis . . . I have to get going to work now, but first I'm off to vote, as today is election day, this is where we watch the market/stocks fall some more . . . anyhow I know who I'm voting for. I gave up voting for parties, they turn out to be the same, and have the same problems when they get into office, so now I vote for the person and I like Larry Bagnall ; he is always available to talk to, he is visible, goes to all of the functions—he was even at the dinner for the children's group the other night. The one Zoey and I went to, he was the only candidate there, he gets my vote . . . he has also helped me out a couple of times . . . anyhow, I need to get going. I love you very much. I will check my e-mail at work shortly . . . love you Davis . . . ti amo.

Amore. Tess

From: Tess

Sent: October 14, 2008 10:56:09 AM My Darling Davis,

I just tried to call you, I heard your hello . . . And then we got immediately cut off . . . I wish I could talk with you, I know you will write me and let me know how things went. You answered your phone so I take it you are out of the meeting. Were you able to pick up the transfer and I wanted to let you know that Giovanni called, and he verified again with me that he sent the payment, he gave me his phone number so I can call him and let him know as soon as I get the payment and he said he will make another one within the next thirty—four hours. He also told me that with an e-mail transfer he can only send 1000.00 that won't do so, that is out. I hope he will look at doing a wire transfer through the bank. I told him that when he is able to do a wire transfer, I will give him my information so he can do it that way; also the limit to send through Western Union is 10, 000.00/day. And there is probably a charge of around 150.00 to do that, to send the 2500.oo, it cost me 40.00 so. I'm thinking ten thousand would be a little bit more.

I had better get going, I will write later, I hope to hear from you soon, I love you so much Davis . . . and yes I would like to talk about you coming home at the beginning of Nov or end of Oct. I Love you. ti amo.

Amore . . . Tess

From: Davis

Sent: October 14, 2008 12:19:33 PM Hello My Love,

It was nice hearing your voice again, I hope work is treating you well. I just got to the hotel, and want you to know Mr W brought the money. I am so grateful, thanks so much. The lawyer is here with Mr W, we have to talk about somethings, and after, I will send you an e-mail if I am not able to talk to you on the phone. I love you so much and appreciate everything you do for me. I will show you how grateful I am now I am home, and will pay you everything you have spent on me. I Love You. Will talk to you soon. Ti amo.

Amore . . . Davis

From: Tess

Sent: October 14, 2008 11:16:23 PM My Darling Davis,

I love you . . . I have been waiting to hear how things went for you yesterday. I'm a little concerned about what is happening at the mines, with the workers wanting to talk with you . . . do you know what is happening there, my one big concern is . . . when are the workers expected to get paid and is this what they wanted to talk with you about ? I did tell Giovanni that we needed to get the money to you as soon as possible. I will talk to him again about the wire transfer when this first payment comes through. My fear, Davis, is that Giovanni told me that they put the payment through on Sunday, if it takes minimum three business days, Monday was a holiday, so that doesn't count, that means three days puts us to Thursday, or Friday, Monday at the latest, and this I don't like. However we can't change it, I will watch daily before I go to work so that if I have to, I will stop on my way to work, also I hope to be able to connect with you online so that I can tell you, yes or not yet . . . so starting tomorrow, today for you, I imagine you're reading this e-mail, it's 2:30 my time maybe 3:00 AM. I will wake around 5 AM-6 AM, If you need or want to talk to me sooner, please call me to join you online, I don't mind if you wake me at 3 or 4, God I would love you to wake me then . . . Mind you it is so much better if you're lying next to me . . . oohhh la la . . . lol . . . Anyhow, I will get up then and join you online, you will have to give me at least fifteen minutes for this computer to get up and running, it is soooooooo sllllllllloooooowwwwwwwwwwwwwww. it kills me at times, I can sometimes fall back to sleep for ten minutes and it's still not finished loading the programs it has to load at start-up . . . anyhow, I will meet you, and I will also check my account to see if it's there or not and I can let you know right away. Given all that, if you don't call me at 3 or 4, I will come online around 6 and check then . . .okay . . . Wow that was a lot . . . Tonight, I want to tell you about our dinner we had this evening, we had Zack and Chad over for supper so all my kids were here, I had put a ham into the slow cooker this morning and I scored and rubbed the ham with Chinese 5 spice, it added a really nice flavour and then I made a baby scalloped potato salad dish. I just cut the baby potatoes in half, I didn't slice them and scalloped them that way and we had mixed veggies, such as broccoli, baby carrots, yellow squash, and red peppers, steamed, and for dessert, pumpkin pie, it was really good. If I do say so myself and the boys admitted it as well. And then after supper we had to play a game with Zoey, Cadoo, it's like a mini version of the game cranium. I don't know if you're familiar with this game or not, it has a little bit of pictonary in it, where you draw what the card tells you to and people have to guess what you drew, also you have to make things with clay and have people guess, a little bit of charades too, it's a fun game really. So we played one game of that and then I put Zoey to bed, late again and Zack and Chad had to go home. I am now making pea soup with the ham bone and stock. I sure wish you could have been here. The boys asked about you, asked how you were doing and when you would get here, I told them that you have to take care of things first and then you will be here in about three weeks.

208

Work was a scattered day for me, I couldn't get done what I wanted to get done as I had to wait to interview people and the staff were busy, so I will have to interview them tomorrow/ today.

When I was grocery shopping after work I ran into one of the doctors I used to work with at the clinic, I don't know if I told you that or not, that I worked at a clinic for three doctors, which was one of the busiest clinics here, and I loved it, I was able to use my nursing skills and I learnt a lot as well, it was great, and the patients loved me. I still get patients telling me when they see me how much they miss me. I would get people in to see a doctor when they needed to be seen, I would go right to which ever doctor, I thought was free and give him the symptoms and the doctor would usually say sure I'll see them, and in they would go. I was so busy it was crazy, in fact one of the doctors whom I didn't work for told me, he finds that the people who are working in my old job cannot keep up. I used to put in so much overtime just to keep my head above the water, so I wouldn't miss something important with a lab result. Anyhow this doctor that I ran into this evening he asked me if I would consider coming back to the clinic as his receptionist is leaving in January. I told him that I had already been approached by one of the other doctors I worked for last week about coming back in January; I don't know if I could go back. I make a good wage with the work I'm doing right now, and I get a wonderful benefits and a pension package, so it's a good position for me to be in. If I go back, I get a fast—paced job that I'm good at and I do enjoy. Unfortunately, with that job there is a certain amount of stress, if Zoey is sick, I can't take the day off to be with her However I do get lunch hours but the pay is considerably reduced, unless I negotiate with them and apparently there is now a benefit package that wasn't there before. Oh I'm sorry, I'm just talking here I hope you don't mind I'm just kind of putting it out there, using you as a sounding board so to say . . . I realise that I'm better off with the job I'm in right now, and when you're here and we want to travel it's much easier for me to take leave from there then it is from the clinic. Then I'll have a lot of excitement, my kind of excitement, with you . . . anyhow my dear, I'm thinking so much about you all the time, I'm wondering if you're waking up around now, I would love to be next to you when you wake, I can feel you wrapping your arms around me and drawing me in close to you,  my cheek resting against your chest, my hands would caress you bare skin on your arms, your chest. I would rub my hands in circles across your chest, your hairs would feel soft against my palm, I can imagine your hand caressing my arm, gently massaging up and down, in gentle wide circles, and every once in a while I would feel your fingers glide across my breast and then against my nipple, teasing it, bringing it to life . . . oh yes I can feel your touch, just sitting here,  I can feel it, I want to feel it so badly. I do want you Davis . . . oh we had better wake early in the mornings so we can get out of bed at a decent time, because waking next to you will definitely take a while . . . I had better get going to bed myself, I love you with all of my heart and soul, I do hope everything is alright with you Davis, please let me know, I am concerned, not worried, concerned . . . I'm concerned because I care about you . . . not knowing what happened, I will try not to speculate, I will wait for you to tell me. I have to go, I could end up writing to you all night if I don't stop now . . . again I love you so much. I hope that I get a chance to talk with you this morning . . . let me know what you are doing today . . . Thank You Davis . . . take care of yourself, promise me . . . I just realized I wrote quite a bit . . . see I just want to talk with you so much . . . I have to get going I love you . . . ti amo

Amore. Tess

From: Davis

Sent: October 15, 2008 6:22:10 AM Good Morning Tess My Love,

I hope you had a good sleep. I had one myself, but it would have been much better if you were lying next to me. Oh, how I wish for that soon, and know it will happen pretty soon. I love you so much. I did not e-mail you again last night because the connection went down. I stayed at the cafe waiting for it to come back till 10 PM when the attender said he had to close so I had to leave with this big disappointed face. Things didn't go that well at the meeting, they have asked me to hold on with work and get all the necessary document before I can continue. And in doing that, I will need money. I just hope everything goes through with the transfer so I can get money to start. The minister was so thankful for the way I stood my ground, he said this was the first time he has seen someone talk to these people like this, and said they are going to take much of the advise I gave them. He said they needed investors to come, invest here, but with the procedures here, he was not sure how many investors will have the patience, and has been talking to them to change the system. He said with their system, and my issue, they would have refer me to the court and I would have had to pay money to the Gov' for working without a permit, but that they did not refer me, means what I said went deep down with them. He sad he was going to help me get all the documents I will need very soon so I will  not have to delay my work. Now all I need is to have the money for the payment. I was wondering the other day what the workers will want to talk to me about, and it came in mind that I have not paid them anything since we started work. I am very sure that is what they will want to talk to me about. It amazes me how all this have to come up at this point, but I am not worried. I just need to focus and get things done as it should. I tell you it's big money we are talking about here, once all this is over and mining of oil starts, we will be making so much money that we will not really need to work anymore, and this money we end from here will take care of us. Our children and grand grandchildren, and we will start living a luxurious life, having everything we want and go anywhere in this world we will want to go. I love you so much and want you to hold to me onto everything I have promised to do, because I am going to make sure it happens. I will have to be at the ministry soon, but hope to talk with you on MSN before I leave, and before you go to work. I will meet the workers at the mines tomorrow. I love you and will call you if I am not able to talk to you on MSN before you leave for work. Ti amo.

Amore. Davis

On 10/15/08,

Tess wrote:

My Darling Davis,

I feel as if I have been spoiled lately, being able to hear your voice and talk with you online has been wonderful, now all you have to do is really spoil me and come home . . . lol. Actually I'm serious, to be honest, if it meant having to give up the mine to be with you, I would, even with all the money you say it would bring. I would still rather have you in my life, than a purse full of riches. I love you and I will be rich with Love, Love for you, and the Love you have for me.

I'm wondering how things went today for you . . . there is still no money in the acct:: I will check at the end of today and three-four times tomorrow as well, Giovanni said he sent it Saturday, so three business days puts the third day as tomorrow, as Monday was a holiday. Once the money starts to come in regularly, things will work . . . and I would like to talk with you about coming home, possibly the first week of November. That would be the best time for me, as I could take that week off and I could spend my time with you, then we could also set something up with the banks here so I can get you money when you need it without this hassle. I have a feeling that with all of these delays it could be another six weeks, that is a long time, and I don't want you to run out of money again . . . or else I may never see you. I would have to come and get you myself . . . if that were the case . . . lol . . . I am serious about that, coming to find you . . . so let me know what you think, I know you would like things to be running before you go . . . again just let me know . . . okay.

I should get going soon, I would love to hear your voice again, hearing you, just melts my heart, I wanted so badly to touch you, to wrap my arms around you and hold you so close . . . I still want to do that . . . I long for the feel of you, for your arms wrapped around me, your lips on mine, your caress, your closeness, I long for . . . I love you Davis Barienda . . . I will write again later, until then you are in my thoughts as I know I am in yours . . . you are wonderful . . . ti amo

Amore. Tess

From: Davis

Sent: October 15, 2008 3:03:55 PM My Darling Tess,

I hope your day is going well, I miss you so much, it's like I have not heard from you for years. I hope work continues soon so I can come home to you. I long to have you close with my arms around you and feel your kiss. My day went well, nothing to write home about. Before any progress, I will need to do payments, and I hope this money can get to you soon so you can get it to me here. I will be going to the mines tomorrow morning, I have to meet the workers and know what it is they want to talk to me about. If it's about payment, I will find a way to talk things over with them. I will let you know the outcome as usual. I just want to say that I love you and thank you for all the love and happiness you've brought to me. You know how hard things have been for me these few days, but knowing you are around makes me feel and know I am not alone. You have been here for me since day one, and I truly appreciate everything so much. You mean so much to me, more to me than anything in this world. I am so lucky that I fell in love with such an amazing person like you. I love you. I will e-mail you hopefully before I leave in the morning, or will try calling you. Good night My Love, ti amo.

Amore . . . Davis

From: Tess

Sent: October 15, 2008 3:15:47 PM

I love you Davis Barienda . . . I don't have time to write a lot right now, I just want to tell you I love you so much . . . and I miss you . . . sometimes I miss you so much it hurts . . . I will write more later I Love you . . . ti amo

Amore. Tess

From: Tess

Sent: October 15, 2008 10:36:48 PM My Darling Davis . . .

I have such a love for you . . . it fills me completely . . . I want you to know that I went online to see if by chance there was money on my Visa and there was no payment yet, so I called Visa to see if they have anything, and they did, unfortunately it was still pending. I talked with the guy and asked him if I could pull it out of my account tomorrow and he did something, came back to me and said yes, so tomorrow morning I am going to the bank at 9:30 when it opens and I will send you 10000.00, the code word, will be the same. I will probably get to Western Union around 9:45, and then I will try and call as I'm racing home to e-mail you the confirmation number, hopefully I get you on the phone, if not check your e-mail around 10:00 or sooner, better yet can you be online at 9:45. I'm going to leave my computer on so I can send it to you immediately. I talked with Giovanni tonight and let him know the payment was here, he said he sent another one today for 9500.00, so that should be here by Friday. If it is, I will send it to you Friday, if not Monday. I also asked him about sending more and he doesn't want to send too much over the credit limit because, he said something along the lines that, that is how money is laundered, oohhh kay so we won't do that. Giovanni did ask me to see if I could increase my credit amount to $20, 000.00, then he could put that much more onto my Visa. I did get an increase, I hate to tell you, because I didn't realize I could do this, anyhow I did increase my credit limit, Visa would allow me to go to 13, 000.00. Giovanni said that he could put the full 13000.00 in, I keep thinking, I could of done that to get you home, but that didn't happen and there is obviously a reason why. Anyhow . . . The money will be there this evening for you . . . I just hope you can get it tonight, I tried to call and hopefully I did get you but I haven't had any success as of yet. I called probably ten times, it rang a lot of those times and I thought maybe you answered but the connection was so bad it was hard to tell. I want to talk with you so much. I know this is the start . . . I hope you get this before you go out to the mines; I want you to know this before you start your day . . . I love you with all my heart. If I dont' get a chance to talk with you, or chat, I will be sending the money at 9:45 . . . give or take five minutes . . . and I will be on my computer hopefully before 10:00. I just hope Western Union stays open till 6 PM your time . . . I love you, I hope you have a good day and I hope all goes well with the workers at the mines . . . the next 10000.00 will come through for sure Monday if that helps . . . I have to go to bed now . . . I will try the phone a couple more times, . . . your voice just melts me. . . . I love you . . . ti amo

Amore. Tess

From: Davis

Sent: October 16, 2008 12:38:17 AM Good Morning My Love,

I hope you are feeling my warmness around you as you sleep, I always feel you around me in everything I do. I can never love anything the way I LOVE YOU, you had my whole heart, soul, mind and me. I woke up about four times when you called, but didn't hear anything when I picked up. I knew it was you, wished I could call back, but I then realized I had run out of calling time. I am so glad to hear the money is in, a sign of relief. I can now pay the chief and start the so called right procedure at the ministry. I am leaving for the mine in the next 15 to 20 minutes, I will arrive hopefully, 12 noon, that will be 5 AM your time. I don't know how long the meeting will take, I am going to meet you online at 2 PM, your time 7 AM. I hope we can talk online for a while before you leave for work. Talking with you just makes everything look perfect. You are so wonderful, and I will love you till my last breath on earth, and will continue loving you wherever I found myself after life here. I LOVE YOU so much Tess.

You mean the world to me and I care about you so deeply that it hurts that we are not together. My every thought and breath, I draw from you and I truly do love you.

I love you and you are my world. You are the most sweetest, most precious woman in my life. All my life I prayed for someone like you and I thank god that I finally found you. I know in my heart our love will never die. You will always be a part of me and I am a part of you indefinitely.

I don't find enough words to describe how I feel about you. You possess all the color and beauty of heaven. I hunger for your touch and the warm embrace of your body. I love you; you are my every heartbeat and my every breath. I hope to meet you online at 7 AM, till then, know I love you so much. Ti amo

Amore. Davis

From: Tess

Sent: October 16, 2008 3:14:05 AM My Darling Davis,

You make me swoon, with your words, and your love, you just warm me so much Davis . . .

I am so glad that you checked your e-mail before leaving for the mines, I just felt it important that you knew the money was here, before talking with the workers. I will meet you online at 7 AM. Just in case we can't get onto MSN, will you still be at the mines at that time, I'm asking because, I'm wondering if I have to race back home to e-mail you the confirmation number, if you're not going to be able to get the money today, then I can drive to work and e-mail you from there. Mind you I'm going to try and phone first, if you can let me know, either through e-mailing me or when we talk . . . I wish so much that we could have talked early this morning, I was wondering if I had woken you, I kind of have this thing now for waking you, it's your voice, when you first wake in the morning . . . lol.I would have loved to have talked with you. I am now going back to bed for the next three hours, and I will meet you here at 7 AM. I love you with all of my heart and soul Davis, you are it, you are the man I have been dreaming about, I want my dream, I want you . . . I Love You . . . ti amo

Amore. Tess

From: Tess

Sent: October 16, 2008 8:34:38 AM My Darling Davis,

I'm not too sure what happened this morning, but I lost you just after you asked me about Zoey, I thought maybe you got busy, I know that you may have still had to meet with the workers.

I have to get going right now, I will get in touch with Mr W as soon as the money is sent and I will e-mail you as well, I love you so much, I will hopefully get a chance to talk with you later, if you can send me an e-mail, let me know if we can meet tomorrow morning and what time if possible, now that you have money, it's going to be busy again for you . . .

I love you, have a great day . . . I am with you . . . ti amo Amore. Tess

From: Davis

Sent: October 16, 2008 9:55:32 AM My Love,

I lost my connection, I guess you are on your way to the bank. I had the meeting with the workers, as usual, it was about getting paid. I will go down into it more later, nothing to be worried about. For now, I am coming back to Accra. Let me know when you send the money by trying to call me, and send the confirmation number to Mr W. I told him to check his mail at 10:00 if he does not hear from me by then. If you are able to get me on the phone, I will then call him. I have to get going, I will get in touch later. I love you so much. Ti amo.

Amore . . . Davis

From: Tess

Sent: October 16, 2008 11:33:34 AM My Darling Davis,

First let me start off by saying I love you very much, in fact I know I love you more . . .

I was being real smart and went to Western Union at 9 AM to fill out the paper work, get the amount that I could send and the fee amt . . . Then I went to the bank for 9:30, in fact the doors opened earlier   at 9:25. I went right to the counter, then the clerk called Visa and they put him on hold for twenty minutes, I had to talk with Visa and they released the funds, so then it was 10 AM and over to Western Union where it took another thirty minutes. The amount she told me I could send over was too large the computer would not accept it to send to Ghana, it would only accept 7000 and the lady in the main office, put the clerk on hold at Western Union here for over twenty minutes, anyhow it was a waiting game and then I couldn't get online at home.

I am so glad I got you on the phone at the last minute . . . I know what to do now to avoid these hassles, it will mean sending you money almost daily 6000 one day and then 4000 the next day, that way they do not have to phone to clear the larger amt, I may do more the next day, it all depends on what Giovanni can send me, which reminds me I have to call him . . . I am very eagar to hear how things went with the workers . . . I hope you are doing okay. I love you so much . . . I have to go I just wanted to e-mail you . . . in case you may need it again, the comfirmation # is 190-777-4444. I hope you were able to get the transfer today . . . have to run . . . I love you . . . ti amo

Amore. Tess

From: Davis

Sent: October 16, 2008 4:16:31 PM Hi My Love,

I just got to Accra, and Mr. W was at the hotel with the money. I just want you to know I love you so much. My day was good, and I hope yours is good too. I was wondering if you could send the rest of the money today so I can have Mr W pick it up tomorrow morning so I can pay the workers something for now. I will be leaving to the mines in the morning, and will meet you online at 7 AM. If you can send the rest of the money today, let me have the confirmation number so I can have Mr. W pick it up in the morning and meet me at the mines later. All I want to do now is to finish with work here and come home to you to show you how much I love you and make passionate love to you as I have always wanted to do. I am sure you can send the rest of the money today once I have cleared the first one. Tess, I love you, those simple words always bring a smile to my face and song to my heart. I am just writing this here because it's the only way I know that I can shout to the world I love you! The day you came into my life, a miracle happened. One minute I was resigned to the fact that love was a part of my past, something although painful to think about, was nothing more than mere memory. And then there you were.

You opened my heart in ways it had never been opened before. You awakened a part of me that had lain dormant all of life. We share a love so true that I have never before experienced the true joy of complete empowering, soul-felt love as we share. The comfort I feel in knowing that we can love forever, we can get through the roughest of times and still know in our hearts that we can't live without each other is what makes it even more special. "It wouldn't matter if it didn't matter . . ."

217

Baby, you matter to me and I know in my heart I truly matter to you. I am secure in your love as I know you are in mine. What more could we ask for than to be truly loved as we do each other and have found the one we have both been searching for all our lives.

I cherish, respect, and love you so much. This kind of love is rare and special beyond words. You mean the word to me. So, in closing, let me shout this to all . . ., "I LOVE YOU, TESS, WITH ALL MY HEART AND SOUL. Hope to talk to you in the morning. Ti amo.

Amore. Davis

From: Tess

Sent: October 16, 2008 6:43:56 PM My Darling Davis,

I was able to send you some more money I transferred 5300.00 under Mr. Warleh's name. I couldn't remember who you wanted me to send it to, you or Mr.W so I played it safe and sent it to him. I reread your e-mail once I arrived home and saw that I had made the correct choice. Sending smaller amts is much easier. Anyhow I am going to keep track of the payments made by Giovanni to my Visa and the amounts that I send to you. I was also wondering, I imagine you will be paying the workers cash, are there government taxes that you have to be concerned about regarding paying out wages? This is the bookkeeper in me talking now, are you keeping track of who you pay and what you pay? Oh I'm almost forgetting one of the most important things, first one is I Love You, I read your e-mails and you make my heart flutter, your words, your feelings, it's like looking in a mirror. It is amazing, as I said it feels like a fairy tale—a dream I don't ever want to wake up from . . . second, the confirmation number is 415 585 7777, after this one, I will change the question and answer, I will let you know what it will be. I have to get going I'm going to pottery this evening, I wanted to get this to you just in case you left early in the morning. I will try and check my MSN at 3 or 4 AM, you are my world Davis . . . I love you so much . . . ti amo

Amore . . . Tess

From: Tess

Sent: October 17, 2008 12:02:21 AM My Darling Davis,

Goodmorning My Darling, I Love you . . . I hope you were able to get the money this morning. I'm hoping that there will be another payment through tomorrow and then I maybe able to send it tomorrow evening. If it's not in tomorrow it will have to be Monday, I hope that this will cover what you need until then. I am hoping that with one of these payments I send you, you will be able to book your flight to come home for a week or two, I would settle for just one week, the first week of Nov. I need to feel you Davis, I need to touch you, I don't want to dream anymore I want the real you, I know it will be soon, it seems the longer I'm away from you, the more I miss you, I haven't even physically met you yet I miss you . . . Sometimes I feel like I've known you forever, I feel I know you . . . yet I've never seen you . . . physically . . . and I do believe you understand what I'm talking about . . . Davis, have you ever felt that we've been in another life together? I feel strongly that we have experienced different lives throughout our time, and each one, brings us closer to a meaning, to a beginning, to what we need . . . I feel that when we have loved deeply in another life, we search for that love, I never gave up on believing in love, I always longed for true love, a love that was respectful, giving, and complete, and as I said I've always believed that it was out there, and then I wasn't finding it. I still believed, I wanted to believe. I too had almost given up, thinking that my true love would be something that I would be writing in romance stories, and then you found me and you wanted to talk to me, and you gave me my belief back . . . Davis, sometimes I still feel as if I'm dreaming without being able to touch you, feel you, see you, sometimes it's hard for me to believe that this incredible, wonderful man loves me as you do, it fills me, I am so scared sometimes that it is just a dream. I know you love me, it feels wonderful and I love you . . . so much . . . It's almost midnight, I need to get to bed so that I can get up and be ready before meeting you online . . . in case for some reason I miss you, I wanted to ask you one more thing, regarding Giovanni. I tried to call him several times today to let him know that the payment went through to you, he was going to send another one, but also I told him, as I mentioned to you, to send one hundred thousand in instalments and then send you the rest in a cheque. Do you want him to send the cheque made out to you, here in Whitehorse, or do you want him to send it to me, and I can put it into a bank account which I will set up for you? Would you be able to call him and let him know what you want him to do regarding the cheque . . . I just think it would be better coming from you, as he does not know me and I would be more comfortable with you telling him . . . Are you okay with that? . . . I had better get going to bed so I can dream of you, you do some amazing things to me in my dreams, in fact we share a lot of amazing moments in my dreams, I often wonder if we share the same dreams sometimes . . . I will talk to you soon . . . I Love you . . . ti amo

Amore . . . Tess

From: Davis

Sent: October 17, 2008 7:42:53 AM Good Morning My Darling Tess,

I Love you so much, and will forever LOVE YOU. I hope your day went well yesterday. Yes, I am keeping track of who I pay and what I pay. I am also concerned about paying out wages. Thanks for your reminder, you are so sweet. I love you. I will be leaving to the mines just after sending this mail. I will go with the lawyer. We have to first meet the chief and his people to settle the rest of their money, and I will meet the workers. The money will not be able to pay all the workers, but I will pay what I have and let them know they will get the rest by end of next week. I have the second confirmation number, and will let Mr. W pick the money and meet me at the mines later with it. I know I am working you out by going to the bank and to Western Union of late, but I assure you once this is over, we will be together soon and will be so happy having each other. This business is for you and the kids, and it will be ours forever.

I am glad that finally, I have found someone like you. Now that I have you here with me, I would like to let you know how happy and grateful I am to have you in my life. I love you with all my heart and my soul. You mean so much to me.It is you that I want to see waiting for me at the altar, it is you that I want to spend my life with. Now that we're together I promise to be always true to you, to love you and trust you. I love you more than anything this life can offer me.   I am happy to have you and as long as it feels right for me. I guess destiny has lead you to me so I guess we're really meant for each other. Now I know everything's going to be okay because I have you with me now. I will meet you online at 7, till then, know I love you so much. Ti amo.

Amore. Davis

From: Tess

Sent: October 17, 2008 8:21:27 AM My Darling Davis,

I wanted to write to you as I'm afraid that I'm not going to be able to finish our chat, I did write you a lot more, I hope you will still receive the messages once I sign off . . . I love you so much Davis, you make me feel so alive, and today, today we had such a good connection on the phone. I love hearing your voice, you just make me melt, I'm going to be a jiggling, melting, wobbly kneed, teenage-like woman when I see you, you may have to pick me up off of the floor . . . and do with me what you want . . . lol

I have to get going to drop Zoey off at school, and myself to work, I will write again later, I also wanted to let you know, that I know you are going to be busy and you probably have to see how things go before you can confirm as to when you can come home. I'm hoping that you will be able to set a date because I do have to put in a leave form, to ensure I get my time off while you are here, and the sooner the better, so that is why I ask, and I want to see you as well . . . I want to touch you, and I want to kiss you and I want to feel you, as we make passionate, sensual, erotic, wild, uncontrollable out of this world, complete loss of control . . . love . . . it is going to be all that and more being with you . . . have to go now that I've worked myself up . . . I will talk to you later, if you can get a chance to call me . . . I have my cell . . . I Love you so much . . . ti amo . . .

Amore . . . Tess

From: Tess

Sent: October 17, 2008 11:34:43 AM My Darling Davis,

I'm taking a quick break, so I can write to you and tell you that I'm thinking about you always, every step I take, you are with me . . . I hope your day went well, I imagine that the chief is happy now and do you think a little more trusting of you, or was that ever an issue? Also, what has to be done with the Ministry, how much do you have to pay there? Is that another $5000.00?

I have tried to call Giovanni a couple of times to let him know that the first transfer has come out and gone to you but I have been unable to reach him, he is not answering his phone, I did leave a message so if you are talking with him at all, could you ask him if he did get my message about that. I think about you always, Davis. I wonder what you are doing right now, are you still at the mines or are you on your way back to Accra? . . . Are you back to mounting the machines, and how many were you able to get done before this all put a stand still on work?, how many are left to do? I know I ask a lot of questions . . . that's me . . . I'm curious. And about me having to go to the bank and Western Union, I don't mind, yes it was a hassle, but I think I have it figured out where it won't be such a hassle anymore, it will still take time at the bank, one of the biggest concerns that visa brought up with me is that this is a fairly new credit card for me with them, so they really don't have a history with me . . . I still have to establish this, and that is why all these questions, again I am new to the world of credit, this year, to be exact so yes, they will be asking me lots of questions . . . believe me, I don't mind doing this whatsoever, as you said it is for the both of us . . . but it is for you, and it will get you home . . . for a chance to see you . . . I will do anything though, wait hours if I have to . . . my main concern and frustration was making sure that I got you the money before the Western Union closed on your end . . .

I should get going . . . I have to enter some more data into my computer, and go and do another interview after lunch . . . and then once the day is over it is the weekend . . . Yes . . .

It snowed here this morning . . . and it is still snowing, I hope this will melt shortly, I'm not ready yet for snow . . . I can't remember if I asked you or not . . . Do you cross country ski? . . .

I love you Davis with all of my heart and soul, I will hopefully get a chance to talk with you later or maybe tomorrow, take care of yourself, and know I go with you . . . ti amo

Amore. Tess

From: Tess

Sent: October 17, 2008 10:42:07 PM My Darling Davis, Goodmorning . . .

I missed you today; I know you were thinking of me, as I have been thinking of you. I was wondering how things were going? Have you started everything back online at the mines? I imagine if you had, you would be busy . . . I sense that you are man who gives more than 100%

when you're working, you give more than your all . . . I imagine you are the same in a relationship? I want you to know that I give more than my all, more than 100% in a relationship. I love you Davis . . . and I will give you my all. I was wondering if you received my e-mails I sent you late last night, one was titled I'll meet you at 7, I asked you a couple of questions about talking with Giovanni and if you like to cross—country ski?. I also sent you an `I miss you card` which hasn't notified me that you've received it yet, if you didn't get these e-mails let me know and I will resend them, Me not receiving your email this morning has me thinking, that it was the same for you . . . I feel tired tonight I'm going to be going to bed soon, I was hoping that I might be able to meet you at 7 AM my time? If that will work for you, I will check online for 7, if you're unable to make it, as I know you are busy, let me know.

Zoey and I have a busy day planned for today. Zoey has dance at 10:30 and then we have a birthday party, my friend's daughter is turning one tomorrow so we are celebrating from 1-2:30 and then at 3:00, I am taking Zoey to see the Irish Dancers at the Art Centre. They are supposed to be like the river dancers, (I would love to be able to go to concerts at the Art Centre with you.) Our day will definitely be full . . . I will always be thinking about you throughout my whole

day, wishing you were with us, sharing these experiences. I hope to meet you this morning, my time, for you this afternoon; it seems with our talks being interrupted I feel as if I've been missing you so much. How can I fill my nights without you? Wanting you . . . I had better get going, I need to get my beauty sleep . . . lol . . . I will be dreaming of you . . . all night . . . you are my dream Davis, please let me know if you received my e-mail from Friday am . . . I find it so hard signing off from you . . . I will go now and hope to be talking with you first thing this morning . . . my morning . . . I Love You . . . ti amo

Amore. Tess

From: Davis

Sent: October 18, 2008 5:08:04 AM Good Morning my Darling Tess,

I miss you so much, and love you with all that I am. I got disconnected yesterday while talking with you online, and the connection never came back till some few minutes ago. I tried calling Giovanni, but someone picked it up and told me he was out of town and will be back

Sunday evening. Anywhere he knew I have the first transfer he sent you, and told me the second one would be in Monday. That was when I spoke with him yesterday morning. I wanted him to know I need much money so he should try to speed up things. I have not yet had the card you sent to me, and will be expecting it. I will need about $15, 000 to settle the workers and some little things here in the mines, and will need over $50, 000 for the taxes and some little more money for other things like the document. And Giovanni is going to get you that money so you can send it to me here. I told him this transfer will not let me have the money soon as I want, so he said he will find another way to make sure you have all the money I need before the weeks dead line I gave him. I am at the mines now, I will be busy, but will try to meet you online at 8 AM.

Like you, I put my all in my relationship. I always want the best out of it, but with you, I want more than the best, and going to put more than my very best into it. More than 100%. There are no words that I can speak, no song that I can sing, and no gesture that I can show, to prove my love for you, for the love I have for you has no definition. How can I describe the sheer joy I feel with the very thought of you?

How simply hearing your voice causes my heart to beat faster, my pulse to race and my smile to widen. You have opened my heart and awakened my soul. You are my one and only true love. That is how I know that our love is everlasting. I have to get going, I will try to meet you at 8 AM. If I am not able, I will try calling. I love you so much and will be thinking about you in everything I do as usual. Ti amo.

Amore . . . Davis

From: Tess

Sent: October 18, 2008 6:24:02 AM My Darling Davis,

I love you. I figured the connection was down, it's frustrating at times when it seems to be our only way of being together, to lose these connections is like having to let you go, but know that you are with me, and when you go away like that, just cut off, I know it usually is the connection. As it usually is on my end as well . . . I will be online at 8 and hopefully you will be able to meet me, I look forward to that. My son locked his keys in his car, including the house key for here, so he woke me just before 5:30am to let him in, as I have his spare car key. It seems like I just missed you online, mind you, you probably

224

wouldn't have had time to talk when you first sent me the e-mail. I am re—sending you the e-mail and the card that I sent you yesterday.

I am so glad you talked with Giovanni, I hope he can just send me a cheque that I can put into the bank and then I can take what I need to send you for the week, and in one week you should have $80, 000. I could possibly send you $13, 500.00/day without hassle, So here's hoping Giovanni can do this. By the way, do you have my address just in case he does send me a cheque? He could UPS or FedEx it to me. I should get going and maybe get a couple of things done before I meet you online, I thought maybe I could go back to bed, I don't know, it would be much more inviting if you were lying there waiting for me to come back to bed to join you . . . and of course I would bring you a coffee with cream. I don't have an espresso machine at my house, we would have to be at your place if you wanted a latte in the morning . . . I will talk with you soon . . . I love you . . . ti amo

Amore . . . Tess

From: Tess

Sent: October 18, 2008 9:30:51 PM Goodmorning My Darling Davis,

I wish that I could have been with you last night, I imagine you were tired, I would have lain next to you in bed, you would have been so tired that you would have turned your body in towards mine and laid your head against my breast, your breath I could feel against my nipple, I would have stroked your hair next to your ear, and caressed the top of your head, I would have bent my head towards yours and kissed the top of your head. You could hear my heart beat, and soon your breathing would match the soothing rhythm and you would sleep, a deep relaxed, wondrous sleep, and while you slept, you would move your body and take me against you, so my head would be lying on your chest. I would be able to hear your heart beating, and I would close my eyes, my hand; I would caress your chest, and I would feel your heat, and we would sleep, until the early hours of the morning, and then I would wake to the feel of your kiss against my lips, I would open my eyes and look into yours, I would get lost in your wanting me . . . I would open myself up to you and I would feel you as you came deep inside of me . . . the thought of you making deep passionate love to me . . . This is how you would be starting your day today, if I was with you . . . you would be starting your day with a big smile . . . lol I love you . . . so much Davis . . . I am missing you . . . does it show? . . . Know that

I am content with loving you . . . Content in the way that I know that our love is for each other with each other, I still very much want to see you as soon as we can . . .

We had a good day today, Zoey and I, while she was at her dance lesson I went for a brisk walk around town, and then we went shopping for a birthday gift and then to the birthday party, a lot of people, moms, dads and lots of little kids and babies, lots of food and punch, and then it was off to the Arts Centre to watch the Irish Dancers, they were incredible and the band that played for them, I don't know if they even had a name. They were just introduced by their individual names, they were excellent, in fact the band got the standing ovation at the end. Zoey wanted to get the music CD, which we did. She then came home and proceeded to dance the Irish way . . . it was quite cute, unfortunately she had a meltdown with one of her friends, I think she was tired, she calmed down and now all is well. Zoey will do that once in a while when she has had too much stimulation and gets tired, if things don't go her way, she can't control her emotions at times; She needs a lot of understanding and firmness at the same time. What can I say, she is a girl . . . my boys were so much easier to raise, there was less hormonal situations. I'm going to dread puberty. with you in my life, I'm not going to feel alone in these situations, just having you to talk to will make things so much easier . . . Just to let you know as well Zoey does listen better to a male than to her mother it seems. Single parenting can be trying at times. She comes up to me afterwards and gives me a great big hug; my heart just goes out to her . . . my little angel . . .

I'm hoping we get a chance to talk this morning, I usually wake sometime between 3 and 5, so when I wake I will check my e-mail to see if you're online, but if you're able to let me know if there may be a chance to meet and when, I know that you may be busy and/ or the connection may not be there, but I will check and wait for you, if there is a chance . . . I thought about you being with us today, and the thoughts were wonderful, and when I was walking I felt you next to me, we would walk and talk, laugh and make plans, it feels so wonderful Davis, knowing that soon you will be more than just a thought, but a reality walking next to me . . . I'm going to bed now, I'm going to be dreaming of you . . . and I hope to meet you online . . . I love you. ti amo

Amore. Tess

From: Davis

Sent: October 19, 2008 1:45:06 AM Good Morning My Love,

I couldn't talk with you yesterday, and it seems I have not talked with you for years. I miss you so much I could not have a good sleep. I kept waking and wishing I had a computer in the room so I could talk to you online. I kept trying to call you, but could not get the connection. I hope your day went well yesterday. I couldn't meet you online because the connection went down and was down all day all night yesterday. I am sure Zoey and you had a busy weekend, the birthday party, Zoey's dance and some other things you people might have done. I love you.

You are a dream come true, you have stolen my heart so innocently with care and grace and perfect love. The perfect thought is us together forever, the greatest thing is your love. From day one I knew there was something very special about you. I felt you were the right one for me, and I am glad I did not let you go, but rather loved you with all that I am. I love you so much, those five words I tell you so much can't have more meaning than anything else ever possibly could. I love you with all my faults and all my achievements. I love you with all that I am. I love you for who you are. I need you to know I will forever love you. I will be online at 4 AM, hope we can talk by then. I love you so much. Ti amo

Amore . . . Davis

From: Davis

Sent: October 19, 2008 4:09:03 AM Hi My Darling,

I was hoping to talk to you online at this time, I guess you were so tired last night and still sleeping. I am going to the lawyer's place, we have to talk about a lot of things that we will have to do this week. This week will be a very busy week, but it's good, because once work is going on well, the sooner I will get to come home to you. I will try to get to a cafe around this place so I can meet you. If I am not able, I will call you. And please try to call me if you can. I have been having a difficult time getting to you on phone. I love you so much. Ti amo. Amore . . . Davis

From: Tess

Sent: October 19, 2008 5:17:57 AM My Darling Davis,

I do love hearing your voice, I wish I could talk with you all day. I love you so much, you get my heart going, with your words, your voice, the thought of you coming home . . . SOON . . . who needs cardio exercise, I just need you . . . lol

I felt the same as you yesterday, not talking with you was like having something undone for the day, I kept telling myself, that at least I had your e-mail from the morning, I just reread it . . . once or twice throughout the day . . . and I also stared at your picture lots . . . you are with me Davis all of the time . . . I want to see you and talk with you so much . . . not to mention, as we talk, I am in your arms, I hope you don't mind, but I plan on being in your arms a lot. I want to hold hands when we walk down the street, I see couples holding hands, walking, and I'm envious, I want that to be you and me . . . I will meet you here at 6:00 AM, or close to that, (In fact I will be waiting for you) that should be an hour from when we talked, I tried to call you back several times but I just got the message that the number I dialled could not be reached at this time . . . I don't like that message. I am so glad I got you, mind you I tried for about five times before I got through to you, one thing you will learn about me is that I am persistent in things that I want bad enough . . . Oh, Davis, I love you . . . I could say these words to you all day . . . they fill me, you fill me, I will be yours forever . . . I will meet you soon, and hopefully we will have time to talk, I never got a chance to ask you as to how much time we will have, as I'm not sure what you have planned for the rest of your day . . . I am looking forward to hearing what you've been doing these past couple of days and how things have been going for you . . . okay . . . until we talk, I love you with all my heart and soul . . . ti amo

Amore . . . Tess

From: Tess

Sent: October 19, 2008 8:14:38 AM My Darling Davis,

When you came online the first time, it never showed you as being online nor did it show any messages if you typed any, just said, you had signed out at 7:30, and now, at least we got the I love yous and the miss yous, in before we were disconnected. Davis these connections are cruel, I can't get through on the phone . . . I will continue to wait to see if you get reconnected, I wanted to talk with you so bad . . . I've been wanting to hear what has been happening with you. . . . just wanting to talk this just proves you have to come home real soon, we really do need to sit wrapped up with each other and talk . . . amongst other things It's 8:11 and I will wait Davis, I hope if you can't get back online that you are at least able to get through to me on the phone maybe we will have better luck later on in the day . . . Oh Davis, I miss you. I love you . . . completely . . . I will wait . . . ti amo

Amore. Tess

From: Davis

Sent: October 19, 2008 12:16:39 PM My Love,

I am here thinking deeply about you and how wonderful it will be to have you next to me right now. I miss you so much, and love you with all that I am. You are all that I want in life. You make me dream and believe in life. You bring me up when I'm down. You tell me I can reach my goals if I keep trying. You love me for me, even the mistakes I might do. All you do makes me love you more. I could never find anybody as special as you are. I love you, Tess, and will continue to love you forever. I hope to talk to you online soon. I love you. Ti amo.

Amore . . . Davis

From: Tess

Sent: October 19, 2008 1:03:52 PM My Darling Davis,

It's 1 PM and I'm online, I just read your e-mail, I hope we get a chance to connect, I love you so much, I want to talk with you so much, there is almost a pain inside of me not being able to reach you . . . I am going to try and call you again . . . I will keep myself online until 3PM. I love you. Hope to talk with you soon. ti amo.

Amore. Tess

From: Tess

Sent: October 19, 2008 3:12:20 PM My Darling Davis,

I have tried to call so many times, and it sounded as if you picked up once and then that was it, I couldn't get through again I'm hoping that we can meet tomorrow. I will wake and check online again around

3 AM. I don't know if you're going to the mines tomorrow or not, there is so much I wanted to talk with you about. Oh, Davis these connections not working is very frustrating, my heart is sinking, I want to talk with you so bad, it is so wonderful to hear your voice, I wish today that we had a better connection, it did sound loud coming from your end, sounded like a party . . . I wish we could be together. I'm taking Zoey to Arts Underground, we are going to do some pottery her and I . . . I will try again to phone you around 11:00 your time, and please try to call me, you may get through as well, I used all my minutes this morning on one phone card and on this other one I have eleven minutes remaining, I will have to get another phone card later today . . . I Love You Davis, again if you can try and meet me tomorrow AM, please let me know and if not let me know a time when we may meet . . . I Love you . . . ti amo

Amore. Tess

From: Davis

Sent: October 19, 2008 4:23:51 PM My Love,

Its has really been very frustrating trying to get online today, I never gave up, and just got connected. I was hoping you will be here, but I guess the frustration we were going through made you log out. I told the guy at the cafe to let me talk with you for thirty minutes before he closed, just for the time taken, and he agreed. But since you are not around, I will go back to my hotel room and get some sleep. I will be going to the mines tomorrow, but will mail you before I leave, and hope to talk to you on phone or online. I Love you so much and miss you. Ti amo.

Amore . . . Davis

From: Tess

Sent: October 19, 2008 10:01:26 PM My Darling Davis,

You are so wonderful, I just keep falling in love with you more and more, each day and then you do something like this and I fall even more . . . oh Davis, the fact that you never gave up on me, just fills me, I'm so sorry that I wasn't online, I promised Zoey that I would take her to pottery, they have a drop in on Sundays from 2:30pm to 6pm. I was going to go at 3pm because I knew that that was when the internet cafe at the hotel would be closed, however I called you from 3:00 to 4:00 and then I left because I was not getting through, I got another phone card online, and I thought you might have picked up once during that time, but it was cut off immediately . . . oh Davis, if I would have known I would have stayed online. This is killing me, today was just a big frustration not getting to chat to you online but at least we did get to talk briefly, which, hearing your voice, oh Davis, I wish now that we could have talked longer, but even when we did talk I know there was a lot of noise on your end, and it wasn't always clear; I could just hear you, and that alone was good enough. I miss you so much when we don't get a chance to talk, I want you to know that sending me the e-mail after you waited for so long, my god Davis, I just want to make love to you, I want to hold you so close to me . . . even though you're not here, your e-mails, what you say to me, the effort that you make to contact me, that means the world to me, more in fact, it alone says so much . . . you bring tears to my eyes, Davis. You make me feel so loved and cherished, you make me feel special. I've always wanted to be special to someone and I am forever thankful that, that someone is you. You make me melt, oh I want to be with you forever, I want to be the best for you. I want to do things everyday to show you what you mean to me . . . even with the frustrations and disappointments of not being able to talk to you, your e-mails, bring me so much . . . again I am so sorry I wasn't there, I do feel like crying at times, tears tend to build, I then bring your picture up. Did I tell you I have it on my computer, as well as my phone, and I look at you, and I feel you, you are so handsome, sometimes I can't believe that you are the man who loves me, I just go Wow, I am the luckiest girl alive. Davis, I love you, beyond words, I will wake tomorrow at 4 AM to see if you may possibly be online, I figure by 11AM your time you should be at the mines, again I don't know if you will be busy at that time or not, but if you get this before then and you won't be able to meet please let me know, and if possible maybe we could meet at 7 AM, oh, Davis, I do want to talk with you, talking with you just makes my day complete, and more . . . I Miss you so much, I Love You So Much . . . you are my everything . . . ti amo.

Amore . . . Tess

From: Davis

Sent: October 19, 2008 11:34:45 PM Good Morning My Love,

I just want you to know I am falling in love with you deeply every passing day. I love you so much. I am going to the mines just after sending this mail. I should have been at the ministry today, but I don't find it necessary going there when I don't have the money to get things done there. I will be at the mines taking care of some stuffs and will be online if not at 4 AM, then it will be 7 AM. The feelings that I've felt for you all along begin to resurface. Only this time, I am free to act on them without fear of upsetting anyone. Thank you, Tess. What more can a man say to the woman who opened her heart to him, allowing him to feel the warmth of her love across the great distance that separates them? You truly have no idea what I feel for you. I try to put this feeling into words, but fail miserably. This feeling of being both scared and at peace, of having both butterflies and a sense of calm, is a feeling that I have only dreamed about. As the days continue to pass, my love for you continues to grow. I never thought I had the capacity to love anybody as much as I love you right now. Yet, my love for you continues to mature, growing beyond the realm of my heart. It seems that you have become the fiber of my soul, the very reason for my existence. I have no other words to describe the way you make me feel. No words, no actions could even come close. I believe that Ronald Regan said it best to Nancy in a letter, telling her only that, "I more than love you". Their love was a strong love, surviving everything, even death. I believe that even after his passing, Nancy felt Ronald's love for her raining down upon her. That is why she has always seemed at peace after the death of such a truly loving husband. That is the love that I feel for you. I have to go now, I will talk to you later. I love you. Ti amo.

Amore. Davis

From: Davis

Sent: October 21, 2008 1:08:32 AM Good Morning My Darling,

I had a good sleep last night and hope you are having a good sleep. I guess my good sleep was the outcome of talking with you before going to bed. Oh how I wish I could talk with you and hear your voice all the time. I would not get Giovanni on the phone last night, I will try again when I get to the mines, and will let you know the outcome of our talk.

I love you so much, you are all I have ever wanted, and so glad to have you in my life. I know there's an ocean between us, and I wish that it weren't true, for every day when I rise, I yearn to be with you. Though a lot of distance lies between us, you will always be in my mind, my heart, and every night beneath the stars, I pray for the day we willl never be apart.

I think about you all the time. When my eyes are closed, when I sing and dance to a love song, when I'm checking my e-mail, I think about you. When I go to sleep in the loneliness of my room and give in to wonderful dreams I definitely think about you. I know in two weeks we will meet and spend our lives with each other. I have waited for someone like you, and now that I have found you, I will never let you go. I love you so much, Tess, and will always love you with all that I am. I will be online at 7AM. I hope we can talk then. Ti amo.

Amore. Davis

From: Tess

Sent: October 21, 2008 4:50:24 AM My Darling Davis,

I love you, I tried to e-mail you before I went to bed last night as I usually do, however my internet was down, and this morning I'm still trying to sign in to messenger it has been attempting for over ten minutes now, so I'm hoping that it will work at 7 AM, if I can't get signed in, I will phone you. I love talking with you, I could talk with you all day and night, we would never sleep . . . lol . . . between talking and making love, you never know you may need to go back to Accra for a rest, once you come home . . . lol Anyhow, I woke at 4 AM thinking of you, so I just had to check to see if you had e-mailed me and you had, you are wonderful, my kiss for the morning, how do you like my analogy regarding your e-mails, I hope that it is for sure only going to be another two weeks, but I also want you to think about what I mentioned about coming home and getting the money straightened out by using this next payment, if you can't get a hold of Giovanni. I think in the long run, it would be quicker to get the workers paid, and could they not continue working if you were not there, next week, I know that is a lot sooner than what you thought, but if Giovanni doesn't come through for some reason, do you have another option? I will also check my Visa before we chat at 7AM so I can hopefully tell you that the money is in and I can send it to you. I had better get back to sleep for a short time, I'm still not doing all that well, my head is now feeling like it is being hammered on from the inside out. I don't normally get headaches like this; I don't like this at all. I need some tender loving care . . .

I had better get going, I will talk with you soon . . . I love you so much Davis, you are my world . . . my everything . . . so do you sing and dance to love songs? I would love to sing and dance with you, arm in arm, we would waltz . . . love you . . . ti amo

Amore . . . Tess

From: Tess

Sent: October 21, 2008 10:05:13 PM My Darling Davis,

I love you Davis, it has been wonderful being able to talk with you on the phone and absolutely wonderful for me, that you took the time to meet me online, I know that it is busy for you today. And what you said about your family being most important to you, you absolutely make me feel so loved and so wonderful, thank you Davis. You do things that show me you love me, even at these great distances, and I love you, beyond what anyone can imagine, I hope you know just how much I love you, however I don't think you will realise it fully until we are in each other's arms and can literally feel the sensations . . . then you may discover that my love for you is beyond what you have ever known . . . I love you completely, it's so incredible that it even takes me by surprise . . . I wanted to say to you I love you, and I wanted to wish you a good night's sleep last night on the phone, I also wanted to tell you that I wanted to be lying next to you in your arms. I tried to get you on the phone several times after we got cut off, just to say I love you to you, but I couldn't get through . . . it was so nice hearing your voice Davis, I love the sound of your voice, so tell me do you sing? If not out in the living room/kitchen or car, do you sing in the shower? . . . maybe you would sing to me, with me (not that I can sing, but I don't let that stop me) one day maybe . . . I do sing in the shower . . . and in the car . . . that'll be a test to our love . . . lol. I'm feeling much better this evening. My headache—and I think fever finally went away this afternoon just after talking with you . . . I slept for a little bit, and I made a homemade vegetable soup for supper, and I made some cereal bars for Zoey's lunch tomorrow, so I had a little bit more energy tonight than what I have had in the last couple of days. I imagine tomorrow, (today) I will be going to work . . . I will check as soon as I get up or before I meet you online to see if the payment is in. I did check tonight and it is not there yet, and the guy I talked to tonight, told me not to be surprised if it's Thursday or Friday if it's coming from the States. I did tell him that it didn't take this long with the first payment, he said sometimes it does take longer—it all depends on when they process and how fast . . . I'm hoping that it will show up today . . . I will let you know as soon as I find out . . . I will probably call you right away, I want to wish you all the best today with your meeting. I hope all goes well and you can show them a couple of things, maybe they'll end up hiring you as a consultant and pay you . . . wouldn't that be good ?. I should get going, my eyes are getting heavy, I need to get some sleep, even though I've slept today I still feel tired. I'm going to take my vitamin Cs, lay my head down, close my eyes and dream of you holding me in your arms, my head, resting against your chest, my hand caressing you, stroking you . . . you bending your head towards mine and kissing the top of it, complete comfort, that is what I will feel with you . . .complete . . . I love you my darling, I love you so much . . . I will see you soon, but before that I will be online at 7 AM, hoping that you may meet me . . . I will be constantly checking my computer . . . in case you are able to get online, I won't call until later just in case you are still in the meeting. If you are out and unable to get online, please phone me if you can get through, that would be great, otherwise I will just keep watching for you, I will have to leave here to go to work and drop Zoey off at around 8:20—8:25 AM . . . I should say goodnight now, when you read this I will be dreaming of you . . . love you . . . ti amo

Amore. Tess

From: Davis

Sent: October 22, 2008 12:31:30 AM Good morning My Love,

It was so wonderful talking with you online and on the phone last night and all the time. I had a good sleep, with you in my dream. I don't have much doing today, I am waiting for Mr. W and the driver to pick me up to the lawyer's place. We have something to talk about before the meeting. I will keep you informed as to whatever goes on in the meeting, and will meet you online at 7 AM. I wish I didn't have to miss you. If only you could be with me always. I know I could never be any happier. But then again, I know that the day will come soon when I will be able to spend my every waking moment with you. I even miss you when I am sleeping. I love you, Tess. You are my first and my only love, and I thank you for being so kind with my heart. Hopefully, soon I won't have to hate missing you. From the very first moment I met you on eharmony, I knew that we were destined to be together. It has been so long since a woman has captured my attention so fully or made my heart beat the way it did that cool day. Your smile in the picture lights up my entire spirit. Your laughter in the phone fills me with joy, and your mere presence will warm any room. I have no doubt you are the woman Heaven has made especially for me. Thank you for the comfortable conversations and for asking me to be yours. Most importantly, thank you for sharing your love and wanting to make me your husband. Vowing to be your partner for life would be the easiest decision I could have ever made.

Each day that passes makes our love for each other grow stronger. Although I know it's hard for us to be apart, I know there is nothing that can keep us apart forever. Our desires will continue to stretch across any distance, over every mountain and ocean between us. Nothing can stand between us, and nothing will stop me from meeting you. You are my future and nothing can ever keep us from our destiny. I miss you

more every day. I am here with open arms where you will soon finally belong. Right where you always belong. I love you so much, ti amo. Amore . . . Davis

From: Tess

Sent: October 22, 2008 7:30:53 AM My Darling Davis,

You take my breath away, you fill me so completely Davis, what you write to me, what you tell me from your heart and how you feel, it overwhelms me at times, yet your words, your feelings wrap around me and hold me . . . I love you so much Davis, I know that soon, we will be in each other's arms and we will both be where we belong. I hope you are able to meet me this morning, I will wait for you to come online, I will be doing a few things so if you should come online, and I don't reply right away, just give me a couple of minutes as I will be checking every two minutes or so, non the less, I will be waiting, if for some reason you're not finished with the meeting, and we can't meet online then please try to call me that is if you have any luck with the phone I will have my cell phone on me all day long. I also wanted to let you know that I checked with Visa again, before coming online and there is no payment pending. She said to check after midnight tonight, as any payment coming in today will be posted after midnight. So I'll call around 3 this afternoon, and again around 7 PM. If it doesn't come today, then I will call Giovanni, or would it be better for you to call him? Anyhow, Visa suggested asking him if he can check with the bank that he sent it through to see when they sent the payment out as the bank it was made from might not have sent it when he made it. And they were asking me, how he made the payment, by cheque, money wire, or cash.since that will make a difference. Let me know my dear, as to what you would like me to do. I would prefer not to call Giovanni from work, as there will be a lot of people in and out of office today, so I would have to call him this evening. I will check my e-mail throughout the day. I wish I had Messenger on my work computer so I could talk with you; however that would never be allowed. Facebook is banned from our work place, so Messenger would also be outlawed . . . Well it is 7:20, I hope everything is going well for you with the meeting; I'm very interested to hear about it from you . . . to see if there are going to be changes made . . . and what. I have Zoey in the bathtub, I should check on her, she has been in there for the last half hour, she loves the water, my little one. I love you with all of my heart, with all of my being. I know that the decision I made, to be your wife, has been one of the biggest decisions I have ever made, even at not seeing you or touching you physically, but wait, you still have to ask me, and for that you have to see me. You are the best decision I have made, all my belief, trust, hope and faith, that I have in the word Love, as well as the strength that comes with the word Love, I have in you, I believe in you Davis, I trust you, I have faith in you, in us, and I know that the strength that our love has and will continue as we grow with our love. We will both forever be loved by each other, I can promise you that. I love you ti amo.

Amore . . . Tess

From: Davis

Sent: October 22, 2008 8:43:32 AM My Love,

I just want you to know I LOVE YOU SO MUCH. I am going to rest for a while and will call you and send you mails when I am awake. Take care, have a nice day, and know I cherish, care and love you so much and MORE. Ti amo.

From: Tess

Sent: October 22, 2008 11:30:55 AM My Darling Davis,

I can't stop thinking about you . . . my mind has been doing nothing but wandering to what you would have done to me this morning . . . oh my god, Davis, this is really bad . . . what you do to me, or what I imagine you would do to me, the only way to make this stop is for you to really do to me what I think you're going to do to me . . . see, it's so bad. It's good . . . I have to go . . . I love you so much . . . ti amo . . .

Amore. Tess

From: Davis

Sent: October 22, 2008 Hi My Love,

I too can't stop thinking about you and how wonderful it would have made us felt if we were able to continue with what we were imagining this morning. I wouldn't say nothing till we are able to talk continue from where we left. I love you so much. While I was resting this afternoon, I dreamt about us again, it was so wonderful. We did so many wonderful things together. Things I really look forward to in doing with you when we are together soon. I love you so much and my love for you can only grow stronger and stronger forever. You are the best thing to ever happen to me. I need nothing more than your LOVE, I need to feel your touch, to kiss you and make passionate love to you. If you were here right now, I would have taken off your dress, and lick you right from your neck to your feet. Then I would suck your breast and Mmmmmmmmmm, will talk about what would have happen later. I want you so badly, I LOVE YOU TESS, and can only love you forever.

Honey, you have changed my life completely. You are the one who makes me beautiful. You are the one who makes me strong. You are the one who makes me feel so important, you are everything to me. You show your love to me everyday. I thank God that I have found a woman like you. Please forgive me for not giving you enough time to chat with me sometime, but I promise I will make up for it once we are together. All that I can offer you is true love to you and our family. I can offer you a family that will stick together through the good and the bad. I can offer you a family that will support each other everyday. Darling, that is part of so many wonderful things I can give, and know that is the most important part of life . . . FAMILY FIRST. I really wish that you were near me. I wish that I could just call your name when I needed you and that you would be there. However, knowing that you love me so much is enough for now, and if I can be your husband and a father to your children, then I would wait forever to be with you. Ti amo tesoro mio, meaning I love you my treasure. You are the only one that I want. I hope work is treating you well. I will try calling, if I am not about to get through, I will come here again to send you a goodnight mail before I go to bed. I love you, ti amo.

Amore . . . Davis

From: Tess

Sent: October 22, 2008 1:44:43 PM My Darling Davis,

I'm quivering from just reading your e-mail, I know your touch is going to completely have me lost in you . . . Oh Davis, I can't write a lot right now, I have to go and do an interview I should be done around 3:00 with my interviews. If there is any chance you can get through to me, please call. I love hearing your voice, you are an amazing, wonderful man and I'm so glad you want to be with me. I think I would die if I were to ever lose you . . . I want you so bad Davis, I want you to be a part of our lives and a part of me . . . I have to get going . . . you are going to have to teach me Italian, I want to learn Italian. I can see it is a beautiful language; you will also have to teach Zoey. I do look forward to hearing from you, please let me know if we can meet online, and if possible sooner than 7 I can meet you sooner, even if it's at midnight or if it works for you, before you have to start your day . . . I love you Davis, so much, I do have to run. until later. ti amo

Amore Tess

I love being your little treasure . . . thank you . . . Love you with all of my heart

From: Davis

Sent: October 22, 2008 3:50:21 PM My Love,

I have been trying to get you on the phone, but I have had no luck. I am lucky the cafe attender realised how important my family means to me and give me this charge to mail you just to say goodnight and let you know I Love You so much. The more I think about you, the more I know I have made the right choice. I once told you that if you really loved someone, then everything would work out just fine . . .

that if our love was strong we could make it through anything. I have realized that is what true love is all about. I want you to know that while I am gone I will be completely faithful to you. You will NEVER have to worry about that. You have completely taken my heart. It's funny, because I told myself I would never fall in love again. Yet when I was least expecting it I fell the hardest. I have finally found my partner. No matter what we may face, I will NEVER give up on our love. I know that God brought us together. No doubt about it, we were just meant to be. I love you, I will love you forever. I will try to be online at 11 PM or 12 midnight so we can talk before I leave to the mines to meet the workers. I love you so much. Ti amo. Good Night.

Amore . . . Davis

From: Tess

Sent: October 22, 2008 10:52:33 PM My Darling Davis,

I love you so much, I can't express it or say it enough to give the absolute complete realm of what it is that I feel, and how I feel. You take over my every thought, my every move, my every sense of being, you are a part of me, and it is that that I feel, the whole complete sense of the love that we share. I have never felt this before, this wonderful feeling of knowing that you love me as I love you . . . there is no question, no wondering, it is wonderful. And Davis I want you to know as well, that when you're away, you will never have to worry about me. I will be completely faithful to you, I would never be with any other man, I want only you that is a promise that I make to you. My Love for you is very real, very strong, I would never jeopardize or break what we have, because what we have and what we share is very rarely found, so what we have, we must cherish . . . and that I promise you, I will do . . . I love you . . . I called Visa, and if we've met online before you've had a chance to read this you will already know that there is a payment made on my Visa account for around 10, 500.00. I will send you money so that you get it at 5:00 PM, I will contact Visa to ensure that I can access it in the morning. I will also send one payment to you and one to Mr W, so that I can send you more at one time, and again I need to make sure I can do that, I should be able to as it is two separate people, if not I will have to do one tomorrow and then send another in the evening, I will let you know . . . I will probably be able to only send 11, 000.00, as there was only 10, 800.00 put into the account, but then there should be another 4000 coming which may arrive Friday. Can you please call Giovanni and let him know that the ten thousand has arrived, and hopefully he is able to do a wire transfer or bank draft. Now enough with Giovanni, I hope to meet you online shortly, I love talking with you, today I was talking with a very special lady that I used to work with. She is a wonderful person and she was asking me how things were going, I of course, have told her about you, she thinks what we share is very romantic and very special; and while we were talking I told her that the only way we have to communicate right now is by talking, either on the phone, or online, and through our e-mails. She told me that she immediately thought, well isn't that the only way, and then she said she realized that no, there are so many different ways, through touch, through sight, through body language, and that us sharing ourselves first by the talking, the writing that we are doing now, will allow us to blossom when we are able to explore our other forms of communicating when we meet, but for right now, we are growing and building a very good strong foundation, My friend, her name is Rose, she is a very kind soul and she wished the best for the both of us. She said I deserve to be happy, and I totally agree with her. I think Davis that both of us deserve to be happy you and I, together . . . I had better go now, and see if you're online. I love you so much . . . I hope to be talking with you soon. ti amo

Amore. Tess

*Davis and I met on MSN messenger and during our conversation, I asked Davis if he would help me to get undressed. And no, there was no webcam. I asked him to tell me what piece of clothing he would like me to remove and I would describe what I was doing and how I was removing it. we were right in the middle of things, I was down to my panties and bra being the only items of clothing that I had left to remove and the internet was disconnected. just at the good part too.*

From: Tess

Sent: October 23, 2008 1:35:30 AM My Darling Davis,

I have this feeling that the only way I am going to be able to get naked around you, and you naked around me, will be when we are both standing in front of each other . . . I was so enjoying you helping me to get undressed, we'll have to try this again sometime, oh Davis, I tried to call you back, but I couldn't even get through to the calling card number. I guess I will have to go to bed frustrated and yet happy that I was able to talk with you and hear you say to me You Love Me, before

I go to bed. Davis I want you to make love to me, I want to feel you, I think about you touching me, feeling me, kissing me, entering me, loving me, passionately. Sometimes I close my eyes, and it's as if I can feel you . . . I know I've told you this before, but I often wonder, that when I have this sensation of feeling you, if you're thinking about me and feeling me at the same time . . . Oh Davis, I wish we could close our eyes and meet in a dream that we would both know that we have met there . . . does that make sense, better yet, I wish for us to meet real soon in person . . . and I know that is one wish you will grant me . . . I love you . . . so much . . .

I am now going to take off my bra, I slip the straps over my shoulders and then I reach around the back and undo the clasp and as I remove my bra, my hands feel my breasts, I imagine your hands, my breasts aren't very big, somewhat on the small side, they would rest in the palm of your hand. I feel my breast resting in the palm of my hand, my breasts are soft, I take my finger and my thumb and I gently rub my nipple, imaging you doing so, I then caress my other breast, again, I'm thinking of you, touching me, and here, this is where I need to stop, for I need you to help me continue. I want to do this with you . . . Davis . . . I love you . . . It's almost 1:30AM, I have to go to bed, I will talk with you tomorrow. I will try and call you with the confirmation number as soon as I send the money, again if I can't get through, I will e-mail Mr. W. Do you want me to send it to you as well, or just to Mr. W.? I know you said you would be at the mines . . . and it was 10, 800.00 that Giovanni sent. I should get going to bed now and dream of you. I wish we had better connections, but hearing you, being able to talk with you, fills me, we will try again, okay . . . hopefully we will have better luck staying connected . . . Davis . . . I love you . . . have a great day . . . know I am with you. I will talk with you soon . . . ti amo

Amore . . . Tess

From: Davis

Sent: October 23, 2008 2:48:17 AM My Love,

This whole disconnection thing is soo frustrating. I wish we could continue from where we left off, and surely know we could sometime soon. I love you so much Tess, you are my world and my everything. I am here to stay forever, and to love you the BEST way I can. As I read your e-mail, I felt your breast in my palm, I felt the softness of it, and wanted to make passionate love to you right away. I love you more than words can say. My heart will always belong to you. My love for you stands as strong today as it ever has. It hurts to be far away in a place filled with heartless violent people. I miss you more and more every day. In everything you do, just remember one thing: I will always love you deep in my heart. Ti amo. Amore . . . Davis

From: Davis

Sent: October 23, 2008 2:49:50 AM

Forgot to tell you I will meet you online at 7 AM. I love you so much.

Ti amo.

From: Davis

Sent: October 23, 2008 7:10:50 AM Hi Love,

I hope you are awake by now, and had a good sleep. I will meet you online soon, but want you to do something very important for me. I will brief you more when we meet online Okay. I had a call about 20 minutes ago; it was about the meeting with the committee. It's coming on tomorrow. According to the lawyer, we will need at least part—payment before they will allow us to continue work. Looking at things now, I don't think Giovanni will be able to get us the kind of money we will need if he still sends this little amount. So I want you to call him and tell him your acct:: has been blocked and you have been asked to come to the bank this morning, but you don't want me to know about your acct:: being blocked because you know I really need the money so badly. So what you and him do about it is right. Whatever happens, he will call me to tell me, and I will pressure him to do the draft to you before Monday. By that doing, I can get the amount of money I need and can come home soon to you. I love you so much and going to sign in to MSN now. We will talk more about this. Ti amo.

Amore . . . Davis

From: Tess

Sent: October 23, 2008 10:47:05 AM My Darling Davis,

Hello my darling . . . What I was trying to tell you on the phone, is that I talked with the First Bank and asked them about someone sending me either a bank draft or a wire and how long that would take to process. Both would take approx five business days, as they are

243

coming from the States. They still have to be verified, I'm going to call the Canadian Bank to see if it's any faster.

Canadian Bank with a wire can take up to 1-3 business days, the one lady told me if it was done on Friday the funds should be in my acct:: on Monday. There is coding that Giovanni would need that I have:

SWIFT CODE—########### (that is for the Canadian Bank) and if in US funds Routing number is #########

Transit number for my bank is 0000010 acct: 0010010 Whse YT Y1A 0I0

I hope he can do this, today Davis, this would solve so many things for you, but it needs to go through the Canadian Bank as the other bank is, what's the word . . . ridiculously slow . . .

I will talk with you soon, I Love You so Much ti amo. Amore . . . Tess

From: Tess

Sent: October 23, 2008 10:18:03 AM Hello Mr Warleh

I have the control number for you, 670-674-7777, and again the security word is my daughter's name, thank you again, I will be writing you again later . . .take care

Tess

# 10

## CONNIVING MEN

From: Davis

Sent: October 23, 2008 3:23:30 PM Hi My Love,

I just got back to Accra, and as usual will do anything to let you know what happened. I am with Mr W, and I have the money. So you can send the rest anytime today. I want you to also call Giovanni. Tell him that you had a call from the bank that your acct:: has been blocked and you should come over, but you were not able to go because you had a call to be at the hospital. And you will go first thing tomorrow. Tell him you don't want me to know because you know I need the money so badly and I will break down if I hear about this. But you will let him know what happens when you go to the bank tomorrow. If he asks you any question, tell him you don't know what is going on till you go to the bank tomorrow morning. I will meet you online at 11 PM. And don't let him know the transfer is in. He will then call me to inform me, and I will pressure him to do the draft tomorrow when I talk to him. I am so grateful for everything, you have really shown me how family should live and understand each other and also do things together. As the day fades away and slips into night, I find myself once again clinging to my prayers. Every night I pray to God that he will keep you in his arms. I pray that he keeps you out of harm's way until we can finally be together again. Just because we will not be able to see each other doesn't mean we have to give up hope. If you really love someone, the time and distance apart should not make a difference. I love you, so you have my answer. I feel the same way you do. I love you Tess. I have loved you from day one, and I don't think I am going to stop loving you anytime soon. I will meet you online at 11PM, and let me have the confirmation number so I would have Mr W pick the money. Talk to you soon. I love you so much. Ti amo.

Amore . . . Davis

From: Tess

Sent: October 23, 2008 4:29:18 PM Hello Giovanni,

Here is the information that the Canadian Bank provided for me, to send a wire transfer. The lady I talked with told me that if the money is sent Friday it could be in my account on Monday. Davis is meeting the committee tomorrow and requires this money immediately, I appreciate you doing this, I really need to get this money to Davis, And I will let you know as soon as I hear from Visa regarding the payment.

Thank you Tess

I sent Giovanni all the account information that he needed to wire money to my account.

From: Tess

Sent: October 23, 2008 4:49:20 PM Davis, My Darling,

I finally got hold of Giovanni, I talked with him and stressed the wire transfer, as you can see he gave me his e-mail to send him the info, Davis, I could not tell him anything about the hosp, I'm not good at telling untruths, I get very uncomfortable, it's not in my nature. I did tell him that the payment was not there and that I had to go to the bank to clear things up, and that this was ridiculous and that I was very concerned about you and that I didn't want to tell you, I told him again you need the money NOW, that was not untrue, the 4000 payment is not in, I do know how to bend the truth. Anyhow, I stressed my case with a quiver in my voice, female traits, and he said he would forward this info to his banker and see what he could do. I told him if he does it tomorrow I could have the money by Monday, I hope this works . . . I told him as you will see that I will call him and let him know that Visa payment came in, which I will do tomorrow afternoon or once the 4000 comes through. And then I will talk to him again about the wire transfer.

I will meet you online at 11PM and I will give you the confirmation code at that time as well. If I don't' see you; I will call you to see if you are able to get on or not. I love you Davis, so much . . . I have been thinking about you all day, wondering how things went with the workers, I do get concerned about you, I know you are under a lot of stress with these money issues, but I do know and I believe that Giovanni will get things settled tomorrow. I will push him okay, and or if he calls you . . . he needs to do this, and he sounded like he would. I believe it will work . . . I have to get going I have to leave work and get to Western Union to send you the other transfer. I have tried to call you several times today, I started with a ten dollar card, I believe we talked for that short brief time, once and I am now down to five dollars, even when there was no answer, I was charged . . . oh Davis, I just keep thinking SOON . . . you will be home soon and we can fix this . . . so that you will not have to deal with this type of stress again when you have to go away . . . okay . . . I have to run. I will talk with you later, maybe we will get lucky tonight and you can help me get completely undressed and dressed for bed . . .

Until we talk again . . . I Love you . . . ti amo

Amore. Tess

From: Giovanni Ortona

Sent: October 23, 2008 10:06:11 PM Hi Tess,

I got the information and has given instructions to my account officer, he will know how to work out the wire transfer to your bank as soon as possible.Please try get the 10, 800 CAD already available in your credit card and send to Ghana today, I will be greatly encouraged if you achieve that today.Keep me informed as soon as it's done to enable us move further.Thank you and God bless you

Giovanni Ortona

From: Tess

Sent: October 23, 2008 10:53:34 PM My Darling Davis,

I wish I could be with you right now, I am so tired, I feel like I would love to just put my head on your chest, close my eyes and be comforted by the sound of your heart beat, and your breathing, I now know why I was feeling so bad on Monday and Tuesday and it wasn't because I was sick . . . oh no. These thing cause great exhaustion   at times, men are so lucky . . . anyhow, business first before I fool around with you . . . I'm forwarding you the response I got from Giovanni, I almost feel like he is telling me, to make sure I get the funds before he sends anything else, such as a wire. I could be reading this wrong . . . but I am asking you what you think I should do, call him in the morning and tell him that the one transfer is in, for the 10, 000.00 but not the 4, 000. It does sound like he will do the wire, let me know what you would like me to do, I would prefer for him to know that the money is in, but that I don't want it to go through my Visa anymore . . . mind you . . . today the teller, never asked me questions, and they never phoned Visa like the other guy did the first time I went in, and everything was smooth . . . but it's the time that it is taking, I don't like it, I would prefer to tell him not to do the Visa or I could tell him that I have placed a lot of security features on my account which I have, because of that, they are calling me about any transaction done on my account. It is probably the movement on my account lately that Visa is asking me to verify myself all the time. Bottom line is, I will tell him not to go through my Visa anymore, and to just do the wire. Does that sound okay with you? I would be comfortable with that. What would you advise? And you can tell me when we're online together, Now, I'm hoping to be talking with you right about now, so I won't write too much more right now, I did want to forward this to you though . . . and I wanted to tell you I love you, in writing, my kiss for your day . . . I hope all goes well at the meeting today. I will be with you, my thoughts, my heart, my love, my soul, are all with you Davis . . . I had better sign in I don't want to miss you . . . I will wait until 11:30. If I don't hear from you I'm calling you on the phone . . . If you get this, and it doesn't seem like I'm online, please try to call me . . . I Love you. ti amo

Amore . . . Tess

*I emailed Davis the previous message from Giovanni. In fact I forwarded all the e-mails that I received from Giovanni to Davis so that he would know what was being sent to me.*

From: Tess

Sent: October 23, 2008 11:38:12 PM My Darling Davis,

If you should happen to come online and not see me, I had to sign out and I'm trying to sign back in again to Messenger, please wait for me, it's 11:36, I am tired, but I will wait another half hour to an hour to hopefully catch you online, I'm also trying to call you but obviously with no luck, the phone is ringing however, I don't know if you're hearing it, or even if it's getting through to you . . . I hope we can talk soon . . . I Love you . . . ti amo

Amore . . . Tess

From: Tess

Sent: October 24, 2008 12:03:00 AM My Darling Davis,

I'm still trying to get connected to Messenger, I'm just sending this quickly just in case you are sitting there waiting for me . . . I will try some more to get online, if I can't I will e-mail you the confirmation number . . . I love you . . . ti amo

Amore. Tess

From: Davis

Sent: October 24, 2008 12:06:27 AM My Love,

I am online, but can't find you. I will wait for a while. I hope your day went well. If you were able to send the rest of the money, please let me have the confirmation number, so I can have Mr W pick it up this morning. I want him to go to the mines this morning and do the payment while I go for the meeting. I am not going to be able to do all the payment, but I an going to pay what I have for now.

Secondly, I am going to take care of Giovanni. Don't let him know the money is in, and please let him know your visa acct:: has been blocked, and you don't know why, and the bank called you to come there in the morning. Once you are able to tell him that, I will be able to attack him and pressure him to do the transfer. I can see you are online now, so we will talk there now. I love you so much. Ti amo.

Amore . . . Davis

From: Tess

Sent: October 24, 2008 1:14:21 AM My Darling Davis,

I have tried calling you several times with no luck, I am finding my eyes are starting to close, I'm afraid that if I let them close I will fall asleep and I will miss you coming back online, then I realized that you may not be able to get back online for a while, it could be a short time, but my eyes are starting to close so I think I need to go to bed, and get some sleep. I don't want to have these bags under my eyes when you come home and see me for the first time . . . so I will go to bed now. I will dream about you, as I always do, I will dream about watching you walk towards me and me wrapping my arms around your neck and you holding me so close to you, and finally, being able to look into your eyes and feel your lips on mine as you kiss me, possess me . . . that is what I know I will dream about . . . Please let me know how things go today. I never got a chance to ask you as to what time the meeting was this morning, if you told me, I have forgotten. My memory is usually pretty good, I totally blame you for my head being in the clouds. Okay, it's getting hard to type, I have to go to bed now . . . I wish I could have talked with you more online, we will, I know. I never got to ask you if you will be able to meet me at 7 online, if you get a chance to please let me know, I usually wake around 6. I will check my e-mail then . . . I love you so much Davis, you are my everything . . . I wish I could take you to bed with me . . . lol . . . when I get tired I get frisky . . . did I ever tell you that? . . . until later. I Love you. ti amo

Amore . . . Tess

*I called Visa this morning to see if the $4, 000.00 payment that Giovanni said he had made was showing up on my account yet. The customer service clerk that I was talking to asked me if I had phoned the bank and to tell them that the payment made on my Visa was fraudulent. "Of course not" I asked her what was she talking about?*

*She explained to me that Visa had received a call from the bank the payment was being sent from and they had been told that the money used to make that payment was made with fraudulent funds. She told me that Visa would have to look into this and if it was fraudulent, then the funds would have to be returned to the bank and it would be taken from my Visa card. So if I had the money that I took off my card the day before, it would be best to return it until this got cleared up.*

*My stomach got that gripping sick feeling inside. I told her I didn't have the
funds, I had already sent the money to where it was supposed to go. I told
her that this had to be a mistake, a big mistake. I gave her Giovanni's name
and phone number so that they could contact him directly to clear things
up. I had to get a hold of Davis.*

*I tried calling Davis five times before I finally got through to him. "My
Account is on hold!"*

*A drawn out "Whaaat' was his response,*

*I told Davis what the lady at Visa had told me, I was quite upset, Davis
reassured me that he would contact Giovanni immediately, I had called
him during a meeting but he would step out and deal with this. then I
e-mailed Giovanni.*

*I didn't want to think that Davis had anything to do with this, I honestly
felt that Giovanni had called the bank himself and said that the funds were
fraudrlent. Why I thought this, I don't know. I didn't want to think it was
Davis so it was easier to think that it was someone else. Davis was the one
person who could fix this for me. At this time I was in complete denial.*

From: Tess

Sent: October 24, 2008 7:41:45 AM Giovanni,

The Bank contacted me, the money, the payment of 10, 800.00 that
you put onto my Visa, the bank said that is was fraudulent so they are
holding my acct:. Apparently, Visa received a call from the Financial
First Bank, where the payment was sent from and they were told by
the Financial First Bank that the payment is fraudulent . . . Giovanni,
what is going on, please. Giovanni, the funds were in my bank acct:
yesterday afternoon, so I pulled the funds off of my Visa late yesterday
afternoon, and sent it to Davis. I was going to write you this morning
about it and tell you that the one payment arrived and now, this . . .
What is happening? . . . My Visa account has been frozen, and I need
you to contact, your bank and clear this up please. Call me as soon as
you have done so, or e-mail me back, Visa will be getting back to me
sometime today.

Thank You Tess

From: Tess

Sent: October 24, 2008 8:00:00 AM My Darling Davis,

I am sorry I am upset this morning, I must sound frantic, I dont' like the words fraudulent and big money, involved in the same sentence . . . I e-mailed Giovanni, I told him that the payment was in, because I think this is his doing, because he probably called his bank and they verified that the funds were on my Visa so when I told him they weren't, he is thinking I'm pulling a fast one on him . . . this is what I'm thinking . . . I say this because the Financial First Bank, where the funds came from received a call stating that the funds were fraudulent. Visa was calling me asking me if I had called and stated that to the Financial First Bank, this is why I'm thinking it is Giovanni, at least I hope this is what it is. If it's a fraudulent payment, I want to know what is going on . . . because, I've taken that money now . . . I told the bank that the money was a business transaction for my finance ( I told them you were my fiancé) and that I sent the money to you already. Davis, please straighten this out with Giovanni. I don't want anymore activity on my Visa Period. Oh and are you psychic? Well at least I'm not going to have to tell him untruths anymore, as you suggested . . . I have to get going, I'm sorry but I'm upset right now, and I'm worried. Please call me when you can. Davis, I know you can fix this. I will check my e-mail from work, and please tell me how things went this morning, today . . . I love you. ti amo

Amore . . . Tess

From: Giovanni Ortona

Sent: October 24, 2008 10:08:51 AM Hi Tess,

You guys were trying to be very smart. You certainly had to refund all the money to the banks. Next time do not connive with evil men Giovanni Ortona

From: Tess (Tess)

Sent: October 24, 2008 10:40:13 AM Giovanni,

What is going on, did you do this? Giovanni, I think you have made a big mistake about me, I think you need to call Davis, and what do you mean about evil men . . . I would like for you to also call me and straighten this out with me . . . This is very wrong . . .

Tess

From: Tess

Sent: October 24, 2008 10:52:25 AM My Darling Davis,

This is the response I received from Giovanni, what in the hell is going on, Davis, we don't need this, he thinks we are tricking him, so please, you have to straighten this out. I have done nothing to deserve this type of treatment from him . . . Thank You for calling me . . .

I love you ti amo. Amore . . . Tess

I forwarded Giovanni's response to Davis, and just as I was doing so, Davis called me on the phone. I told him what I had just sent to him, I was so upset my voice was shaking. Davis sounded not only angry, but concerned about me and concerned about how I was doing. He told me that he would deal with Giovanni and that I would not have to talk to him again. He sounded so sincere, I felt I had no other choice then to believe him.

On 10/24/08,

Tess wrote:

My Darling Davis,

I am so upset, I am writing you because I want to write Giovanni again and tell him I want an apology from him and that he should be ashamed of himself . . . Davis, what is this man? . . .

I don't think you want me to write to him again, so I'm saying this to you, I want an apology from him. I'm not calling him a bastard yet, but it will come . . . what in the hell does he think you are doing? What does he think I am doing? I have a tendency to go on the attack when I'm being attacked and he is attacking me and I think threatening me as well, at least I feel a little bit of a threat there from him when I'm told not to connive with evil men . . . I don't like that . . . I am holding back on calling him or writing him anymore . . . but man I want to . . . so I'm venting to you . . . I know you will clear this up . . . I have payments coming out from my Visa that will not go through if it's not cleared up soon. One is my cell phone payment which comes out on the 26th of the month, this is not good . . . the bastard . . . does he think he is protecting you? Again I ask what in the hell does he think you and I are trying to pull, this is your money after all, is it not? I told him we received the money and I sent it to you. He seemed to get pleasure out of knowing that I am going to have to pay back the money to the bank. The bastard, I want to slap that smile off of his face . . . not literally, I've only punched one man ever in my life, and he deserved it . . . there was a mistress involved . . . anyhow I am upset, and I'm venting because I can't do it any other way. The only person I can talk to about this is you and I can only do this through e – mail . . . my fingers are flying over the keyboard . . . I need to take a deep breath, and know that you will talk with Giovanni, he needs to know that he can trust me, and that you are getting your money, this is just not right, Davis, please tell me that everything will be okay, I am so sorry that this has to happen, we don't need this, but we will deal with this, I will calm down and you will get in touch with Giovanni, and things will work . . . all things will work. I had better get going, I'm feeling calmer now, now that I have vented to you, I'm normally a calm reasonable person, but this is beyond reason for me . . . I had better go, please do call if you can, or e-mail me, let me know what is happening . . . I know you will . . . it's hard for me to sit still, I want to call, e-mail, confront, but I'm going to go about my work and wait for you . . . I Love you Davis . . . There you have now seen the mad side of me . . . this man has made me mad . . . I love you Davis, and I know you will do what you can. ti amo

Amore. Tess

I honestly believed that Giovanni was responsible for what was happening to my Visa. It was easier for me to have Giovanni responsible then it was to think that Davis was involved. I have to admit that I was in complete denial at this time.

From: Davis

Sent: October 24, 2008 1:38:37 PM My Darling,

I am sorry for everything. I apologise for all that he said to you. I spoke with him and he said he was the one who asked the bank to put a hold on your acct:. He said he did that because he didn't understand why you said you never had the money he sent. I am to be blamed, and very sorry.

He said he was going to call you and to clarify things, and will pay back the $20, 000 dollar. I am now going for dinner and will try calling you soon. I love you so much. Once again, I am very sorry. Ti amo.

Amore . . . Davis

From: Tess

Sent: October 24, 2008 3:09:10 PM My Darling Davis,

I forgot to mention in my other e-mail, that you will definitely have to make this one up to me, I think a massage by you, while you are naked . . .would be a good start . . . and there has to be oil involved and at least thirty minutes to start . . . I want you to know that, I understand why you asked me to tell him that, there is a lot of frustration and stress involved, and a lot of money. I don't' blame you, understand that . . . I have to run, I love you . . . ti amo

Amore . . . Tess

From: Giovanni Ortona

Sent: October 24, 2008 2:09:02 PM Hi Tess,

I am sorry if I have got you wrong but Davis never told me he got the money, I was believing that you got the money and never sent it to him as my account officer confirmed to me at the time you picked up the money from your card.I will talk to my bank and get everything straightened, please do not worry anymore about them as I am sure my bankers will make them to stop the freeze on your account. I will inform you as soon as the 50, 000 CAD is available in your bank account.

Thank you Giovanni Ortona

From: Tess

Sent: October 24, 2008 2:26:32 PM Giovanni,

Thank you for your apology, I can appreciate you having a concern regarding sending money to a stranger, and the amount of money you are dealing with adds an extra concern. We just received the money, yesterday, and I would never do anything to harm or hurt Davis in any manner, you can be assured of that. I must admit that this did upset me and I do appreciate that you said you will be clearing things up at the bank for me as they are going to have my bank account on hold for ten days or until this is cleared up. Again I accept your apology, and I hope that you feel like you can trust me now.

Sincerely Tess

From: Tess

Sent: October 24, 2008 2:51:26 PM My Darling Davis,

I will be looking forward to your phone call, my phone cards are almost all used up, I don't know if I even have enough minutes to call you. I will get another card on my way home this evening. I am sending you the e-mail Giovanni sent to me along with my response to him, thank you for clearing things up. I knew he was responsible for this, anyhow, I didn't blast him as he is a business associate of yours, again, thank you. I'm curious as to what you said to him . . . I love you, Davis, with all of my heart. I am taking Zoey to see a movie tonight and then I am hoping we may get a chance to meet online at 11:00 I don't' have to work tomorrow morning so we can hopefully have a chance to talk . . . I have to go so you can hopefully get this before the cafe closes . . . You are my Hero . . . I Love you so Much . . . ti amo

Amore . . . Tess

From: Tess

Sent: October 24, 2008 11:38:24 PM My Darling Davis,

It's 11:30, and I have been trying to call you I was hoping to wake you up and hear your voice. I am online, I'm hoping when you sign in, you will be able to see me. I want to talk with you so much, I miss you . . . I just need to talk with you, it was so wonderful being able to talk with you this evening, I know it was late for you, I'm wonder if you were still sleeping when I called, it's so hard to say if I'm actually getting through to you or not, these wonderful phones, anyhow, just in case you do come online. I'm sending you this e-mail, so you know I'm here, and I will wait for you, no matter how long it takes . . . I love you . . . ti amo.

Amore . . . Tess

From: Tess

Sent: October 25, 2008 12:21:19 AM My Darling Davis, My Love,

It is 12:18, I have had no luck getting you on the phone, and I'm not too sure if my messenger is freezing up on me or not, so I am signing out, and restarting my computer, this will take about fifteen to twenty minutes to do, so please if you come online before it's finished rebooting, please wait for me, give me at least until 12:50 just so I can get back online . . .

I love you and I hope to talk with you soon . . . ti amo Amore . . . Tess

From: Tess

Sent: October 25, 2008 12:44:15 AM My Darling Davis,

I'm back, I will be online, but please do Buzz me, as I may have my eyes closed . . . I will be waiting for you. It is right now 1242 . . . I send you a kiss to wish you Good morning . . . ti amo

Amore. Tess

I met Davis online. it was our first time and all I can say is. Wow.

From: Tess

Sent: October 25, 2008 3:49:56 AM My Darling Davis,

I am still breathing hard, and my heart is still pounding, all I can say right now, is Oh my god, I want you Davis, I want you so bad . . . you have turned me on and heated me up. I haven't so much as touched myself, since we've met, so what you did to me tonight felt so good. Oh Davis, I wish it was your hand, your fingers, your mouth, your tongue caressing me, and not just my hand, and my fingers, and I want to stroke you, taste you. I want to take you deep into my mouth, and feel your hardness against my mouth, in my mouth . . . you have opened up a door, which I want to go through with you . . . Oh Davis, thank you . . . Thank you for giving me a little bit of release, I want to come again, but I want to come with you . . . I was so hoping you would be able to come back online, I did want to ask you how things went at the ministry yesterday, but I never got the chance, so please do tell me . . . I'm still quivering Davis . . . Wow. How are you doing?

Our lovemaking is going to be amazing, I know it, oh Davis, this is just going to make things worse, you realize that, it just means you have to make sure you're home in a week's time, so we can feel each other and make love to each other, and do what we want to with each other . . . Oh Davis, I love you so much . . . I want you so much . . . I'm going to have to get to bed pretty soon, mind you I don't know how much sleep I'm going to get, I may have to touch myself some more, as these thoughts of what you've done to me are repeating themselves in my head, and I'm wet again. As I mentioned to you at one time, I love sex, and I'm going to love making love to you, and I will love having you make love to me . . . I hope you are a man who loves to make love anytime of the day . . . in fact I'm hoping that you are . . . Now see, you've unleashed the wanton woman in me and that is all I can think about right now. I don't think you're going to make it back online for a while, my eyes are starting to feel tired, I do need sleep. Today has been a very emotional day, and you have made my night extraordinary.

Oh Davis. I know you said you are going to meet the workers today at the mines, so I'm not too sure as to what time you will   be back in Accra. If you get a chance to e-mail me, please let me know if there will be a chance for us to meet online, and even if it's again at midnight Saturday night, I would love to meet you . . .

You completely turn me on, you fill me in every possible thought, in every possible emotion, in every part of my being, I love you . . . I should get going to bed now, I am going to lie in my bed, naked with thoughts of you beside me, caressing me . . . touching me . . . I will be doing to myself, what I imagine you would do to me . . . oh yes . . . I will talk to you later . . . I Love You . . . and Davis, Thank You. ti amo

Amore . . . Tess

From: Tess

Sent: October 25, 2008 9:22:37 AM My Darling Davis,

I love you, I was wondering if you were able to get connected last night. After we were disconnected the timing of these disconnections is just not nice . . . I have a feeling that you weren't able to connect either . . . I do hope that I will be able to meet you later today, I will continue to check my e-mails . . . I wanted to let you know that I called Aeroplan regarding my points, and the flight is booked right online through their website, you can use the points from London, there is a flight on

Nov 1st. It leaves London at 12:05 and arrives Van 3:05 and then you can go Van to Whse, not too sure what the timings are for that flight out of Van, anyhow, it requires 60, 000 points, which I don't have, but I have 35, 000.00 and they require for you to only have half and you can purchase the rest of the points, so saying that, it would cost from Lon to Whse, $784.07.Davis, I can book this for you right online, the only flight arrangements you would have to make is from Accra to London. If you are in agreement, if my Visa account gets cleared up I could book this online for you or you could do it yourself as well . . . which ever . . . I don't know how much it costs from Accra to London. The only thing is, that you have to fly Air Canada, are you okay with that? Anyhow let me know if you would like me to do this for you . . .I love you Davis so much . . . I will hopefully talk with you later . . . ti amo.

Amore . . . Tess

From: Davis

Sent: October 25, 2008 10:12:55 AM My darling Tess,

Oh how I wished I was there in person to make love to you, I really felt your presence, and felt the closeness. I love you so much. You are so wonderful. The truth is that I have not done this for a very long time, and this was my first time of making love online. I am glad I did it with you, and will only do this with you. I will love to make love to you anytime. I love you so much.

I will be leaving for the mines right after this mail. I hope to meet you online when I get to the hotel, and will try calling. Let me know if you have a webcam. We can have the chance to see each other while we make love again if we have the chance. I love you with all my heart, you make the best out of me. I knew from the first day, you were the one I would spend forever with. You took my heart in just a second, and put a smile on my face. That smile follows me everywhere I go. I am so happy I have you in my life. I couldn't ask for anything else in this entire world—'cause, baby, I found all I have ever wanted or needed in you! The times . . . we shared together talking on phone or online are times I will always cherish. I am looking forward to all the times we will have in the future. I love you lots, you are my queen. my sweet love.

I know it has been hard for you to be alone there, but remember one thing . . . Sweetie, I am always here, and there, in your heart. Think of me and my warmth will be the blanket for you to sleep tight in the night. Look to the sky at night, and when you see a sparkle of a very shining star, that's me, love, thinking of how much I love you and miss you. Look to the moon, thousands of miles away from you . . . I will be looking at the moon too—thinking of you. I am struggling a lot here, through thick and thin, but I am doing fine so don't worry—you live in me and will always.

In your deep eyes I fell in love, victimized by the spell your eyes shows and I am trapped in you. Please don't ever let me go—as our love starts at forever and ends at never. I love you so much. Talk to you soon, ti amo.

Amore . . . Davis

From: Davis

Sent: October 25, 2008 10:17:57 AM My Love,

Again, I guess we were mailing each other at the same time. we will talk more about this later. I Love You. Ti amo.

Amore . . . Davis

From: Tess

Sent: October 25, 2008 9:35:38 PM My Darling Davis,

I love you so much, I miss not being able to chat with you online this afternoon, (last night), I tried to call several times and the one time I heard you answer, the phone cut out almost immediately and then I couldn't get through to you. I finally figured that at 6 PM which would have been 1AM your time, you were not going to be getting online . . . I'm hoping that you will be able to get on this morning, your morning. I'm going to be going out this evening, my neighbour, called me this evening and asked if I wanted to go to Lizards bar, there is a musician there Harry somebody, who plays blues, jazz, soul, and a little bit of rock and roll . . . so we are going out around 10 PM and we will be back home around midnight, so I am going to check online just as soon as I get home . . . Oh and Davis, I do have a web cam . . . Do you have access to a web cam as well? . . . Anyhow I will call you if I don't see you around 1:00 . . . I love you so much Davis, It hurts sometimes, missing you, wanting you . . . there comes a time when I'm going to need to touch you . . . to feel you, I want to be with you for the rest of eternity, I don't know how many more lives I'm going to go through, but I want you in each and every one of them.

Davis, there are so many things I want to ask you, so many things I want to find out about you, learn about you, I want you to know that what you did, the way you did it, telling me what you wanted me to do . . . I want you to know that, that turns me on, and completely excites me. There are so many things I want to be able to do with you and to you, and I think that both you and I, (the sense that I am getting from you), is that we were made for each other . . . I am going to enjoy learning everything about you . . . and introducing you back into the experiences that you haven't had for a very long time . . . Oh Davis . . . I had better get going, I need to change and get ready to go, I think I'm going to wear my jeans with a leopard camisole, and my black blazer over top of it, with black shoes . . . know that while I am out, I will dance with my friend, and I will dance by myself and you will be the only man on my mind tonight. you are the only man I want . . . again as soon as I get back I will check online. I love you so much, I hope you slept well, I also want to find out what has been going on with you, the workers and the ministry committee. We still didn't get a chance to talk about what the outcome was of your meeting on Friday. I Love You My Dear . . . ti amo

Amore. Tess

From: Tess

Sent: October 26, 2008 12:15:22 AM My Darling Davis,

It's 12 ;10, and I've been back now for about a half of an hour, my messenger does not seem to want to work so I'm going to have to reboot my computer which could take about twenty minutes. If by chance you come online before 1 AM my time, please would you wait for me . . . I also tried my webcam and the Vista Beta version of Yahoo Messenger that I have does not support a webcam, so you can't see me and I cant see you, if my MSN messenger was running then it works on that. I'm so sorry, I was hoping that we could see each other . . . there is a solution to this, when you are here, before you go back, I can take my computer in and get it nuked and paved. I guess that is what it is called and then I can reload my msn, then we can do the webcam . . . I don't want to do it now because they will have to keep my computer for a couple of days and this is my only link to you . . . I'm going to shut my computer down now, please do wait for me and again if I haven't heard from you by 1AM I am calling you . . . I love you so much . . . ti amo

Amore. Tess

From: Tess

Sent: October 26, 2008 1:20:13 AM My Darling Davis,

It is now 1:15, I've tried to call so many times, and then some strange man answered this one time, I think the phone gets re—routed at times. Anyhow, I'm not able to get through to you and I'm not able to catch you online as I was hoping that I would . . . I'm starting to fall asleep now, so I had better go to bed, I miss you a lot . . . I love you very much. I guess I will wait for you to contact me somehow, and maybe you could let me know when we may possibly meet online, I have no idea if you're going to the mines today or if you're at the hotel . . . Again I will wait for you to contact me . . . I would really love to talk to you at some point and time. I have to go to sleep now . . . I will be dreaming of you . . . I Love you . . . if you can please call me, my cell is right next to me beside my bed . . . ti amo

Amore. Tess

From: Tess

Sent: October 26, 2008 2:42:59 PM My Darling Davis,

I guess the connection just didn't want to work this evening, I'm sitting here watching the time, and realizing that it is almost 9:30 PM, I am so hoping you're able to get online before the cafe closes, I will wait. If you're able to get on after 10:00 PM, you can call me, or e-mail me and I will check my e – mail regularly . . . I want to talk with you so bad . . . it was great talking with you this morning . . . I did go back to bed and I slept for a couple more hours, Zoey had crawled into my bed while I was talking with you and she was so nice and warm to cuddle up with, I slept for two hours, in a very nice deep sleep, you are in my thoughts before I go to sleep, you are in my dreams, and you are in my thoughts as soon as I wake . . . I keep picturing you here, with me . . . You just feel so right . . . the images of you feel so right . . .

I had a couple of things I wanted to talk to you about. I wanted     to talk to you on a very personal level . . . I do hope that we get a chance to talk . . . Let me know when you may be able to talk/chat with me

... again phone me if you can ... will you be going to the mines tomorrow? Can we meet online tomorrow morning at 7am ... or earlier if possible, I have to be at the workshop at 8:30 so I have to leave at 8AM tomorrow morning to drop Zoey off at school and get a coffee before going to the workshop.

I love you so much Davis ... I wish you could hold me right now, hold me and make love to me I hope to talk with you soon ... if not today tomorrow morning ... ti amo

Amore. Tess

From: Tess

Sent: October 26, 2008 4:56:13 PM My Darling Davis,

I was just missing you ... I am missing you, it is wonderful being able to chat with you but the time goes by so fast. One hour seems like twenty minutes if that ... at least we were able to have some time today to chat ... I Love You so Much Davis ... When you asked me about the airlines that I had checked, I told you I wasn't sure but I thought it was African airlines, that is not correct, it is Ghana International Airlines, and I looked into things a little further, just in case you would like to take this info to the agents, here is a flight suggestion:

Ghana International Airlines

Flight 101 leaves Accra Friday Oct 31 1140pm Arrives London Sat Nov 01 6:25 am

This flight also leaves Oct 29 and Nov 01. so then I checked out London to van and

Flight 85 Departs London 17:05 Nov 01

Arrives Vancouver 19:10

Flight 8449 Leaves Nov 01 22:10

Arrives Whitehorse and to the arms of the woman who loves you and will love you forever ... This is just a suggestion, and it gives me something to do as well ... Tomorrow I will be booking the first week of November off. I will talk to you sometime soon ... Oh I wish I could have given you a hug last night. I wish that we could have been in each other's arms and wrapped around each other for the night and I wish that I could have woken this morning and watched you while you slept, and just felt your love all around me and in me . . . I love you so much . . . Have a great day today . . . I will let you know as soon as I know that the money from Giovanni is in my acct:: . . . love you with all my heart. ti amo.

Amore . . . Tess

My main concern was getting money that I could send to Davis. I felt that if Davis were to come here, that he would be real, so I had to get him home.

From: Tess

Sent: October 27, 2008 12:02:42 AM My Darling Davis,

I'm just getting ready to go to bed, I was so happy that we were able to chat this afternoon, as I said in my previous e-mail, time with you goes by so fast . . . I really want to ask you about your picture, next time we're online I am going to ask you. You just have to promise me that you won't think I'm crazy . . .

This love that we share, that we have, just overwhelms me. I am praying that all will work out this week, everything has to work out . . . I am going to e-mail Giovanni and see if he has been able to take care of the payment regarding my Visa so they will take the hold off of my account . . . I also wanted to ask you, I am hoping that Giovanni has also put the $4, 000.00 onto my Visa. I am almost out of oil and I have to put it through on my credit card as I don't have an account with any of the oil companies which means I have to get a full tank and that is about $800.00, are you ok, if I keep 1000.00 on my Visa to pay for the oil. That is if Giovanni puts the $4000.00 on it. Anyhow, let me know. I ask because I know you need a lot of money and hopefully with the $50, 000.00, things will be okay . . . Oh also I forgot to ask you if you and the lawyer came up with anything about getting the money to you in a faster manner? I was also thinking, can I send a transfer in the lawyer's name as well that way I can send over, three payments of 6500, in the AM and three in the PM. I should be able to get you 29000.00 in one day, at least in my one day, two for you. Let me know and I will check with Western Union as well to make sure that I can transfer to three separate people in the same city. I have to get going to bed, I'm looking forward to going to bed with you . . . I feel so content in that thought . . . I will say goodnight to me and good morning to you . . . My dear . . . I love you . . . ti amo.

Amore. Tess

From: Tess

Sent: October 27, 2008 7:03:02 AM My Darling Davis,

I love you . . . I guess it's not good morning for you anymore, just for me now . . . I have to e-mail Giovanni and ask him if he can let me know as soon as he can verify that the wire has been put into my account. I hope he has the ability to text message, then I can excuse myself from this workshop for about an hour an get the transfers taken care of. I also phoned Visa, so far, no payment on my acct: and until there is a payment made my account is on hold and when a payment is made it will be on hold for ten business days or until the funds are verified. So. oh well . . . there is not much I can do right now . . . I just hope Giovanni will take care of things quickly. My main concern is filling my oil tank as it is going to be getting cold. I'm at a quarter of a tank so I should be okay for a couple more days but I need to do something before the weekend. It is not a good thing to run out of oil on a weekend, mind you if you were here I could use you to keep warm, we could stay in bed the whole weekend and create lots of body heat . . .now that opens up a lot of possibilities . . . and a wonderful image. . . .

My dear, I love you so much     I was hoping to see you online for a bit

this morning, but again we are at the mercy of the network connection. I wasn't able to ask you what you were doing today, so I have no idea if you will be able to meet me or not, I will just keep my line open and check my computer as I'm getting ready for work. I should get going, I have to get Zoey up and into a bath this morning     and make lunches

for her and me . . . I love you . . . I miss you . . . I want you     with

all my heart. I will talk to you soon ti amo

Amore. Tess

From: Tess

Sent: October 27, 2008 10:28:49 AM Hello Giovanni,

How are you doing? I was wondering if you were able to transfer the funds on Friday. I am in a workshop for the next two days so please could you e-mail me as well as text me on my phone (if you have the ability)to let me know when the funds have cleared. I would really appreciate that, as I need to get the money to Davis no later than Wednesday. Also I was wondering about the funds going onto my Visa, apparently it is going to take ten business days once funds are put on my card before the hold comes off, unless the funds can be verified before then.

Thank You

Tess again my phone number is 311-555-2121

From: Tess

Sent: October 27, 2008 12:52:33 PM My Darling Davis,

I'm sorry I don't have a lot of time to write, my computer again is taking so long to boot, anyhow, I sent you the copy of the e-mail I sent to Giovanni, whatever correspondence I do with him, I will address to you as well, so he knows that I am sending you the emails. I hope that helps, you may need to call him to make sure he has sent it already. I called the Canadian Bank and as of 12 noon, there has been no monies wired yet. If Giovanni could talk to his bank or he may already know, it is his bank that dictates how long the wire will take. I have to get going back to the workshop, it's interesting, I just wanted to write and tell you I have been thinking about you all morning, almost to the point where I realise I have no clue what the speaker was just talking about because I'm thinking of you . . . it's bad . . . so bad . . . I love you with all my heart, I will hopefully be able to talk with you later . . . I wish you were here . . . or I was there, with you. I have to run . . . Love you . . . ti amo

Amore . . . Tess

From: Davis

Sent: October 27, 2008 3:38:45 PM Hi My Love,

I hope your day is going well. I have been trying to send you a mail for over three hours now. I am so glad I am now able to do that. I spoke with Giovanni this evening, he said the hold has been lifted, and the transfer will there by end of the day today. I have to go now, the cafe is closing. I LOVE YOU SO MUCH and will forever love you with all that I am. I will try to be online 11 PM. If you are tired please go to bed. I will talk with you in the morning. Take care, I love you. Ti amo Amore . . . Davis

From: Tess

Sent: October 27, 2008 5:25:52 PM My Darling Davis,

I love you too . . . so much . . . it scares me at times. Actually I don't think scare is the right word, it overwhelms me, that's probably what it is, because I'm not scared of the love we share. I'm not scared of my love for you or your love for me, what scares me, is that I don't ever want to lose you . . . losing you scares me . . . Loving you . . . overwhelms and yet fills me and makes me feel so good inside, it's takes my breath away, you take my breath away, and I Thank God, everyday, for you being in our lives . . . I Love You . . . Now I will be online at 11:00, I will wait until midnight and of course you may have received a call from me. Anyhow, just to let you know I called the Canadian Bank and there is nothing posted there yet, but my branch was closed when I talked with the agent and he said that if a wire came through today, or this evening, it's my branch that will post it and they will only do that when they're open, so I will check again tomorrow morning. I can use my phone to check I don't have to go online so I will do that around 9 AM, the bank doesn't open until 9:30 but I do know that the tellers are there earlier, so by 9AM they should have things posted to my account. If it's not there tomorrow morning it could possibly show up during the day, and if Giovanni, checked with his bank and found out that it went through today, then it should be there . . . it will be there . . . Now on another note regarding my Visa, I just called and there is still a hold on it, however the customer service office is closed until tomorrow morning as well, so it's a matter of waiting to speak to anyone about whether or not a payment has been applied to my account, again this is The First Bank who seem to take longer than any other banking system . . . I have to get going; my neighbour has just stopped by. I will write later .

. . I love you so much . . . ti amo

Amore . . . Tess

From: Tess

Sent: October 27, 2008 11:09:36 PM My Darling Davis,

It's 11:00, I have phoned a few times, the phone rings but I don't know if it's ringing at your end. I imagine you would be up by now, 6 AM, I'm hoping you'll come online. I love talking with you; I wish we could talk longer on the phone. At times it seems when we get a good connection it's hard to have to say good bye . . . I love hearing your voice, my darling. I'm sitting here and my eyes are getting real tired, I'm tired, I'm going to go to bed, right now. I don't know if you'll come online or not, but I'm afraid sitting here, I'm going to fall asleep. Are you able to meet me at 7 AM? I get up around 5:30-6 AM and I check my e-mails at that time to see if you've e-mailed me, let me know if you can meet me . . . or if you can't meet me at 7 AM or sooner if possible before 6 AM. Call me, wake me, and I will meet you. I love you so much Davis, you are my dream . . . I'm hoping we can get a chance to meet online . . . I love you . . . ti amo

Amore. Tess

# 11

# GETTING IN TOUCH WITH JOHN

From: Davis

Sent: October 28, 2008 3:19:14 AM Good Morning My Darling,

The phone never rang at my end. I am sorry about that. I was trying to get online at that time, but had no luck. I am on my way to the mines, had to do a stop over just to tell you I LOVE YOU SO MUCH and FOREVER. I am sure the money should be in by end of the day tomorrow. I have up to tomorrow to pay for my flight. That is what is most important to me right now. I want you to get in touch with one John Sigman. Send him an e-mail telling him I am your husband, and out of town for now. I called you telling you there was some payment to be made to me by him, but since I am not around, I will want him to wire the money to you. His e-mail acct: is jsigman@yahoo.es. I want you to forward every e-mail you send to him to me and every e-mail you receive from him. I know you are my destiny. No body had ever captured my attention so fully or made my heart skip a beat the way you do to me. Your smile lit up everything around, your laughter on the phone is delightfully contagious and your mere thought warms my heart and soul. I have no doubt you are the woman God made especially for me. I want to thank you for everything you do for me. Thank you for waking just to talk with me. Most importantly, thank you for falling in love with me. I look for the day I stand before God and our family, vowing to be your partner for life. Each day that passes me by only makes my love for you grow stronger. Please remember my love for you knows no boundaries. It will continue to stretch across any ocean and over every grain of sand between us to get to you. I want to be your husband, you are my life. No war or distance can ever keep me from my destiny. I miss you so much and will be home soon, where I belong. I have to get going. We have two more hours to get to the mines. I will be online at 7 AM so we can talk for a while.    I love you so much, you are my everything. I will forever cherish you, and adore you. Ti amo.

Amore . . . Davis

From: Tess

Sent: October 28, 2008 4:00:34 AM Hello John,

Davis told me that you have monies to wire to him and being that he is not home right now, he has asked that you wire it to my account until he gets here. He did tell me that he talked to you about this. I am sending you the banking information that you require to send a wire to my account at the Canadian Bank. If you have any questions or concerns you can either e-mail me or call me, my cell phone number is 311-555-2121.

Thank You Tess

Again, I sent John my bank account information so he could do a wire transfer.

From: Tess

Sent: October 28, 2008 4:31:23 AM My Darling Davis,

Good morning, I Love You . . . I was awake just after 3 AM and   by the time my computer was up and running, I just missed you, I finally got online at 3:30, and as you can see, I sent the e-mail to John. Davis, more than anything, I want to be your wife, and you to be my husband, but please understand, that after what happened with Giovanni, I don't want a business partner of yours questioning me as to why I'm saying I'm your wife if he knows you're not married, that will just make people suspicious of me, I wasn't able to ask you, as to how well he knows you and if you had already mentioned that I was your wife? If you've told him I am your wife, that is fine, anyhow I didn't mention it in my e-mail to him . . . You are wonderful Davis, it means so much to me that you do take the time out of your trip to stop and e-mail

270

me, to let me know when you're going to be online, I love you, your consideration of me is so warming in my heart.

I am counting on the money being in today, Davis, and at the latest, tomorrow. It should only take 2-3 business days from the States for a wire, so it should be there . . . and again as soon as it is here, I will be calling my bank throughout the day, I will go and get the money transferred to you. Now in case I miss you at 7 AM, do you want me to send it to the lawyer as well? So that would be three money transfers of $6800.00 each. I guess I should get back to bed for another hour or so, I will be online at 7 AM . . . I love you so much Davis, and I know you will be here soon, nothing will keep us apart this time, you are going to come home to me, you are my destiny. I want to be with you, I want to be the one, who stands next to you, and says the words for all to hear, and for all eternity, I do, I do take this man to be my lawful wedded husband . . . to love for eternity and beyond . . . I love what you wrote the other day, my love for you starts at forever and ends at never . . . I love you Davis, with all my heart I love you . . . I'm going to go back to bed now and dream of you with me. . . .

oohhhh yes ti amo

Amore. Tess

Date: Tue, 28 Oct 2008 13:32:19

From: jsigman

Attn: Tess,

I am Mr. John Sigman of JS & Associates, attorney to the Finance company approached by your partner for a loan to help you finish your transaction and I have been mandated by my client to liaise with you as regard this matter.

It will interest you to know I have been briefed by your partner on what the loan is required for, so as soon as the fund is release to you I shall monitor the whole process to ensure the fund is used for the exact purpose it's meant for to be certain that my client's fund is safe.

Therefore, be informed that as soon as the fund is transferred into your account you shall send out the fund immediately through our company representative based on the agreement reached between Mr.

Davis and myself, so all relevant and important documents require to complete the transaction could be procured to enable him complete the transaction.

Furthermore, the loan attract a 20% interest upon maturity and the total fund plus interest must be paid paid back within 72 hours as soon as the transaction is completed, as these are part of the conditions by which the loan was granted. If this is agreeable by you, I shall commence the process and hopefully the fund would be in your account on or before this weekend. Feel free to call me on my direct line +447029876543, for any clarification and further information. Note: you would be required to reconfirm your details.

I am looking forward to your urgent response. Regards,

Mr. John Sigman.

While I was reading John's email, I got that gut wrenching, sick feeling in the pit of my stomach.

From: Tess

Sent: October 28, 2008 7:16:36 AM My Darling Davis,

I am not too sure what this is about, but it is not what I thought it was going to be. I thought you said that this money was owed to you . . . this sounds as if it's a loan and I'm to send it to you which I can't send that much money to you in seventy—two hours and I don't understand what this is . . .from the sounds of it, he is expecting me to send it to somebody else who will send it to you and I am responsible for it if it is not sent. I'm not comfortable with that, I would be willing to hold your money for you until you get home, and send you enough so you can get home if need be. Now, if this is a loan for you and you will be here on Sunday and you can get it on Monday, I am fine with that, but the way this sounds it says I'm responsible to pay it back . . . please tell me what is going on here. I'm shutting my computer down and I will be online soon then you can let me know what this is . . . ti amo

Amore. Tess

From: Tess

Sent: October 28, 2008 12:22:10 PM Hello Giovanni,

I don't know if you received my text message this morning or not, so I'm e-mailing you as well, I contacted the bank and the wire still has not come through as of 10 AM. I was wondering if you are able to track it and let me know where it is, I really need to get money to Davis tomorrow at the latest. I also contacted my Visa and they don't have any payment on my account as of yet. And the first payment you put on my account for $9, 620.00 is also being returned to your bank and I will have a debit of close to or over $30, 000.00 and it is slated to go to the collection agency soon, apparently. I am asking you to please fix this, please . . . Davis said that you had made the payment onto my visa, can you tell me when it was done and does it cover the $9620.00 as well. Please, could you get back to me today . . .

Thank You Tess

From: Tess

Sent: October 28, 2008 12:36:31 PM My Darling Davis,

I contacted the bank just now and they suggested that I contact the sender to do an investigation as the payment should be here by now, which I did, so please find out what is going on, ask Giovanni to please tell you where it is, and to fix my Visa, at least get him to tell you when he put the funds into my account as it will take 3-5 business days to go through. But, in the mean time, Visa said within the next couple of days it will be going to collections, Davis, I don't have money to cover this. I don't even have the equity in my house to take out a loan to cover this. If Giovanni doesn't come through, what do we do . . . I love you Davis, please get a hold of me, somehow, I am going to be in the workshop until 4:30, I am going to be having a break around 2:30 so maybe I can try you on my cell phone or if you call I could step out real quick, maybe that's what I will do. Davis, please tell me what is going on . . . what scares me is Giovanni calling himself an evil man . . . is that what he is? . . .

I have to get going back to my workshop, we're learning relaxation techniques, so I should be able to put the techniques to good use . . . I love you . . . I know you will take care of this for me . . . ti amo Amore. Tess

From: Tess

Sent: October 28, 2008 4:45:16 PM Attn Mr John Sigman,

I spoke with Davis about this, this morning, if you have not heard from him today please contact him immediately.

Thank You Tess

From: Davis

Sent: October 28, 2008 4:48:18 PM Hello My darling,

I just got back to Accra, there was a little traffic on the way. I had to call the manager to let me use the cafe to send you an e-mail since I was not getting through with the call. I love you so much and will make sure everything is being fixed as soon as possible. I called Giovanni, and he said he will check out everything and get back to me soon. I promise you everything is going to be fixed out and will be well soon. All I want now is to get the money to pay for the flight tomorrow, and hope Giovanni would get the transfer to you before the end of tomorrow, so can get money to pay for the flight. I also talked things out with John, he has the reason why he said it was a loan was to be sure you had a connection with me. He said they gave money to someone before and the person never paid the money till now, and they can't find where the person is right now. They are still trying to get him. I want you to e – mail John or call them and tell him you have spoken with me and now agree that the money be wired to you. So they should try to let the money be there by the weekend. If Giovanni is able to get the money wired to you by the end of tomorrow, I will be home by the time the money is in, and will let you know everything about our oil business. I can't write much now, I hope to talk with you online at 11:0:0. Try calling me if I am not there by then. I am so tired today and may sleep very deep to wake at that time. But I would be so gald if you wake me. I love you so much, and will always love you witth all that I am. Ti amo, goodnight. I love you.

Amore. Davis

From: Tess

Sent: October 28, 2008 5:13:20 PM Hello John Sigman,

I just received an e-mail from Davis and he mentioned that he talked with you and that you only said it was a loan to ensure that Davis and I have a connection. Again, I want to be clear, that this is not a loan to me whatsoever; this is money for Davis, which he will receive once he is home next week. He has asked me to tell you to proceed with the wire transfer so that it can possibly be in my account for Davis by the beginning of next week. If you have any concerns or questions, please contact me, my cell phone number is 311-555-2121 I have my cell phone with me at all times, so please feel free to call me at any time.

Sincerely Tess

From: Tess

Sent: October 28, 2008 5:29:44 PM My Darling Davis,

I love you. See, you have the ability to make everything better, thank you . . . When I came home, I got home about 4:15, I checked for your e-mail and you were obviously just writing it at that time. I tried to call you but with no luck, so I e-mailed John asking him to call you, that e-mail I sent to you and then I received your e – mail. I sent him an e-mail, as you can see, I hope you are okay with what I said to him, about it not being a loan to me . . .I also phoned and talked with Giovanni, I think he was surprised to hear from me. Everything was good, I asked him to please track the wire. I told him that my bank suggested he do so, also the wire was sent on Monday and not Friday which for some reason I thought it was Monday; so tomorrow I'm just wanting to get you home I guess, so bad, that today seems like Thursday . . . But I just thought about what I just wrote, that means that this week is going to be a long week, I want to ask you, if you could please check with the travel agent to see if you can still get a seat on Friday ( was that when you were leaving?) if you paid Thursday . . . If the transfer is in tomorrow, I will leave work and get it to you asap . . . Oh Davis, I am praying . . . I love you so much . . . Giovanni said he would also check into the money going on my Visa and make sure that it gets taken care of, I stressed to him that my priority was getting the money to you, first, then comes my Visa . . . I love you I will be online for 11:00 and I will call you . . . Thank you Davis, whenever I talk with you, I just feel that you will make everything work . . . you calm me, and thank you for making sure that I received your e-mail, you made me feel so much better, and I don't feel alone when I hear from you . . . I love you . . . I will talk with you soon . . . ti amo Amore . . . Tess

From: Tess

Sent: October 29, 2008 12:06:05 AM My Darling Davis,

It is now 11:40, I have been trying to call you but unable to get through, all I get is the recording saying that the cellular number is not available. I am imaging you sleeping in a deep sleep, you probably needed a good sleep my dear and I hope you were able to have one. I wish I could have woken you, I love hearing your voice when you wake. I'm looking forward to hearing your voice right next to me, when I wake you. I now have to go to bed. I'm sorry I couldn't wait any longer, my eyes are getting tired and I'm falling asleep. I wanted so bad to talk to you about what we started to discuss this morning, I wanted to hear what you had thought about . . . I love you Davis, I love you so much . . . you are my everything . . . I will check my e-mail when I wake, will you let me know if we can meet at 7 AM . . . I'm taking my time writing this e-mail, hoping you will come online, but no, not yet, I even just called and still the same recording, it could also be that you aren't able to get online right now as well . . . Have a good day today, I will be thinking about you, actually, dreaming about you . . . Today, I pray that the money will be in, as I said in my earlier e-mail to you, I contacted Giovanni, and stressed to him that you needed the money today, so hopefully he is able to track the wire and it will get into my account before 10 AM am, I will be checking, if it comes in later today, could you check with the travel agent just to see if there is still a seat available on Friday's plane, if not there is a flight Saturday night getting you into Whse Sunday at midnight. No matter what, you will still come home . . . I have to go to bed, I will check in the morning for the money. I love you Davis. ti amo

Amore. Tess

From: Tess

Sent: October 29, 2008 6:43:35 AM My Darling Davis,

I just received this from John, I don't really understand what is going on, I know you will tell me, Should I phone John and talk to him in person? I want him to know that this is not a loan for me Davis . . . I

Love You ti amo.

Amore. Tess

Date: Wed, 29 Oct 2008 11:46:26

From: John Signam To: Tess

Attn: Tess,

It is obvious you do not know why this loan is required, so I would want you to clarify issues with Davis very well before we go any further.

Thanks.

John.

From: Tess

Sent: October 29, 2008 8:08:04 AM My Darling Davis,

I wish I was there right now with you. . . . I feel a sadness coming from you . . . Davis, we will be together, and you will get the money this week. It may not be today, but it will be tomorrow . . . and you will come home this weekend, and when you walk through the doors at the airport, you will see me standing there waiting for you, and you will feel me in your arms, and you will feel my lips, my mouth, my tongue with yours . . . we will be together . . . I just keep holding onto your image, and I keep seeing you with me . . . everywhere, and in everything I do; I keep seeing you, I know you will be here . . . Today, as you're walking around, or just sitting, having a coffee, or something to drink, think of me sitting or walking next to you, while we are walking, my hand is in yours, and you find me looking at you often and I'm smiling at you, you can see the love in my eyes that I have for you . . . and when we're sitting, my hand is touching your arm, and then your leg, and every once in a while I lean over and kiss you on your cheek. Sometimes I will lean over to you and kiss your arm, or I'll take your hand in mine and I'll bring your hand to my mouth and kiss the back of your hand, but as I do this, I will look at you, look in your eyes and you will know that I'm thinking of kissing more than just your hand, and we will both smile . . .

I'm hoping you will come back online before I have to go. I will try calling, I've tried a few times already but have had no luck, it's almost as if the phone lines and the internet are connected, even the cellular phones don't want to work here . . . I will sign off, I do look forward to

hearing from you, take me with you today, I know I'm in your thoughts and I am with you no matter where you go and no matter what you do I will be there. Think of me in the description that I mentioned to you, I will be holding these thoughts close to me and I will sense it every time you think of us holding hands, every time you think of me kissing you, every time, you lean towards me and kiss me, I will feel the whisper of a breeze against my lips and I will know that it is you thinking the same thing . . . I love you Davis . . . with all of my heart . . . I Love You . . . ti amo

Amore . . . Tess

From: Davis

Sent: October 29, 2008 12:19:12 PM My Darling,

I tried getting in touch with Giovanni and John just after talking with you, but it was difficult getting them. So I went to see the agent and went back to my hotel room to have a nap. I woke and tried again, this time I got them. Giovanni said he was doing this joy ride and will make sure everything is fixed, but can't send me money through Western Union. I told him how important I needed the money, that is why I wanted him to get it through Western Union to me, but he said his bank has already wired the money to you and they were monitoring it and will let you and I know soon as it's there. I have now lost hope with him being able to get me the money for the ticket tomorrow. With John, he said after looking through the documents very carefully, he and his associate decided to give me the money that I needed, so I can continue with the mining since I told him about the problems I was having with my bank. But the money his company owned me is not ready yet, due to some delay at the other end. And truly speaking, the contract I signed with him was to get pay when the deal is over. So the money they are sending me is not what they have to pay me, but rather a favor they are trying to do for me. He said it's not a loan to you, and you will not need to pay anything. They have my documents and with my signature, so they are going to hold me responsible and not you. You have only taken the money on my behalf. He also said you said you will keep that money till I get back, and that was not the agreement I had with them. The money is for the business and they want to see it being used for what it has to be used for, and they will be monitoring every step. I told them you misunderstood things, and I was going to explain it well to you. All I want you to do is to co—operate with them, so we can get the money and use it for the work here. One reason why I want you to do that is because I am losing faith with Giovanni to get the money to us soon, but John said the money will be in your acct: before the weekend if we will allow them to monitor the use of the money which I agreed to. I am doing and saying all this because the agent said if I am not able to pay for the flight tomorrow, but able get the money by Saturday, he would be able to let me leave Saturday night with a private flight. I want so much to be home and to be with you for a while before I come to continue work here. So if we co—operate with John, we will have the money, and then part of it would go to the mines so work can continue while they also monitor it, and I can pay for my flight ticket back home. I think this is the best way we can get me home.

What I want you to do now, is to e-mail John, and tell him I have explained everything to you, and you have understood everything, so they should wire the money to you so you can get it and wire it for the project to continue. And that you understand they will be monitoring the money and where it goes, and you will make sure you let them know every step of the way. I want you to do this right after reading this mail. I will try calling you before I go to sleep. If I am not, I would e-mail you then. And let me know every step of the way.

I love you so much and look forward to having you in my arms come Sunday. I am sure that is what has kept me down today, not having the money yet to pay for the ticket yet. I promise you once you do things the way I have told you, I will be home on Sunday and we can do all the wonderful things we have planned to do together. I love you so much, I cherish you, and I will always do anything just to show how much I Love You MORE. Take care and have a good day. You are always in my thought in everything I do, and feel your present in anything I do. Ti amo

Amore. Davis

From: Tess

Sent: October 29, 2008 12:49:42 PM My Darling Davis,

Oh Wow, I will contact John and talk with him, I just have a concern, how much money is he sending? Can I send you all the money right away, as I am only able to send max of 13, 500.00 if I send to both you and Mr W, that is, if I have the money in my account by Friday before the bank closes. I can send you money Friday evening and Saturday AM and PM. So what are they expecting me to send to you and you are to be home on Sunday evening . . . so the rest you will get when you are here, so I will be holding it for you until you get here . . . I am trying to call you. I love you Davis . . .I will contact John and then get back to you . . . ti amo.

Amore. Tess

From: Tess

Sent: October 29, 2008 1:20:06 PM John,

This is the banking information that you require to send a wire to my account. This is the information that the bank has given me to do a wire transaction.

Sincerely Tess

Once again I e-mailed all of my bank account information to John

From: Tess

Sent: October 29, 2008 2:12:34 PM Hello Giovanni,

I just talked with my bank and they said they have not received any transfer as of yet, I was wondering if you or your accountant has had any luck in tracking the funds to find out where the wire is at, again the bank said if it is coming from the States, it should only take two business days, this would be the second business day, I apologise if it seems like I am hounding you regarding this, but I am wanting to get Davis home not only to see him, but so he can clear up his financial matters as well. I know you understand the importance of this. I do appreciate you taking the time to look into this and if you can get back to me and let me know when I can expect the funds. I would appreciate that as well.

Thank you Giovanni. Tess

From: Tess

Sent: October 29, 2008 3:42:07 PM My Darling Davis,

I'm finding it hard to focus on work, I'm just wanting to find out what is happening with the money situation. I keep trying to call you and call my bank. I keep checking my e-mail to hopefully hear from Giovanni or John, there is just too much going on, but if the money does not come through by Friday, Davis, there will be a way to make things work, there has to be, if it means you coming home and being able to take care of everything, there has to be a way. and I truly believe that we will be able to get the money to you by Friday . . . there is a flight leaving Saturday at 11:40 as well out of Accra, the same itinerary that I sent you before, goes Saturday. I love you Davis, I have booked my time off for next week, so you have to be here, no two ways about it, I will keep trying to get a hold of you by phone, if not I will check online and wait from 11 PM to midnight tonight for you to come online. I have to go . . . I love you . . . ti amo

Amore. Tess

From: Tess

Sent: October 30, 2008 12:23:10 AM My Darling Davis,

It's midnight, I have been trying to call you, but I'm unable to get through, I keep getting that wonderful recording. I miss you Davis, after talking to you about John, I never did hear back from you, are you doing okay? Davis, I checked the flights and there are flights out of Accra on Saturday night getting into London Sunday morning and into Whitehorse Sunday at midnight, Davis, the money will be here and you will be coming home either Friday night or Saturday night . . .

either way you will be home Sunday or Monday. I am keeping that thought real close to me.

Zoey and I went over to a friend of mine tonight, she decorates for conferences, and banquets and I sometimes help her. She has a contract to decorate a banquet room in one of our hotels for Saturday night. So Saturday, during the day we are decorating the room. Tonight we were making centerpieces for seventeen tables; they're beautiful center pieces.

Oh Davis, I wish I could talk with you. I know that today you have the meeting with the committee and you have to go to the mines, so I don't know if you'll be able to meet me online or not, if you are able to meet me at all and it's earlier than 7AM, please call me, and if you're not able to meet me, if you can e-mail me, I would love to hear from you. Davis, all day yesterday I felt down, like you, but I'm not giving up hope, I'm not giving up on you, I have to tell you something, remember in my e-mail yesterday I told you that when you think of me, kissing me, and I am thinking of you, I will feel the breath of your lips against my lips, Davis, I was getting a coffee at Tim Hortons, before going to work, and as I was standing there waiting for my order, I was thinking of you, and I felt, literally felt a breath, a breeze against my lips, it was so obvious, that I looked at the time and it was 12:15. When I got to work, I received your e – mail and you sent it to me at 12:19, you were thinking of me, Davis, no matter what, we feel each other. I know I feel you, we need to be together . . . I love you . . . I have to go to bed now . . . I'm getting very tired, please do call me if you can, wake me, I would love to talk with you . . . you are in my thoughts and in my dreams . . . I will love you forever . . . ti amo

Amore. Tess

From: Davis

Sent: October 30, 2008 3:28:17 AM Good Morning My Darling,

I am in a meeting, but I had to come and send you this mail because I know you would be worried about not hearing from me after we talked yesterday about John. I couldn't get him, and tried get in touch

with you, but had no luck. I will meet you online at 7AM so we can talk. I am not there at that time, then I would still be in the meeting, but I would excuse myself so we can talk. Please wait for me. I have to go now. I love yu so much and look forward to talking with you and having you in my arms soon. Ti amo.

Amore . . . Davis

From: John Sigman

Sent:    October 30, 2008 5:59:25 AM Attn: Tess,

I am in receipt of your mail and your details were well received. Like I stated over the phone everything the transfer would be done by next week to give us time to finish all necessary paper work here in our office. I have told Mr. Davis.

I shall keep you informed. Regards,

Mr. John.

From: Tess

Sent: October 30, 2008 7:13:17 AM My Darling Davis,

I love you . . . I want to thank you for your e-mail, and for you taking time out from your meeting to send it to me. I was getting concerned about not hearing from you, and I know the connections are not the greatest, I keep telling myself that, but I still am concerned after our phone call yesterday. So again I thank you for thinking of me . . . I love you so much, you have the ability to make me feel special Davis . . . I'm e-mailing you what I received from John this morning . . . I'm hoping to talk with you soon. If for some reason we miss each other, please let me know how things are going and how things went this morning and again I will check with the bank later this morning to see if they have received the wire and I will let you know as soon as I know . . . I love you . . . ti amo

Amore. Tess

From: Tess

Sent: October 30, 2008 8:21:01 AM My Darling Davis,

I have been watching and waiting for you since 7 AM, I hope everything went well for you in the meetings, I have to go to work now. Please e-mail me and let me know how things are going, and how you  are doing . . . Davis, do you believe Giovanni when he says that he transferred the money not just by wire but onto my Visa? I don't know the man, I just hope he isn't playing a game here . . . I hope he is a sincere man, because I need you home, I need to see you, to touch you, I need to hold you . . . I will keep checking my bank account throughout the day . . . I love you . . . I have to get going . . . ti amo Amore. Tess

From: Davis

Sent: October 30, 2008 9:18:41 AM Hi My Darling,

Pardon me for keeping you waiting and not able to meet you at the end. I couldn't leave the meeting because we were having serious talk. We went deep into things, and I tried getting them to let me pay part and pay the rest later. That they would not accept. I will still keep pushing, and hope they would hear me out soon.

About Giovanni, I am not sure the money was wired as he said. If it was, then why has it taken so long to get to your bank? I spoke with him today, and he told me there was a problem on his bank side, and would let me know soon as the money is in your acct:. He could feel the high level of disappointment in my voice. He later called me back to apologise, saying the problem was from the bank's end. I also spoke with John, and it doesn't seem like we are going to get the money this week. I promised the money would be in your acct: early next week. So I went to see the agent before going to the meeting. What I want us to do is to put a little pressure on John, so we can have the money early next week. If the money is in by Tuesday, I can have it on Wednesday, pay for a flight that same day and leave that night. If I have to come home for a day just to be with you and spend that special time with you, I promise I would do that. I really need to see you and feel you. I want to kiss you, hold you, make love to you. I want to cook for you and Zoey, I want to feel at home, even if for a day and come back to work here. I would do that. I love you so much, I believe much. I have always wanted someone I can truly love and go all out for her, and I found that is you. I have to see the lawyer, I would e-mail you again soon. And please e-mail John and tell him you have his e-mail and are looking forward to hearing from him soon. I Love You so much. Ti amo.

Amore. Davis

From: Tess

Sent: October 30, 2008 9:56:03 AM My Darling Davis,

Thank you again for e-mailing me, I love you, I can't write for long right now, but I will e-mail John and let him know that I hope to hear from him soon. I have to run, I hope all works with Giovanni, I sure hope he didn't screw things up for himself by reporting to the bank that the money he sent to my Visa was fraudulent, that apparently is what the bank was told by Giovanni himself . . . that is my guess. Anyhow Davis, I do need to talk with you about something else as well, which I will do later, I have to get back to work . . . after I e-mail John, I will e-mail you as well with what I send him . . . I love you my dear . . . I love you so much, and you need to come home so you can take a large sum of money back with you because I'm not going to be able to get a large enough sum of money sent to you at one time, which is what you need.

I would give everything for just a day . . . with you . . . I love you . . . ti amo Amore. Tess

From: Tess

Sent: October 30, 2008 10:00:16 AM Hello John,

Thank you for your e-mail. I look forward to hearing from you soon, and if you are able to send the transfer so I am able to get the funds

Davis requires at the beginning of next week, we would really and truly appreciate that . . . thank you John,

Sincerely Tess

From: John Sigman

Date: Thu, 30 Oct 2008 12:59:23

To: Tess Attn: Tess,

I am in receipt of your mail and your details were well received. Like I stated over the phone everything the transfer would be done by next week to give us time to finish all necessary paper work here in our office. I have told Mr. Davis. I shall keep you informed.

Regards, Mr. John.

From: Tess

Sent: October 30, 2008 12:46:13 PM My Darling Davis,

I am going to ask a favour of you, I am also going to ask for your understanding in this. I know that the normal natural response to what I'm going to say and ask of you would be a defensive reaction, possible anger, but I'm asking you to not be, and to understand things from her side. The her I'm talking about is my mom. Davis, my mom is worried about me, she is getting concerned because she keeps asking me about you and I haven't really told her anything other than that you are coming but I don't know when. I have been somewhat evasive on telling her anything about your situation and about our situation, I have told her about how I feel about you and that I have fallen in love with you and Zoey has told her that you are going to be her new step – dad. She is concerned because she is my mom; she doesn't want to see me get hurt, she can see how much I love you, and of course what goes through her mind is that we've never met and you're not here. So when she asked me if I had sent you any money I told her no I haven't been sending you any of my money, she asked me what I meant by that, and remember when I told you, I can't lie, I really can't tell a lie. I can skirt around the truth, anyhow I told her that I was sending you your money but that I wasn't going to tell her anymore, and she said she's really worried now . . . Davis, she wants you to be you and she wants me to be happy, she is just scared that you are not who you say you are and anything I say is not going to take the worry away until she sees you in person. I told her that you are coming . . . Anyhow, I am sorry about this, but would you do me a favour, would you be willing to . . . e-mail my mother, and just introduce yourself to her, to let her know that your intentions are good and honest and that you understand her concern and could you just reassure her that you will be in our lives. I feel so foolish asking you this but I love my mom very much, and I want her support for us. She doesn't know you, but I'm hoping if you e-mail her, you would be able to assure her that you do love me and that you will be coming and that you would never do anything to hurt me. Please understand as well that my mother is a very wonderful person, she is feeling protective of me, and she told me she is worrying so much, until she sees you that she hasn't been able to get any sleep. She keeps telling me that she hopes you are real, because you sound pretty extraordinary, in fact, you sound perfect, she just doesn't' want me to get hurt, she's watched me go through a lot in my life, oh Davis, let me know your thoughts on this, please . . . unfortunately with all the corruption that goes on in this world, that is what she is afraid of, that I am going to get hurt, and that my money is going to be taken from me somehow, I have not told her about the computer, or the money that I sent you or about my Visa, I don't want her to know that, that is between you and me and Giovanni, I'm just asking you if you would be willing to reassure my mother that you are who you are. Would you be willing to tell her what you are doing in Africa, a little bit, and that you will be here soon? Coming from you it might be easier for her to hear it, and she has contact with you. In fact at one time she said she would like to talk with you on the phone, I didn't tell you that . . . the women in our family are strong independent women, and truly my mother is a lovely wonderful woman, but she is my mom who hasn't really let go, it has something to do with me being on my own, she has this need to make sure I'm okay . . . If you were to do this for me it would really make me feel like I have support, if she hears from you, and you have a wonderful way with words, she won't be feeling as if you're not real . . . does that make sense? Anyhow I hope I have given you a little bit of the picture. Please understand as well that this just happened this morning, my mom is wanting our relationship to work out, because she knows how happy you make me, and she wants you to be you, anyhow I can go on and on, bottom line, would you do this for me, with understanding . . . I love you Davis, and no matter what anyone says or does that is not going to change how I feel about you. I want you, and I believe in you, and I know that you would never do anything to hurt me or put me in any type of jeopardy . . . I love you so much I had better get going . . . I'm sorry about this . . . if you are willing to do this I will send you my mother's e-mail address . . . I had better get going . . . I love you so much . . . ti amo

Amore . . . Tess

From: Davis

Sent: October 30, 2008 2:27:28 PM Hi my Love,

I have not been myself since yesterday. I am hating myself for keeping you through a whole lot and for not yet having the money to pay for the ticket. I so much want to be with you, and to always make you happy.

The last thing I would do is to hurt you. I truly believe I would end up hurting myself twice if I try hurting you. I love you so much with everything I am, and will do anything to be with you, show you how much I love you and alway make you happy. If writing to your mom is what you want me to do to reassure her, I would do that with all my heart. You are all I want, and I would do anything you want or ask of me. I love you. Never did I imagine that I would ever love this much, especially not in the form of a chat friend. God has got his own reasons for us to meet and come this far. But I hope our love will flourish beyond what it is right now. I am sure our love for each other is way far stronger then any oceans can come across. I want you to know my love for you is so real that I can't find any words to describe my feelings for you. At the same time I would like to thank you for all your patience while going through high waves and hard rocks. My love for you has grown so strong that I can never imagine a life without you now.

I will always be yours no matter what the world turns out to be. My heart will always yearning for your love and care forever. I love you always. Ti amo.

Amore. Davis

From: Tess

Sent: October 30, 2008 2:50:07 PM My Darling Davis, My Love,

I would love you to do that, please talk with her, and would you be okay if you were to write her soon, I love you Davis, I would die if you weren't in my life, I don't want a life without you . . . I want you, you have given me so much in the way of making me feel alive, you have given me hope, I did tell them that I was sending you your money, and that is what is scaring her because she doesn't understand why you can't access your own money, again she is not aware of the difficulties that you have had . . . I have not shared that with her, I did tell her though that when you first got to Accra, everything was stolen from you. Davis, I have to get going, I love you so much . . . Thank you, thank you so much, you are my hero, everything will work for us . . .we just have to hold onto each other . . . my mom's e-mail is mom@klon. com her home number, in case you want to talk with her is 311-555-1212 and her name is Kate, my step father's name is Preston. Again I love you so much . . . I have to run, I will try to call you again ti amo.

Amore . . . Tess

From: Tess

Sent: October 31, 2008 1:01:08 AM My Darling Davis,

I Love You so much, I am missing you so much, I feel that you are somewhat at a distance from me, I know you have not been feeling well yourself these last couple of days, I have been concerned about you. I'm wondering how you are feeling? I have tried to call you all day, I just really needed and still need to hear your voice, Oh Davis, I love you so much, I have been waiting online for you as well, I guess this is just not going to work, trying to meet you at 1100, Davis, please try to call me, wake me, I want to talk with you . . . I should get going to bed now . . . I love you so much . . . I miss you, I miss talking with you . . . ti amo

Amore . . . Tess

From: Davis

Sent: October 31, 2008 3:04:30 AM My Darling,

I saw your calls, but they cut when it rings once. I started to worry, because I knew if it was, you calling, you would be worried why you can't get me on the phone. I am doing fine, and taking good care of myself, so you need not worry about that. I am on my way to the mines, there was an emergency and I needed to be there. I couldn't mail you the time I was leaving the hotel, because the connection was done. So we stopped over because I could let you know I am fine and everything is well.

I have your mom's e-mail, and will e-mail her when I get to the mines, or better still try calling her. I will also try to be on MSN 7 AM, so we can talk. I miss you so much, it's like I have not heard from you for years. Never am I going to leave for this long time once I come home. I love you so much, you give me the strength to face anything that comes my way, and I know soon we would be together and be happy forever. You are the best thing to ever happen to me, and I know I can't live without you in my life. You are the air I breathe, and the pillar I lay on when I am weak, and want to be the same for you. Have to go now, I would talk to you 7 AM. ti amo.

Amore . . . Davis

*I had a hair appointment today; I was preparing myself for if and when Davis was going to be coming home, I wanted to look good for him. I was early for my appointment so I went over to the Java Connection to get a cup of coffee. There was Steve. It was the first time that I had seen him in three months. We had talked a few times on the phone, always our conversations were good but I had not laid eyes on him until now. We had the brief how are you. good. how are your kids, his kids. good. he told me something about what he was planning on doing, I can't remember exactly what it was, he was with a co-worker for coffee, so we walked outside together and said our good-byes and I walked back to get my hair done. It was good to see him.*

From: John Sigman

Date: Fri, 31 Oct 2008 14:32:13

To: Tess Attn: Tess.

I am in receipt of your mail and thanks for same.

I will do my best to make sure the funds get to you by early next week but I hope you understand you shall not be sending the fund directly to Mr. Davis but to our representative base on the agreement reached between Mr. Davis and myself.

This is in view of the fact that some people have set a bad record by not paying back loans given to them because there was no proper monitoring by our team and they come up with different flimsy excuses why they've not been able to pay back and we found out that the funds were used for something else instead of the original reason by which the loan was given.

Therefore, as soon as you receive the funds in your account I shall give you instruction on how to disburse the fund through our representative to the appropriate authority to enable Mr. Davis conclude his transaction.

E-mail for any clarification. I am looking forward to hearing from you ASAP.

Best regards, Mr. John.

*When I read this, I felt scared for the first time, I felt real fear, and that sick tightening feeling in the pit of my stomach, I think it started to finally make itself known, I was starting to think that I had better start listening to it. I just didn't know what to do. My mom has phoned me several times now and has asked me to stop by as they would like to talk to me about Davis. I couldn't, not just yet. I felt lost, and alone.*

*Who could I turn to, I was adamant with all of my friends about Davis being real and not being involved in a scam, and now, here I may be involved in something bigger than just a scam, but money laundering as well, because that is what it sounds like. And what about my Visa, if the funds are fraudulent, I'm responsible for that. My own money that I sent to Davis I could cover that, but not the funds that Giovanni put on my Visa, that would hurt me a lot. I felt like an idiot, like a fool, and I wasn't too sure as to what to do, I just knew that I couldn't let Davis know how I felt, not right now, the thought of losing him made my heart ache, he made me feel what I wanted to feel for so long. I was such a fool. what was I going to do. I e-mailed Davis.*

From: Tess

Sent: October 31, 2008 12:20:52 PM My Darling Davis,

I just received this, and I'm not too sure what this means, can you please clarify this for me, who am I supposed to be sending this money to? And if it's not going to you. why do they need me, why not send it to their representative directly? I thought that I was going to be sending you the money to enable you to pay the wages and of course so you could get home . . . to get the money, that was my understanding . . . If I can't do that . . . can you please clarify this for me. How is the representative going to be able to get the money to you? Again please clarify this for me, and given everything that has happened with Giovanni, would you object to me or could you ask John to inform me of these disbursements he is talking about to their representative before I receive the funds, as I may not be able to disburse the funds that he wants me to and I don't want to be responsible for not being able to do that and if something happens . . .

Davis, I love you, I have fallen in love with you so deeply, so please believe me when I say I am so torn here, I want so badly to help you, to get you home, but I don't feel comfortable being a middle man between John and his representative, I don't know what to do Davis . . . I'm sorry, I don't want to make things difficult for you, but please assure me that in what I'm being asked to do they will not come back to me and say I did something wrong, or kept the money as Giovanni did . . .

By the way, now I'm in trouble, I went for a loan today so I could put some money on my Visa, but the way things are standing this fraudulent transaction may affect my credit and the bank won't even look at me right now. Davis, I'm going to be home this afternoon at around 2 PM my time, I'm hoping we can talk then, I feel like crying because of this, this is tearing me apart right now . . .I love you. ti amo

Amore. Tess

From: Tess

Sent: October 31, 2008 12:29:57 PM Hello Giovanni,

Well today is Friday and I haven't heard from you as to how things have been going, Davis did tell me that he had talked with you and that you mentioned you were having problems at your end with the bank transfer. I was wondering if you were able to get things resolved and if you have an idea as to when we could be expecting to see the transfer into my account. I would like to send the money to Davis by the beginning of next week. Also I was wondering about the payments onto my visa—have you been able to clear that up yet? I have already had two payments that I make on a regular basis through my Visa come back to me as being declined, so I really do need to get this resolved as quickly as possible.

Thank You Tess

From: Tess

Sent: October 31, 2008 1:41:30 PM My Darling Davis,

I'm leaving work now it is 1:40 I should be home and online just shortly after 2 PM, if you come online before then would you please wait for me to join you . . .I love you ti amo.

Amore . . . Tess

*My Mom called me again and asked if I would stop by and see her and my step—father, I told her that I would try but I wasn't sure if I could. Every time she asks me, I feel like I'm sixteen again and I've been caught sneaking around with a boyfriend and now I face getting a lecture and being grounded. Why is it, no matter how old you are, mothers still have the ability to do this, I knew I had made a mistake sending money to*

*Davis, but the feelings he instilled in me and the way he made me feel alive, those feelings were real for me and they made me feel so good, I didn't want to have them taken away, and to hear it coming from my mother, I guess I felt I couldn't defend Davis anymore. and to face that. that tore at my heart, I wasn't ready to face that just yet, to give Davis up, so I told her I wouldn't be able to stop just yet.*

From: Tess

Sent: October 31, 2008 9:38:10 PM My Darling Davis,

I Love You, I'm missing you as well, I was hoping we could have talked this afternoon, I assumed that you weren't able to get connected, I tried to call so many times, I'm not sure if you get the call or not, it rings and then there is nothing, and when that happens, my minutes go down.

I wanted to tell you about our night, Zoey and mine, we went up to my friend's house, she has costumes galore at her house that she rents out. Zoey is really good friends with her little girl. We went up there to join them for trick or treating. Her brother and his wife and their two kids were there as well, anyhow my friend had costumes for all of us. Zoey had her costume, she was a kitty cat, I put on a jester outfit and we went out for about an hour. Zoey got two bags of candy and chips and one juice box, it was a nice night, it wasn't too cold and there was no wind so it was perfect. We had a good night. I thought as we were walking, I wish you could be with us, sharing this experience, I'm sure we could have come up with a costume for you . . .

I'm hoping that we get a chance to talk today, or that you at least will get a chance to e-mail me, and let me know how things are going with you. I am feeling really tired lately, today I have to help my friend, decorate the banquet room, Saturday, my mom will be baby—sitting Zoey for me, so I won't be back until after 4 PM, I have to go at 9, I'm not going to be able to talk with you during the day, I'm hoping that I may get a chance to meet you online this evening, if not this evening. I am feeling like I need to get some sleep, so I may not be able to stay awake until 11:00, maybe we could meet tomorrow morning, please let me know . . . I love you Davis, I love you very much . . . ti amo Amore . . . Tess

*I had to stop by my mother's house to pick up Zoey after work. My mother and step father were waiting for me with a letter that they asked me to please read. My step father informed me that they had not received an email or a phone call from*

*Davis and that they hadn't really expected to get one. As I was leaving with Zoey they again asked me to read the letter right away. I told them that I would. When I got home, I read the letter. It was a print out from the website titled, Anatomy of a Romance Scam. Dated April 21, 2008 (1), as I read it, I could follow mine and Davis's relationship with what this document was stating, almost scenario by scenario. The only thing that was missing was that there had been no major accident or hospitalization as of yet. I felt sick, and I felt like a fool, an idiot. I felt absolutely alone and I felt scared. In this document it stated that in some cases, the people that sent money, which ended up being fraudulent, were personally responsible and in some cases innocent people were charged with fraud.*

# 12

# I NEED HELP

*After getting back home from trick or treating, I reread my e-mail from John, I knew that I was in trouble, I couldn't talk to my parents, or my friends, there was only one person that I could think of that I could talk to because it wouldn't hurt so much hearing him say to me, you're an idiot, and I needed to hear that, I needed to hear someone say to me what I was feeling. Steve would do that. I called him, the phone rang, there was a pause when he answered,*

"Hello "Steve said. "Hi" I responded "Hello" Steve replied.

*I asked him if I could talk to him, I needed to tell someone, Steve listened to me while I told him about Davis needing money and about how Giovanni sent me the money through my Visa and once the payments were taken off of my Visa and I had sent them to Davis totalling $20,000.00 that I was then notified that the money was fraudulent and now this John Sigman was wanting me to move money from my bank account to "his representative". there was silence on the other end when I finished talking.*

*Then Steve said to me " Tess, you need to go to the police"*

*I could feel the tightness in my throat as I responded " I know" and then I cried, I had to now face the facts and hearing Steve take this seriously, I could no longer deny the fact that Davis was using me.*

*"I'll go with you" Steve responded,*

*"Thank You" I said. "I'm scared Steve, I can't afford this. I'm not too sure what to do"*

*"Well start by going to the police, I'll pick you up in the morning" Steve said*

*We arranged for Steve to pick me up just after 10:00 AM. I felt such a relief, I wasn't alone, but what surprised me, and problably scared me more than anything was that Steve didn't tell me that I was an idiot as I expected him to, he didn't even say to me that I was whacked, which was one of his favorite sayings to me. I was in trouble and he was showing me understanding and compassion. Just being able to talk to him about what was going on with the money was like a wave of relief that washed over me and lifted a tightness from inside of me, I was going to be okay. I still felt like an idiot. One thing though that I wasn't ready to do, was to let Davis know how I felt and that I was going to the police, not just yet.*

From: Tess

Sent: November 1, 2008 9:12:40 AM My Darling Davis,

I had to get going, I never got a chance to say I love you to you, so this is my I LOVE YOU . . .I wish we would never get disconnected . . . on both the phone and the internet, there is only one way to solve that isn't there . . .

Davis, I will meet you online at 5 PM if you can't get connected, or the manager is not able to set the internet up in your room, then please e-mail me or phone me, which I know is difficult, I find that usually by the 10th try I can usually get through to you . . . I am a determined woman . . . and persistant . . . I love you Davis . . . I Love You so Much . . . I do have to run . . . We will talk tonight . . . ti amo.

Amore. Tess

*Steve picked me up just before 10:00 AM, we went to the police station and we met Constable Alex Ramsy. She directed us into a room just off of the front entrance. As soon as you walked into the room there was a couch against the wall to our left, a large corner desk against the wall to our right and two chairs in front of the desk. Steve sat on the couch and the constable and I sat on the chairs that were at the side of the desk. I could see Steve if I turned my head just a little bit to my left, knowing he was there made this easier. I told the constable what had transpired from the beginning, starting with meeting Davis, sending him the computer, I didn't have to look to my left to know that Steve was rolling his eyes, I could just feel it. his eyes would be rolling right to the back of his head before I was finished because I never did tell him everything last night, now he was going to hear it all.*

*The constable, when I had finished my story, suggested that I cut all contact with Davis immediately and that I cancel my Visa card and my bank accounts. I told her that my Visa card was on hold right now and that no one was able to access it, including me. She told me under no circumstances was I to send anymore funds to Davis whatsoever. She said that she would get hold of an officer in Commercial Crime and see if there was anything that could be done as far as the money transfer. I told her that if there was a way of getting these guys through the money transfer wouldn't it be worth trying to stop them? She said she would ask commercial crime and get back to me. Being that it was a weekend, I would have to wait until Monday before anything could be done. She asked me to send her the e-mails that I had received from Davis, Giovanni and John regarding the money, I told her I also had a picture of Davis, she said she would like to see it. I showed her the one I had of Davis on my phone; she too mentioned how handsome he was. Damn, it's not fair is it. was my response to her comment.*

*As we were walking down the stairs outside of the policestation Steve looked at me and said "the whole time we were in there I kept wondering what was bigger—her gun or her ass".*

*It's good to know somethings never change.*

From: Tess

Sent: November 1, 2008 2:08:49 PM My Darling Davis,

It looks like we will be working later than 5, maybe home by 5:30 in case you can get online . . . Hope to talk to you, I need to talk to you about this . . . I am sorry . . . I love you ti amo

Amore . . . Tess

From: Davis

Sent: November 1, 2008 3:13:43 PM Tess My Love,

I am sorry we can't talk online as we planned. The technician did not come to do the set up. But if you can call me so we talk, I would be very glad. I miss you and LOVE YOU SO MUCH. I am going to my room and sleep for a while. I hope you can wake me so we talk. Take care and know you are always in my thought. I love you . . . ti amo Amore. Davis

From: Davis

Sent: November 1, 2008 5:12 PM My Darling,

It didn't look like that the manager would be able to set up the Internet in my room, I called him and he said I forgot to tell the technician, and he has now gone home. He is trying to get him on phone to come back and do the set up in my room. If he is able to come and do it, I would let you know. If he is not able to come, I would let you know that also. I guess I need to explain what has been going on at this point, because I am not too sure if we can talk this evening, and don't want to keep worrying what is going on. I am sorry I couldn't and have not been able to tell you till now. I just didn't want to get you worrying about me.

Two week ago, there was a disaster at the mines, and there were some injuries. Mine was not that bad, but I have about six of the workers still at the hospital very seriously injured. We couldn't get to the stage where we could break from mounting the machines when we were stopped, so the machines were not supported. They came down on us. What happened was terrible. And that was when the workers started complaining that they needed to be paid for what they had done so far, and the hospital also needed money to take care of those at the hospital, and that was what I was using the money you sent me. I needed money to get this all thing fixed up, and that was when I started putting pressure on Giovanni to send you the money. I realized I was not going to get all the money I needed from Giovanni, so I contacted John to come to my aid. He asked me to send me all details and documents and he would see what he can do, so I did that.

After going through everything, he contacted the suppliers of the machines, and others, and they all admitted they have done business with me not once or twice. He asked me to reorder the machines and he would get the money to them directly, and I agreed. Later, he came back telling me he wanted the money to be wired to my acct:, then my bank would wire the money to all the people I would have to pay. I asked him why, he doesn't want to pay it direct and he told me he wants the money to pass through me. I told him I had a little problem with my bank transaction, and if it was possible I would have you, as my wife, take care of that and he said it was fine with him. All he wants is for the money to pass through me to the people. My plan is that, once the money is with you, I would let you send part to the people, then you would send the rest to me. What you would be sending to me is for the hospital bills, and payment of the workers and the ministry. But I would use part of that money to pay for my flight so I can come home to resolve things with my bank and to spend some time with you. I am very sorry I have not been able to tell you this. I didn't want you to get worried while I was still here, and was going to tell you once we are together. I want you to know it's been very hard for me living with all this, but talking with you, your thoughts and knowing you are always there for me is what has been keeping me going. If you have to get mad at my I will understand, but please don't leave me. I am very sorry. I promise this would never again happen. I would tell you everything that happens from now on, even if it would get you worried. I know once you know what is going on, we would be able to talk things out and find a way to resolve them. I love you so much, all I want to do is be the best man for you forever, and to love you and everything that makes you. I have to go now, we have about an hour and half to get to Accra, I would call or mail you to let you know if we could be able to talk more deeply at 5. And please send John an e-mail telling him you understand the agreement between him and I, and you would make sure the money goes to where it belongs. Talk to you pretty soon. Ti amo.

Amore . . . Davis

*I read Davis's e-mail and reread the Anatomy of a Romance Scam*

*—again it was uncanny how it basically described the romance that happened between Davis and me. It could have been our story, the way we met. The scammers pretend to be living locally with the pretense that the person would eventually meet you and then that person would have to go to some foreign country for work, that's when tragedy strikes and the person ends up in the hospital needing money; and there again is Davis's e-mail. I think the wind was knoecked out of my balloon, I felt deflated, how could he do this to me. I gave him my love, I opened up to him, I wanted him to be real. I felt numb. it was just all a fantasy. I still couldn't believe it, it was all there. Davis just filled in the missing piece with a tragic accident happening at the mine and having some of his workers end up in the hospital of which payment was going to be needed for medical help. Yes I felt deflated and I felt like a complete fool. I also felt a saddnes come over me that left me feeling so empty. Davis gave me such wonderful feelings, I honestly didn't know if I wanted to give up having someone give me those feelings. And now I had to go and talk with my mom and step—dad*

*At least now I was able to face my parents because I could tell them that I had talked with Steve and that he had come with me to the police and that I had told the police everything. I knew my mom would be worried for me because of the money that I had given away to Davis, and not to mention that I may be responsible for the fraudulent monies on my Visa. At least I was starting to do something about it.*

# 13

# PLAYING THE GAME

From: Tess

Sent: November 1, 2008 6:35:16 PM My Darling Davis,

I am sorry for what happened at the mines, I can't believe that you would not tell me something as serious as this . . . I'm sorry I still have to think about this . . . Davis, there is so much going on, with you, and then now, I may be in serious trouble here Davis with my Visa, I mean serious trouble, I can't do anything, and my Visa, I relie on it to pay my bills. My oil is almost completely out; I have been keeping the heat down and using the baseboard heaters. I've had my regular payments that I make from my Visa come back as declined, and Visa is asking me to make a payment, and if it's not made by next week, I will be going to collections and if I still don't pay they will be contacting the police as there was a fraudulent claim made . . . Davis, I am scared, I am concerned about you and what happens, but I need you to tell Giovanni he has to replace that money. I can't do anything until that money is replaced, I need it done on Monday Davis, if there is nothing in my account by Thursday then I will be in trouble, so please, I am asking you, to help me . . . please contact Giovanni and make sure he does this, I don't want to talk with him anymore, I am upset, . . . once the money is back on my Visa I will feel a lot better about everything, please will you do this for me . . . My computer has been acting up today, I have been trying to get connected for the last half hour, I have been trying to call, and I get nothing . . . Davis please . . . I need your help now . . . I love you . . . I love you with all my heart . . . ti amo

Amore . . . Tess

*I started to embellish a little bit with Davis at this point, I needed to stress to him that I was in trouble. I also didn't want Davis to know that I had gone to the police.*

From: Davis

Sent: November 2, 2008 1:04:16 AM My Darling,

I am sorry for putting you into all this trouble, I am going to make sure it's been fixed before Thursday. You also say to me sometime you need a 1000, what about you take it from the money that you will have to send to me. I am going to contact Giovanni right after writing, and I am going to tell him we are reporting him and his boss to the police if he doesn't get your visa fixed by Wednesday. I want you to trust me in this, and I assure you everything would be fine soon, and we would be happy together forever. I PROMISE YOU. I am going to the hospital and then to the mines. I would be online at 7, so we can talk. Once again, I am very much sorry for all this. Just help me get home and everything would be fine. I love you so much and thank you for everything. I know it's hard for you, and it's very hard for me here too. I am very sorry Tess. Look forward to talking with you soon. I love you. Ti amo.

Amore. Davis

From: Davis

Sent: November 2, 2008 6:39:21 AM Darling,

I have been here waiting for over 30 minutes now, and trying your cell too. Is everything okay with you? I am getting worried. Hope to hear from you soon. I love you . . . Ti amo.

Amore . . . Davis

From: Davis

Sent: November 2, 2008 7:27:55 AM My Darling,

I don't know how soon you can get your computer work to read this mail, but I hope it works soon. You have now got me much worried after talking with you. This is what I was trying to avoid. I can feel from your voice that you are not okay, and that will affect me, because the last thing I want is you getting worried about stuff I am taking care of. I promise you everything is going to be fine. This I assure you. I have worked too hard to get to this far with work, and we have had our hard times so soon together, but one thing I believe is that the best things don't come easy. All what is happening now makes me believe the more that you are the best thing to happen to me, and I am going to do anything and everything to have us together and to be happy together forever. I need you in my life more then any other thing, this I know deep inside. Because you coming into my life has chanrged so many things. I feel so alive, I feel love and being loved, and I feel for a very long time, I now have a family I am coming home to. I am going to try calling you, and hope we can talk. Please don't worry about a thing, everything is fine with me and everything would be fine soon, and we will be together. I love you with all that I am, I need you more then anything in this world. Send my love to Zoey, and take good care of yourself for me. I am managing here. I love you Tess, and want you so much. ti amo.

Amore . . . Davis

From: Tess

Sent: November 2, 2008 2:19:00 PM My Darling Davis,

I finally got my computer working, I don't think it is going to be reliable though I have this feeling I am going to have to take it in and get it checked out, my Yahoo just did not want to sign in and my Internet Explorer, wouldn't even open up . . . I can see why you wanted an Imac, this Vista, is frustrating . . . This is more so because it is my only link to you . . .Davis, I want to thank you for e-mailing my Mom and Step father, they are concerned about me, they don't want me to be hurt, and given everything I've been through and given where you're at, Ghana has a bad reputation and unfortunately, you are there . . . Davis, I want you to understand that I love you . . . I have fallen so deeply in love with you . . .

I know that you will make sure Giovanni puts the money back into my account, you may want to remind him that he has actually stolen that money from me, as the money he sent, your money, went to you as it was supposed to, and I agree with you and thank you, for saying that if he doesn't come through by Wednesday, I don't want the police knocking at my door first, I haven't been able to make a payment on my Visa and Visa is not happy about the whole situation. I don't want to think about money, it's too stressful right now, and I know that you need it . . . Davis, please let me know how things go, and please let me know how things are going with you I miss talking with you, I wish we could talk about making plans to go somewhere when you are here, I would love to go to dinner when you are here, I would love to go to your favorite restaurant, and then we'll go to mine. I wish I knew more about you . . . What you like, what you don't like, what you have done in your past, what different places you've been to, I just want to know more about you Davis . . . I love you . . . and I want to know about you . . . who could blame me? . . . I have to admit I am feeling quite down, I haven't been able to focus very well these last couple of days, I had better sign off, my computer is acting up again and I want to get this to you before it crashes again . . . I love you so much Davis . . . ti amo

Amore. Tess

The following e-mails are first, the one Davis sent to my parents and then the second is from my step—father to Davis

From: Preston and Kate

Sent: November 2, 2008 10:20:21 AM Good Morning Tess,

We received the following e-mail from Davis this morning and I must admit I was quite surprised when it came. The problem is that from the content of the letter I am more suspicious than ever. I have replied to him and have sent you a copy of my e-mail. It should be very easy for him to prove to me that he is who he says he is by answering my questions. Maybe you already have the answers and just haven't told us. For your sake we hope this thing is for real and I hope you understand why we are so concerned.

Love, Preston

— Original Message — From: "Davis Barienda"

Sent: Sunday, November 02, 2008 7:58 AM Hello Kate,

I hope you and Preston are doing well and having a wonderful Sunday. I am Davis; I guess you have heard a little about me from Zoey and Tess. I met Tess on an online date, and I might admit we have fallen in love seriously. It feels so wonderful to fall in love with someone who loves you that much too, and that is what Tess and I are feeling for each other. I thought it nice to e-mail you just to say hi. Tess keeps talking a lot about you, and how wonderful you are. You and my mom seem to have things in common. Tess and I are very proud of you people because of the love, care and good motherhood you shown us, and I found that quality with Tess.

Work had to take me away from home just when Tess and I were getting more involved, but we talk a lot and even now much closer than ever. I always say things happen for a good reason, I guess my trip has taught Tess and I how to understand, care and love each other the more. It has also taught us to go for what you believe is the best.

I am coming home soon, hopefully by the end of this week, and looking forward to meeting you and the whole family. I feel like I am part of the family already, and feel so comfortable meeting every single person. I would not stay for long, because I have to get back here to make sure work is moving well, but I hope my short stay would bring us together and we can start to live as one family. I want the best for Tess and I, and I am going to do whatever it takes, to make her happy forever. You can take my word on that. I Love her and love you all. Take care and have a wonderful Sunday.

Yours Truly Davis

From: Preston and Kate

Sent: November 2, 2008 10:06:12 AM Hi Davis,

Thanks for the e-mail. I hope you can appreciate why Kate and I are quite concerned about your online romance with Tess. I guess after being a policeman for thirty years, and still working as an investigator, things like this raise my suspicions.

We understand that you have lived in the Yukon for five years and travel extensively because of your employment. Do you have a home here in Whitehorse and is your house unoccupied while you're away or do you have someone living there or looking after it for you? What is your address? Having lived here for five years you must know someone who can vouch for you—give us a name. I have already done some checking and know you don't have a vehicle registered in the Yukon; you don't have a Yukon driver's licence, and don't have a phone listing here.

It sounds like you have been in Ghana for quite some time. Where are you staying (what is your address in Ghana)?

I guess what I'm saying is that I would like you to prove to me you are who you say you are and for Tess and Zoey's sake we truly hope you are legit. We would appreciate a reply as soon as possible.

Sincerely, Preston

From: Tess

Sent: November 2, 2008 2:51:08 PM Hello Const Ramsey

Here are some of the correspodence with Giovanni, the man who put the money onto my Visa that was fraudulent. I will continue to forward you some more e-mails, I look forward to hearing from you. Thank you for your information about the phone call id, I have to admit that this is hard for me to take all of this in. I wanted Davis to be real. He e-mailed my mom and step—father this morning, and told them how much he loves me and wants to be with me. My stepfather e-mailed him back mentioning their concerns and the fact that he has these concerns being that he was an RCMP officer for thirty years and now works in the justice system. He also asked him some pretty straight forward questions about living here, so he could prove to them that he is legit. I guess we'll see if he responds to their request and if he continues to try and contact me. Have you had any response from the Commercial Crime Unit? I hope to hear from you soon.

Thank You

Tess.

From: Tess

Sent: November 2, 2008 3:01:17 PM Hello Constable Ramsey,

This is the e – mail that Davis sent to me yesterday . . .

I e-mailed the Constable the letter about the accident at the mine and the worker's being in the hospital.

From: Tess

Sent: November 2, 2008 3:12:09 PM Hello Constable Ramsey,

I know you told me not to have any contact with Davis, however, I want to get the money paid back onto my Visa, I need to at least try and see if it will happen. I can assure you that I will not send any more funds to Davis; I have also implied to him that my computer is not working very well and that I haven't been able to get online very easily. I will forward to you his picture as well with this e-mail. I can tell you that I do know for sure that he is not registered with motor vehicles and he does not have a Yukon Driver's licence.

I will talk to you later . . . Tess

From: Davis

Date: Sun, 2 Nov 2008 01:04:14

To: Tess My Darling,

I am sorry for putting you into all this trouble, I am going to make sure it's been fixed before Thursday. You also say to me sometime you need a $1000, what about taking it from the money that you will have to send to me. I am going to contact Giovanni right after writing, and I am going to tell him we are reporting him and his boss to the police if he doesn't get your visa fixed by Wednesday. I want you to trust me in this, and I assure you everything would be fine soon, and we would be happy together forever. I Promise You. I am going to the hospital and then to the mines. I would be online at 7, so we can talk. Once again, I am very sorry for all this. Just help me get home and everything would be fine. I love you so much and thank you for everything. I know it's hard for you, and it's very hard for me here too. I am very sorry Tess. Looking forward to talking with you soon. I love you. Ti amo.

Amore . . . Davis

I wanted the constable to see that Davis was saying that he would make sure my Visa was going to get fixed, I sincerely felt that there may be a chance to get my visa fixed so that I wasn't responsible for the $20, 000.00, and in order to do that I had to keep in contact with Davis as there was going to be a larger sum of money involve. I also felt that somehow I had a chance to get information that I could give to the police. Information that may lead to who these guys really are, surely that would be something.

From: Tess

Sent: November 2, 2008 11:47:49 PM My Darling Davis,

I'm sorry I woke you, mind you I do like to hear your voice and the way you sound when you first wake up, you have that deep, sexy morning voice. I wish you could be lying next to me this evening, this is where you should have been this weekend, next to me . . . I miss you Davis, I do love you with all my heart, it's 1138 right now, we had the time change this morning, I don't know if that happened where you are or not, but when I called, it was 10, and you said it was 6 your time, I was hoping we could chat online, I do miss talking with you. I'm hoping that my internet stays working, if for some reason I'm not able to get back online, please do try to call me and know that I love you Davis, I love you with all my heart. I will stay online until midnight, then I will have to go to bed, if you get online, please call me so I can join you, I used all of my minutes up on my calling card trying to get a hold of you, I think I have fifty cents left, not even enough to connect. So the phone calls will have to be up to you . . . I love you, I hope all goes well for you today, and I hope that Giovanni will keep his promise this time to fix things. I love you Davis . . . ti amo

Amore . . . Tess

From: Davis

Sent: November 3, 2008 2:37:50 AM My darling,

I am so sorry I couldn't meet you online, I went to the cafe right after we talked, but the connection went very bad. I tried calling, but had no luck. I am going to call again and hope I would be able to talk with you this time around. I love you so much Tess, and mind you I love it when you wake me. It was so wonderful, because I was dreaming about you when the phone rang. And before I checked, I just knew it was you. I just left the hospital, and on my way to the mines. I spoke with Giovanni yesterday and this morning, he said his bank was going on it and every thing is going to be fixed this week. I also told him I have documents to prove I worked for his boss and the payment they did into your visa was wrong. And how to get him is not a problem since I know how to get his boss. I love you and going to make sure I fix this mess okay. Preston wrote me, he seems to think otherwise about me. We would talk about that later. I am to get going now, I would call you when I get to the mines, and hope to meet you online. And please try and send John a mail. Let him know we are expecting to hear from him soon. That is now our only way of getting me home. I love you so much, and cherish and thankful for everything you have done for me. I love you with all ny heart. ti amo.

Amore . . . Davis

From: Tess

Sent: November 4, 2008 12:39:10 AM My Darling Davis,

Undressed myself . . . sniff, sniff-

I guess I m on my own tonight, I ve been waiting since I talked with you, but I guess you weren t able to get online, I was so looking forward to you telling me what you wanted me to take off first. Oh Davis, I wish we could at least share an experience together . . . I will be spending my day tomorrow with my cousin, she has just arrived in Whitehorse, just before Thanksgiving, and we have just got together this evening. She came for supper and is spending the night, we will be spending the day together tomorrow, or I should say today. I was so hoping to meet you tonight; I just hope that we will have a chance soon to meet online in the evening, your morning. I'm stalling here hoping you will soon be able to make it online, but I guess its wishful thinking on my part, I have done a lot of wishful thinking lately. Oh Davis, hearing your voice first thing in the morning, just makes me wish I was beside you, waking you, you have such a sexy morning voice, you do have the ability to turn me on with just your voice. again, I'm taking my time writing it's almost 12:30 and still nothing. I'm going to try and call one more time . . . no Luck, tried 5 times . . . Oh Davis . . . I wish things were different . . . I wish you were here, really here . . . I guess I had better go to bed, I love you . . . have a great day today.I hope things work for you as they should . . . ti amo

Amore . . . Tess

From: Tess

Sent: November 4, 2008 7:50:52 AM Hello John,

Davis has asked me to e-mail you and ask you if you could please call him as soon as possible. He has been trying to get in touch with you and has not been able to so as of yet.

Thank You Tess

From: John Sigman

Date: Tue, 4 Nov 2008 18:18:59 +0000

To: Tess

Okay. I will call him

From: Tess

Sent: November 4, 2008 4:23:23 PM My Darling Davis,

I'm just forwarding John's response to you, I hope he was able to get in touch with you. I miss not receiving an e-mail from you, it kind of leaves an empty feeling inside of me. Having an e-mail from you, I'm able to read your letter over and over, mind you, talking with you on the phone is equally wonderful, actually more so. I have enjoyed our last few conversations, it seems like we have been able to really talk and have the time to talk without getting cut off.

Davis, I may have access to a computer that has Messenger, so I can access my MSN Messenger which would allow me to use the webcam, if you are able to access a webcam, I would love to have a webcam date with you, to see you . . .if you can get the computer hooked up in your hotel room with a webcam maybe we could have a coffee together, and just see each other, and we could do other things as well . . . but you have to have access to one as well . . . Oh Davis . . . I miss you . . . I love you so much . . . let me know how things are going for you . . . I hope we get a chance to meet tonight . . . I love you . . . ti amo

Amore . . . Tess

*My thoughts on asking Davis to try and use a webcam was because I was told that these scammers use other people's pictures so the scammers themselves will never meet*

*you on a webcam that will allow you to actually see them. I guess in my thinking that if Davis agreed to meet me using a webcam then I would get to see if he looked like his picture. I still wanted him to be real, even knowing that he was using me in a scam.*

On 11/5/08, Tess wrote:

My Darling Davis,

I am feeling as if we will never get our chance to meet . . . online . . . I have tried calling several times, I thought a couple of times you may have picked up but there was just dead air from the other end . . . it is now 11:20 and I have now gone from 8 dollars on my card to 3 in the last hour, I am hoping you have not given up on me . . . I love you so much Davis . . . I'm missing you, I feel like this morning when we talked on the phone, it feels as if it has been forever.

I was wondering if you had heard from John and if he has agreed to let me send you enough money to come home . . . Oh Davis . . . I hope everything is okay . . . I do love you, I feel as if I have been calling you and waiting for you I hope you don't feel as if I've been forcing myself on you, so maybe what I should do is let you get a hold of me when you are able to . . . I will be here waiting . . . I love you Davis . . . I don't want to live my life without you . . . You have become so much a part of my life right now, my life feels empty when I don't get a chance to hear from you . . . I Love You Davis . . . ti amo.

Amore . . . Tess

From: Davis

Sent: November 5, 2008 3:06:05 AM My Darling,

I hate it when the connection and phone come in between us, I wake when you called me, I could hear you clearly, but guess you were not hearing me. I then went to the cafe hoping to catch you there, but the connection was still down and there was nothing I could do about it. I tried calling, but had no luck. I really got mad not being able to talk with you. I want you to know I love you so much, and you are not forcing yourself on me. It's the love YOU have for me, and I do have that much love for you too. This kind of love will make you do anything for that one special person. I love you so much and will do anything for you. I could kiss you a thousand times and still not be satisfied. My love for you is endless, so tender, so hot and complete. I swear to God I want you in my life. I love you more and more with each day passing and it eases me to know as tomorrow approaches, that I will love you more than yesterday and tomorrow will be more than today. My love for you cannot be measured by words alone as love does express my true feelings for you. When I think of our love it reminds me of all the things you are to me. You and only you have given me so much hope and have made me realize how much I want you. You show the true meaning of how a woman should treat a man.

Darling Tess, please accept my heart as your own and listen to both of ours beating as one. You are my reason to live. Without you I'm nothing. The years will be a test, but nothing will keep me from loving you, or from being by your side. I love you more than you could even know, you are my world. I just wanted to let you know how much I love all that you are and will be. You're truly my love, my soul mate, and my best friend. For the first time in my life I have something to believe in. I thank God for you every day because I know you're heaven—sent, you are my angel. I love you from now till death do us part. Me being far away from you is killing me but I know in my heart that we are going to be together soon, and do all the wonderful things we have planned to do together. I don't want to lose you to anyone else, and would never listen to the wrong things people might say about you. I love you the way you are, and would forever love you with all my heart. I want you to know I love you from the deepest part of my heart. I am always so lost for words when it comes to you. I want you and always will and there is nothing that will ever change the way I feel about you . . . I love you. Love can make you do things that you never thought possible. I hear your voice whispers softly echo. It's the place where a part of you will forever be a part of me. I promise, you will always be in my heart. I love you.

John called, but we couldn't talk. The connection was very bad. He said he would call again. I would let you know the outcome of our talk soon as I am done with him. I hope I can get online at 7 AM so we can talk. I would make love to you if you want me to. I love you. Ti amo. Amore . . . Davis

From: Davis

Sent: November 5, 2008 7:22:31 AM Good Morning My Darling,

I hope you had a good sleep. I have been trying to get online, but msn is not working. I spoke with John; he had a problem with sending money for personal use. I told him it was not for personal use, but I needed to get back home to fix some mess. He said he just couldn't take the company's money and have it sent to me for personal issues. I tried confronting him, but had no luck. So I had him to send you part of the money. I know this is going to be hard, but I really want you to do this for me. It's our only way of getting me home. And I need you to accept the money. I wished I could talk this over the phone or online, but the connections are very bad because of the heavy rains last two days. I want you to do this for me, send John a mail, and remind him today is Wednesday, and he said the money would be his early this week. This would put pressure on him to send the money soon. I really need you to do this for me. I have to go now, I would check on you again in 30 minutes and hope I can get online so can we talk. If I am not able to get online, please try calling. And do send John the mail. I love you. ti amo.

Amore . . . Davis

From: Tess

Sent: November 5, 2008 7:45:10 AM My Darling Davis,

I love you, you make everything seem alright. These bad connections are keeping us from talking and it is so frustrating, I tried to get on at 7 AM to MSN and have just succeeded, however, if you were online, I have missed you. Davis, I want you to know I love you with all of my heart, your words have captured my soul, your voice has captured my whole being, and your picture, the way you look, has melted me completely . . . I want you Davis, I want you as you are, I love talking to you, I want to plan things with you and do things with you . . . When I think of you, I think of you next to me, next to Zoey, I can see it so clearly Davis, that thinking about not ever being able to have that, have you, tears me apart inside, and leaves me with such an emptiness, and when we have no communication, I feel an emptiness I don't like, I don't want . . . Thank you for your e-mail . . . you have no idea how much your words mean to me . . . I love you my dear. I love you Davis, with all my heart . . . ti amo

Amore . . . Tess

From: Tess

Sent: November 5, 2008 8:03:26 AM My Darling Davis,

I get knots in my stomach when I read this, I want you home, but    I want assurance that what happened with Giovanni won't happen here, I don't know John, I want to know the company's name, along with the name of his client who is giving you/loaning you the money. I want assurance I am not responsible for the money and that what he is asking me to do is proper and that I won't get into financial trouble. I don't like this middle man thing, where he is asking me   to send it to his representatives, can you get him to explain that to me, as I don't understand, this is a large amount of money, even if it is half and I don't like moving it on a personal basis. I would prefer to move it on a business basis; John's reluctance does not make any sense to me, so that is why I am questioning why he is doing this or wanting to do it this way. I will agree to accept it from John, but Davis, I want my Visa cleared up . . . get that done for me, and I problably wouldn't be so leary, but right now I'm out thirty thousand dollars, so I am leary . . . Give me some assurance, and my Visa back . . . and then I'll feel better, and given the circumstances, I think that you would understand where I am coming from. I love you with all my heart, you know that, but please can you do this for me? . . . And can you tell John, he can get a hold of me if he needs to . . . Again  I love You . . . ti amo

Amore. Tess

From: Davis

Sent: November 5, 2008 11:20:15 AM My Darling,

I have been trying to call you for hours, I would have love to talk with you about the issue with John on the phone. I need to hear your voice, it made my day, and makes me feel you are with me in everything I do, which you are. I love you so much, I love you with all my heart and all that I am. I wished there was another way to make you trust me about this, I understand, and didn't want to involve you anymore, but without you, I would find it very difficult coming home. I don't have any money on me now, I am owing a lot here. I am just lucky some of them understands, but others are really giving me a hard time. I give you my word, and I want you to trust me about this. I am not going to let what happened with Giovanni happen again. I am also going to make sure your visa is fixed. I spoke with him today, and he said he would call me, so I am waiting for his call. I have no time to wait, so please do what I tell you to do and I promise everything would be fine soon and we would be together and happy forever. I need to hear your voice, so please try to call me. I know you are trying, and I am trying too. I am sure one of us will get through and we would be able to hear each other's voice. I love you so much, and miss hearing your voice. You are my everything, and I would forever do anything to make you happy. I am yours forever . . . I love you Tess, and I would always love you. Send my love to Zoey. We will soon be together, and I want you to trust me about John, and everything would be fine. I am going to keep trying the phone, I sure hope one would get through and I would be able to talk with you. I love you. ti amo.

Amore . . . Davis

-

From: Tess

Sent: November 5, 2008 10:47:42 PM My Darling Davis,

I have been trying to get in touch with you, again no luck, I was hoping you would come online at 10 PM but I guess that is not going to happen either. Again I'm missing you . . . I love you Davis, know that no matter what, you will always be my fantasy, you will always be my love . . . the man I will always dream about . . . and I hope one day to be with you for the rest of my life . . . I love you . . . I hope you have a great day today . . . I hope that with Giovanni, that you have heard from him and he has put the money back onto my Visa by today . . . I will feel a lot better about everything, if that happens . . . I know you will make this happen . . . I love you . . .

I am going to be going to bed soon, I'm feeling sad because I haven't had any chance to talk with you what so ever, I can't believe the emptiness I feel not talking or hearing from you . . .

I hope that maybe tomorrow we will have a chance . . . Take care of yourself Davis; You are my Love . . . ti amo

Amore . . . Tess

From: Davis

Sent: November 6, 2008 3:23:06 AM My Darling,

I have missed you so badly, its like I have not heard your voice for years. I hope you are doing well and had a good sleep. I spoke with Giovanni this morning, he said your visa has been fixed, but it would take five or more working days. I am going to still keep getting in touch with him till you confirm the money is finally in. I want to know if you were able to mail John. I am out of money, and need to do a lot of payments here. I told the hotel manager today that I would pay him when I get back, and he understood, but there are other things that have to be taken care of. Please keep a little pressure on him so he does it soon. It's hard getting in touch with him from here.

I never expected to fall so deeply in love so fast, but I did with you. What's your magic, honey? I am very pleased to be part of your life. I'll always be in love with you . . . ONLY to you, Tess. You have my heart and soul. Tess I love you with everything that I have inside of me. I love you. I wish you were here with me, holding you tight in my strong arms. Every night I lay in my bed dreaming of you, so sweet and peaceful. You are the one I want to spend the rest of my life with. Missing you so much is breaking my heart into many pieces. I want to come home to me, I need to. I love you more than anything in this world. I want to walk on the beach with you. It would be so peaceful and romantic as we sit and watch the sun as it sets. The ideal of being with you makes me happy. You keep me alive. I am so lucky I found you, the woman of my dreams. I hope I never lose you, if I did then it would break my heart so badly. Thinking of you makes me smile because knowing that you love me so much means the world to me. You are so sweet like the smell of roses and you are so romantic like the sunset. Your love is what's keeping me strong. I am so depressed right now and your love is all that is keeping me strong. I love you so much. I want to be with you physically. I would try to be online at 7 AM. I love you so much. ti amo.

Amore . . . Davis

From: Davis

Sent: November 6, 2008 9:51:19 AM My Darling,

It was so nice talking with you, I miss you so much, and was about to try calling again when your call came in. How wonderful. I hope we can get to talk again soon. I want you to trust me as I am going to get everything fixed and we would be happy together forever. Giovanni said everything was in place, and it would take five or so days to get to you. Please try to mail John to fasten things okay. I am sure he slowed because we did not give him the go—ahead. I have been trying to get him to go ahead, but have had no luck. So please do that for me. I love you so much, Let me share a kiss with you as you read these words with your own lips, my beloved. I will soon be with you, my love. I will try calling now. I love you with all my heart, and would do anything to prove that. ti amo.

Amore . . . Davis

From: Tess

Sent: November 6, 2008 2:48:13 PM My Darling Davis,

I finally got into my Internet Explorer, unfortunately my Messenger seems to be stuck. It only goes to a certain point and then stops, I hope it doesn't have a virus, I am so frustrated and now I'm out of minutes. I will try to e-mail John, but I am asking him for all of the details as well, can you e-mail him just in case I am not able to and can you ask him to send me the assurances that I asked of you, can you explain to him what happened with Giovanni and why I am asking these questions? I know that you need this right away.

I should get going, just in case I lose my internet again, I miss you so much Davis . . . it's not fair, and now I can't even phone you as I have used my limit up on ordering the calling card, this is ridiculous, because of all of the scams and corruption going on in Africa, there is a card limit that you can order per wk and I have reached that limit. Why does there have to be so much corruption, is it because that is the only way these people can survive is to steal from others? It's sad really, and it's frustrating . . . no matter what I do, this corruption is thrown in my face, do you see it Davis, being there? How do you deal with it?

I should get going, I love you so much . . . I wish you were here, I have to cook a big meal for my dad and step—mom's 25th anniversary. I'm going to have a dinner party here. See, if you were here, you could help me cook. I'm thinking of doing coq au vin as the main course. Well I had better go; I just remembered that I promised Zoey that I would pick her up from school today. I also wanted to say Thank You for checking with Giovanni, to make sure that he is doing what he says he is doing . . . Oh darn my internet is acting up I will send this now while I can . . . I love you . . . I hope you can call me . . . it's up to you now. I love you . . . ti amo

Amore . . . Tess

From: Davis

Sent: November 7, 2008 4:30:40 AM My Darling Tess,

It was nice hearing your voice this morning. I really miss you and want you next to me. I would e-mail John and let you know when I hear from him. I wished I would be home before 11th, so I can help with the cooking. If that does not happen, we would have to plan another dinner when I get back. With that, I can meet everybody. What do you think?

I wish we could talk on the phone when the Internet Explorer acts up, but now I feel that would not be possible and I am wondering how I am going to live without hearing from you for a day if Internet Explorer is not working. I just can't believe the kind of corruptions going on here in Africa. Everything needs something from you before they would do what they have to do. It's not been easy for me at all here. I would one day tell my experience here to you when you are lying next to me on bed. I love you so much Tess. I know it is difficult for you, as it is for me, to be separated for so long. Life seems to   be full of trials of this type which test our inner strength, and more importantly, our devotion and love for one another. After all, it is said that "True Love" is boundless and immeasurable and overcomes all forms of adversity. In truth, if it is genuine, it will grow stronger with each assault upon its existence. Tess, I know our love has been assaulted many times, and I am convinced that it is true because the longer I am away from you, the greater is my yearning to be with you. I cherish any thought of you, prize any memory of you that rises from the depths of my mind, and live for the day when our physical separation will no longer be.

Until that moment arrives, I send to you across the miles, my tender love, my warm embrace, and my most passionate kiss. I love you

MORE. ti amo

Amore . . . Davis

From: Tess

Sent: November 7, 2008 4:05:06 PM My Darling Davis,

I am so sorry I wasn't able to talk with you when you called, it was so good to hear your voice. I kept waiting for your call to come but I guess once again the connection wasn't very good, please do try to call me again if you can . . . I Love you so much, this is hard Davis, wanting to be with you, yet unsure as to when we will be together. No matter what, promise me, that we will meet one day, we will touch and finally kiss. Have you given any thought to the webcam date I mentioned a while ago?

I can't write for long, I am using mom's computer and I have to get going, so I only have time to let you know that I am thinking about you always. I love you very much, and I wish and pray that all will work out in the end and allow us to be together the way we should be. Please try calling. I am hoping that my internet will work, I hope that I don't have to take it in, but it may come to that, and will you try to call me and let me know if and when you hear from John . . . I have to get going My dear . . . again I love you and know that I am thinking of you every minute of the day and throughout the nights . . . ti amo Amore. Tess

I MISS YOU

-

From: Tess

Sent: November 7, 2008 7:32:36 PM My Darling Davis,

I love you, I love what you write to me, it fills me with such wonderful feeings inside. I finally got my Internet Explorer working. I just don t know how long it will work for, it seems to be a hit and miss situation. Oh Davis, if you should read this as soon as you wake, I will try and be online, again I don't know if my Messenger is working or not, but I will try it. I am hoping that we can meet online when you wake this morning. I miss being able to call and wake you. Davis, your voice, hearing your voice, just makes my heart melt. God, I wish you and I could be together, it just isn't fair, I meet the man of my dreams online, and I can't be with you . . . I find myself watching couples as they walk holding hands, as they sit in a restaurant, and lean into each other as they talk to one another, everytime I see them, I wish it was you, with me, and my heart aches longing for you. Oh Davis, I think that that is one of the reasons I am feeling so sad lately, it just seems like time and distance is keeping us apart and our only contact with one another is going to be this computer. Mind you, your e-mails are what keep me going, keep me believing, your e-mails and hearing from you on the phone, as well as chatting with you on Messenger. If that is the only way we could have a relationship, I would . . . just so I can be with you . . . I have fallen in love with you Davis . . . no matter where you are, this man, the man in the picture, who has the most amazing sexy voice, and the most breathtaking words that leave me weak and wanting, this man, called Davis, I have fallen in love with and I have given him my heart and my soul, please remember that . . . I love you . . . I will hope to meet you between 10PM and midnight . . . ti amo

Amore. Tess

From: Davis

Sent: November 9, 2008 6:28:11 AM My Darling,

I hope you had a good sleep. I miss you so much, It's very hard for me not being able to get to talk with you in the phone and not being able to meet you online. All I want you to know is that I love you so Soooo MUCH, and would love you forever. I am never going to give up on you. You are the best thing to happen to me, without you, there is no life for me anymore. I don't want to ever lose this wonderful feeling you bring to me. You kept me alive, and showed me what it feels like to have someone special. To have someone you love and loves you that much. I am so excited about you coming into my life, and nothing would take me from you. I love you.

I got back to the hotel very late last night. We were able to fix the flat tyre because we had a spare tyre around 10 PM, and we left the place half past 10. For a moment, I thought we were going to have to sleep there. The place was so dark and scary. I got to the hotel so tired, took my shower and headed to bed. I spoke with John yesterday, he said the money would be in tomorrow or Tuesday. You need to be e-mailing him everyday to put a little pressure on him, with your pressure and mine here, I am sure he would fas—track things. Send him a mail today, ask him what is going on with the money, and keep doing that everything till the money is in okay.

I have not heard from Giovanni this weekend, I would get in touch with him and let you know what he says. The last time I heard from him, he told me everything was fixed, and it was going to take five working days for Visa to get the money. So I am sure it would be in by mid-week. I will still be calling and keep the pressure on him till Visa confirms that the money is in. I love you so much Tess. Although we've never met, I feel as if I know you well, and I promise you we would be together someday and that is very soon. I knew from the start that there was something special about you. You have touched my heart and wouldn't let go. Our relationship has given me a lot of dreams, and now I feel hope. You entered my thoughts and magically erased all of my fears with your sweet and caring ways. Now I look forward to each day and feel so much at ease with you. I am so grateful that we are able to share our problems and aspirations with each other. You are truly a part of me, our time together is a welding of souls. The thought of you fills me with smiles, and I can't wait to hug you each day. I love you and would forever love you with all that I am. I would keep trying the line, and hope I can get to talk with you soon. Even if it's for a second. Hearing your voice makes everything looks right. ti amo.

Amore . . . Davis

On 11/9/08, Tess wrote:

My Darling Davis,

I woke thinking you may be online, so I got up and came downstairs and turned on the computer and had to wait again for about fifteen minutes for it to boot up and set up Messenger and when I saw the time you sent your e-mail to me, 6:28, it seems I just missed you . . . I feel like crying missing you like this, and then my Messenger just shut itself down, so I am hoping it will be working this afternoon. You never did mention in your e-mail whether or not you will be able to meet me at noon, I will be online at noon and I will hope that we will be able to meet. Oh Davis, I miss you so much, . I am sorry you had to wait for so long to get the tyre changed, hopefully now, they will keep a spare tyre in the car at all times if that is possible, by the way what types of cars are there in Accra? I keep picturing cars like Volvos, or Toyotas, and of course there are the Jeeps, but I think I get these images from shows that I've watched from Africa. Speaking of Africa, there is a show being held on the 13th at the old fire hall, an auction really to raise funds to help children living in a mission in Tanzanis there is going to be a lot of African art, and jewellery. I must say it seems that no matter where I go, I'm running into items or foods from Italy and Africa. Anyhow I'm going to go to this auction.

There is going to be appetizers and refreshements, it starts at 5 and I'm just going to go and just check out the art and jewellery and then I'm going to go to my pottery class at 7, I'm looking forward to it. I don't know who or where the artist is from, but I'm sure I will find out soon enough. Well my dear, being that it is Sunday, and it's only 7:30, and I've missed my chance to talk with you, I'm going back to bed and I'm going to snuggle up with Zoey, she is sleeping with me, she is so cuddly that one. Anyhow I'm going back to bed for another hour before getting up and facing the day. I will be closing my eyes and dreaming of you. I keep dreaming of you walking through the airport doors towards me, I figure if I have that image strong enough in me, that one day it may actually happen, and we will meet. I keep hoping . . . I love you Davis; I hope to see you at noon, 8 this evening for you . . . and thank you for not giving up on me . . . ti amo

Amore. Tess

From: Davis

Sent: November 9, 2008 12:11:31 PM My Love,

I hope your day is going well, I didn't talk about we meeting at noon because of the way the connection had been misbehaving these days. I don't want you waiting for me and I would not be able to make it. I feel you get so disappointed when that happens. I tried calling since 1 AM your time to tell you I was online, so if you could come online so we talk because I really miss you and wanted to make love to you. I waited and waited, called and called, and finally had to send you a mail. I love you, I want you to know I would do anything when it comes to you, and know you would do the same for me. I am trying to get on MSN, but I am having problem doing that. I would keep trying to tell I leave here at 10 when the cafe closes. I love you more than I can say. You are the most important thing in the world to me and I would do anything for you. You make my life complete and I would be much happier when we are together. I know that things have been a bit hard for us lately, but I am assuring you everything would be fine soon, and we would be happy forever. I really do believe that it will be okay. I want to spend the rest of my life with you. I want us to grow old together. Oops, I guess you were the one trying to call me right now, it cut just when I was about to pick up. I am trying to get online, and get you are online. Hope to meet you there soon. I love You Tess. ti amo.

Amore . . . Davis

From:John Sigman

Date: Mon, 10 Nov 2008 14:09:27

Dear Tess,

I am in receipt of your mail and thanks for the same, I just got off the phone with Mr. Davis and I have explained the position of things to him, so if you can immediately open a new account with The Corporate Bank and send me the information, I would be more than happy because my financier has just requested for this information to enable him to make the deposit right away.I am waiting for your urgent response.

Regards, Mr. John.

On 11/10/08,

Tess wrote:

My Darling Davis,

I wish when we talk that we can talk longer, it was a little bit difficult to hear you this morning and by the way. I called the number several times, and on one of those times a woman answered the phone? I believe your phone number is getting re—routed as this is the third time that someone other than you has answered, and each time it has been, someone sounding African. Just thought you should know that, there is a distinct ring for when it goes to you and then you answer the phone; a very strange phone system.

Now, I have attached John's e-mail that he sent to me, can you tell me what he explained to you regarding the position of things, and Davis who is the financier?. If you can get back to me as soon as possible, I should be able to go and set up the account this afternoon . . . however, why the Corporate Bank? There are a few things I haven't told you about myself as of yet, and I may have problems at that Bank. I will let you know as to what I can do. I should get going, I love you very much, I will check my e-mail again around 11AM, hopefully you would have gotten this by then . . . I love you Davis . . . ti amo

Amore . . . Tess

From: Davis

Sent: November 10, 2008 11:26:43 AM To: Tess

My Darling,

I am sorry we keep getting cut off when we are on the phone. I really need to explain everything to you before you left home, hoping you could set the acct: before going to work. Anyhow, I sure hope you can do it before the end of today. I spoke with John about what happened with Giovanni, and told him Giovanni said he had fixed things out and I wanted the money to be on your Visa before I think of transferring any money to be, but I really need work moving here, and have to be home soon, because you are expecting me, and there are other things you and I needed to take care of. He said it would be best if we could open a new acct:, and I told him you and I are planing to open a joint acct: for the company, so I would not have to go through this hell of a time the next time I am out for business. I told him I needed the money soon because I couldn't handle the pressure on me anymore. The Corporate Bank came up because I did transaction with them before and the money went through within two days. So if you open the acct: as you suggested to me before, John can have his financier (accountant) transfer the money to you today or first thing tomorrow, and the money would be available to you Wednesday or Thursday. Then I can start planning on my trip back home. I would keep calling and hoping I get through. When you are done with the acct:, send the details to John and forward it to me too. I would explain it better when we get to talk on the phone. But please go and open the acct: at the Corporate Bank and send the details to John as soon as you can. I Love You so much and so grateful for everything. I promise you I would never disappoint you. Hold me to that. I want you so much. you are my life, without you, there is no life for me. I hope my darling Zoey is doing well. Let me hear from you soon. And hope we can meet online at 10. I want to make love to you. ti amo.

Amore . . . Davis

On 11/10/08,

Tess wrote:

My Darling Davis,

I have been trying to call you, I want you to know that I phoned the bank just after getting your e-mail and they don't have anyone in today who can open a bank account. Tomorrow is a holiday and Wednesday is the earliest I can meet with the bank. I have an appt at 10:15. Will you please, before then, fill me in on the details, as to what you want or expect me to do . . . and the amount of money that is expected to be wired into the account. Also who/what is the company that is wiring the money to me, as it is not coming directly from John, is that correct? The Bank is going to want to know this information. I know John will problably fill me in, but can you tell me before I set the account up so I know what type of account to open, and what will be the best one to get regarding interest rate ect . . . so please fill me in . . . I am hoping that as soon as I send you some money, you will book your flight asap, because, when you get here, we can take care of a lot of other things as well and I know you won't be able to stay for long, but you can then take a large sum of money back to Accra with you to take care of everything there. I will need to know as well how much you want me to send over to you before you come home . . . and please come home immediately, I do know that things need to get paid, and when you are here we can continue to send the money to Mr. W or to the lawyer and I'm sure that they would be able to take care of some payments for you in your absence . . . Oh Davis, you coming here, and getting things set up with the bank, will make things a lot smoother and easier for both of us. I Love you very much, and I want things to be okay, and you are the only one who can do that. I will write to you again later this evening, maybe we may be able to meet online 10 PM my time if you can get connected, if not please keep trying to call me. I recieved your calls but they were cut off as soon as I answered, I love you with all my heart . . . ti amo.

Amore. Tess

*I received a call from Constable Alex Ramsey, she told me that she had talked with the Commercial Crime unit and was informed that because the phone calls were coming out of Africa and there was no MLAT (Mutual Legal Assistance Treaty) with Ghana, which meant there was not much that the police could do, other than warn the victims of these scams to stop all contact with the perpetrators. After talking with Constable Ramsey I phoned the commercial crime unit myself and I left a message for the officer in charge to contact me. A Constable Lawrence Walker returned my call. He explained to me that there was not too much that he could do as these internet scams usually originated in Africa and again he told me about MLAT. He told me if the calls had originated in either the United Kingdom or the United States then there may be something that could be done. I told him that the guy that was going to be sending the money to me was supposed to be in England and that Giovanni was calling from the States. Constable Walker asked me to send him the details but couldn't give me any reassurance as to being able to do anything from his end. He gave me the phone number to contact PHONEBUSTERS (2) and report all of the phone numbers that I have been receiving calls from, which I did.*

*I talked to Constable Walker about the money wire that I was being asked to accept and transfer to whomever; I wanted to know if I were to accept the money would I be breaking the law? He told me I could accept it, just that I couldn't touch it. As soon as I touched it or transferred it out of my account in anyway, I could then be liable for it, if the money was found to be fraudulent. I could also be considered an accessory to the fact if there was illegal activity regarding the money if I were to move the money. I told him about my Visa, and that the only way I felt that it would get cleared up was to let them (them being Davis, Giovanni and John) think that I would move this larger amount of money for them, if they cleared the fraudulent payments on my Visa account. I told the constable as well that they all sounded Italian, I was a bit concerned as to who I may actually be dealing with. He told me again, just make sure, you don t touch it. He asked me as well to let him know how things went with me.*

-

From: Davis

Sent: November 10, 2008 11:08:42 PM Darling,

I was hoping I would be able to undress you to bed as I promised, and have been calling to get you online. I guess you were not prepared for that today/night, because I made that clear in my last mail. I would get in touch again soon. I love you so much. ti amo.

Amore . . . Davis

From: Davis

Sent: November 11, 2008 5:46:25 AM My Darling,

I hope you slept well, and are doing fine. Pardon me for not being able get online as I said I would. There was an emergency at the hospital with one of the workers, and I had to be there. Things are getting reallyy bad here, and I need money to fix things. The only work these people know here is cash and carry. This is making things difficult for me because I am not able to raise the kind of money needed to take care of the workers at the hospital. But I know things would be fine so, and I would finally have you next to me and we would be happy forever. I love you so much Tess, and was looking forward to undressing you last night. I know you would be very busy cooking for your dad and mom today, but please try to make time for me to undress you before you go to bed tonight. I would be most grateful to have the opportunity to undress you before you go to bed after the hard and tiring day. Please promise me you would be online to have me undress you tonight because I am going to wait for you. I love you. I know we are so far apart from each other and I try so much to be with you. I know, this is so hard but nothing on earth can make me lose my true love for you.

Although we've never met in person, I really love you. The distance is our problem but if we look at it in a different view, we will know this is the thing that can prove our true love, and I promise I am going to be with you soon, and we will smile with a tear of happiness together when we talk about the past, in our house with our little darling Zoey beside us. I have to get back to the hospital to check on the condition of the worker in the emergency, I hope to hear from you soon. I would try calling. I want to wake you. I want my voice to be the first you hear each time you wake. I love you more every minute. I will wait for the day we are together and I hope you will wait for me. ti amo.

Amore . . . Davis

On 11/11/08,

Tess wrote:

My Darling Davis,

I was dreaming about you, thinking about you, and you called me, and I heard your voice, I wish you could call me everymorning and wake me, and I want to wake you. Actually, I wish I could just turn onto my side and there you would be, lying there next to me. All I would have to do to wake you is just reach up and caress your bare chest. I would nuzzle into you and kiss your chin. I can just imagine your arms wrapping around me, holding me close. These are my thoughts of waking you . . .

These miles, oceans, and lands that we have seperating us, have not kept me from falling in love with you, and I will keep falling in love with you. I know it has been hard for you, I don't know how you are managing, you must have some really great people who are willing to advance you credit . . . such as the hotel manager. I often wonder what you are doing for gas, and the driver, you must have to pay the driver as well? . . . One of the most important things that we haven't really talked about is the workers who are injured and still in the hospital, this is a long time for someone to be in the hospital. Davis, what are their names? And what happened to them and what are their injuries? How are they doing? How much longer are they expected to be in the hospital? It must mean a lot to them that you are there everyday at the hospital . . . Davis, will you give me the name of the hospital, please . . . I know I ask a lot of questions but I too am concerned . . . I love you Davis . . . I wish I could be with you . . . talking with you fills me and keeps me going, and getting your e - mails, I need to see your e - mails. It's like a daily dose of Davis . . . I need you . . . and I get a part of you that I can re - read whenever I want to feel close to you and that is usually often throughout my day . . .

My day today will be busy, Yesterday I cut up a couple of chickens and I have had them marinating in red wine overnight. I made a carrot cake last night and I will be icing it and decortating it today. I put together a center piece with silk flowers last night which will be our focal point on the buffet table, and then later this morning, I will cut the veggies and get everything prepared so it's a quick put together, oh and for the appetizer I have, smoked salmon with peppers, as well as smoked honeyed halibut. I will serve this with thinly sliced white onions and capers and I'm going to do a cream cheese with fresh dill . . . how does that sound? . . . I will take a picture and send it to you . . .

I will definately make time for you tonight I will be online at 10PM and I will be waiting for you, and yes I want you to undress me, and put me to bed tonight, I have been waiting for you to do that to me for such a long time . . . I will be here . . . I want you Davis, I should get going and start my day . . . Davis thank you for calling this morning . . . waking me, I love hearing your voice when I wake . . . I love you so much . . . ti amo Amore . . . Tess

On 11/11/08,

Tess wrote:

My Darling Davis,

I wanted to show you a picture of what I looked like tonight, I thought maybe if you were undressing me, then maybe you should see what you were going to be taking off, just to give you an idea . . . I will wait for you until 11 PM, I hope you are able to make it online, I love you . . . If you're not able to make it online tonight, maybe you will be able to meet me tomorrow. I hope to talk to you soon, by the way the coq au vin was sensational, and marinating the chicken in red wine overnight and then all day gave the chicken a purple tinge before it went into the oven. I was wondering if we would be eating purple chicken but once it was cooked it looked normal. It was really great, I wish you could have been here My picture may be sideways, so you'll have to lie down to view me . . . lol

I had better sign off now, I am hoping you will come online real soon.

I love you Davis

ti amo . . .

Amore . . . Tess

I sent Davis a picture of myself, one that was taken of me at the dinner party. At this point I knew that Davis wasn't who he said he was, however I found it easy to pretend that he was still the person that I had met. That is one thing about the internet a person can be who they want to be, say what ever they want to say and the person that is being emailed will never know what is really true because they can't see your face. I was able to pretend with Davis because I kept thinking about him as being the Davis that I had met, the man who generated such wonderful feelings inside of me, I was able to work with those feelings to keep up the facad. I also feel that I didn't want to let Davis go just yet, I didn't want to give up the feelings that he gave me.

I met Davis online and he did undress me as he said he would . . .

From: Davis

Sent: November 12, 2008 5:18:29 AM Hi My Darling,

I hope you had a good sleep. I love you so much. I am sorry I had to leave this morning while we were talking, I wished I never did, but I had to. It was really difficult for me leaving, but I couldn't do anything about it. Thank you so much for making my day, it was so wonderful undressing you and feeling you deep inside me. I love you with all my heart and all that I am. You truly make me feel alive. I hope I do make you feel this wonderful feeling you give me. It's not been easy for me at all here, and someimes get surprised by the way I am able to handle things. I guess it's your strength in me that is helping me. There are five more workers still at the hospital, Ema, Lahna, Kompi, Sally and Palaki. They might spend this month at the hospital. Three broke their legs, one his arm and back, and Lahna, broke his legs, back and is in coma as of now. They are all in a private hospital called Nii Bach now, because the government was demanding cash before treating them.

Yes this brings me to this another important thing. I want you to try and open the acct: if possible before you go to work this morning. Then you can send the details to John when you get to work, and forward it to me too. After what we shared this morning, I feel I need to be home as soon as I can so we can experience everything we have done online. I want you so much, and would book my flight right away once John sends you the money. One thing I want to know is would it be okay with you that I make love to you when you pick me up from the airport? I would love to make passionate love to you first thing when we get home. Please let me know if that is okay with you. I need another favor from you, I know it going to be hard for you, and I am not forcing you. If you have the means you do it but if you don't, don't force yourself. I would understand. I was wondering if you can send me $400 today, I don't have any money on me, and need to go to the mines tomorrow. If you can, send it to my name. Davis Barienda. Don't worry If you can't, i understand. I have to get going, I hope to talk to you at 7 AM, and would keep trying the phone hoping to wake you and be the first person you talk to today. I love you so much and thanks for the wonderful feelings you give me and for making time for me last night. It was so wonderful and I look forward to having such a wonderful time with you again tonight and in reality very soon. I love you Tess. ti amo.

Amore . . . Davis

From: Davis

Sent: November 12, 2008 5:23:17 AM

Baby you were looking so beautiful in the picture you sent me. It was wonderful undressing you, and hope we can do it again tonight. I have printed out the picture you sent me, and would paste it beside my bed, so you would be the last thing I see before falling asleep and the first when I wake. I love you. Ti amo.

Amore . . . Davis

On 11/12/08,

Tess wrote:

My Darling Davis,

Last night I must say, you were wonderful . . . I can only imagine what making love with you will be like when we are together, I get a sensation deep inside of me that takes my breath away when I think about what it will be like and what it will feel like . . . WOW . . .

Anyhow, what I was trying to say to you on the phone, is . . . can you give me the particulars to what the money is going for . . . John said I was to send money to his representatives? But also how much money is he sending to you? And what exactly do you want me to do with it, then I would have an idea as to what type of an account would work best . . . might as well get a bang for your buck right . . . Also Davis, please understand again where I'm coming from, and why I'm asking this of you. Also can you send an e – mail to John and send it to me as well a letter stating that I am not responsible for this money, and if anything should happen to you, God forbid, that what John's financier owes you, will cover the loan they are giving you . . . You did say that once the contract was complete that you have with them, then they would be paying you the money that they owe you, is that correct? I just want to make sure that I am covered, because if anything should happen, there is no way I can cover this loan and they need to know that, and I would like it in writing to them and to me . . . would you do that please . . .

I had better get going; I have to be at the bank soon, by the way which bank do you normally deal with when you are in Whitehorse? I love you so much and again last night was wonderful . . . oh and when I pick you up from the airport, there is no question; we will be sharing our nights together right from the start. I hope you are okay with that . . .

Have to run . . . I love you

ti amo Amore . . . Tess

From: Davis

Sent: November 12, 2008 9:53:15 AM Hello My Darling,

I hate it when the connection starts acting up like this. It was wonderful to be able to hear your voice anyway. I love you so much. As I told you already, the money is going to take care of the payment of the new machines I ordered, some is going to take care of the hospital bills, the ministry as to the getting the right documents and permit, the workers, and some other little things that don't come in mind right now. I told him to send you $50,000 first, hope that can take care of part of everything and get me the ticket home. Then he would send another 150,000 for part payment of the machines. By then I hope to be home to take care of the rest. He wants you to send the money to his representatives just to make sure the money is being used for its purpose, but I would have my part of the money to pay the workers, take care of the hospital bills and other things and that is part of that money that I am going to pay my ticket from I am going to e - mail John and his financier as you said okay. There is no need to worry about a thing Okay, they also own me some money, because in the agreement, we had the understanding that there would not be any payment made to me until the contract is done. And that money can even take care of the loan and more, so you need not worry, okay. The connection is acting up, I better send this now before I loss everything. I Love you so Much and would explain thing much better when the connection gets better. ti amo.

Amore . . . Davis

On 11/12/08,

Tess wrote:

My Darling Davis,

These phones are terrible. I wanted to tell you that I set up the account at the bank and I gave the bank your info as a third party. I also told them you were my fiancé, so please if anyone should ask, you are my fiancé. I will call you my husband, once you marry me, and I do want to call you my husband, but to the bank and to Visa as well, as they are calling and asking me questions I have told them you are my fiancé . . . I love you Davis . . . I hope you are not upset with me, I will try to call you again, I love you

ti amo . . .

Amore . . . Tess

I didn't actually set up an account; however I told Davis that I had . . .

From: Davis

Sent: November 12, 2008 1:30:43 PM Hi My Darling,

It is always nice to hear your voice, even if it's for a second. These phones are really terrible, and I get upset when we keep being cut off. I love you so much and thanks for the money. It is better than none as you already said. Thank you for always being there and for the wonderful things you do to me and for me.

I understand everything you say, and I am not upset at all about you addressing me as your fiancé. I would also do likewise till we are finally married. Something I truly looking forward to really soon. I tried getting John to tell him you have set up the acct: but have had no luck yet. I sure know he would also call me and keep us informed as to when the money would be in. I can't write much because the connection is still acting up, and I understand that you are not able to get online tonight. We can do it another time. Take care, enjoy the rest of the day and know you are always in my thought, and I would dream about you as I go to bed. I Love You so much and more. Ti amo.

Amore . . . Davis

*I received a call from a gentleman by the name of Hudson Clark who is a security officer for The First Bank's Visa Fraud Detection department. He was extremely concerned about what had happened with my Visa. I explained everything to him; I even gave him Davis's contact information along with Giovanni's phone numbers. I told him that I had been in contact with the police and gave him the file number. He asked me to send him a letter authorizing him to release information to the bank that the payment had originated from, as this was the bank that wanted to have their money back. Nothing as of yet had been taken off of my Visa account. I wrote, signed and faxed the letter to Mr. Clark, he also gave me the phone number to the security office at that bank so that I could speak directly to their fraud department and maybe I would be able to make arrangements to pay the bank back without having to go through my Visa. I thanked Mr. Clark, he said he would get back to me and in the mean time he told me not to let Davis know that they were investigating him. When I finished our phone call, I called and left a message with the bank's fraud department, hoping that maybe I could clear things up and possibly get some answers.*

From: Tess

Sent: November 13, 2008 12:54:22 AM My Darling Davis,

I got in late this evening I tried to call you, I was missing you so much, I stopped my vehicle and tried to call you, I felt just like crying, I was listening to a song on the radio, the lyrics went something like this, how do you expect me to breathe when you are not here . . . miss you so much Davis, it hurts, please promise me, no matter what, you will come here to me . . . I have fallen in love with you and I don't want to be without you, I love you Davis, please call me when you can . . . tonight I have pottery and I get home around 10:30, so maybe we can meet online again, and you can help me go to bed again. I'm going to bed right now, to dream about you . . . I miss you, I want you . . . ti amo

Amore . . . Tess

From: Davis

Sent: November 13, 2008 3:48:14 AM My Darling,

I hope you are doing well, and had a good sleep. I tried getting online so I could undress you and put you to bed, but the connection was so bad. I just got to the mines, I had to be here to see how things are going with the other miners who didn't get hurt that badly.

I miss you and love you so much. I promise you no matter what, I am coming home to you. I had told you before, I telling you again, that without you, there is no life for me. You have shown me true love, and brought me alive. I will never want to lose this wonderful feeling, and coming home to you.

Babe, you are always lighting up my heart with the things you do and say. As the lyrics in the song on the radio say, how do you expect me to breathe when you are not here. And I promise to be home soon so we can breathe. You are my babe, and will forever be my babe. You will always be the love of my life. You are my theme for a dream! Every moment we share together we grow closer. I love you with all that I am, all that I was and all that I will ever be. Please know that my love and I are inseparable and I would want it no other way and if time could express my love for you, then it's forever and a day, I can't wait to be with you, see your smile, look in your eyes, feel your sweet touch. I really love you. Tess.

I have been trying to get in touch with John, but have had no luck. I want you to e - mail him and found out when the funds would be available. I have to go now, I hope to be able to wake you. I love you. ti amo. Amore . . . Davis

From: Davis

Sent: November 13, 2008 3:52:46 AM

OH AND THANKS SO MUCH FOR THE MONEY, I PICKED IT UP BEFORE LEAVING THIS MORNING. I LOVE YOU.

AMORE . . . DAVIS

On 11/13/08,

Tess wrote:

My Darling Davis,

I'm in tears writing to you . . . The bank called me and told me they were going to refuse me and close the account. Davis, I think I'm being investigated for what Giovanni did. You see, I took the money and I sent it to you and because it was a fruadulent payment -according to the bank, I am responsible for that money . . . so I think my name will be flagged with every bank now . . . I'm basically screwed . . . I am so upset . . . not just because of this, but Davis, I have this fear that I will never meet you . . . I cant' help you . . . there is nothing I can do, unless you are here, the only thing that can get you here is if you can get John to send you money via Western Union. Davis, I am so sorry, but I don't know what to do . . . there is nothing I can do from here . . . the banks will not touch me . . . and my Visa, Giovanni he has lied . . . I was set up by him . . . and I will pay the price - the greatest price is losing you . . . Davis . . . this, excuse my language this fucking hurts me . . . my heart is breaking . . . I don't know what to do . . . will you e - mail John. I'm too upset . . . I dont' know what to say to him . . . and he hasn't e - mailed me either.

Davis I have fallen in love with you, I will always be in love with you . . . I feel like I have failed you . . . please think of something, if you really meant what you said about me, about us, I dont' care what the situation is, if you are the man in the picture, if you are the man who talks with me on the phone, if you are the man whose words I have fallen in love with, if you are the man who made passionate love to me the other night, if you are the man in my dreams, if you are the man I love and you love me, and you truly want to meet me, please . . . get someone to send you enough money via Western Union to fly here and we can straighten things out . . . Please be my man, please . . . I love you so much . . . ti amo

Amore . . . Tess

*I actually felt a desperation inside of me. I can't explain it other than feeling like I was going to be loosing something, that I wasn't ready to let go of just yet . . .*

From: Davis

Sent: November 13, 2008 1:33:53 PM My Daring,

I don't understand what is going on, is it the acct: you just opened yesterday or what? I am going to call Giovanni to find out what is going on. I love you so much and would keep trying the phone hoping to talk with you. I don't even know what to say now. I would fix everything up soon okay. Ti amo.

Amore . . . Davis

From: Tess

Sent: November 14, 2008 7:24:38 AM My Darling Davis,

I'm very worried about you, I haven't replied to John, I was wondering if you talked with him . . . If you would like I will send an email to John and tell him that he can't deposit to that account as it was closed . . . for some reason, I don't want to do that . . . maybe because John felt like the last chance to get you home, . . . Davis, please don't shut me out . . . I need to know that you're physically okay . . . if John is any kind of man, he would not leave you there Davis . . . if he doesn't agree to help you . . . that would be mean, as he does have the means to help you I'm sure. .I Love you Davis . . . please let me know that you've received this e - mail . . . ti amo

Amore . . . Tess

*I e - mailed John and asked him to wire the money to my original account. I felt that I needed to do this to get the $20,000.00 cleared up regarding my Visa. I also kept thinking that there has to be a way to get these guys and I felt if there was a chance it was going to be through the money.*

From: Tess

Sent: November 14, 2008 11:56:28 AM

John, I'm not too sure if you were able to get hold of Davis yet, so I thought that I should write and inform you that The Corporate Bank will not allow me to open an account, so the only way to get money to Davis is for you to wire money into my other Account. Here is the information that is required *Once again I sent my banking information to John . . .*

Please forward to your financier as soon as possible, Thank You

Tess

From: John Sigman

Date: Fri, 14 Nov 2008 12:35:58

To: Tess Attn: Tess,

I am sorry for not responding to your mail, I was away for a few days. I have received the new account information and forwarded same to my Financier to make the deposit into your account. A soon as it is done, I shall give you the necessary information.

Regards, John.

From: Tess

Sent: November 14, 2008 8:00:29 AM My Darling Davis,

I have thought of a way to get you home; however this is the only way I will do this, as you can see from my previous e - mail I have asked John to transfer into my other account. Davis, if he does that, I will send you only enough to book a flight from Accra to London and my airmiles will take care of the rest. When you get here you can then get the rest of the money, I will not touch it until you are here. Considering everything that has been happening to me regarding my accounts, I am not going to take that chance. I don't know why I didn't think of my other account until this morning, I guess I was so upset, but if we can get you home, you can fix everything else, if John does not agree to this then I don't know what there is left that can be done . . . I love you Davis . . . ti amo

Amore . . . Tess

From: Tess

Sent: November 14, 2008 11:15:12 AM My Darling Davis,

Please contact me, I am very worried about you, have you read my other e - mails? There is a way to get you home . . . Please call me, or write me

I love You, ti amo.. Amore . . . Tess

From: Tess

Sent: November 14, 2008 2:07:42 PM My Darling Davis,

Please don't shut me out . . . I Love You . . . Ti amo . . .

Amore . . . Tess

# 14

## DAVIS, DAVE, DAV OR JACK?

Will the Real Davis, please stand up . . .

From: Davis

Sent: November 15, 2008 2:57:21 AM Hello My wonderful woman,

First of all I just want to thank you for coming into my life. You took me by surprise, I wouldn't ever think that I would be as lucky to have you, but now that I have you I don't ever want to let go. You have brought so much love, joy, and happiness that no other woman has ever shown me. I love you so much!! You mean the world to me, and I know that we have problems but I know we can get through it. Hatred stirs dissensions but love can cover all wrongs! Thanks for sticking by me through thick and thin, I will always be here for you. You and I have shared so much together, and have been through everything, we have just taken over a special part in each other's lives and can't let go . . . I will always be loving you and be proud that i have a woman like you in my life. I will always be thanking the lord for bringing you to me and i will always Hold on to you and share so much together with all I count on is when I get home.

I love you and I am all yours, Dave

From: Davis

Sent: November 15, 2008 3:03:50 AM Hello Tess,

Thank you

How are you doing?I feel so worried and disturbed for putting my problems and worries on you but I want you to know I apologise dearly and as soon as I get home I will be paying you all the money I owe you and so we can continue with our life story. I love you with all my heart and I want you to know that I never had someone to care for me this much and to cherish me like you do. Babe I will do anything in this world to support you with all your needs and wants as tha'ts the responsibility of a great responsible man, I want to be that man in your life and to share so much happiness and love with you. Tess, I told John everything and he said I have heard me but nothing from him again he said he will see what he can do but I have not heard from him and also I dont know what to do . . . I feel so lost and also empty in this world and to let you know I have never been in a situation like this before and I believe in life everything happens for a reason and the lord wants me to know those who love and will always be by me when I need them.

But I have strong hopes and faith that I will survive but I want to get home and spend my life with you as you know Christmas is near the corner and I want us to start preparing and build a great and a wonderful family together. I dont even know what to eat but I will have to go and relax and be thinking of what the future brings i have tears in my eyes now . . . Hmmmmmm I LOVE YOU.

Dav

From: Davis

Sent: November 15, 2008 3:04:20 AM Hello sweetone,

My reason for writing to you was just to let the feelings flow. This is to the one I love. Everyday, I fall over and over in love with you again . . . as the time goes on and a new day shows, your presence enlarges and my love grows. I just wanted to thank you for sharing and making me laugh . . . I will always be loving you. Thanks for being the most awesome girl a guy would ask for. Thanks for the warm moments, caring times, and loving experiences. Thanks for understanding me and most importantly, thanks for just being there for once I have found someone who stands besides me and not over me and I'm so lucky to have you. There are so many reasons; so many causes that make me love you. Thanks for all the happiness you bestow upon me. Thanks for making me see what   I don't see. Thanks for camouflaging my faults. Thanks for tolerating my idiosyncrasies and playing along with them. Thanks for making me overexcited. Thanks for holding my hand when I need your touch. Thanks for hugging me hard when I need your warmth. Thanks for wiping my tears when I cry so foolishly and last but not the least, thanks for loving me the way you do . . . I love you all the way down to my toes and up to my brains and a lot more in the middle I will always be loving you Yours forever

Jack

From: Davis

Sent: November 15, 2008 3:07:11 AM Hello Tess,

Sorry for writing Jack at the end of the mail, I was contacting an old friend of mine called Jack to see if there might be any help from me . . . and I ended up typing Jack at the end of the mail.

Take care and I will be resting whiles thinking of you Dave

*I believe that these last four e-mails were written by someone else, Davis never used the expression Hmmmmmmm.in his letters and Davis and I always gave our final salutation as ti amo. Amore, and who was Dave, Dav and Jack. I also looked at the timing of these e-mails they were one to five minutes apart from each other, there was not enough time inbetween the letters, given the length of them, to write and send them as quickly as they were sent which also led me to believe that they were cut and pasted in.*

From: Davis

Sent: November 15, 2008 3:09:24 AM Hello my wonderful woman,

Thank you for Loving me and thinking of me, I do that very much and now my problem is that i will be pleading with you so that you can forgive me for putting so much of my problems on you.Hmmm babe please can you send me a mail later when you are on the computer to let me know all the money I owe you and as soon as i get home I will be paying you back and with interest.

Thank you I love you Take care

From: Davis

Sent: November 15, 2008 3:11:47 AM To:    Tess

Hello babe I was online but it seems you didn't show up. I couldn't have a chance to call you because of the Phone Bills

From: Tess

Sent: November 15, 2008 10:36:53 AM My Darling Davis.

When I woke this morning I had a knot in my belly, I wasn't sure if I would hear from you, I was so worried about you Davis, and to see that you sent me all these e-mails . . . made me cry . . . Thank you . . . Davis I don't ever want to lose you . . . I meant what I said NO MATTER WHAT. . . . I WILL ALWAYS LOVE YOU I have to ask . . . you have never signed off from your letters like you did today . . . there was Dav . . . Dave . . . and Jack I know you told me why you wrote Jack I have always called you Davis . . . what do you prefer, what name do you normally go by?. Can you tell me how you were yesterday, I was very worried, and I felt so helpless, I phoned so many times, and I keep phoning but the message kept coming up that the mtm number could not be reached, and when I didnt hear from you at all yesterday, I was actually getting scared . . . having these feelings, I know that I don't want to ever lose you Davis . . . I love you so much . . . you have become a part of me, a part of my life that I don't want to live without . . .

How do you expect me to live alone with just me, when my world revolves around you . . .

I love you Davis, Dav, or Dave, . . . I had a thought this morning . . . how long does it take for a ship to go from Africa to London . . . ever think of working on a ship for passage? . . . I can get you home from London . . . I have to get going, my cousin and I are going to go to a few different craft fairs this morning, I will write again later this afternoon, we wont' be back before 2 PM, but I will write you a letter when I get home and I will be online this evening at 10 PM and I will wait until midnight for you to come online . . . I need to talk to you . . . I need to hear you . . .

I love you with all that I am . . . I send to you my heart and my arms wrapped around you, my body leaning into you and my lips on yours

. . . ti amo.

Amore . . . Tess

From: Tess

Sent: November 15, 2008 4:35:17 PM My Darling Davis,

I Love what you wrote to me Davis, I will hold onto your words and
your love forever, I promise you that. Davis, you thanked me for loving
you, you make me feel so special, I want to always make you feel those
special things, because you are special to me. I want to thank you as
well, you came into my life when I needed you, you made me feel
wonderful, the attention that you gave me, your e-mails everyday, was
more attention than what I had been given in years, you treated and
you still treat me with respect, and you made me feel as if you were
interested in me, as a person, I hadn't felt that in years either, I started
to fall in love with your words . . . and then it dawned on me, it wasn't
your words, it was you . . . you are your words Davis . . . I want to
thank you for your words, for all the special feelings that you have
given to me, you make me feel alive . . . when things were getting
difficult, and I talked with you, heard your voice, you made everything
seem like all was going to be okay, you have the ability to make me feel
supported and not alone, and most of all, you make me feel loved . .
. Thank you Davis, for loving me, and one of the biggest things that
I love about you, is you ask about Zoey, already you have included
her, you have made her feel special, that means so much to me Davis,
promise me, you will come here, to be with us, to be with Zoey and
me, I want to be with you, the man whom I've fallen in love with, you
have completely swept me off of my feet.

I have sent you something, the attachment is your birthday gift from
Zoey and I, it has been a while since your birthday, and I wanted you
to have this now, I saw this print, and it just spoke to me of us, you see,
Eagles mate for life . . . l love you Davis . . . ti amo

Amore . . . Tess

*I bought a print of two eagles sitting on a branch of a tree looking at each other
for Davis's birthday. I took a picture of the painting, scanned it into my computer
and e-mailed Davis a copy of it. I guess I felt that I had bought it for him so he
should at least see it.*

From: Tess

Sent: November 15, 2008 5:03:20 PM My Darling Davis,

In my last e-mail to you I forgot to list what you asked of me, so here is the breakdown,

Computer . . . 2800.00 Fed ex . . . 1480.00

To you for chief 2500.00 from Visa . . . 2000.00

That was with the money Giovanni sent you, he sent 10, 800.00 and I sent you an extra $2000.00, Giovanni had asked me to increase my limit . . . which I did so I was able to send you more than the 10,800.00 . . .

I believe that covers the money I sent you for the "business aspect of things" that is a total of $8, 780.00 Wow I guess that is why my Visa is maxed out . . . I never added it up until now . . . but right now, this money is not a concern to me, what my concern is, is you getting home, to me, I want to know that this wish we have of being together is not just a fantasy, but a wish that will come true . . . I love you Davis with all of my heart.

I had better go, I am making spagetti, I bought some Riggato cheese, I think that is how it is spelt, anyhow, I bought it from the Bent Spoon that has authentic Italian foods for sale, I go in there to get a piece of you, a little bit of Italy.

I will be online at 10 tonight and as I said earlier I will wait until midnight for you . . . I am hoping we will meet . . . I Love You Davis . . . ti amo

Amore . . . Tess

From: Tess

Sent: November 16, 2008 12:11:16 AM My Darling Davis,

I am so tired right now, I don't know when or if you will be coming back online, I'm torn between going to bed and missing being able to talk with you online. I will wait until midnight and then I will have to go to bed, but I will wake and check again at 3 AM to see if you will be online, I want so badly to talk with you . . . I want to feel you

. . . I love you Davis Barienda . . . would you make love to me again, sometime? I love the way you make love to me . . . I hope to meet you soon . . . ti amo

Amore . . . Tess

From: Tess

Sent: November 16, 2008 4:51:16 AM Davis, My Darling

I guess you weren't able to meet me online, I'm wondering if the connection is down again? I just tried to call you, it rang several times, but it was a different ring then what you would normally answer to, I'm wondering, if you haven't been able to pay the phone, are you still able to receive calls on your cell phone? Davis, does the hotel have a phone number that I can call you at? Even a main number and I can arrange a time to speak with you on the hotel phone . . . ? Davis I will try again to be online at 7 AM . . . I love you Davis . . . ti amo Amore . . . Tess

From: Davis

Sent: November 16, 2008 12:13:02 PM Hello My sexy woman,

You have touched my life in so many ways like being there for me at a time when all hope was lost. When I was deserted and thought that the world has come to an end, you stood by me all through the rough and tough times. You made me understand that life is all about appreciation and understanding but must be appreciated first before understanding. I want to make this promise based on the love that you have shown me and the things you have done to keep my hopes alive; Treasure, today, I declare my love for you alone, no one but you and it's from the bottom of my heart. I promise to be there for you in good and bad times because you are worth dying for.I have such a hunger for you, honey. I want and need you in my life to make me whole. I love hearing your voice and sharing sweet moments together. I want to spend my life with you and grow old together. Be safe for me, Love, and be mine. I pray that the Good Lord watch over us till the end of time. I will always be loving you, You are Mine forever,

Dav

From: Tess

Sent: November 16, 2008 1:14:33 PM My Darling Davis, . . .

I will be yours forever . . . my love for you is true, is real, if you were to take all of the outside, outlying factors away, and removed them so all that was left standing was just me and you, that is all that is there, is just me and you, no matter what the outlying factors are, they don't exist, the love I have for you, that is all that I care about, I have fallen so deeply in love with YOU . . . your words have touched me, your thoughtfulness has touched me, your dreams have touched me . . . Davis . . . you have touched me, just you . . . I will hold on to you, no matter what, please believe that . . . I don't know what is happening with you, I wish you would be able to tell me, honestly, I would like also for you to tell me why you have changed the way you sign off from your e-mails, as Dav . . . I want you to know that nothing is going to change the way I feel about you . . . the way I love you . . . you have come into my life and have given to me and have shown me love, hope, respect, and you have listened to me . . . and have made me feel special, and you made me feel loved, I LOVE YOU, and I want to grow old with you . . . I want you to be by my side, forever . . . I want you to me mine . . . and I want you to know that you are the only man in my life . . . I Love You and I will always love you . . . please will you let me know what is going on with you, I have read and reread your last few letters which have brought tears to my eyes, but Davis, I can't help thinking that you're in someway saying goodbye to me . . . please promise me, you won't, I know what you've been saying in your letters, it's just a feeling I get when I'm reading them . . . so please, tell me, I don't ever want you to say good bye to me, I don't ever want to stop talking with you, I don't ever want to lose you . . . I wouldn't want to live without you . . . I hate not being able to talk with you on the phone, to hear your voice, is there another number we can arrange for me to call you at? Even if it's the lawyer's number or Mr W . . . please . . . tell me when we could possibly meet online, . tonight at 10pm or 11pm if we could try again? I just need to talk with you, to know things are okay . . . I love you . . . ti amo

Amore . . . Tess

I will be yours and I will love you forever, I promise you that.

From: Tess

Sent: November 16, 2008 1:50:36 PM My Darling Davis,

I know this is not much, but I am sending you a phone card it is not accessible through a mobile phone, but it should work through a land line, the access number is 019019 and the world wide card code is 68, you then put in the pin number which is listed below and then the number . . . this is the instructions I got off of the speedypin site, calling from Ghana to Canada, so I am hoping that you will be able to call me . . . somehow . . . I really want to hear your voice . . . I love you Davis . . .

TRV25-DL $25 MCI World Traveler 1.0000 x $25.00 25.00 Here are your new TRV25-DL PIN(s):

32-4888-1234

Remember access code 000019

World wide card # is 86 and then the pin which is above.If you have any problems e-mail me and I'll send you the link for the speedypin website regarding international calls. ti amo

Amore . . . Tess

From: Tess

Sent: November 16, 2008 9:51:38 PM My Darling Davis . . .

I'm hoping that I will be meeting you online around 10:00 PM-11:00 PM, in case that I miss you, I will try and meet you at 6:30 AM, will you let me know if that will work for you . . . or you could try and phone me . . . I love you Davis . . . Zoey has a CD that we've been listening to every time we get into the vehicle, and there is this one song by Jordon Sparks that when I hear it, it reflects how I feel, how I feel without you . . . Davis, I know I need you in my life, and I don't want to feel empty, which is how I will feel if you're not in my life, I need to hear from you . . . my world does revolve around you Davis, my thoughts are always of you . . . I want you to be a part of my life, no that is not true, I don't want you to be a part, I want you to be . . . be in my life . . . BE my life . . . I love you

No Air

If I should die before I wake

It's cause you took my breath away

Losing you is like livin in a world with no air I'm here alone didn't wanna leave

My heart won't move it's incomplete

Wish there was a way that I could make you understand

But how do you expect me To live alone with just me

Cause my world revolves around you it's so hard for me to breathe

CHORUS

Tell me how I'm supposed to breathe with no air Can't live can't breathe with no air

It's how I feel whenever you aint there Theres no air no air

Got me out here in the water so deep

Tell me how you gone breathe without me If you aint here I just can't breathe

Theres no air no air No air

ti amo Amore. Tess

From: Davis

Sent: November 17, 2008 7:54:09 AM Hello My Tess,

Thank very much for the card but I want you to know that I cant get it working down here In Ghana, so I am really sorry about that and the only communication we can be on is the Internet and I think you will be comfortable with that. I have been thinking of you and also to let you know I am working on things to get home and be in your arms as I think I have put much on you already.

Thank you for the mail and the try, I love you

Dav

*Davis met me online this morning and asked me if I could send him some more money as he needed not only medication as he was extremely sick but some food as well. I have to admit, he did sound sick, anyhow I told him that I just didn't have the cash and that I may be able to send him $100.00 "Please don't insult me" was his response." if you can't do it, you can't do it". I wasn't sure as to what else I could say.I did feel though, and this is going through my head. what if, he is sick and I'm the one person he can turn to for help, what do I do. in some way I did feel like I had the ability to help him, what if. there is that little voice inside my head that was always questioning, what if he is real. however I did know that Davis wasn't who he said he was. I still wasn't ready to give him up. again I calculated if I could give away a couple of hundred dollars, because I knew that, that was what I was doing, giving my money away.*

From: Tess

Sent: November 17, 2008 12:07:25 PM My Darling Davis,

I do love you very much, I feel terrible that you felt as if I was insulting you this morning, it wasn't meant as that . . . please do accept my apologies, I don't know the extent of your frustrations, stress and worries, all I can do is imagine what it must be like, and from where I sit, it's not good, that too is why I worry, because I don't know, and I don't know how you are doing . . . and now that I know that you are sick . . . I wish there was something . . . Davis, I will send you 200.00 . . . at least you can get some food, and that may help with your sickness, food that will help if that is possible. I'm expecting a cheque in the mail today if I receive it, I will send you 200 this evening so you should have it tomorrow morning. Western Union is open until 8 PM. Davis, I want to ask you before I do this, to make sure you are okay with this. I would like to call John myself and ask him about sending you enough money to get to London, a personal loan, and I want to ask him why not if he says no, you said he was a business associate of yours, would you consider him a friend at all? Can I do this for you? Like I said I can get you from London to Whitehorse. Here is another idea, once you said that the travel agent was willing to accept half payment for a ticket, would he be willing to do the same on a ticket from Accra to London, if you were to send money to Mr W on your arrival in Whse?. Money enough to cover the balance of the ticket, if I knew he would do this, I could send you enough to cover half, in knowing that you would be here in two days, as I would be using the funds to cover my bills, but I would do that, just to get you here . . . Do you think you could check with the agent? It's worth a shot anyways right? Also I wanted to ask, are you able to access your own funds when you get to London? or maybe funds from John? . . . I was thinking, I don't know if this will work but if there is an airline that will use airmiles from Accra to London, which I haven't been able to find out yet, I have been trying to call aeroplan and I just get put on hold, anyhow, I don't know if there is a carrier, but I want to check with them if there is, then you can use my airmiles to go from Accra to London. Anyhow these are ideas that I'm thinking of, I will check them out, today when I can . . . Please let me know what you think . . . I Love you my Dear, I Love you very much . . . I will write again later . . . ti amo

Amore. Tess

*I e-mailed Mr.Hudson Clark with The First Bank fraud department I wanted him to have as much information as I could possibly give him regarding Giovanni. Mr Clark was genuinely concerned about my situation. I felt he was treating me as if I was a victim of these men. in retrospect, I guess I was.*

From: Tess

Sent: November 17, 2008 1:36:28 PM Hello Hudson,

Here are the phone numbers for Mr Giovanni Ortona; I've also attached the e-mails between Mr. Ortona and myself regarding the payments made to my Visa. The first one is from me to Davis regarding the first payment I am hoping that this will help to clear things up . . .

Just to let you know I never did recieve or accept the 50, 000.00 Giovanni's #'s are

641-555-3131

689-555-4141

Thank You Hudson Sincerely

Tess

*I e-mailed Mr Hudson Clark the same e-mails from Davis and Giovanni that I sent to the police.*

From: Tess

Sent: November 17, 2008 8:58:22 PM My Darling Davis,

How are you doing today? I hope you are feeling better. I wish I were there to nurse you back to health. I do take good care of my patients, and I can give a pretty good sponge bath, that's supposed to bring down a fever but can sometimes get things heated up. I love you . . .

I called about the phone card and it can't be used from Ghana, even though they give an access code, Ghana is one country in Africa that prepaid phone cards are not allowed, it'll work in South Africa . . . Anyhow, I can still use it so it will not go unused. I just wish I could call you.Is there a phone at the hotel that I can call, a house phone of some kind? Please let me know . . . and we can arrange a time when I can phone you. I would love to hear your voice . . .

I have sent you 200.00 the confirmation number is.306-232-1122. Security question and answer are the usual. It's better than nothing Davis, so please accept it, from me . . .

I love you very much, and I hate the thought of you not well and not eating properly so I am sending you what I can. Davis, I want you to get better . . . most of all I want you home, I will call aeroplan in the morning to see if they have a carrier from Accra to London, that I can use points for. I should get going, I am tired tonight, I want to thank you for coming online this morning, it was good talking with you . . . I just wish things were different, but what is happening is happening and the only way we're going to get through this is to hold on to each other, so I am going to hold onto you very tightly Davis, very tightly, and I'm not going to let you go . . . I love you Soooo Much . . . I will be dreaming of you, in fact last night I had these wild thoughts of you and me on a pool table, do you like to play pool? It started with me bending over the pool table to make a shot, I had to lean way over the table and you came up behind me and reached your hand under my skirt, that was when you discovered I wasn't wearing any panties, it was very difficult for me to concentrate on making my shot, so it was taking me a long time to shoot, and you kept moving your hand along my thigh until you felt my warmth, and then you began to tease me, and you teased me so that I kept spreading my legs wider and wider, giving you more access to my wetness and then I was bent right over the table my breasts pressed right into the pool table, I was completely exposed to you . . . and then I could feel you taking me from behind, taking you deep inside of me, you leaning over me and kissing my neck and nibbling my earlobe as you slowly but firmly enter me over and over again; slowly, firmly and then I can feel you grab my hips with your strong hands, the heat between us builds, I moan, and call your name, Davis, I feel like I'm going to explode, the intensity of our need, overwhelms my senses, you can feel my release as I tighten around you, and then I can feel you, as you let yourself go, and collapse on top of me: that was my dream last night . . . well now I have to go to bed and dream again . . .

Davis, please e-mail me and let me know when we can meet online, I'm going to be sleeping tonight, I really need sleep so I don't get sick, I will check online at 7 AM, I'm hoping we may be able to meet then . . . I had better get going . . . I love you ti amo

Amore . . . Tess

*I had to continue with my charade, it was easy to do this because my feelings were still there and it was done through e-mails. It is so easy to create an illusion online indeed, . that's the frightening part. I myself hate deception; however I excused myself with this one, I was on a mission.*

From: Tess

Sent: November 18, 2008 1:16:47 PM My Darling Davis,

I was hoping that I would hear from you today. Not hearing from you, leaves me wondering how you are feeling, I hope you are alright. Please let me know how you are Davis. I care deeply for you and I am worried about you . . . Can you tell me what is wrong with you, maybe I can send you some medicine from here, if it's possible to send via Fed—Ex, please let me know what you think. I have to get going, I have to get back to my work . . . please e-mail me and let me know when we can possibly meet again online and if there is a number I can reach you at, at a certain time, I would even get up at 3 AM to call you Davis, just to hear your voice . . . I love you . . . ti amo

Amore . . . Tess

From: Tess

Sent: November 18, 2008 2:44:30 PM My Darling Davis,

I thought I would send something that I found written that is very much me . . . It's my zodiac sign that describes the type of person I am. My zodiac symbol is Cancer and the description states that I am a MOST AMAZING KISSER. Very high appeal. A Cancerian's Love is one of a kind. Very romantic. Most caring person you will ever meet in your life. Entirely creative Person, most are artists and insane, respectfully speaking. They perfected sex and do it often. Extremely random. An Ultimate Freak. Extremely funny and is usually the life of the party. Most Cancerians will take you under their wing and into their hearts where you will remain forever. Cancers make love with a passion beyond compare. Spontaneous, not a fighter, but will kick your ass good if it comes down to it. Someone you should hold onto!

That is so like me Davis, it is uncanny, again, I hope you are doing okay, not hearing from you makes me think that you're not doing very well, I'm hoping that you are sleeping, and getting better . . .

I love you . . . ti amo

From: Tess

Sent: November 18, 2008 2:59:31 PM Hello Hudson,

I thought I should let you know that the RCMP officer called me and she gave me another RCMP file number. It is 2008-111111. I did try to contact the security agent at Financial First Bank; I only got his voice-mail so I left him a message to call me. Would you be able to keep me informed as to how things are looking for me. I would appreciate that very much

Thank You. Tess

*Hudson Clark emailed me and thanked me for the information, I talked with Hudson a couple of times on the phone about what happened with the fraudulent payment and he told me that these scammers are very good. They know the timing that is needed to get the money into the victims account and how long they have to move the money. Hudson was very informative; he also reiterated calling Phonebusters and giving them the phone numbers that I had for all of these guys. He also gave me the names and phone numbers of the three credit bureaus(3) that I should contact and inform them that I have been a victim of a fraud and if anyone tries to use my personal information to try and get a loan or any form of credit, then I am immediately notified before anything transpires.*

*I met a friend through eharmony, we had chatted and talked with each other on the phone for just about a year and developed a friendship, he may be one person who could help me find out whether or not Davis truly existed or not, I e-mailed my friend.*

From: Tess

Sent: November 18, 2008 3:03:44 PM Hello Josh,

You may be able to help, are you able to search data bases to find a person or to find out if a person exists or if they are real? I think I have been taken for a scam and fraudulent activity has taken place on my Visa, I have lost some money, oh Josh I feel like a fool, but I know that the situation is not real but I want to be absolutely sure. So if I were to give you phone numbers are you able to trace their origins?

Thank You Josh, from your snow covered Northern Friend who just wanted someone to love . . .

Tess

From: Josh Harrison

Date: Mon, 10 Nov 2008 07:40:59—0800

Hello Tess

I am doing fine. There does not seem any lack of work here. So I just stay busy.

I actually work with the Special Police Force. I dont know how that or if that can be any help but I will try if I can.

You take care and stay warm

Your friend who had snow but lost it. Josh

From: Tess

Sent: November 18, 2008 10:19:18 PM My Darling Davis,

I don't know what is going on with you, how you are doing? I can only hope that you are feeling better, I know that if you were to read your e-mails you would get back to me, so I'm hoping that I will be hearing from you when I wake I miss you, it seems like we have not had a chance to talk in a while, I am praying for a miracle Davis, one that will find you and bring you home. Know that I am here, thinking and caring about you with every fibre of my being. Davis, how am I to find out if you're really sick and what if you end up in the hospital. I don't know who I would call other than start trying to find a phone number for the hotel and go from there, or call every hospital in Accra . . . Davis, I am praying that you are okay . . . I feel lost not knowing . . . I know you were saying you feel lost, use me as your light in the window, to guide you home, there has to be a way, and I know if there is a way, you will find  it . . . Come home to me Davis . . . Stay strong, come home and be with me, and Zoey, I need and want you in my life . . . I want to cook meals for dinners, breakfasts and lunches with you, I want to bring you coffee in bed, and lay in your arms as we talk about what we're going to do for the day, I want to hold your hand as we walk down main street window—shopping, I want to hold you, when you need to be held, I want to caress you, when you need to be caressed, I want to love you when you need to be loved, I want to heal you when you need to be healed, I love You Davis Barienda,  I love you . . . ti amo

Amore . . . Tess

From: Davis

Sent: November 18, 2008 10:31:10 PM Hello my sexy woman,

How are you doing today?? It will be really nice to know that you are so safe and I will always want you to know that I will be loving you forever because you complete me. You have a place in my heart and you hold the key to my heart.I will always be thinking and loving you, yu complete me because I will always be loving and cherishing you forever. You will always be my woman no matter what, you are my everything. Thank you for loving me the way no one can. You understand me and you know just how to make things right. You will never know just how much I love you, but I will spend the rest of my days trying to show you. You saved me from the worst, and you are always there for me.

Fighting is never an option and making love is always as sweet as the first time. No matter what, there will never be another for me and I will always keep you safe. I love you . . . for all eternity I will always be loving you,

Love always

Dav

From: Davis

Sent: November 18, 2008 10:39:11 PM Hey ya,

Hmmmmm I am so lonely and all I need is to feel you in my arms and to let you know that I will always be loving you forever . . . You are the woman that holds they key to my heart . . . Baby, I love you, that's always how we start. Those five simple words always bring a smile to my face and song to my heart. I am just writing this here because it's the only way I know that I can shout to the world I love you! The day you came into my life a miracle happened. One minute I was resigned to the fact that love was a part of my past, something although painful to think about, was nothing more than mere memory. And then there you were. You opened my heart in ways it had never been opened before. You awakened a part of me that had lain dormant all of life. Although I had loved and been loved before, never had it been so intense and so deep as what we feel for each other. This much I am sure of, we share a love so true that I have never before experienced the true joy of complete empowering, soul-felt love as we share. I will always be Loving you

Dav

*This e-mail seemed and felt so strange to me. Reading these e-mails I felt as if I was losing the Davis that I knew. I wasn't ready to let him go yet, I guess the feelings of being in love is a feeling that is so hard to let go of. these e-mails started to scare me. I can't explain the reason why, I just know that I felt this sensation of fear when I read them.*

*These emails were being written by someone different then the man that I first started emailing with, however when I talked with Davis on the phone, which I was still able to do once in awhile, the voice sounded like the man that I had orig- inally talked to. It was at this point when I began fabricating scenarios that put Davis into a situation where something had actually happened to him, thoughts that maybe he did start to feel close to me and he was not allowed to email me any more. Apparently having these thoughts are not uncommon.*

*In the research that I did there were some cases where the scammer tells the person that they are trying to scam the truth or partial truth and tells them that they have fallen in love and now want out of their scamming ways and the country that they are in, sincerely stating that their love is real. So the victim begins to feel once more like they are the only person that can help and an almost "desperate" feeling sets in to save the scammer and get them out, however all that this does is draw the victim in deeper, and possibly getting involved in the criminal activity as well. Once involved, these "victims" become accomplices and can be charged and end up in jail. The scammers remain in a different country and in a lot of cases can not be located or caught. It is the victim that takes the fall.*

*These feelings or scenarios sneak in and take over your thoughts, at least that is what they were doing to me, I think I was able to keep them from taking me completely over because Steve was back in my life as my friend, and he kept things real for me.*

From: Davis

Date: Wed, 19 Nov 2008 06:43:25 +0000

Hello Tess,

I was so weak because I couldn't have anything to eat but bread and water, and I was thinking you could wire me some little money to eat something and then later see where it goes. Hmmm but it seems it was not in your Budget, anyway I was online to see if I could talk to you for a while, I feel so ashamed that I am putting my problems on you as I think you should be taking care of Zoey and me supporting you but look at me in this bad situation . . . Hmmm everything happens for a reason but I will check back and see if you are on so we can talk for a while if you want to. I love you forever,

Your Husband, Dav

From: John Sigman

Date: Wed, 19 Nov 2008 13:07:05 +0000

Attn: Tess,

How are you today? I hope you are doing fine.I am writing to inform you that the fund would come into your Canadian Bank Account tomorrow, so you can check your account later to confirm and let me know immediately. As you already know, I shall be giving you instruction base on the agreement between your partner and myself on the disbursement of the fund to ensure the fund is use for the purpose by which its meant for. I will be waiting for your urgent response.

Best regards, John.

From: Tess

Sent: November 19, 2008 7:02:19 AM My Darling Davis,

Do you not check your e-mails that I send you? I sent you 200.00 on Monday when you first asked me about money, I sent you the confirmation number and everything, so it is there for you . . .

I just got an e-mail from John, which I will forward to you, Davis, I'm not going to tell him this—I will accept the money, I will send you enough to get to London as I said, and to get you home, but I will wait until you get here to take care of the rest, with this fraud thing over my head I don't want to move anymore money. Once I send you money you can be home in 48 hours, so maybe this will work. I love you Davis . . . please read your e-mails from me . . . ti amo.

Amore . . . Tess

Here is a copy of Mondays e-mail . . . with the confirmation code . . . and it was a good one too . . .

*I resent Davis the e-mail with the confirmation number and the pool table scene.*

From: Tess

Sent: November 19, 2008 7:04:15 AM Hello John,

I will be checking my account, you said it should be Thursday when it should be in my account?

Thank You Tess

From: Tess

Sent: November 19, 2008 8:16:58 AM My Darling Davis,

I hope you were able to get the money I sent you on Monday, you should have been able to pick it up yesterday . . . I hope you got it today. I am sorry I missed you last night, at 10:30 PM, I was on the internet, I sent you a letter before going to bed, I didn't think you would be online, as I never got an e-mail from you all day . . . I hate not being able to phone you at the hotel . . . to wake you and get you online . . . Davis, I will be online tonight at 10 and I will wait for you until 1130 . . . okay and then hopefully we will get a chance to talk. I had to leave early this morning so I couldn't wait anymore. I just missed you, I saw that you signed off at 7:05, and I came online at 7:06, this is not fair . . . I love you Davis Barienda, and I'm going to get you home . . . I need to see you and we need to get things set up so you can continue smoothly with no more money problems . . .

I Love you with all of my heart . . . Tess

From: Tess

Sent: November 19, 2008 10:40:13 AM My Darling Davis,

Hello My Handsome Man, I'm still wondering if you were able to get the money I sent to you on Monday . . . Please tell me you picked it up. And let me know about meeting you online at 10:30 PM tonight my time. I love you.

Tess

From: Tess

Sent: November 19, 2008 12:20:35 PM My Darling Davis,

Hi Hon, I'm sitting here at work, its lunch time and I'm wishing I could talk to you. Davis, Please e-mail me as soon as you can . . . I did phone western union to see if you picked up the money and they said that the money was received, so I'm glad that you were able to get it. Again I'm sorry it wasn't more, I hope you are feeling better, I'm praying that things will go better now, I was surprised actually to see John's e-mail, as soon as I get it I will book your flight to London, and then I will book you from London to Whitehorse, we're going to get you home, by the way I need a date for December 5th, would you be my date? I Love You Davis so much . . . I want you in my life, no matter what . . . I miss you terribly, not being able to talk with you is killing me here . . . I had better go, I love you Dav . . . with all my heart.

Tess

From: Tess

Sent: November 19, 2008 9:20:58 PM My Darling Davis,

Please get a hold of me . . . important

I'm hoping that we will meet online this morning for you . . . 10  PM 10:30 for me . . . I can get you home this weekend . . . are you interested?

I Love You . . . Tess

*Davis and I talked on the phone, and he sounded like the man that I had been talking to originally, he sounded like the Davis that I knew. He was sounding so down, it broke my heart really, knowing that I was wanting him to show himself, I wanted to make him real, I thought that if he came here and he was the man in the picture then there could be a chance that he was real. I had such a strong feeling that I needed him to come here; I needed him to clear things up and to tell me the truth. So I decided I would take my chance, and one way or the other I was going to end this. I was going to get him home if that was what it was going to take for the scam to be exposed. and if he did show up, I had no idea what I would do or how I would feel I decided to send Davis 1500.00 to end this*

From: Tess

Sent: November 20, 2008 6:09:16 AM My Darling Davis,

You do know how to make me glow inside, I couldn't sleep, I've been lying awake, I think since 4AM when I woke, I should have come online, I would have met you then, Davis, I want us to build a life together, a family, and I think our faith that we've held onto, the love that we've shown and given each other up until now, will only continue to grow and get stronger. I do feel that we need to meet, it is important for both of us, to be able to gain strength from each other, by actually being able to touch and feel one another . . . I know I want to feel you, and I need to feel you, I need to know that you are alright. I do hope that you are feeling better today, if you were here, I could make you chicken soup, my specialty, lots of garlic, and maybe some ginger it will cure anything. Davis, as soon as you can get your flight arrangements to me, I will book from my end . . . again I will go to the bank at 9:30 and I should be at Western Union by 9:45 and if all goes well I should be here back home to send you the e-mail before 10 AM my time, I know that that is cutting it pretty close to 6 PM your time, I will try and do my best to be as fast as I can.Attached, below, is the e-mail I received from John, so Davis we may be timing this just perfect, this will not get into my account until next week, even if they wire this to me today, at which time you will be here, I feel so much better about this, because I will not touch this money until you are here . . . I guess I had better get going and get my day started, I am on a mission, and that mission is to get you home . . . to us . . . I Love You with all of my heart,

Forever Yours Tess

From: John Sigman

Date: Thu, 20 Nov 2008 07:53:19

Attn: Tess,

The fund is coming from within Canada, in fact, it is actually from J BLACK OPERATIONS LTD under the name of Mr. Joseph Black. The amount is $57, 800.00, As soon as you confirm the fund in your account endeavour to notify me immediately for further directives as per our earlier agreement.

I am looking forward to hearing from you ASAP. Best regards,

Mr. John.

# 15

# BANNED FROM WESTERN UNION

From: Tess

Sent: November 20, 2008 9:51:23 AM My Darling Davis,

I won't take much time to send this confirmation number is 214-566-4322 for 1500.

Come home to me Davis, I will be waiting to hear from you I love you

Tess

Davis called me and he was having problems picking up the money I sent him at Western Union. he told me that I needed to call the main Western Union office to clear a few things up.

From: Tess

Sent: November 20, 2008 11:05:46 AM My Darling Davis,

I have called Western Union and I was given another 1 800 number to call because they want to interview me regarding the money I sent over. I had to leave my number for them to call me back. Davis, I'm sorry about this, I put Mr Earl Warleh Totoei Tayamer's name on the transfer like you asked me to . . . I think my name has been marked, no matter what, I will get this money to you, It would have been there before 6 your time . . . this is not right, please, can you see if you can get a seat on the Fiday evening plane, the money will be there for you to pay . . .

It sure was good to hear your voice again . . . I love you Tess

From: Tess

Sent: November 20, 2008 11:55:54 AM My Darling Davis,

This is so frustrating, I talked with the manager of Western Union and she said she would call me back as she had to locate the information about my past transfers being that I am a frequent user of Western Union. She has to ask me questions as to the transfers I have made, and that my information needs to be updated, which is completely ludicrous, anyhow I will do what I have to do to get this money to you, but I want you to know that I am telling them that I am sending this money over for my fiance, Davis Barienda, but that you were unable to pick it up today so I sent it to your friend as you instructed me to, this is personal money, the other money I sent you was for business purposes, some sent to Mr. W and some sent to you, this is what I am telling Western Union as it is the truth. She said it would take about fifteen minutes for this interview and then the money could be released. The agent from here just called me and she said she talked to them and they are doing this because of the scams that are happening in Ghana. Davis, you need to get out of there . . . I have to go, I'm trying to do my work but I need to be by my phone, this is so frustrating, I can imagine that it is frustrating for you as well. More so problably . . . we just have to keep proving ourselves it seems. Everything will be okay, and we will be together, soon . . . I love you ti amo

Amore . . . Tess

From: Davis

Date: Fri, 21 Nov 2008 06:53:39

Hello My Love,

I have such a hunger for you, Honey. I want and need you in my life to make me whole. I love sweet moments together and I can't wait to get home and be in your arms so that we can be together forever as one family. I want to spend my life with you and grow old together. Be safe for me, love, and be mine. I love you always and forever, Your man

Dav

From: Tess

Sent: November 21, 2008 12:50:06 AM My Darling Davis,

I am sorry I couldn't wait up any longer for you to come back online, my eyes are starting to shut, I think that I have been up since 5 AM this morning. I didn't get much sleep last night, so that is why my eyes are closing fast now, but please do call me and wake me when you get the flight details. Tell me when you will be here in Whitehorse, it will either be Air North or Air Canada/Jazz that I will be meeting, and I will be there before the plane even touches down, I will be waiting for you, and I will be running into your arms as soon as we see each other. WOW . . . Oh I wish we could have talked more, I wanted to ask you if you have a warm coat with you? Because if you don't I can bring one to the airport for you to put on before walking outside, as it is cold out now, lots of snow, and minus temperatures, so a coat you will need. If you don't have one, let me know your size, and I will pick one up . . . and have it here for you . . . I love you my dear, my eyes are now real heavy, you're not coming back online so I am now going to go to bed. I love you with all my heart, and I am going to be dreaming of seeing you at the airport, and how it is going to feel with your arms around me, and how your lips will feel against mine, as we kiss . . . I love you . . . now I will say goodnight, to you a good day . . . and stay safe, and come home to me Davis, I love you ti amo

Amore . . . Tess

From: Tess

Sent: November 21, 2008 6:58:25 AM My Darling Davis,

Pretty soon, I'm hoping to be whispering your name in your ear to wake you . . . whispering to you, my darling Davis. I woke this morning, thinking that I will be waking up next to you Sunday morning, I have this wonderful feeling inside of me Davis, and it's building . . . I was hoping you would have called to wake me and tell me your flight details. I am eagerly waiting to find out when you will be here. Oh Davis, you are my dreams, I have fallen so deeply in love with you . . . stay safe for me, and get to me because I need you . . . and I want you . . . and you have to prove to me that you love me more, more than I love you, and you have a lot of proving to do, because I love you more than what you could ever imagine . . . I'm hoping to be able to meet you online before I leave for work . . . ti amo Amore . . . Tess

From: Tess

Sent: November 21, 2008 1:44:31 PM My Darling Davis,

Looking forward to seeing you and touching you . . . Western Union just called me and the lady that I talked to yesterday who released the payment for pick up said that her supervisor returned the file back to her and needs more information. They want receipts as to what the money was used for . . . I don't know if they can actually do that. This is being done for my protection I guess. anyhow this is what they want, I told her that I dont' have the receipts, that if anyone does it would be you, but you were still out of the country, anyhow, my name is going to be blackballed from Western Union if I can't produce these reciepts. She said they want to make sure there has been no illegal activity going on. Davis, this is all because of the corruption and the scammers in Ghana that take advantage of people. I guess I'm asking, do you have any records that I can show to them, if you have receipts, bring them home please . . . until I can produce the receipts I am banned from using Western Union.

I am waiting patiently for your flight details, patiently jumping up and down with anticipation . . . YEEESSSS gotta run, I've got to finish at work and relieve my son, he's watching Zoey . . . I love you ti amo Amore . . . Tess

# 16

# GETTING DAVIS HOME AND OUT OF AFRICA

From: Tess

Sent: November 22, 2008 7:26:51 AM My Darling Davis,

I don't know if you checked my other e-mail first, the one containing your ticket info from Montreal, I just wanted to let you know that I had to book a return flight so I picked a date in Jan, however that can be changed, and it does not necessarily need to be used at that time, it was cheaper for airmiles to book a return flight, otherwise it was triple the amount of airmiles for a one—way ticket. I hope the date works for you, the coming home date, and if we have to change it we can, but this is the soonest I can get you out of Montreal. I have been trying to call, but no luck . . . I love you

Tess

From: Tess

Sent: November 22, 2008 8:31:50 AM Hello John,

I have been checking my account twice a day, Thursday, Friday and again this morning and I still do not have the transfer in my account. Please be aware that I have checked regarding the length of time that the bank will hold funds to verify their origin and it can be anywhere from five to fifteen business days if it is a large amount. And with the

Canadian Bank, money transfers or wires are entered into the accounts by the receiving bank; my bank is closed on the weekend, so anything that the main wiring center receives this weekend will not be put into my account until Monday if it is cleared. Please be assured John that as soon as I get the funds into my account I will let you know immediately. I can promise you that . . .

Sincerely Tess

*Davis and I met online this morning, he asked me for one more favour. In order for him to leave Accra, he needed to give the hotel manager some money towards his bill, otherwise the manager was not going to let him leave. I told him that was ridiculous because anywhere else, if you can't pay your bill the hotel would kick you out, not keep you. He said that he had to do this because the hotel manager had been really good to him and they needed some sort of reassurance that he would be coming back to clear up his bill which was over $10, 000.00. The hotel manager was willing to accept $2400.00. I told Davis, I couldn't come up with $2400.00, possibly half $1200.00 but not $2400.00, I pointed out as well that even if I could do this, I had no way of getting it to him because I was banned from Western Union until he could produce receipts. He suggested that there could be another way to send the money, through moneygram.*

From: Tess

Sent: November 22, 2008 10:14:25 AM My Darling Davis,

I was up and out the door before 8:30AM, I had to wait for the post office to open, on Saturdays it's 9:30, only to find out that the one in the mall does not do moneygram only money orders, so she said the one under shoppers on main may do moneygrams she was not sure, so I went over there, and they're not open until 11 AM, so I still don't know if they do moneygrams or not . . . not all Canada posts offer that service, and here in Whitehorse, I don't think that they do them, but I will call them at 11 AM to see if they do. I will let you know as soon as I find out. I have been trying to call you as well since 9 AM, if you get a chance to call me please do, I love you Davis . . .

Tess

From: Tess

Sent: November 22, 2008 11:11:04 AM My Darling Davis,

I have done everything in my power that I can do, I have the $1200.00 but I have no way of getting it to you. There is no moneygram service here in Whitehorse That is a service offered only in the big cities, Here are the phone numbers for the post offices in Whitehorse, in case you want to double check 311-555-5544 Also if you want to contact Western Union regarding me being blocked and I believe your name and Mr W is also blocked for receiving funds through Western Union. If you want to talk to them to straighten things out so you can once more receive money their number is 1-800-555-1155. Davis, I don't know what else I can do . . . You have a ticket for the plane from Montreal to Whitehorse, the hotel manager has to understand that I can't do anything and the only way he is going to get paid is to trust that you will send him money as soon as you get home. Davis, I feel absolutely numb, I don't know what else to say, please don't tell me you've wasted the flight, please don't, I love you, and I want you in our lives, Zoey wants you as a father, I want you as a husband, please come home . . . I love you Davis . . . with all my heart.

Tess

From: Davis

Sent: November 22, 2008 11:35:14 AM Hello Tess,

Ever since you walked into my life, I have been smiling. There hasn't been a night when I have gone to sleep with a frown on my face, and it's all because of you. Honey, I am glad that you came into my life. I have always wanted the love of my life to be understanding, loving, caring, and faithful. I wanted someone who would accept me for who I am. I know that I've found that person in you. My heart told me that my princess was there when I first said hello to you over the phone. I didn't have to think twice when I asked you to be my wife. I knew that you were the perfect match for me. I don't think that there is, or that there ever could be, anyone better than you out there for me.

I love you with my whole heart. I have never trusted anyone the way I trust you. Sometimes I even doubt myself, but I know I will never doubt you because you are my true love. I know deep down inside that you will never break my heart or let me down in any way.

Thank you for everything, honey. I pray to God every day to bless you with everything you deserve. I will love you until the end of time.

Always and forever yours. Dav

From: Davis

Sent: November 22, 2008 11:39:47 AM Hello My wonderful woman,

How are you doing once again??It was really nice to talk to you this morning and to know that you are safe and doing great for me.I know you are having problem with western union and I don't want you to use there but I want you to drive into the city and wire the money with Money gram so that I can get home babe. I want you to do it in the name of love . . . Hmmm Babe I need to get home and I have parked all my things and looking forward to heaing r from you.Honey I know it's really hard for you to drive distance where Moneygram is located, but just try and do for me so I can get home. I am having tears in my eyes while talking to you.I need to get home so that you can take care of me as you know my health is not in good condition.I will call you I love you Your Husband

Dav

*I have to say that the reference from Davis as being my husband was making me feel weird, in a very creepy way.*

From: Tess

Sent: November 22, 2008 1:27:34 PM My Darling Davis

You know if I could drive to a city to send you a moneygram I would, there is only one problem: the closest city to us, in Whitehorse, is Vancouver, that is a 2 hour plane ride from here, or a two day drive in good conditions, Davis . . . I don't know what I can say, other than, I don't care about anything else other than you coming here to meet me and Zoey. You have a ticket from Montreal to Whitehorse; I have done everything you have asked me to do, that I could possibly do for you. Whitehorse does not have a moneygram; we are a small city located thousands of miles from any large city. Davis, I am asking you to come here to meet me, I've sent you the money for the ticket, I have used my airmiles to buy you a ticket in order for you to come here I'm not able to do this last thing for you because there doesn't exist the means to get the money to you. I have been banned from Western Union; I am being investigated or watched for fraudulent activity by the banks. I need you here to take care of the money situation and to help clear me . . . Please don't let the manager come between us, I can't do anything, I'm sorry . . . Dont' throw us away because he won't accept the fact that you can send him money when you get here . . . no matter what, I want to meet you . . . I fell in love with YOU . . .

Tess

My messenger is not working I can't sign on . . . I am sorry

From: Davis

Sent: November 22, 2008 11:14:56 PM Take a Look

Thank you for booking with KLM! print Print Flight details

Departure From Accra (Kotoka Airport) to Amsterdam (Schiphol) Flight number KL0590

Departure time 2155 Tue 25 Nov 2008

Arrival time 0550 Wed 26 Nov 2008 Class Economy Class

From Amsterdam (Schiphol) to Montreal (Pierre Elliott Trudeau

International Airport) Flight number KL0671

Departure time 1520 Wed 26 Nov 2008

Arrival time 1700 Wed 26 Nov 2008 Flight duration 24:05 h

Class Economy Class

Re Total journey time: 24 hours 5 minutes Price Breakdown

Passenger Type No. Excluding tax Tax Total Adult(s) 1 978.00 325.33 1, 303.33

Price USD 1, 303.33

Accra (Kotoka Airport) to Montreal (Pierre Elliott Trudeau International Airport)

Economy (Flexible)

Passenger information (First Passenger) Name Mr. David Bagnad (Adult)

Seat preference Aisle Special meal Fruit meal Selected ticket type Ticket Type E-Ticket

Selected ticket type E-ticket

I must say that this itinary looked pretty good. There weren't any spelling errors.

# 17

# JOSEPH BLACK AND FIFTY THOUSAND DOLLARS IN MY BANK ACCOUNT

Late in the evening of November 22, after 10 PM I received a phone call from Mr Joseph Black, calling from someplace in Ontario. He told me he had sent a cheque by Federal Express to my bank and that the tracking information on his computer showed the cheque as being delivered to the wrong address, he asked if I could double—check in the morning with my bank to ensure that they did indeed have the cheque. First of all, this took me quite by surprise; for starters, I thought that they were not going to go through with the money transfer after all, I had made it clear to Davis that I was not going to forward the money like they wanted me to. Also, I was expecting a wire transfer, not a cheque. Secondly, he wanted to establish a code word with me, which was Black 123, and I was not to give out any information unless he stated that coded word. Every time Joseph called me he would start asking me questions and I would ask him the code word and he would have to say it before I would answer.

The money transfer was actually happening, they were going to go through with it. All I had to do now was see if Davis showed up, that was my test, deep down inside, I felt that if he arrived, looking like his picture, I wasn't too sure what I would do.

From: Tess

Sent: November 23, 2008 9:04:44 AM Hello John,

I talked with Joseph Black last night regarding the Fed Ex delivery of the cheque, when he called me I did not get his phone number as he is going to call me tomorrow which will be Monday, however I would like to talk with him today as well. John are you able to get a message to Mr.Black to call me after 6 PM my time, which would be 9 PM for him, I would just like to give him an update. Thank You

Tess

*Davis and I met online, he was sounding desperate as to what to do in regards to the hotel manager, he had to leave him with something, he would leave the computer but that would not be good enough on its own. I couldn't stand it, I agreed to attempt one more time to send the money that he was requesting, I did look at whether or not I could afford to lose anymore money, I decided I had to, in order to finish this I had to send the money. I asked my cousin to help me out. She agreed to send the money through Western Union for me.*

*Davis of course was elated when I came up with this solution and he promised me again that he would repay everything that he owed me, I just wanted to see if he would show up. One way or the other I had to find out the truth.*

From: Tess

Sent: November 23, 2008 9:53:59 AM My Darling Davis,

I have changed your flight leaving Montreal to Thursday Nov 27. I believe it leaves at 7:05AM and arrives in Whitehorse at 2 PM . . . Davis, I will be waiting for you . . . I want to welcome you with me in your arms, I want to look into your eyes and I want to feel your kiss on my lips, this image is all that I can think about. It is what I see . . . it is what I've seen in my dreams, I believe in dreams Davis, you are my Dream I love you If you have trouble opening the attachment please let me know, it was taking a long time to open for me, so I just forward the e-mail that aeroplan sent to me, with the attachment . . .

My Cousin's name is Jamie York The security question: What's my favorite colour, answer is Blue. She is telling Western Union that she is sending the funds to her friend as it is close to Christmas as a gift.

I am hoping that I could meet you online. I will keep my Messenger open, my buzz sound, just so you know, sometimes doesn't work, so if you come online and I'm not responding very fast, will you be able to call me? I will be getting Zoey into a bath and cleaning up my kitchen, I will keep checking as well.

Jamie will go tomorrow at 9 AM to send the money and then she will call me at work with the confirmation number. I will then email it to you so you should have the confirmation number before 5:30PM your time. and then Tuesday you can leave . . . Davis do you think you can write down that phone card that I sent you and take it with you so you can call me when you get to Montreal, I'm hoping that from there we may be able get a good connection and have a chance to hear each other and really talk without getting cut off. . . . Oh Davis, this is it, you are coming HOME . . .

I Love You Tess . . .

Oh and Mr.Joseph Black, just called me and I told him that the Fed Ex was recieved by a lady whom I know is the receptionist at the bank. However, I will call the bank to see what is happening with the cheque as it is not showing up in my account.I hope to talk to you later, I hope you are feeling better today, I love you and take care of yourself, stay safe.

I love you Tess

From: Tess

Sent: November 23, 2008 9:16:47 PM My Darling Davis,

I was hoping that we could have talked today, I do hope that you are feeling alright, when you come home, if you're still not feeling well, I will nurse you back to health. I will take very good care of you, I promise. I was going to stay up tonight until 11 PM to see if you would come online, but I am feeling exhausted right now, and it's only 9 PM, so Davis my darling, I am going to go to bed right after e-mailing you. I really need to sleep, I think I am emotionally exhausted, we've both been through a lot these last couple of weeks, and I think finally knowing you're coming home, my body is telling me, it's time to get some rest. Jamie will be at Western Union at 9 AM, and she will call me at work with the confirmation number as soon as she is done, and I will e-mail it immediately. Then I will call the bank and find out what happened to the cheque that Joseph Black sent, it was delivered at least that is what the Fed—Ex tracking report states. Anyhow, please will you let me know how you are doing . . . I care about you Davis and I worry about you, please keep yourself safe and come home to me where you belong . . . I love you.

Were you able to open the flight itinerary I e-mailed you? I haven't been able to open the one they sent me . . . ti amo. Amore . . .

Tess

From: Davis

Sent: November 23, 2008 10:35:29 PM Hello My love,

How are you doing?It's really nice to hear from you and I have smiles on my face now because you are in my life and I will always be loving and cherishing you.You are all I have been praying and hoping for . . . But now that you and Zoey are in my life I will hold on to you and let you know that I will always be loving you . . . I am online now like always to see if I could reach you but no luck . . . I love you

Yours forever Husband, Dav

From: Davis

Sent: November 23, 2008 10:41:23 PM

Hello My wife, life can be cruel but when it all comes together there is no moment as sweet. That is how I feel about you entering my life. You have rekindled the flame called love in me. You have given one more reason to look forward to tomorrow. Now, you are a significant part of my life and I look forward to the day when we can make it permanent. I love you so much. I love you for your kindness, for your caring and giving nature, for your beauty—both inner and outer, and most of all I love you because you are you. The fact that you show me who you really are and not what you think I may want. Sweetie, let this letter be a testament to my true feelings for you. The whole world can see and know how I feel for you, I will always be loving.

Your lovely man Dav

From: Davis

Sent: November 24, 2008 9:38:24 AM Hello My wife,

I love you because you make me look forward to each day. You're my everything, a dream come true. There are no words to express what I feel for you. There are no songs as beautiful as the music that fills my soul when I hear your voice. There are no roses as lovely as your smile. Nothing moves me like you do. There are no days brighter than the days I spend talking to you on the phone. You're my light in the darkness. There could never be words strong enough to express my love for you. I love you with my body, soul, and mind. You're my everything. I love you so much,

Your Man Dav

From: Tess

Sent: November 24, 2008 7:04:56 AM My Darling Davis,

I am sorry I was not able to meet you online last night at 10:30, Davis I couldn't even keep my eyes open anymore at 9:30, and believe me I tried. I went to bed and I dreamt of you; you were laying next to me, your arms wrapped around me, I fell asleep feeling your arms around me, and I woke feeling your presence as well. Davis, we will be in each other's arms soon. I am counting the days, the hours, minutes and seconds, until we can look into each others eyes and feel each other's arms holding us together . . . Oh Davis, I just keep thinking, my God, you will be here, and our lives will finally be able to begin . . .I am looking forward to seeing you, to talking with you, to touching you, to kissing you, to holding you, to laughing with you, and most of all to being with you . . . I love you Davis.with all my heart. I will be e-mailing you just after 9 AM. let me know how things go . . . I love you

Tess

From: Tess

Sent: November 24, 2008 9:22:59 AM My Darling Davis,

Here is the control number . . . 807 444 0897 I hope this works. Please e-mail me or call me and let me know that everything is taken care of and that you are able to come home . . . tomorrow. YEESS. I love you ti amo Amore . . . Tess

From: Davis

Sent: November 24, 2008 9:41:17 AM To:     Tess

Hello My lovely Tess,

There are no words to express how I feel about you. I constantly search for the words, and they all seem less than I truly feel. You are my life, my heart, and my soul. You are my best friend. You are my one true love. I still remember the day we first met. I knew that you were the one I was meant to be with forever. I thought of you every day, and dreamed of you each night. Just when I thought you had forgotten me, you would call and make all my dreams seem real. The sound of your voice on the line was the sweetest sound I would ever find.My heart was beating hard within my chest. My hand was shaking and I could barely breathe.

Your love forever, Dav

*I went to the bank today and talked with the account manager. The cheque did arrive at the bank, however it was made out to the bank with only my account number to deposit to, no name and no other information. I explained everything to the bank manager, and that I had been in touch with the police. I also told him that I didn't want to be able to have access to the money even if it cleared. The bank manager told me that it will show up as being in my account but I will not be able to access it and that the fraud department would be looking into the cheque because it did appear questionable. The bank managerdid ask me if I had taken a look at the cheque, I told him no, he said that just the way the business logo appeared on the cheque with just my account number raised quite a few red flags for the bankingpersonal. The bank was going to put my account on deposit only; however that account was my main banking account so the manager allowed me to still access the original amount of funds that I had in my account before the cheque arrived, otherwise I would have not had any access to any monies. This incident could and did mess up a lot of my own personal banking transactions that caused me a lot of anquish and a lot of frustrations.*

From: Tess

Sent: November 24, 2008 11:19:17 AM Davis, My Darling,

You fill me with love through your words. You express beautifully your love, I feel and sense it and know it, through your words, now I want to feel it through your touch. I wanted to let you know that I just talked with Joseph Black. I went down to the bank personally and I talked with them, the cheque arrived on Thursday, however, today it is still in the manager's office, he will be verifying it before it shows up into my account and the bank wanted to know what it was for . . . I told them that it was for my fiancé's business, which is what I explained to Joseph Black. It could take another 48 to 72 hours for this to happen, but I reassured him that the cheque was here, it had been delivered. And again it will be here for us to deal with when you get home on Thursday. We can go to the bank on Friday if you would like . . . it should be cleared by then.

I love you . . . I have to get going, people are coming to my office . . . I will write you later, and if not, is it possible to meet you online at 10-10:30 tonight . . . I love you ti amo Amore . . . Tess

From: Tess

Sent: November 24, 2008 1:38:24 PM My Darling Davis,

I just had to take a minute from work to write you, to tell you that I love you so much, and I think of you every minute. I'm picturing you walking into my office at the end of the day, coming to pick me up and take me home and Zoey would be with you. I have this feeling I may have to set up some ground rules for when you two go shopping. Otherwise, we may have to get a big house. I want to do so much with you Davis, I want to show you so many things, but most of all, this feeling of actually being a family with you and me, Zoey and the boys, is one of the best feelings I have ever had. Knowing that you will be here by my side, and that we will be together, I have dreamt of this day Davis, and you are the man to make my dreams come true. Thank You and I will forever love you, for being the wonderful man that you are, for being my man . . .

I love you . . . Tess

From: Tess

Sent: November 24, 2008 10:30:30 PM My Darling Darling,

I was just looking at your ticket, I'm hoping that you've already noticed this: your name is wrong, on the ticket—it is David Bagnad. I hope you've changed this or are able to change it with the travel agent. Davis I would hate for something like this to keep you from me . . . I want you with me, with us more than I've ever wanted anything in my life . . . I love you Davis, and I'm waiting for you.

Your love for life . . . Tess

From: Steve

Date: Mon, 24 Nov 2008 22:55:07

Hey Tess

I would like to know should I look to you for a couple of dates? I am looking for a date for a movie, I want to see Bond and then there is the work xmas party. Should I be asking you?

I would like to . . .

*I called Steve and told him that I would love to go to the movies and to his Christmas party with him, if he would come with me to mine, however I just had to wait until Thursday to see if Davis arrived or not. I was not prepared for Steve's response, he told me not to go to the airport alone, whatever I did, do not go alone. Steve said that he was going to be out of town that day for work otherwise he would be there himself, he was adamant that I not go alone. I was quite shocked and I think Steve was too, he told me he was quite concerned about this. I started to think about what Steve was saying and realized that maybe I should have someone with me, maybe I should be somewhat cautious. I told Steve I would call him and let him know and I promised him I would take someone with me.*

From: Tess

Sent: November 25, 2008 9:43:34 AM Hello John,

I just wanted to keep you posted, the cheque did arrive at the bank, it is now showing as being deposited into my account but I still do not have access to it until the bank verifies the cheque. When I talked with the bank yesterday, the manager said it could be anywhere from forty eight hours to five days. So I will let you know as soon as it is verified and accessible.

Sincerely Tess

# 18

# DR PHIL BYMAN

November 26th the day Davis is to leave and fly home. We talked online this morning; Davis was getting ready to leave for the airport. I told Davis that the money was here, that the bank was holding it, and if they released it I was not going to send it as John had instructed me to, but rather I was going to hold onto it until Davis got here, and then he could deal with everything. Davis told me not to worry about the money because as soon as he got home, he would take care of everything and the first thing he was going to do, was pay me back. He told me he had to leave to get to the airport; Mr W was picking him up. I wished him a safe and speedy trip, he was coming home. everything just didn't seem real, it was a dream. For so long this had gone on and now it was coming down to these final hours. All day long I kept checking my e-mails; was I expecting one from Davis saying he couldn't make it? I'm not too sure. but I kept checking. By the time I went to bed, there had been no e-mails from Davis, I guess that meant he was on his way.

My phone rang at 12:30am.

A feeling of complete dread washed over me as I picked the phone up, pushed the talk button and whispered a strained " hello"

"is this Tess?"

"Yes" I replied, my throat feeling tight

*"Tess, do you know a David Bagnad?" He asked me "No, do you mean Davis Barienda?" I asked*

*"Yes, Davis Barienda" I could feel the numbness starting to take over my body, I had been expecting this, but I hadn't been expecting it to hurt like it was starting to hurt.*

*" My name is Dr Byman, I am calling from the hospital, Mr Barienda collapsed at the airport and was brought to the hospital, he is unconscious, we found your name and number in his wallet so we are calling you to let you know what has happened to him."*

*I couldn't respond, I was numb. "Are you there madame?"*

*"Yes" I whispered into the phone. I asked "what is his diagnosis?"*

*The Dr replied, "He could have Malaria"*

*I asked the Doctor what were Davis's vitals signs and asked what his temperature was, the Doctor quickly responded that they were a poor hospital and were not able to provide that. The Doctor gave me his phone number and asked me to call him right back as he was running low on minutes.*

*I told the Doctor that Mr Warleh would be the best person to get a hold of as he was Davis's friend, and business manager and he was in Accra.*

*The Doctor said he would keep me informed as to how Mr Barienda was doing. I thanked him and hung up the phone. I then called Steve and told him that I could be his date for the movie and Christmas party if he would be mine. Steve said he was sorry that things didn't work out for me and that he would be seeing me soon. I thanked Steve for being there for me and sat down at my computer and wrote a letter to Davis.*

From: Tess

Sent: November 26, 2008 1:05:57 AM Davis,

I guess this is it . . .Please forgive me, but everything that has been said will happen has happened. You know I did fall in love with your words, they were beautiful, I just wish they were real. I'm sorry if it doesn't seem real, the Doctor calling me and telling me that you collapsed at the airport, and you were taken to his hospital, he couldn't tell me the name of the hospital, he told me his name and asked me to call him back, which I tried to do, but couldn't get through. Everything is numb right now, numb with the realization that you are not coming. I'm sorry I can't help you . . . I can't go on with this. You made me feel alive, loved and beautiful, the only real sad part is that Zoey, my daughter believed in you, and she is going to get hurt as well . . . I'm sorry that this had to happen, I wish it was real, I wish you were real . . . we could have made magic together, the way we talked,

Goodbye to the man I fell in love with, for now I am numb. My fairy tale was just that, a fairy tale, it's too bad fairy tales aren't real . . .

# 19

# MY INTRODUCTION TO MR EARL WARLEH

From: Earl Warleh

Date: Thu, 27 Nov 2008 05:14:31

Hello Madam Tess,

This is Mr W and I want you to know that your husband collapsed at the airport on his way home. He even told me that he was very excited that everything that he has gone through is over and he is getting home to be with you (His Wife I believe) be leaving to the airport. hmmmmm I was at the hospital when the doctor taking care of him asked me if i know him and all I could say is yes but he has been like a father to me because he is very nice to me and also he has helped me a lot.For the doctors information he said Mr Dav has a grown appendix and malaria.

The name of the hospital is Lungetown Hospital and the name of the doctor taking care of him is called Dr Phil Byman.

When I saw Mr Dav in his condition I nearly had tears in my eyes but I am a man so I had to pull my self together and be strong, but Dr Byman assured me that he will be okay. But he is running some test on him.

As soon as he told me that I had hope and became strong, Madam Tess, please I want you to hold heart and be strong. I promise I will do anything to get your husband home . . . He told me a lot about you and he said he wants to get home and build a great family with you and that was the last word I heard from him before he left for the airport.

Thank you for your time and I will contact you again I have to run to the hospital and check up on him because I am the only person I think I can help him out.I promise to do all my best to make sure your husband gets home to you,

This is my number +233242345678 and please you can contact me as well as I will do the same.

Mr W

Have a Good day

*I felt that I had to continue with letting these guys think that I didn't know what was going on, I felt I needed to get some information from them, I wasn't too sure as to what information I was expecting to get, but I had $57, 000.00 sitting in my bank account and I wanted to make these guys squirm a little.*

*Steve called me and had asked me if I wanted to go with him to his cabin for a couple of days, I told him that I would. He even told me that he wouldn't take advantage of me, being that I was in a vulnerable state. I completely did not believe that and knew that he would totally use my vulnerability to his full advantage and his own benefit as well as use my situation for his complete entertainment value. I think I needed that at this point, Steve's sense of humor laced with some sarcasm, laughter and some understanding from a "good" friend and maybe some loving as well, I did miss Steve. I must admit, our sex life was amazing. and it had been a while.*

From: Tess

Sent: November 27, 2008 9:22:48 AM Mr Warleh

Thank You for getting in touch with me, all I can think about is Davis being in the hospital and I don't have any idea as to how he is doing or what his condition is. I tried to contact the doctor with the number he gave me but the number is not working from here. The doctor told me that Davis was in a coma. I have been in tears and I have been very scared. I love Davis with all my heart, yet I dont know if I will ever see him . . . If he is in the hospital and needs treatment, who is going to pay for this treatment? I dont have any money and I am no longer allowed to send money, so even if I had any money whatsoever, I can't send money through Western Union as I am blocked from using it and there is nobody else here that I can ask for help. My cousin can't anymore. I did what I could to get Davis home, now that chance is gone and when he really needs me, I can't be there. I feel as if I have failed him. I am asking you, and thanking you to be there for Davis, as he thinks very highly of you, you are the only one he can turn to right now, please, even if he is in a coma, please tell him I love him, I miss his words and his voice . . . I am very upset, I am going away for a few days to a place where no cell phones can reach me. I may be able to check my e-mail, but that is not a for sure thing; I have to get away as my heart is breaking. I fear that my world is crashing down around me, it is best that he doesn't know this as he needs strength of which I don't have. I wish I was there then I would be able to do something. I need to go now, again thank you for your letter and your phone calls and for being there for Davis. I love him so much, please tell him . . . Thank You

Tess

Please can you give me the address and the phone number of the hospital. Thank you again.

From: Earl Warleh

Date: Thu, 27 Nov 2008 21:56:55

Hello Madam Tess,

Thank you very much for the mail, It's good to be in touch with you. Your leaving out of town won't solve the problem, but to make Mr Davis lose hope when he hears about this and Davis will lose the chance of being alive for you.I am a very kind hearted man and I have some good news for you and some bad news too. The good News is that Mr Davis opened his eyes and was able to talk a little but all he could say was your name and he wants to talk to you . . . When I saw him like that I nearly had tears in my eyes but I couldn't help to hold the tears but to drop it, anyway you can come to Ghana and see him if you want to, but Dr Byman told me that in his condition he needs a flight back home directly ASAP for serious check up and I learnt you are a nurse so you can look for a good hospital where you think they can do a good and clean work on your husband. Madam Tess I want you to take heart and I told you I will make sure everything is under control and please stop crying. Okay it won't help but to leave the situation unsolved . . . I want you to be strong and help him in prayers.

The doctor taking care of him told me they dont have some of the equipments they will need to save him due to the under developing of this country. Anyway I will go to the Hospital Early In the Morning to find out his condition is and if he can try and say a word to you.

Thank you,

I hope you have my number you can contact me Best Regards,

Mr W

From:John Sigman

Date: Thu, 27 Nov 2008 11:02:42

Dear Tess,

Rest assured that the fund would be available today because it was supposed to be held for only five working days. I want you to check your account today and once the fund is there, go ahead to transfer the sum of. $3, 500 by Western Union in the name of Mr.Jileon Behgoh, Location: Lagos

Nigeria.

Thereafter, transfer the sum of $45, 000 into the account stated below and send me all relevant information and transfer slip for easy collection of the fund by the authorities.

Below is the banking details of the agency;

BANK NAME—BANK OF CHINA

BRANCH NAME—BANK OF CHINA BANGKOK BRANCH. ACCOUNT NO.—0136 1280 2222 1499 916

SWIFT CODE—BKCH###BK001

BRANCH ADDRESS-No . . ., Bangkok, China. BRANCH PHONE—008601 2345678

BANK NAME—BANK OF CHINA.

It is very important you send the Western Union today and let me have the necessary transfer information and as soon as the rest of the fund is transferred into the account stated above, also let me have the transfer slip, so as to submit same to the concerned agency.

I am looking forward to hearing from you ASAP. Regards,

Mr. John.

I think that this is what I have been waiting for. this is the information that I needed to pass on to the police. I had a feeling I wasn't supposed to get this until there was no doubt in their minds that I would move the money for them. someone made a mistake in sending me this info. I felt as if I was holding a valuable piece of information and I wasn't too sure as to what I should do about it.

From: Tess

Sent: November 27, 2008 4:17:44 PM John,

Please can you get a message to Mr. Black, because of what has happened with Davis, I am so distraught that I have gone out of town, I have come back into town today to check my e-mails, and on seeing yours I thought that I should reply asap. I checked my bank account and the funds have not been released yet. I do have a call into the bank manager to see what is happening, but John, are you aware of what has happened to Davis? I am so upset that I feel like my world has come apart; I will have to call the bank manager tomorrow as I do not have my cell phone with me. Please let Mr.Black know this as well. While I'm in town tomorrow I will e-mail you and let you know what is happening. I have to go,

Tess

From: Tess

Sent: November 28, 2008 8:39:44 AM Hello Mr Warleh,

Thank You for your e-mail, I know you may not understand this, but I have a place that I go to, where I gather strength and I go there to heal. It is in our wilderness, it is a beautiful place with mountains, trees and a lake and a cabin. It is a place where I could go and have my heart break without falling apart in front of my daughter. Feeling as if I have lost Davis, has torn my world apart, I still don't know how he is doing, but you have given me a little bit of hope. I want Davis home so I can take care of him. I am hoping that the travel agency will still honor his ticket, please can you talk with them, I will not be in town for another hour or so, I have to go to the bank as there is a problem there, and then I will try and see if I can phone you . . . I am hoping I will be able to talk to Davis . . . Please tell him I love him . . .

Thank You Tess

From: John Sigman

Date: Fri, 28 Nov 2008 09:29:18 +0000

Attn: Tess,

I am in receipt of your mail and thanks for same. However, I was a little bit worried when I did not hear from you because I was under the impression the fund has been confirmed in your account that was why I sent you that details base on our last correspondence

Nonetheless, I want you to try and get in touch with Mr. Black by phone to let him know what is going on because he is very worried at your silence. Also, Mr. Davis is alright, he just had a little fever but he is fine now.

It is very important you check your account immediately and follow the instruction I sent you previously, to enable us to move ahead with the transaction because we have wasted too much time already. I am waiting to hearing from you ASAP.

Best regards, John.

From: Tess

Sent: November 28, 2008 8:33:04 AM Hello John,

I am just leaving for town, I will be there by the time the bank opens, however I went online and just looked at my account and it is telling me funds are not available. When the bank is open this morning at 9:30 I will be able to see what is going on. Please can you get a message to Joseph Black as I do not have a phone number for him with me or an e-mail address, and it is going to take me an hour to get to town. I hope you recieve this e-mail before then. John, Davis had more then a fever, he was in a coma, and it wasn't looking good for him, he needs to come to a proper hospital, I don't even know if he can talk to me . . . I am so upset, I am hoping and praying that he will be okay . . . I don't know what I would do if I lost him . . . I will e-mail you as soon as I find out what is going on.

Tess

*I waited for what would seem like a reasonable time if I were to really have gone to the bank and then I emailed John once more.*

From: Tess

Sent: November 28, 2008 11:15:45 AM Hello John,

I am sorry but the bank is not releasing the funds. I have talked with Joseph and have asked him to call you regarding wiring the money directly to where you want it to go. I did offer to e-mail him the info but he said he would call you instead, also John I am unable to do any Western Union transactions as I have sent Davis a lot of monies already and the manager at Western Union wants to see receipts to prove that the money was used for business so unless that can happen I have been blocked from doing any Western Union transactions . . . I feel terrible that I cannot help Davis, please, if you can help him I would appreciate that . . . again I am sorry . . .

Tess

From: Earl Warleh

Date: Fri, 28 Nov 2008 17:27:45

Hello Madam Tess,

You talking about traveling to heal your broken heart that's what I dont understand, Davis still loves you and its because of you that he wants to get home and be with you but things didnt go that way . . . Tess, I want you to take heart and please be strong. I promised you something, I want you to know that with this situation we need to be in good communication I think so that we can work on things possible for Davis to get home. I dont want the idea of him still being here because his health is really down and you should be here to take care of him as you are a nurse, You can call me tomorrow morning. I was at the hospital tonight but Mr Byman was not on duty so there was nothing I could do but to just go and sit by Davis and tell him that you called and you are communicating with me and, madam please, Dr Byman told me you have his number but you never called him.

Thanks for the mail and I have to run now,

Mr W

From: Tess

Sent: November 28, 2008 6:17:56 PM Hello Mr Warleh,

I am glad that you are there for Davis, please tell the doctor that I have tried to call the number that he gave me and all I get is that the number can not be reached as dialed. It is very hard for me to be here and not be able to talk to anyone, so I thank you very much for keeping in touch with me, you are my only link to Davis . . . this means so much to me . . . Earl, can I call you Earl?, I would be in Accra next to Davis right now if I could, if I had the ability I would not be here, believe me, I want to be beside him right now, but I have no money to get me anywhere. This is what scares me, because my only hope for Davis to be able to come home is that the airlines will give him a credit as he collapsed at the airport. I pray and hope that they will do that.

Please tell Davis that I am praying for him, I wish I could talk to him, Earl, there is nothing I can do for Davis from here other than send him my love and my prayers; please tell him, that he is in my thoughts every minute of the day, Zoey is very sad that he is not here, and she wants him better so that he can come home and be her step—father, she cried last night, wanted to see Davis, this breaks my heart, to see her upset. I need to be strong for my daughter, and in order to be strong I need to have a cry and gather my strength and then I can go on . . . Please tell Davis that I am gathering my strength and energy for him, he is my dream . . . please tell him . . . tell him I love him with all my heart and soul.

Please can you e-mail me a phone number for the the hospital, so I can talk to one of the nurses and check on Davis, anytime, and also the address of the hospital I would like to send him a letter via mail if I could. I could get it there in two days if you could send me the address. Saturday AM for me I would love to send him a card via courier.

When I say that I go away to heal, it is not like travelling, it is driving to a place that is two hours from where I live, to a small town that is nestled in the mountains and this place is my home town. It is where I spent many happy memories as a child, it is small, spacious, only about 300 people, it is quiet, and it allows me to gather my strength. It is a special place, I have told Davis about this place, in fact I have told him that I want to take him there when he comes home, I think he would understand. Please don't ever let him think that I am not thinking about him, he is always with me, and reassure him that I love him.

Again Thank You so much for everything you are doing for Davis . . . Tess

From: John Sigman

Sent: Fri, 28 Nov 2008 22:41:52

Attn: Tess,

Thanks for your response.

If you cannot do any Western Union transaction go ahead to transfer the fund into the account stated in my previous mail and send me the transfer slip. At the moment there is nothing I can do for Davis till the transfer is done by you, so as to be certain everything is going on accordingly.

I am sure the funds would be in your account before the end of today. Regards,

John.

From: Tess

Sent: November 28, 2008 3:43:51 PM Hello John,

I am sorry, maybe I did not make myself clear enough before, the bank is not allowing me access to the money, they have threatened to close my account completely. I am unable to access any funds at this time, they will not accept any wire transfer either so I am unable to do any transactions whatsoever, I explained to Joseph Black that it would be best if he could wire the money directly to where you want it to go as I am not able to. My bank will not allow it, all I can hope is that they will reconsider closing my account completely as I have banked with this bank for years. I do not understand why this is happening. I cannot help you, I cannot help Davis and this is killing me . . . I am very sorry . . . Please talk with Joseph Black

Tess

From: Tess

Sent: November 28, 2008 11:21:00 PM My Darling Davis,

I don't know if and when you will be able to read this, I have fallen apart since hearing what has happened to you, I apologise for not being able to be there for you, Davis, I would have flown over if I had the money, in fact I checked to see if I could, and it was not possible. I have felt so helpless, I have felt so numb, I have cried a lot, I have prayed a lot, right now, Mr W with his phone calls and e-mails has given me some hope, he said that they would do whatever they could to get you home. I am hoping that they can do that soon, Davis, I read my e-mail I sent to you, please, understand when I wrote that letter I felt all was lost between us, I thought you were gone. I was so afraid for you and I couldn't do anything, Davis, I feel so empty without you, not hearing from you has left me feeling so alone; I miss you so much, I wish I could talk to you to know how you are doing, if you are reading this, you must be better, enough at least to be able to get to a computer anyway. Please write me and let me know how you are, I wish I could talk to you, to hear your voice, Davis, I left town when I heard you were in the hospital uncounsious, sick with malaria and appedicitis. Davis, I had to go and cry, and then I had to build my strength I'm missing you so much, you have come into my life and you gave me so much with your words, you made me believe in love again Davis, I wished for you, I wished for you in my dreams—I will continue to dream for you and wish . . . You are my Dream . . . I Love you so much Tess

*What can I say. I missed getting e-mails from Davis. I was thinking that maybe he would e-mail me back, but I never did received another e-mail from him, I did miss getting the e-mails and I guess deep down I missed the attention that Davis gave me even if it was only through the phone, the emails and the online chats. I shared something with someone for a period of time that made me feel good, even though I knew it wasn't real and that he wasn't real it was still hard to let go of, I knew I had to let go. Dealing with Earl made it easier because I didn't have any emotional connection with him. When Earl would call me, I became a pretty good actress according to my friends who overheard my phone conversations, I would sound genuinely upset, I had Earl convinced that I was having a complete breakdown over Davis.*

From: Earl Warleh

Date: Sat, 29 Nov 2008 07:58:07—0800

Hello Madam Tess,

How are you doing today? I have not heard from you today so i had to send you a mail to know how you are doing . . . Anyway this is the doctor's number +233275554444 you can call him because I spoke to him and Dr Byman said you need to talk to him as you are the wife for his Noticed and not me come and talk to him about you talking to Davis on the phone . . .

Yesterday I was at the hospital but it seems he was not on duty so I had to sit by Mr Davis and be praying for him and all I could see is that he was having tear drops from his eyes and mentioning your name.

Madam Tess, I have to run now and check on his health. I will contact you as soon as possible.

Thank you Earl

From: Tess

Sent: November 29, 2008 11:22:09 AM Hello Earl,

Thank you for the phone number, I have been trying the number and it is not going through. I will keep trying as I do want so badly to talk with Davis, please again tell him that I love him very much and he is in my thoughts every minute of the day, tell him that I am praying for him to keep his strength and get stronger, tell him to picture white light surrounding him, and in the middle of the white light, I am standing there, my hands are touching him, and I am sending the white light into him to help heal him. He needs to visualize this, this is important, I will be visualizing this as well, he needs to do this, please can you tell him this, and please tell the Dr that I am trying to call him. It just is difficult for me to get through, can you ask the doctor, if he is able to e-mail me if we can't talk on the phone? I would very much like to talk with Davis, if he is able to talk. I have to get going I will try and check my e-mail again later today . . . again tell Davis I love him with all my heart . . . and thank you so much . . . I consider you a friend . . .

Tess

*I was at my pottery class when I received over 20 calls on my cell phone within 10 minutes, one right after the other, I never answered one of the calls. The caller id showed blocked id, and then it would show Joseph Black's number, I imagined Joseph was just stressing out not hearing from me, then I started to get a little worried when the phone calls started to become closer and closer together, I began to think that I may be playing a dangerous game here, after all, it seemed that all the players except for Earl and the doctor were all Italian, thoughts of the Italian Mafia kept going through my head.*

From: Earl Warleh

Date: Sun, 30 Nov 2008 11:56:52—0800

Hello Madam Tess,

How are you doing today?I have not heard from you today and hope everything is good with you. Take care and I hope we connect soon. Thank you

Earl

From: Tess

Sent: December 1, 2008 12:05:28 AM Hello Earl,

I am sorry I haven't been able to get back to you sooner, my internet has been acting up for most of yesterday and today, I think the telephone company has been working on the lines Anyhow I haven't been able to get through to the doctor either, I did receive a message from him and have been trying, and finally I did manage to get a hold of him, he wasn't at the hospital but on his way, so I am hoping he will be calling me soon. Please tell Davis, if he hasn't talked with me by the time you see him, that I love him and I am trying to get through to talk with him . . . Thank you

Tell him as well, he needs to get strong for us . . . Thank you so much

Tess

*I phoned the Bank of China and talked with their security department and explained to them about the information that I received and how I obtained it. The woman I talked with, Mary, suggested that I send her*

*what I had and she would look into it. I then e-mailed Mary all of the information that John had sent to me as to where he wanted the wire transfer to go to. I didn't know if they would be able to do anything but I passed the information on that I had. I think that was all that I could do right now.*

From: Tess

Sent: December 1, 2008 1:29:14 PM Attention Mary,

This is the information of where I was to send this money that was sent to my account. As I mentioned to you, this is a questionable money transfer. I have talked to The Commercial Crime Unit and the constable suggested that I pass this information onto you as you may be able to contact the Bank of China in Bangkok and possibly flag this account for illegal activity. Again I'm not too sure what is going on, other than the circumstances around this are highly questionable. Could you please let me know if you are able to do anything about this.

Thank you Tess

From: Tess

Sent: December 1, 2008 12:04:34 PM Hello Josh,

Sorry it has taken me this long to get back to you, I was hoping things would turn out differently, but as it stands I have been a "victim" so to say of a scam, and yes, I was a fool and sent the guy money and a computer, because he needed the help, mind you, I knew that I was taking a risk when I did that, I am willing to pay for my mistake on that end, however what has happened is that when I didn't have any money to send, Davis, that is the guy's' name I was corresponding with he used me to obtain fraudulent funds. The scenario goes that he is in the oil business. He bought an oil mine in Accra, Ghana, and I corresponded with him through this whole ordeal. He started in Whitehorse, I never did meet him face to face, he went from Whitehorse to Orlando, Florida and that is when we first started talking on the phone. He says the right things, I go wow, haven't heard that for a while and I swoon, anyhow, he then goes to England, where he makes the deal to buy the oil mine and asks me if I think he should do this. I told him it was his business, if he felt it was worth doing then do what he wanted to do; anyhow he goes to Ghana and on arrival loses all of his luggage, his briefcase and the expensive imac computer. He is upset about this, he has gone to the police, but he is not worried about money as he has enough on him because he is a businessman and is allowed to bring more into the country, so he goes along doing renovations to the mine, and then he runs out of money. He needs money to continue to work and he makes a good story—anyhow I did send him some money of my own, which again I knew I was taking a risk, but then he said that one of the companies that he did work for owed him money, he could get them to send me money and I could western union it over to him as the banking system is very different there. He was not able to set up an account himself in Accra, I'm gullible I know, however I felt that was okay because it wasn't my money it was his money he was wanting. So the accountant, Giovanni of the company named Makuman, contacts me to arrange to have money sent to me through my Visa. I asked him why not just wire it to me and he stated that it would go faster and easier going through the Visa so he put a payment on of 9, 620.00 onto my Visa, I took a cash advance and sent the money via Western Union over to Accra, Ghana to Davis. I had to do this in two different payments. Giovanni asked me to see if I could get a larger credit amount on my visa so he could send over more money as Davis needed a lot of money . . . I didn't do this, anyhow when the first payment was sent, I contacted him and he then put another 10800.00 onto my Visa and again I took it out, and sent it over to Davis. Well as soon as I did this, the next day I contacted Visa to see if another payment was sent and that is when they told me that the payment was fruadulent. now while this is happening, Davis has told me he has contacted another associate of his who owed him money, a lot of money and because he could not access his bank account if he could get his associate to wire the money into my account and then I could send it to him. I figured that I may have a chance of getting these guys to fix my Visa if I led them to believe that I would move a larger amount of money for them. I got an e-mail from this John Sigman from England about wiring the money into my account. I did go to the police about everything, unfortunately there is not much that can be done as these scammers originate in Africa. Anyhow I have in my account right now "$57,000.00, but do not have access to it.

Josh, these guys have sent me the information as to where they want it to go not realizing that I can't touch the funds (the bank will not allow me to touch it even if the cheque clears), anyhow it is to be wired to the Bank of China in Bangkok. There seems to be a thing happening in Bangkok right now and they were pushing me to wire it asap . . . anyhow I have phone numbers for you and I'm forwarding to you the info regarding the transfer, I don't know if this is anything, but I have sent over 20, 000.00 to Accra, Ghana and now they want 45000.00 to go to China, supposedly to buy mining machines. Josh, if you can't check this out, do you have friends that can check out the possibility that maybe this money is being used for something that is illegal which I think is the case here. I keep thinking of guerilla groups, or terrorist—type organization, or these guys are all Italian, and I'm thinking maybe it's the mafia moving money, I know this sounds far fetched, but it's too much money they want me to move, to be legit . . . I believe that this is definitely an organized group of men and possibly women who are doing this. Here is the list of phone numbers and the Bank of China info I am forwarding to you that is in another e-mail . . .

Davis is now supposedly in the hospital in Accra, Ghana the Lungston Hospital, a new hospital under the care of Dr Phil Byman and he has just asked me to cover the expenses to take care of Davis. The hospital bill comes to 7, 680.00 . . . go figure . . . anyhow I don't know if you can do anything or not or if there is anyone that you can talk to about this. Let me know if anything can be done . . .

Your Northern friend with a story . . . Tess

From: Josh Harrison

Sent: December 1, 2008 6:24:43 PM Hello my friend

Any time Lagos-Nigeria is mentioned I know a scam is somehow involved. Ginger@hotmail.com tried the same scam two years ago on me. I let them have a bank account of mine that was not in use. They tried to run 45, 000 out of my bank. She wanted me to send money through Western Union. Why 45, 000.00?

I will run a check on them when I get to my office tomorrow. You can try and run each of their names through Google right now and maybe find out some things. Please don't feel bad and I wish I could give you a hug.

Your Southern friend

Funny thinking Southern with—3 right now with freezing rain and snow. Send me your phone number and I can add it to the my 5 friends plan again. Your true friend Josh

From: Tess

Sent: December 1, 2008 11:53:22 PM Thank You Josh,

There is something definitely wrong going on here. I just wish there was something I could do to either stop them or mess them up a little bit. My phone number is 311-555-0101, that is my cell phone, my cell phone is with me at all times, so that is probably the best number to get in touch with me.

Again thank you

Your Northern, now cold—20, Friend Tess

From: Earl Warleh

Sent: December 1, 2008 10:27:15 PM Hello Madam Tess,

Thanks for the mail, I want you to know that I will be going to check up on Mr Davis and tell him what you asked me to, that will be done if only he is awake. Thank you Madam Tess, anytime I see your husband's situation I feel like crying. Anyway everything comes our way in life and we must prepare to it.

Your Friendly, Earl

# 20

## SEVEN THOUSAND DOLLARS TO SAVE DAVIS

From: Tess

Sent: December 2, 2008 12:06:27 AM Hello Earl,

I have talked with the doctor a couple of times, he did let me talk with Davis last night, it was wonderful to hear Davis, I miss talking with him so much. Please tell him that I really loved hearing his voice. I am so sorry that he is not well. The doctor called me tonight, and told me that Davis was sleeping, he is asking me for money to help cover the costs of Davis's hospital bill, and I don't dare tell Davis the bad situation that I am in here. I don't want to upset Davis so I couldn't say anything. Earl, the banks are investigating me for questionable activity regarding the money that showed up in my bank account, which was for Davis; however the bank has been holding the funds and are still clearing the cheque. I don't know what is going on, but Joseph Black who was sending the money to Davis has put a stop on the cheque. I e-mailed Davis all of this, I just don't think he has been able to check his e-mail, anyhow, I am not allowed to access any funds, nor am I allowed to send any funds through Western Union as I have sent so much money to you and Davis through Western Union, they have blocked me until I can produce receipts to prove that the funds were used for business. Davis has these reciepts, I don't. The doctor is saying to me that if I cared for Davis I would be able to help him. I can't get any money over there to help Davis, I can't get any money . . . I am so upset right now that the doctor, thinks I don't care for Davis. Please don't let him make Davis think this, I love Davis and I would do anything in my power to help him. But I can't get blood from a stone, if there is no money, there is no money, I have gone to the bank, a different bank to see if I can get a loan against my home to cover these costs and I have an appointment on Wednesday, at which time, I will apply for the loan. I don't know if they will be able to tell me if I qualify for the loan. So please tell Davis, I love him very much. Earl, the only other thing I can suggest is that the doctor directly talks with Davis's friend John Sigman. He may be able to help. If he will talk with him, then I can give you his number.

Please tell Davis, he is everything to me, again I don't want to tell him what has happened with the money, not until he is better.

Thank You Tess

From: Earl Warleh

Sent: December 2, 2008 9:43:13 AM hello Madam Tess,

The Doctor told me he called you and he was telling you that Mr Davis's health is really bad. They don't have the machines down here to help him on the operation so now what they have to do is that they will have to fly him home for the operation and special treatment and Madam, I understand very much because he is in bad health and this place is not well developed and I am scared that if action is not taken Mr Davis is going to die . . . That's what the DOC told me and I don't want him to know because of his health. I will tell him you love him very much and also Madam there could be a way for us to work on things to help Davis concerning his health.

Hmmmm I feel so bad now and thank you for your time, Yours Friendly

Earl

From: Tess

Sent: December 2, 2008 4:08:10 PM Hello Earl,

I feel numb, knowing that I don't have the ability to help Davis, no matter where I go and ask for help financially, I am getting 'no' from everyone. I personally have no money, and even if I did have even $100.00 to send. I am blocked from using Western Union and Western Union is the only way to get money out of Whitehorse to Africa. I am in a small city that does not have what the larger centers or cities have. My only thought is Davis's mother, I do not know her, but maybe Davis can talk to her or the doctor, he can call her, I am sure that she would not want her only son to possibly die in Africa without anyone contacting her first. Earl, I am serious, there is absolutely no way that I can get money. I am so upset, I have failed Davis, I feel awful, I love him so much. I don't want to think of him like this. I will go online and see if there is a volunteer hospital that he can go to, one that will help him, please if you know of one, that takes people in, please help us, help Davis . . . all I can do is send him my love . . . Please if you can call me, so I can talk with Davis, please call me; I will keep my phone by my bed so if you call I will wake immediately . . .

Thank you so much . . .

Tess

From: Tess

Sent: December 3, 2008 3:21:21 PM Hello Earl,

I was hoping to hear from you today, I have tried to call but I am not getting through, I just get empty air, no ringing sound, nothing, this is very frustrating, please if you get a chance to call me while you are with Davis, please, please call me. I am so worried, and feeling completely helpless, I feel so bad that without money, I can't help him. I'm afraid to talk to the doctor, if I tell him they won't give me a loan, what is going to happen to Davis? I'm very scared, but please don't tell Davis this, I dont' want to upset him, he needs his strength and he needs hope and I can't give him that. I have been in tears everytime I think about this, my eyes hurt, my heart hurts, please tell me you were able to check with the travel agent? His ticket they should still honour, as he was at the airport when he collapsed. Please tell Davis I love him very much, he is in my thoughts every minute, every day . . . tell him I am praying for him . . .

Thank you Earl, for everything Tess

*I tried contacting the Medical Association, the police, and I even tried to e-mail the Canadian embassy in Accra; however I never received a response to any of the e-mails that I sent. I looked up the phone numbers for the Accra police and when I dialed the numbers, I kept getting a recording that the number can not be reached as dialed. I was trying to get verification that the hospital and the doctor didn't exist, even though it was obvious that these names and places were fictitious, I still wanted that verification.*

*I even tried e-mailing the Ministry of Mines in Accra Ghana. I felt such a strong urge to verify that Davis did not exist. I knew he didn't, I just needed to continue to search. for what, for verification? for justice?. I can't explain what drove me to search; I just felt I needed to talk to someone in Ghana about this.*

From: Tess

Sent: December 4, 2008 10:52:21 PM

Hello my name is Tess Diamond and I would like to verify with you if possible if a gentleman by the name of Davis Barienda with Millenium Minning Company has or is supposed to be registering an oil mine that he purchased in September 2008 in Accra Ghana. His business registration, which I am not sure if it is authentic or not is dated Sept 19 2008 the Registrar name, is Mr Ushawa Harmona. The barrister's name on the certificate of incorporation is Barrister Lorenzo Knight I am requesting this information as Mr Barienda and myself are listed as owners on the business certificate, please can you tell me if this is real or not— . . . Thank you I am hoping that you can help me with this . . .

Again I thank you. Tess Diamond Canada

On my October Visa bill I had a charge for a renewal with eharmony for $119.00 that I never requested. In fact after meeting Davis in August, I cancelled my eharmony account, Davis told me he cancelled his almost at the same time. I called e-mailed eharmony and mentioned to them that I had a charge on my credit card that I did not authorize. The following letter is the response from e-harmony.

From: Customer_Care@eHarmony.ca

Subject: Response to Notification – Unauthorized Card Use Dear Tess,

Thank you for contacting eHarmony. We understand your concerns. Making your eHarmony experience safe and successful is important to us. Upon review of you account we found that the last charge on your account was an auto renewal charge of $89.95, which was then refunded in August. We do not show a charge of $119.00. If you believe you are the victim of fraudulent or unauthorized charges, we strongly urge you to contact your credit card to report this activity. By doing so, you may be able to avoid additional fraudulent charges from occurring.

We will investigate these charges immediately to ensure that any unauthorized activity is halted and the account connected to these transactions is closed. To assist us in this investigation, please reply to this e-mail with as much of the following data as you can supply:

1. The complete account number for the credit card on which you have received unauthorized charges.

2. The date(s) on which the(se) charge(s) occurred.

3. The amount of the unauthorized transaction.

Regarding your concerns about your match, please know that we take your concerns seriously and will investigate the matter immediately. Rest assured that your report and identity will remain confidential.

Based on the results of our investigation and in accordance with our terms and conditions, we may take action to remove the match from our service. In order to complete our investigation, please respond to this e-mail with the following information as soon as possible:

1. The match's name and city

2. Their age and the date you received them as a match

3. Any additional information that you feel would be helpful

We appreciate you bringing this matter to our attention and look forward to your reply.

Sincerely, eHarmony

From: Tess

Sent: December 4, 2008 10:11:39 PM Hello,

The fraudulent charge of 119.00, has been reversed on my Visa. Thank You, but I would like to know who it was that used my Visa number to renew their subscription. The visa number that was used was 0000 0000 0000 0000. The charge was posted to my credit card on Oct 20 for the amount of 119.85. I believe it might have been used by a Davis Barienda.

In fact I do believe that I am a victim of an organized romance scam. I unfortunately may have had money stolen from me as well by this Davis Barienda. I met Davis online on August 06; he had requested a fast track communication. I responded to him because his profile stated he was from where I lived in Whitehorse YT. It stated that he was 47, Italian and a consultant. We corresponded through eharmony for a short time and then I found that my e-mails I was sending through eharmony were lengthy so I would be timed out and I would lose my e-mail that I had written.So I gave him my e-mail address and we started corresponding through our regular e-mail accounts. We both left town, according to him, around the same time so we were never able to meet face to face. He went to Orlando Florida, then to England and then to Accra Ghana, and that was where he needed help with money and I helped him by sending him some, by this time he had won me over completely and I believed him . . . unfortunately, it has turned out to be a big scam, and I believe he will do this again as I am no longer helping him. He may also go by the first name of Jack.

Could you please let me know if it is in fact this Davis that used my Visa, and could you please let me know if you will be able to do anything such as removing his profile? Also how do you verify that your clients are who they say they are, or are you able to do that? What precautions are you able to take? I paid money in hopes of finding that special someone, I thought that I had, and now I could be financially in trouble because of this man, and my own stupidity, but the want and need to believe in love, was so strong . . . and my heart is sad . . . he was a wonderful writer, or whom ever was writing the letters wrote things that made me feel wonderful. Please I do hope that you will let me know what has and will happen.

Thank You Tess

From: Earl Warleh

Sent: December 4, 2008 12:01:35PM Hello Madam Tess,

Thanks for the mail very much, I know you have really did all you can to help your husband Financially down here but i want you to know that i am willing to help too but you know I am not doing any Good Job. I feel so bad telling you all this but i want you to know that Mr Davis is in Bad health today and i think action should be taken . . . Madam I know you are Not Financially strong now as you tell me but please do your Best to raise something to help your Husband Home . . .

Thanks for your time Earl

From: Tess

Sent: December 4, 2008 12:08:37 PM

Hello Earl,

Please can you call me when you are at the hospital so I can talk with Davis, I really need to talk with him. Thank you for everything you are doing for him, again please tell him I love him, please call me . . .

Tess

From: Earl Warleh

Date: Thu, 4 Dec 2008 11:49:59—0800

Hello Madam Tess,

How are you doing??I was at the hospital this morning and I didn't have any talking time on my phone so I couldn't call you but something really terrible happened today . . . Mr Davis Health is getting really bad and he was vomiting blood today and the doctor is saying he has done his best and if no action is taken, Mr Davis is going to die but Mr David is in bad health so the doctor didnt want to tell him . . . It's really bad that things are going like this. The Doctor confirmed to me that Mr Davis will be sent out of the Hospital in 2 days time because the doctor is saying he has done much already.hmmmmm this is really bad and it makes me have tears when i hear that Mr Davis is going to die.

Thank you very much Yours Friendly

Earl

From: Tess

Sent: December 4, 2008 12:10:25 PM To:      Earl

Hello Earl,

Please can you tell me when you are going to be at the hospital so I can call you, I want to talk to Davis, so please let me know the time and I will call

Thank you Tess

*December 05 2008, Steve was my date for my Christmas party, we had a really good time, it was nice to sit and talk with him. I had missed his colourful comments regarding situations at his work and the people he worked with, as well as the people we came into contact with during our date. And I can't forget to mention the stories about his own life situations, Steve always had a story to tell which had some sarcastic, dry, humourous storyline to it. Steve was being a complete gentleman towards me and was making me feel like he was interested in me and that he cared. It was the part of Steve that I had hoped for when we were together. All I wanted was to enjoy myself with Steve who was real and forget about Davis, Earl and Dr Byman.*

From: Earl Warleh

Sent: December 6, 2008 1:49:30 AM Hello Madam Tess,

How are you? I want you to know that Mr Davis is really sick and he needs to leave this place to get a good treatment home . . . But Madam i don't know what to do now I am so confused and he is really sick I think he is going to die of which the Doctor and I is hiding that secret from him if he is not treated ASAP Because his health is really bad . . . Anyway you have done so much for your Husband but I understand your situation too but please we need to work on things fast to get him out of here . . . Thanks for your time and you can call me anytime you want. Yours friendly,

Earl

From: Tess

Sent: December 6, 2008 1:57:24 PM Hello Earl,

How are you doing? This must be very stressful for you to be put into such a position. Earl, I am sorry but I don't know what I can do, there is nothing more that I can do, and even if I had money, which I don't, I don't even have the ability to send it to Davis, it's not possible. But again I do not have the money. Joseph Black who the doctor said you talked with yesterday; he was the man whom you should have asked for help for Davis. I told him Davis was in need of help and I couldn't help him, he was the one that could help Davis, he could have sent you enough money to cover the hospital and whatever else needed to be done.

He is the one with the money, I believe he knows Davis, and Davis could pay him when he gets back into Canada or the States or where ever he has to go to get better, but I can't. You have to understand, I do not have any money, please can you send me the address for the hospital and the phone number for the hospital because I would like to send Davis a letter. I have to go out now; there are activities here that we have to go to today. I wont' be back until around 4 PM which is midnight your time, e-mail me and let me know when you will be able to connect online and I will try and meet you then.

Thank you Tess

From: JOSH HARRISON

Sent: December 6, 2008 2:32:10 PM Hello my Friend

I have been ever so busy day and night all week with my work getting back logged up on me. Just before your first e-mail I was off work for a week as I hurt my Achilles tendon in my left foot.

The High Comission said that you are in a scam where you can lose all of your savings as they now have full access to your bank accounts. Please close them and move things around so as to limit the damage. He said that there is someone else who got taken just as you are. The couple even went down to see for themselves. They saw people and lawyers and offices. When they got back home they invested all of their savings knowing that they are going to get rich as soon as the oil pays off. The problem was the man who contacted the couple only needed some funds to get the oil released. The couple never heard another thing after sending him the money. They went back and there was no such person as the lawyer or people that they had previously met. They had all vanished. The couple had asked the High Comissioner if he could help. His reply was that if the couple had asked him in the beginning he would have checked out the business. Now there is nothing he can do since they used fake names and accounts. Tess, he will sweet—talk you and promise you everything as he strings you along. Please be careful and run, please. your friend who had snow in October

Josh

From: Earl Warleh

Date: Sat, 6 Dec 2008 16:29:44

Hello Madam Tess,

Thanks for the mail and I will try and connect with you soon, Anyway I will add you to my Messenger in case you are online we can talk. Thanks you

Earl

From: Tess

Sent: Saturday, December 6, 2008, 11:46 PM Hi Josh,

You are so sweet, thank you, I have closed my account and my visa, I am still at the same bank though. Anyhow, you mentioned that the High Commission could check things out maybe? I know this is a scam, but I want to approach these guys with the fact that I know that these things don't exist, such as the mine, the hospital and the doctor. My problem is that the phone numbers that I have for the ministry of mines, the ministry of health will not work from my phone. Josh, are you able to check and see if these things really do or don't exist . . . I just need to know from the Accra ministry of health, is there a new hospital called the Lungston Hospital, and if there is a doctor by the name of Dr Phil Byman. The Mining Company that is registered as a business in Accra is called the Millenium Minning Incorporated, the owners names are Davis and Tess . . . Yes I am supposedly a co-owner to this mine. I do have a copy of the certificate of business registration as well. Davis faxed it to me, anyhow, are you able to check any of this out, I just need verification so I can end this. Oh and the doctor is asking me for seven thousand dollars in order to pay for Davis's hospital stay, drugs and the plane fare to get him home, and of course I have told them that I do not have the money. I do need this information to end this, but I want to give them a run for their money and so far I have given them a bit of a jog.

Josh if you can help me to end this I would really appreciate it Thank you so much.

I too have been busy not just with this but with Zoey as Christmas activities have started and I'm making my gifts as I do every year and this year I am making pottery for everyone, so I have about five more days left that I can actually finish making things. So I am hustling. Anyhow, I will try and text you, I got your message today on my cell phone, I was out last night, Christmas Party, so I never heard my phone, but I did get your voice mail today. I will text you and let you know when a good time to call and we are three hours behind you. You were up late last night; anyhow I had better get going. Thank you so much Josh for your help. I really appreciate this.

Your Northern Friend, who has not seen—25 yet . . . Tess

From: Tess

Sent: December 7, 2008 1:27:09 PM Hello Earl,

I have been waiting to hear from you, I need to know how Davis is, I checked my e-mail address for Yahoo and I gave you the wrong one, it is t@yahoo.com. I will be out this afternoon from my house but I will be checking online at around 10 PM my time which will be 6 AM your time. I hope this will work for you. And please can you get me the address for the hospital.

Thank You Earl Tess

From: JOSH HARRISON

Sent: December 7, 2008 9:34:51 PM Hello dear

I smile as I wonder if you can send me 100 billion for your half of my City Ottawa. I can forward you the registered certificate with your name on it, proving that you own part of Ottawa. Also need your fax number so that I can send you a Registered Classified Document that proves that you now own half of the Pacific Ocean. All I ask is that you put a stop to all the ecological disasters. Okay.

All kidding aside, did you not see that W5 show where the scam was with our homes? They were registering a change of ownership for the deeds to our homes with City Hall. It seemed that as we made the final payments to our deeds that someone took out a big 2nd mortgage. We suddenly owed much more than we thought. The other one was instead of taking out mortgages on us they sold our homes out from under us.

No such doctor sorry. There is a Dr.Phil Byman who is a Doctor of Pharmacy. There is no Lungston Hospital in Accra, Ghana

This week should be easier at work so I will try and check into some more facts

Talk soon

Your cold friend Josh.

My little dog needed to share my jacket as it got to—20, ouch

*Earl called me at home this morning and again asked me if I cared enough to help save my husband. He implied that if I didn't send any money then my husband would be left to die. I told Earl that Davis was not my husband, in fact, I continued, that we had never even met in person. So for Earl to insinuate that I didn't care because I wasn't sending any money, I told him that he was insulting me after all of the money that I had sent in the past. Earl kept telling me to calm down and that getting mad was not going to help matters. I ended our phone conversation abruptly.*

From: Tess

Sent: December 8, 2008 4:44:16 PM Hello Earl,

Hi again, I just wanted to apologise once again for getting so upset this morning, as you can hopefully understand I am very lost as to what I can do to help Davis, as I said this morning, I don't even know who his friends are, to call them and ask for help. I hate not being able to talk with him; I was hoping you could e-mail me the telephone number of the hospital. Earl, you are my only connection to Davis, can you please tell me what is happening with him, can you let me know if and when I can talk with him, I just would like to talk with him, if nothing else, just to tell him that I do love him and I will always be thinking about him . . . if you can please call me, my minutes are used up now on my phone so I am not able to call you. If nothing else could you e-mail me.

Thank You Earl for everything that you have done . . . Tess

*I was contacted by Shea Williams of The Canadian Bank's Security department. She asked me to e-mail her the information that I had from John Sigman and Joseph Black, which I did.*

From: Tess

Sent: December 8, 2008 11:39:00 AM Hello Shea,

Below is the wire information that was sent to me by John Sigman, he was the one who first contacted me about the wire, he is apparently supposed to reside in England, and his associate is Joseph Black who sent the money. I hope this will help in stopping them for a while.

Tess

*When I was talking to Shea with the Canadian Bank security department about the fraudulent cheque in my account, she told me that these groups of scammers are usually involved in organized crime and have warehouses of stolen cheques, and have machines and templates that allow them to put their own logos onto the stolen cheques, and manipulate the cheque to look authentic. She then said to me that unfortunately the fraud department really never gets a chance to find out where the money is going if the money gets held and stopped at the bank, she said that usually where the money is being wired to is usually the final destination of these perpetrators. I told her I had that information, I told her that these guys screwed up and gave me that information because they thought that I could move the money. That was when she asked me to e-mail her with what I had. I just hope that she was able to pass it on to the fraud department and they were able to do something with the information that I had. It's funny, I felt that I had information that hopefully was valuable information, and could be used to stop some sort of illegal activity.*

From: eharmony

Sent: December 8, 2008 2:07:27 PM Dear eHarmony Friend,

Making your eHarmony experience safe and successful is important to us. As a past or present user, we want to inform you that eHarmony has taken action to remove one of your matches, Davis from Whitehorse, from the eHarmony service. This decision was made in accordance with our terms and conditions. Consistent with our privacy policy, we do not disclose the specific reasons for this person's removal. eHarmony disclaims any responsibility or liability with respect to any continued involvement between you and any person whose account is closed by eHarmony. Please visit the links below for further information on our privacy policy, and to obtain safety tips on corresponding with matches

http://www.eharmony.com/singles/servlet/about/terms    http://
www.eharmony.com/singles/servlet/privacy/statement    http://www.
eharmony.com/singles/servlet/safety/tips

To address any questions you may have, please visit our Frequently
Asked Questions section concerning the removal of users from our
service. You can find this information at the following link:

Sincerely,

Customer Relations eHarmony

Fom: eHarmony

Sent: December 8, 2008 2:16:33 PM Dear Tess,

Thank you for contacting eHarmony. I regret to hear that your card was
used without your knowledge. Regretfully, we are unable to disclose
additional information about the account on which this card was used.
We are only able to release this information to law enforcement per
your request. In order to release any information about this account,
we need to receive a letter faxed by you that includes your name, card
number, date and amount of charge and your signature. We also need
the designated police department name, officer name and applicable
fax number to which the information should be sent. Thank you for
reporting your match concern. We have investigated this matter and
have removed Davis from our service. If you have not already done so,
we recommend moving this match to your closed match listing.

If you are still interested in having someone call you about this matter,
please respond to this e-mail. We regret that you have had a negative
experience and thank you for bringing this matter to our attention.

Sincerely, eHarmony

From: Earl Warleh

Sent: December 9, 2008 12:22:48 AM Hello Tess,

Hmmmm thank you very much for the Mail and I want you to know
that I am online as you told me that you will be on so i will want us to
communicate and see how best we can save Davis . . . Now he is out of
the Hospital Because I was not able to raise some Money to Help him
neither did where you able to help . . . Anyway I hope to hear from
you soon,

414

Thanks Once again, Earl

From: Tess

Sent: December 9, 2008 1:31:42 PM Hi Earl,

Are you able to get Davis to the Canadian Embassy? I went online and there is a Canadian Embassy in Accra and they will help with medical emergencies, with flights out etc . . . this is the only way to save Davis. Please contact me or have Davis contact me as soon as he can get to the Embassy. He needs to do this. Can you please help him get there? My phone card is out of minutes and my phone I need to pay the bill, so I have to wait until I get paid again, so please call my other number. 311-555-2121

Thank you . . . Tess

From: Earl Warleh

Date: Tue, 9 Dec 2008 00:22:47

Hello Tess,

Hmmmm. Thank you very much for the Mail and I want you to know that I am online as you told me that you will be on so I will want us to communicate and see how best we can save Davis . . . Now he is out of the hospital. Because I was not able to raise some money to help him neither were you able to help . . .

Anyway I hope to hear from you soon, Thanks Once again,

Earl

From: Tess

Sent: December 9, 2008 11:33:20 PM Hello Earl,

I am sorry I wasn't able to meet you online, it's 11:30, and I am falling asleep, I am afraid that if you come online, I will be sleeping. I am wondering what is happening with Davis. Earl, no matter what, Davis, I fell in love with him, and I do care about what happens to him, so please, tell me if you can, how is he?

I am hoping that he was able to make it to the embassy. Are you able to call me so I can talk to him . . . I am hoping that I can meet you online, please e-mail me with a time as to when you may possibly be online and I will e-mail you back as to whether or not I can meet you at that time,

Thank You Earl, Tess

From: John Sigman

Sent: December 10, 2008 5:01:35 AM Tess,

How are you today? I hope you are fine. I am writing to find out if the fund has been released and access to your account given to you because I have talked with Mr. Joseph Black and he has given the confirmation your bank required. It is very important you get to me immediately because of time constraint, so as to be able to conclude this transaction. I am now in Africa and can be reached at this number +234809876543, for any urgent attention. I am waiting for your urgent response.

Thanks.

John.

From: Tess

Sent: December 10, 2008 6:06:23 AM Hello John,

Being that you are in Africa, can you please help Davis, he does not have just a fever, he apparently has malaria, and possibly appendicitis and with no money, the doctor would not keep treating him in the hospital. Please can you contact Davis's friend Earl Warleh, he knows where Davis is, and as far as having access to my account, John, the bank never released the money to me. They held it in my account, yes, but it was inaccessable to me, and then they have returned it to where ever it came from. I did not and I do not have access to any monies, and my account has been permanently closed, so I don't know what you are talking about in regards to Joseph giving the bank confirmation, as the bank has never gotten back to me, to tell me that they made a mistake. They took the cheque as being fraudelent and they are looking at me as conspiring with you to pass fraudulent monies. I would really like to know as to why . . . And what is going on, if I'm going to be penalized. I would like to know really what it is I am being penalized for. I am going to forward your number to Earl Warleh, so he can call you and

416

talk to you about Davis, John. I do not have any money; I don't even have money of my own . . . anymore

Tess

From: Tess

Sent: December 10, 2008 6:12:17 AM Hi Earl,

I tried to get online last night or I should say early this morning, however, it was not connecting I tried for over an hour I was hoping you would have called me back, anyhow John Sigman e-mailed me, and he also tried to call me He is an associate of Davis's who may be able or should be able to help Davis, I have copied his phone number and I have e-mailed him telling him that I am giving you his phone number He is apparently now in Africa, so maybe Joseph Black has talked to John and John is aware that Davis needs help. Oh, and I'm still not able to get online. But again if I can talk to Davis, please can you call me, I would just like to talk to him, just to hear him. Please can you e-mail me and let me know how he is doing . . . Thank you so much Earl

All the best Tess

P.S. Earl This is from John Sigman

I am now in Africa and can be reached at this number +234809876543 for any urgent attention.

From: Tess

Sent: December 12, 2008 9:17:44 AM Hello Earl,

I have been waiting for your call, I want to talk to Davis, can you please call my cell phone when he is awake so I can talk with him, please . . . How is he?

Thank You Tess

From: Tess

Sent: December 12, 2008 12:58:25 PM Earl,

Please, Please, e-mail me, call me, please, I want to know how Davis is doing, I want to talk to Davis. Please, I have been trying to call you and

I am not getting anywhere, it's ringing, but it keeps getting cut off, so please, my cell phone is working again, so please will you contact me, I just want to talk with Davis. I love him and I miss him so much, I am so worried about him . . .Please Earl . . .

Thank you Tess

*Earl finally called me and allowed me to talk with Davis, it sounded like Davis, the same accent and intonation in his voice as the man       I was talking to earliar prior to Novemeber. However I did not get a chance to talk for very long as Davis started to have a coughing fit which ended our conversation abruptly. Earl came on the line and told me that Davis needed his rest.*

From: Tess

Sent: December 14, 2008 11:29:29 PM My Darling Davis,

It's been so long since I've written you, Davis, talking with you, hearing your voice, brought back so many feelings. I have missed you, I have missed your e-mails, I have been so worried about you, and not able to talk to anyone, and feeling so lost being unable to help you. I am sorry that I can't come up with any money, it just isnt' there, I am so sorry; I will try e-mailing John again to ask him to please help you. I hope you are able to get to the embassy, I looked on their website and they do say that they will help with medical emergencies and flights out.

Zoey and I are getting ready for Christmas, I was hoping that you would be here, I think about you always Davis, you brought me a lot of happiness, and you gave me the ability to feel love again, to feel what it feels like to have someone say to me I Love You. That gave me the most wonderful feeling; you gave me hope and helped me to believe in love again, because of you, I know what love feels like, or what it is suppose to feel like. I will cherish these feelings that you have given to me Davis, I wish I knew magic, and had the ability to make everything different, the way it should be, you better, here with us, not just a dream . . . I will always love you Davis Barienda, you will always be in my heart as the man that made me feel alive.

Earl has been a good friend to you . . . and has been letting me know about you . . . he is my only link to you Davis; he told me that you felt as if I had abandoned you, the only way I abandoned you was by not being able to get money, my heart was always with you, my thoughts were always with you; I tried so many times to get Earl to call me, so I could talk with you, but we had difficulty connecting, and

then I thought that because I couldn't come up with any money, that was it, you didn't want to talk with me. That was why I called Earl, Davis, I am sorry that I can't help you financially, I wish now that I had not sent you the money for the hotel, as I could have sent that to you now, that was the last transaction that I was able to do with the bank's help. Davis, I have also mentioned this to Earl, you should be able to still use your ticket to get out of Africa, as you collapsed in the airport, they should still honour your ticket, it is worth a try. I do hope that we get a chance to talk again. I am praying for you Davis, every night I pray that your body will heal itself and that you will be guided to what will help you and that will make everything right. I will hold your love close, please hold mine . . . I don't even know if you will be able to check your e-mails, here's hoping . . . I Love You

Tess

From: Tess

Sent: December 17, 2008 1:15:59 AM Hello Earl

I'm sending this to Davis as well, hoping that he will get my e-mail, and if he doesn't, I hope that you will let him know that I am thinking of him, please tell him that my minutes are almost out on my phone. I may have two minutes left from when we talked the other day that is why I have not been able to call. I did send him an e-mail however I haven't heard back from him . . . Earl, if Davis doesn't get this, please tell him that I miss him and I love him. I miss his e-mails, it was wonderful hearing his voice. I still imagine his laugh, I fell in love with his laugh, sometimes when I was talking with him, I could picture him smiling, while we talked, he made me feel alive. I really do miss his words,   I miss him . . . I am hoping that you are able to or have gone to the embassy, please let me know how that goes. I am waiting to hear from a friend of mine who may be able to help unfortunately I still have not heard from him. I have to get going to bed now, it is after 1 AM and I have to get up in a few hours. Thanks again Earl for everything and please ask Davis to try and call me if he can or at least e-mail me. I hope to talk with him again soon

Bye for now

Tess

From: Earl Warleh

Sent: December 17, 2008 7:13:20 PM hello madam Tess,

How are you doing today . . . it's really nice to hear from you . . . yes we were able to go to the embassy and the good news is that they are willing to help Davis and I told them you are a nurse so they said you should arrange for an appointment for treatment concerning Davis health . . . But they said they cant do anything about paying the bill of $2000 but they are willing to get David home . . . so now what's on our head now is to get the money to pay for that 2000D . . . So please try and think of something as the chance is now here to get your husband out of here . . . Please I will be on the yahoo Messenger in the morning so you can be on and lets talk.

Yours faithful, Earl

From: Tess

Sent: December 17, 2008 11:29:10 PM Hello Earl,

I am so glad to hear that you went to the embassy and that they will help Davis. I am looking forward to hearing the particulars, tell Davis, that I hope he can call me. Earl, depending on how bad Davis is, the embassy should send him to Vancouver General, I don't have any clout in Vancouver, and here, if Davis comes here to Whitehorse, I would take him straight to the hospital. No appointment necessary, but if Davis is really bad the doctors here may just medivac back him to Vancouver and in order to get here Davis has to go through Vancouver, so he may as well just go there and go to the emergency room there. Much as I want to see him, if it is his health that is on the line then he needs to take care of himself first. I would just be happy knowing that he is in Canada and getting help. And once Davis is in Canada and getting medical attention and getting better, he will have access to his bank account and can take care of everything. I e-mailed my friend and have left several voice-mails, and have not yet heard from him, he was supposed to be back this week, so I am still waiting. but the most important thing is that Davis will have help to come home, everyone else will have to hopefully understand that in order for them to get any money, they will have to let Davis come home and then I know Davis will send them their money. Oh Earl, you have given me hope . . . Thank you

Please tell Davis that I love him . . . and I miss him. Tess

# 21

# EARL IS GETTING DESPERATE

The following is an excerptt from one of my Instant Messenger talks with Earl. I had asked Earl to take Davis to the Canadian Embassy in Accra, as they would help Davis if he needed medical help and had to get out of Africa. As you will see, Earl gets quite frustrated with me, most of our phone conversations followed along these same lines as well, Earl was determined to get me to send money to help Davis.

December 17 2008 2000

Yahoo Vista Instant Messenger with Earl

Earl: Hello . . . Madam Tess

Earl: How are you doing this morning Tess: Hello Earl

Tess: it is not morning yet for me, it is almost midnight Tess: how are you doing this morning for you

Earl: I am doing Good thank you for asking anyway

Earl: I am very happy that things are going ok and davis will be able to get home at last

Earl: i told you that you should never give up but to have hope . . . But God being so Good things are happening the way it should be

Tess: finally

Tess: I have been holding onto hope Earl Tess: so please tell me, how is Davis

Earl: He is doing a little ok.but the most Good news is that the Embassy is saying they will help him get home

Earl: But the embassy said what they can do is to get him home and not to pay for his bill i told you about

Tess: Earl Davis needs to be coming home Tess: then his bill will be taken care of

Earl: The Hospital Wrote an appeal to the embassy already and they are not allowing that

Earl: this country is something different all together Tess: then they are foolish

Tess: the only way they will get their money is to let Davis come home, they should realise that

Earl: hmmmmm thats what i think

Tess: and if the embassy does not help Davis because of that, I would like to be able to talk to the person you talked to at the embassy

Earl: They are saying they will be able to get davis home

Earl: but the embassy is saying that the money davis is owing is his own bill

Earl: but if you dont have the money to help . . . then its ok

Earl: I will do what i can to raise some as the best thing and you try and get some too

Earl: thats the only reasonable idea i think

Tess: Earl, I don't have money, I have no access to money

Earl: My dad was a king and he left me some Gold jewelry i will love to sell and raise some money

Earl: so you mean you dont get paid from your work Earl: or what do you mean

Tess: once the bank said that the cheque that I was sent by the people loaning money to Davis, was fraudulent, it has caused a lot of problems for me.

Tess: Earl, why can Davis not come home first and then send the money?

Earl: Mr Davis didnt tell me anything about that Tess: my bank account has been closed down

Earl: I dont know the hospital said they have a lot of good to foreigners but as soon as they leave they dont apprecaiet and pay back

Tess: and I am on restrictions and I am also being investigated Earl: your account has been closed

Tess: yes

Tess: that is what I was so upset about that day we talked and I was mad Earl: ooh ok if you say so

Earl: so you dont get paid from working any more

Tess: was because of the problems I am having with my bank account,

Earl: I understand but I mean you dont get paid from your work again or what do you mean

Tess: Earl, I am not allowed to send money out of the country, I am being investigated

Tess: and yes

Earl: You are not allowed to send money . . . out of the country Tess: Earl I do get paid, but my paycheck does not go very far,

Earl: Fine you can just let any of your Good friends send the money out for you

Tess: no, I am not, not until I can produce receipts for all the money I sent to Davis, and you, which was a total of 22, 000.00

Tess: so they won't let me send anymore money

Earl: but all we want is that Davis gets home so cant you just sacrifice with one pay check and let me sell my jewelries and add some to it

Earl: your friend can send money through western union for you Earl: and the money can be in the hospitals name

Tess: your name and DAvis's name are being watched as well Earl: I understand Madam

Tess: Earl, does the embassy need money to send Davis home?

Earl: I can see the doctor and he can give me their accountant name or something so you can wire the money through his name

Earl: you can let a friend go to western union and do that for you Earl: NOOOOO

Earl: JUST LISTEN TO ME AND UNDERSTAND

Earl: the embassy is willing to send Davis home without collecting any penny from us

Earl: but now what matters is that the Hospital needs their Money Earl: do you understand

Earl: so now what we have to do is to raise the 2000 and then get davis out of here

Tess: well Earl, I guess the Dr, the hospital will have to take the chance that if

Earl: I can raise some so you should also try something out Tess: Davis doesn't leave Africa, they will not get their money

Tess: so in order for them to get their money, they need to let Davis leave Earl: I spoke to the doc and he said they have helped some foreigners but none have done what they promised

Tess: and if they don't they will be responsible for killing him if he should die

Earl: so you have to listen to my view too Earl: and not only yours

Earl: then i think i have nothing to do to help again Earl: I am even tired of all this

Earl: what they want they should just do to Davis Earl: I am even sick with all this Davis problems Tess: Earl, I dont' know what to say

Earl: Madam please just go to sleep and you will hear from me later

Earl: ok then you have done your best and then the rest is that he should die

Earl: because i am even tired of this whole thing Earl: doing a lot to help

Tess: if the embassy will help Davis leave, then let him leave

Earl: I am even thinking of sellling some jewelry my late father left me and to raise ome money to help

Tess: don't

Tess: Davis has money Tess: the Dr needs to trust

Earl: the embassy will help but they hospital need their money dont you understand

Earl: he said he cant do that again

Tess: if Davis doesn't leave the Dr doesn't get paid

Earl: because he trusted some foreigners and they didnt do as they promised

Earl: ok then

Tess: can you give me the address to the hosptial Earl Earl: Madam this place is a curruped country

Earl: ok

Tess: and the phone number to the hosptial Earl: 1 first street

Earl: accra Earl: ghana

Tess: is that first st Earl: yes

Earl: i dont know the hospital number

Earl: Madam i am even tired of this davis thing ok Tess: what is the phone number

Earl: i am giving up because the doc said without the money he is not leaving

Earl: and he should also not die for all i care Tess: that is wrong

Earl: But now tired and you are not willing to sarifice for him anymore ok

Tess: very wrong

Tess: sacrafice, not willing to sacrafice Tess: I won't even go there

Tess: I don't have anything Earl

Earl: then i will not do anything then Earl: I am tired

Earl: madam you have done much Earl: so you just go to sleep

Earl: I am going offline

Earl: You have done much and you cant help anymore Tess: that is it it is just money that everyone wants Tess: what about the person'

Tess: is there no more humanity

Earl: This country is not like usa, canada and other forrign countries ok

Tess: what about helping, a sick man, you have done much for Davis, the Dr should not be doing this to you

Earl: he is not willing to

Tess: no I believe there is humanity everywhere

Earl: because he said he has helped other but they never showed appreciation when they left

Earl: Madam just listen to me ok Earl: listen

Earl: listen Earl: listen

Tess: the Dr, being a Dr, takes an oath to save lives, not let people die no matter what

Earl: if the doc is willing to accept what you are saying by now Davis should be out of here ok

Earl: listen Earl: listen

Earl: I am sick and tired

Tess: well sometimes he has to trust, and believe that Davis will send him money as soon as he gets to Canada

Earl: i know he will surely do that

Earl: but the doc is not willing to understand Earl: Tess call me now

Tess: and if the embassy helps him then the Dr should know that if Davis doesn't leave then he will get nothing

Tess: I can't—I have no more minutes, maybe 2 on my card Tess: I have to go to bed,

Earl:   me too i have to go

Tess: I don't want to be doing this, Tess: I am sorry Earl

Earl: and i think the best thing is that davis should die Tess: you shouldn't have to deal with this

Earl: take care and bye for now Tess: don't say that

Tess: Davis can come home Tess: let him come home

Earl: I should say that I am willing to help him . . . with some jewelries I have

Tess: I will call the embassy myself

Earl: I will sell them and have the money Earl: i hear you anything

Earl: by bye for now

From: Tess

Sent: December 18, 2008 9:23:53 AM Hello Earl,

I am sorry that you felt so bad when we ended our conversation last night. Earl if I could change things I would. I am still trying today to get a hold of my friend, and if he should get back to town by the end of the week, I will ask him for his help, I personally, have nothing. But Earl, I know that my friend, before he agrees to anything, if there is money that is needed to go towards a hospital bill, he will want to see a copy of that invoice, are you able to talk with the doctor once more and see if he can fax a copy of Davis's bill to me and then I can give it to my friend. That may make it easier for him to loan me money. You can have the doctor fax it to me at 311-555-1212 and please tell him to make sure that the hospital address and phone numbers are on the invoice.

Now there was one thing that you did not tell me last night; when can the embassy get Davis out of Africa and put him on his way home? Oh and there is one more thought that I had, Davis has a business there in Accra, he is not like the other foreigners who leave. Davis will be going back because of the mine, so the doctor is being unreasonable, he should understand that. It is like Davis is being held hostage and I'm being asked for the ransom, this is how it feels, that is terrible. Earl, I would also like to talk to Davis, can you please see if Davis can call my cell phone sometime today or first thing in your morning. Thank you Earl, and no matter what happens, thank you for all that you have done, just don't let Davis die, please get him to the embassy . . .

Thank You Tess

# 22

# SETTING EARL UP

From: Tess

Sent: December 21, 2008 1:43:37 AM My Darling Davis,

I miss hearing from you so much, not being able to talk to you on the phone, or get an e-mail from you has been making my days feel so empty. I am wondering what is going on, the last that I heard from Earl, was that the embassy would be able to help you to get home. But he said that the doctor was saying that he would not let you go unless you paid at least 2, 000.00. Personally, I think that that is completey ridiculous. Earl has asked me to try and do what I can to get this, I personally don't have it, however I have asked a friend and he said that Yes, he will think about it, but before he agrees to sending any money to strangers in Africa, he will only do this because it is me, and he wants to ensure, for my sake that everything is on the up and up so to say, so as I suspected, he is asking for a copy of the invoice from the hospital and he is also asking for a copy ( a photocopy) of your passport—the one page with your picture and information. Davis, can you fax it to my mother's fax number 311-555-1212.

Davis, how are you doing? I haven't heard anything from you, I called the other day and talked with Earl and he said you were sleeping, I asked him to tell you that I called. Davis, I have only six minutes left on my phone. Once more, are you able to call me? I tried to call tonight, it is 1:30 AM I have been up making Christmas gifts for my family, you were supposed to be here for Christmas . . . I am sorry that you are not here, I thought about that today, you should be here, anyhow I called a few times, only to get the message that the phone was either turned off or out of the service area. Please, if you can, please, will you call me . . . I miss you. I hope you are getting better and I hope that the embassy will help you soon. I miss your words Davis . . . I am hoping that I will hear from you soon.

I love you Tess

From: Earl Warleh

Sent: December 21, 2008 1:52:55 AM hello Madam,

How are you doing this Morning, I am really surprised at the way you spoke to me the other time . . . It was not fair at all but I want you to know that you should know how to be nice to a good friend. OOH ok madam if thats what is going to let your friend be able   to lend you the money so that your man can get home . . . I will  be doing that Monday Morning but i want you to know that your husbands health is getting very bad as we dont even get the chance to get some money for drugs. (medicine) but I think we should work on things fast to get home as the embassy is willing to help as well. thank you

Earl

From: Tess

Sent: December 22, 2008 12:17:35 AM Hello Earl,

I'm not too sure as to what you are referring to, in regards to me speaking to you in a certain way. I apologise if my being unable to get money is upsetting to you, I am getting exhausted regarding this money bit. Earl I would like to speak to Davis, I have tried to call your number several times and I am not getting through. If you can call me, I have recharged my phone card so I have more minutes, I would really like to be able to talk with Davis. Please if you can call me, I will call you right back.

Thank You Tess

From: Earl Warleh

Sent: December 26, 2008 12:32:39 Hello Madam,

I am really sorry for you not being able to hear from me . . . I just want you to know that Davis's over stay here is making his sickness really worse and very bad.He collapsed so i had to get enough time for him so i can take care of him so due to that i was not able to get online . . .

Thanks for the mail and we will connect soon. Earl

From: Tess

Sent December 29, 2008 10:07:06 PM Hello Earl

How is Davis? . . . I am sorry I haven't gotten in touch with you sooner. I was hoping that you would call me, so that I could call back and talk with Davis. In some ways I have been afraid to call, I am hoping beyond hope that he is okay, please just take him to the embassy and let them send him home. The doctor will get his money once Davis is back home. I have also been hoping to get a fax from you, without the copy of the invoice and a copy of Davis's passport my friend will not even consider loaning any money. Earl Please e-mail me if you are unable to call and let me know what is going on. How are you doing Earl? Take care of yourself hope to talk to you soon, and I'm hoping I can talk with Davis.

Tess

From: Earl Warleh

Sent: December 30, 2008 10:17:16 AM Hello Madam Tess,

Thanks for the mail and i want you to know that i am really sorry for not being able to send you a mail to let you know what happening concerning the fax . . . we had a bad connection here this few days and town has been really hot due to the election but i want you to expect it within this week okay . . . Thanks for the mail once again and i want you to know that Davis said he longs to hear your Voice.

Earl

From: Tess

Sent: December 30, 2008 7:04:56 PM Hello Earl,

I'm glad to finally hear from you, how is Davis doing?, I am leaving town Earl tomorrow, I won't be back until the weekend, I was hoping that you could have sent the fax by now, I hope it is not too late. Again I urge you to take Davis to the embassy no matter what. Hope to talk to you soon Tess

Please tell Davis that I miss hearing his voice and his laugh.

From: Tess

Sent: January 3, 2009 10:27:30 AM Hello Earl

Happy New Year. Please tell Davis I send him my Love for the New Year, Earl, what is happening, how come I have not heard from Davis? How is he? I have not received any faxes from you, have you been able to send them. Is it possible for me to talk to Davis soon?

I hope to hear from you soon . . . Tess

From: Tess

Sent: January 4, 2009 9:36:37 PM Hello Earl,

What is happening, I haven't heard from you for a while, How is Davis? Can I talk with him, or has he been able to get out of Africa through the embassy, please let me know what is happening, I feel so bad sometimes having to rely on you Earl to get information about Davis, but you are right now my only connection, for that I thank you . . . please call me when I can talk to Davis, or e-mail me and let me know how everything is going. I look forward to hearing from you

Tess

From: Earl Warleh

Sent: January 8, 2009 3:39:27 AM

Hello Madam Tess, Thanks for the mail but we don't have much time and I want you to know that Davis Health is really bad now and All I can say is that if you think you can't help then we should leave him and let him die. Please when you wake up to see this mail I want you to call me ASAP.

Earl . . .

*I finally received a copy of the invoice supposedly from the hospital. Instead of it being faxed to me, Earl told me he didn't have enough money to fax a copy to me, so he e-mailed me a copy. I never did receive a copy of Davis's passport, just the invoice.*

*The hospital invoice had a watermark of a redcross in the middle of the page. It listed the hospital's name, the address and the patient's name as David Bagnad, it listed the admission date as being November 26, 2008. It then listed the Admission charge, the room charge and the tests that were done along with the prices. The dates began November 26, 2008 and ended December 10, 2008. The total at the bottom of the invoice was $ 2, 300.00*

From: Tess

Sent: January 9, 2009 9:56:11 AM Hello Earl,

Earl, I'm at a loss for words, first, I thought that the hospital bill was for $7, 000.00, but more importantly I don't know who this person is, the name on the invoice Earl, who is he? Where is Davis? I want to talk with Davis. My friend is willing to loan me the money to help DAVIS, I want Davis to call me, to talk to me. What is going on? Please help me out here Earl.

Tess

*Earl told me that the hospital made a mistake with Davis's name. I responded to Earl by telling him that, that, was unacceptable, "what would they do if Davis died, that has to be corrected Earl" Earl told me that he would get the hospital to fix things and that he would e-mail me the corrected copy, I kept stressing that unless it has Davis's name on the invoice my friend wasn't going to help. So six days later, after several phone calls with Earl telling him that the invoice wasn't good enough he finally sent me a second invoice*

From: Earl Warleh

Sent: January 15, 2009 12:43:07 AM

Madam just open the file and you will see it . . . I am even stressing now as I dont want Davis to die on me here!!!!!!The Doc said his health is very bad now and he might die soon anyway you are saying you can't help, if he dies I think the government can burry him!!!!! take careYou can call me if you want . . .

Bye bye Earl

*The invoice that Earl sent to me was the exact same invoice: the name still read David Bagnad, however the discharge date November 26, 2008 was added under the admission date. The discharge date was the same date as the admission date.*

From: Tess

Sent: January 15, 2009 8:01:51 AM Earl,

I am talking to my friend today. I don't know how things will work but I will stress to him that I need his help. Is Davis able to talk to me? I will e-mail you later today after I talk with my friend.

Tell Davis he is in my thoughts every minute of the day Take care Earl.

Tess

From: Earl Warleh

Date: Thu, 15 Jan 2009 12:43:28—0800

Hello Madam,

Davis's health is really bad and he cant even talk, always his eyes are closed and he is on drip and the doc said we should work on things fast to get him home because his health is very bad Getting him home is all that we need now, Madam please try and call me!!!!!Davis is in bad condition . . . send me a mail if you can.I will give you all the details you need to send the money!!

Thank you Earl

I am really Tired and frustrated!!!!!!

From: Tess

Sent: January 15, 2009 12:03:55 PM Earl,

I talked with my friend, he did question the incorrect name, but I convinced him that it is for Davis. Earl, he said he would help, he is going to the bank this afternoon before 3 PM my time and he is going to bring me the cash afterwards so I can send the money to Davis.

Please tell me he is still alive, Earl is there anyway I can talk with Davis? Even if it's just for a short time, please let me know, and Earl can you e-mail me his room number at the hospital.

Thank you so much, I will let you know when I have the money in my hands.

Tess

From: Tess

Sent: January 15, 2009 2:41:41 PM Earl,

Please send me the details as I will have the money just after 4 my time as my friend will be coming to bring me the money at work. I am not able to call you from work as I can not access the phone card at this time.

Tess

From: Earl Warleh

Date: Thu, 15 Jan 2009 21:47:39—0800

Hello Madam,

Please this is the details that you need to wire the money!!!! Send it through this name: Leonardo Mosby

15 Bantam St Accra, Ghana 00233

Please send the money through this name okay and send me a mail with the info I will need, Please I just want things to go fast and then I can be free from thinking!!!!!

I am so tired I need to rest with my life!!!!I hope your husband will be grateful to me when he gets back home!!!!!

Earl

# 23

# RUN AROUND EARL.

From: Tess

Sent: January 15, 2009 10:00:56 PM Hello Earl,

I will send the money tomorrow morning before I go to work. Earl, again I feel the need to remind you that Davis is not my husband at this time, I hope that one day that he will be, please tell him to stay alive for me.

I will e-mail you tomorrow with the details as soon as the money is sent.

Tess

From: Tess

Sent: January 15, 2009 11:15:21 PM Earl,

Sorry for not getting to you sooner, the computers at work were being upgraded this morning so I was unable to get online as soon as I got here. I have sent the money to the name that you gave me, the control number is 432 519 0461 the security question is Davis's favorite colour . . . answer is blue.

The amount is for $5000.00 this should cover the hospital bill that you sent to me, Davis's flight to return home as well as any other bill that needs to be paid at the hospital. Earl, when Davis gets back home please tell him that my friend is expecting to be paid back right away.

Let me know how Davis is doing please, I really would like to talk with him.

All the best Tess

After e-mailing this to Earl, I literally sat back and waited for either his frantic phone call or e-mail.

From: Earl Warleh

Sent: January 16, 2009 1:21:05 PM Hello Madam Tess,

What is the senders Name you forgot to give me that including the details i need, As soom as you get this Mail let me know!!!

Thank you Earl

From: Tess

Sent: January 16, 2009 1:54:45 PM Earl,

The Sender was me, the control number is 432 519 0461 the security question is Davis's favorite colour . . . answer is blue. That should be all that you need.

Tess

From: Earl Warleh

Sent: January 16, 2009 2:14:19 PM Hello Madam Tess,

I dont think the details you gave me is correct or i should say there is something wrong!!!!!!

From: Earl Warleh

Sent: January 16, 2009 2:16:12 PM Hello Madam,

We need to get things going fast i already told the doctor that we will be paying the money tomorrow so that Davis can leave to get home for his operation to take place . . . He said you should book an appointment for him so that as soon as he arrives the operation will take place.

Madame I am having problem checking the money!!!!!The Money is not in the system or here . . .

Earl

From: Tess

Sent: January 16, 2009 3:51:48 PM Hello Earl,

I have called Western Union, they never sent the money, they said that I am still banned from sending any funds via Western Union so I am to pick the money up on my way home, Earl, I don't know what to do . . . the only thing I can think of is to send it FedEx if I can do that, the only problem is that the Fedex office will be closed soon and they are not open on the weekend. I'm not sure how I can even get the money sent thru FedEx; I'm not too comfortable sending cash that way. I will think about things over the weekend. I just feel like crying Earl, please tell Davis that I am trying.

I am so sorry Earl, if Davis would have been able to send to me the receipts for the money that I had sent him this would not have happened. Western Union will not allow me to send money, and I have no one here that will do it for me.

Earl, will I be able to talk to Davis? Tess

From: Tess

Sent: January 16, 2009 3:55:48 PM By the way Earl,

What operation does Davis need, I need to know the doctor's s assessment before I can call and book an appt with anyone. Please let me know ASAP so I can book what is needed.

Tess

# 24

# EARL IS GETTING REALLY DESPERATE NOW

From: Ear; Warleh

Sent: January 16, 2009 4:23:54 PM Hello Madam Tess,

Thanks for the Mail, Just check on one of your friends and let them walk to Western Union and Wire the Money we have no time to waste. You have a lot of friends or you can go to Western Union and wait outside in the car and let the baby sitter go and send the money.

Thank you Earl

From: Earl Warleh

Sent: January 16, 2009 4:24:45 PM Hello Madam Tess,

Thanks for the Mail, Just check on one of your friends and let them walk to Western Union and Wire the Money we have no time to waste.

You have a lot of friends or you can go to western union and wait outside in the car and let the baby sitter go and send the money. Drop me your cellphone number and I will call now

Thank you Earl

From: Earl Warleh

Sent: January 16, 2009 4:29:58 PM Hello Madam,

He needs an operation concerning Appendix. Please i told the Doc the money should be here in this weekend so that he can leave because his health is really bad. so think of what i told you let the Baby sitter help you!!!!

Earl. or figure out someone who you think can go and wire the money

*I could sense Earl was getting more and more desperate, I was actually feeling a little bit sorry for Earl at this time. I knew I had to end this soon.*

From: Earl Warleh

Sent: January 16, 2009 4:57:54 PM Looking forward to Hear from you!!!ASAP Hello Madam,

Check if there is Money gram i learnt it's another money transfer agent just like Western union!!!!!

Madam I had to help you see where you can locate some Moneygram stores, here is the address and the number to locate them, shoppers drug mart-canada post: on main st second:coffee tea & spice-canada post Located in the mall You can call and they will help you out, this are all Moneygram agent and they operate just like Western union!!!

Thank you Earl

Use the same Info I gave you

When Earl called me I explained to him that the Post Offices here in Whitehorse did not deal with Moneygrams, he was getting very frustrated, but he kept calling and e-mailing me, and wanting to talk to me through my Yahoo Messenger.

From: Tess

Sent: January 16, 2009 11:59:46 PM Hello Earl,

My Yahoo messenger is not working, it is not allowing me to connect. I am sorry. Please send me an e-mail. I will be going to bed now.

Take care Tess

From: Earl Warleh

Sent: January 17, 2009 12:32:51 AM hello Madam,

Thanks for the mail. Anyway after talking to you I had a call from the hospital as it's going to knock 9 AM here now!!!!They were asking about what am I doing about Davis health!!!!

I told them that they should relax and they said why should they relax if the man is dying!!! You still have not got any idea yet!!!?????Anyway please don't stress. Relax, we will communicate by sharing ideas and this will work.WAITING FOR YOUR MAIL.

Thank you HMM

From: Tess

Sent:January 17, 2009 12:50:08 AM Hello Earl,

Right now I have no ideas other than bringing the money over myself. In fact I will check with the travel agent here to see if I can do that and how much it would cost. Davis's bill is 2300.00 if I can come over for the remainder of the money, I may do that, . I am going to go to bed now Earl, I am very tired and very drained, I will e-mail you tomorrow and let you know what I have found out.

Have a good day, and tell the doctor to please be patient if that is at all possible.

Tess

*Earl called me and I suggested to him that I would be looking into the cost of flying over to Accra, Ghana and bringing the money over myself. I think I had Earl convinced that this was my next step, because this was what he emailed me.*

From: Earl Warleh

Sent: January 17, 2009 1:21:14 AM Hello Madam,

I just called the doctor and made him understand that he should be expecting the Money on Tuesday. I told him you will be wiring the money into my account by Monday!!!

442

He said okay then he will exercise patience and he will put Davis under special treatment till Tuesday. Where they can fly him out of here so please he asked me if you have booked the Doctors Appointment i told you to!!!

You can make the Transfer to this account Bank Name. Ghana Bank

Account Name. Jasmine Uritah Warleh Tayamer Account Number. 1111110000

Address. p.o.box AN 15367, Accra North City. Accra

Country. Ghana

Madam you can make the Transfer on Monday Morning if you still want to help get Davis out of here before we lose him!!!!

Thank you Earl

*After reading this e-mail, it was another assurance that this was indeed a scam, because if Davis was real and needed money as deperately as he did, then he could have had it wired to this account, and Earl could have given it to him. even knowing that everything was a scam to have yet another piece of evidence prove it as such, was still a hard pill to swallow, and that feeling of being kicked in the chest came back to me.*

From: Earl Warleh

Sent: January 17, 2009 5:01:56 PM Hello Madam Tess,

How are you this Morning??I hope you got the Mail with the account info for you to transfer the Money!!!!!!!

Why haven't I got a mail from you, anyway you must be busy have a Good weekend!!!!!!!!!!

From: Earl Warleh

Sent: January 18, 2009 5:04:42 AM Hello Madam Tess,

I have a Good News for you!!!!Today I was at the Hospital sitting Next to Davis and I was sleeping by him when i heard someone mentioning your Name, hey I opened My eyes to see Davis calling for your Name, It made me had tears in my eyes and i had to call the doc. Its like a miracle but the doctor said Davis is a very strong Man and has a very strong cells, Tess I told the Doctor you said Monday you will try and make the bank to bank transfer so that Davis can leave but he asked if you have booked the appointment already for his operation as soon as he arrives!!!

I will try and call you later i don't have any credits on my phone you can send me a mail when you get my mails.

Earl

From: Tess

Sent: January 18, 2009 11:47:30 AM Hello Earl,

That is such good news. Earl I would very much like to talk to Davis ASAP, can you arrange to be at the hospital later on today or first thing in the morning say 9pm your time it would be 5am my time, or even today if possible. If you could call me when you are at the hospital, then I will call you right back. And Earl please can you tell the doctor, and he should know this, that he should contact the hospital himself to set everything up with the doctors at either the hospital here or in Vancouver. I can give you the phone numbers for either hospital, is it Dr Byman who is looking after Davis?

Tell Davis I am so happy to hear that he is thinking about me, and that he is getting stronger.

I will talk with you later Tess

From: Tess

Sent: January 19, 2009 2:03:48 PM Earl,

I am very upset, I don't even want to talk about it right now, all I can say is that I am having problems and it all stems from accepting the money from Davis's associates, I will e-mail you later-tomorrow, I still want to talk to Davis, please can you call me when you are at the hospital so that I can talk to him. again I will talk to you later

Tess

From: Earl Warleh

Sent: January 19, 2009 3:18:47 PM Hello Madam,

Thanks for Making me Hear from you!!!I asked you to open a new account with a different bank so you can wire the money from there as you told me you are having problems with your bank so you need to get to open an account with a different bank in other for you to be able to wire the funds!~!!!!

I told the doc you wanted to talk to Davis and he said you should know that he is not well and what matters now is him getting out of here. He said as soon as they get the Funds they can call the hospital so they can Book the appointment.

Hope to hear from you later send me your cellphone number!!!!!

From: Tess

Sent: January 20, 2009 2:52:38 PM Hello Earl,

I am so sorry about this delay, I am so upset about everything, to be so close to something and not be able to do anything with it, is so frustrating. Anyhow, you have to realise that this town is not like a major city we only have so many banks in this town and I have been to all of them, small towns share information, and there will be restrictions on any account I open. My friend is to return within the next couple of days. I am hoping that he will be able to help me, he was the one who lent me the money, otherwise the only thing I can think of is me using some of the money and flying over myself, however I don't know how much that will cost, I have to give two weeks' notice from here to get a good rate otherwise I'm looking at 1500.00 just to get to a major city to fly out of in order to get to Africa.

I was thinking I could try something, I would like for you to send me the address of the hospital where Davis is at, I would like to send him a card, directly to him. I would need his room number, could you do that for me, Thank You

Tess

From: Earl Warleh

Sent: January 20, 2009 3:11:16 PM Hello Madam Tess,

Thanks for the mail and I keep calling you but it seems you dont pick the call anyway I am getting fed up with all this because we have come this Far and thing are trying to go backwards again.!!!

Madam in the days time when you friend is back let him send the money through western union to the address I have given you that will help.

Thanks for the mail and i will keep trying to call you Earl

*I got the impression from the phone calls between Earl and I that he was getting quite frustrated with me, towards the end of our conversations he would sound worn out. I had to end this, Earl was starting to grow on me, and I was beginning to feel sorry for him.*

From: Tess

Sent: January 20, 2009 6:06:26 PM Earl,

Please can you send me an address as to where I can send something to Davis.

I want to send it tomorrow if I can, Tess

From Earl Warleh

Sent: January 21, 2009 12:16:47 PM Hello Tess,

Thanks for the mail!!!

I will advise you sending the card through post office send it through this address

Jordon Yound p.o.box 81 Accra-Ghana West-Africa 00233 That's the post office box owner

I will get it for Davis

From: Tess

Sent: January 21, 2009 1:02:11 PM Thanks Earl,

I am hoping I will still be able to send it today, if not today I will send it tomorrow and hopefully it should be there by Monday.

Tell Davis, I do think of him often. Tess

From: Tess

Sent: January 21, 2009 2:17:47 PM Hello Earl,

Fed Ex will not send to a post office box, I will need a physical address to send it to.

Tess

From: Earl Warleh

Sent: January 21, 2009 4:17:13 PM Hello Madam,

This is the address Jordon Young #5 first st P.o.box 81 Accra-Ghana 00233 West-Africa

From: Tess

Sent: January 21, 2008 5:10:12 PM Earl,

Will this address work if I address it to #5 First St Accra-Ghana 00233 West-Africa

Tess

From: Earl Warleh

Sent: January 22, 2009 10:51:01 AM

Yes it will!!!!Have you Heard any news from your friend??

From: Tess

Sent: January 22, 2009 3:54:33 PM Earl,

My friend, whom I have been waiting to hear from, called me this afternoon, he is stuck in Tuktoyuktuk, due to weather and is not able to get out, he hopes the weather will change before the weekend, he said he will call me later when I'm not working as he wants to talk to me. I will talk to you later.

Tess

From: Earl Warleh

Sent: January 23, 2009 3:53:01 PM Hello Madam Tess,

If you have sent the card by fedex dont i need the Trackig number????

# 25

# LETTING DAVIS DIE

I talked with Earl on the phone. He kept telling me that if I couldn't send any money then I would be letting Davis die. Earl was getting quite frustrated with me because I told him that my friend would not be back in town for a while and that I was unable to do anything. Earl would get upset and say Thank You Madame Tess, your husband is going to die, have a nice life, then he would hang up and then he would call again fifteen minutes later, he did this twice. I give him credit for being persistent.

From: Earl Warleh

Sent: January 24, 2009 11:52:26 PM Hello Madam Tess,

It's nice to Hear your Voice again anyway I want you to know that you are so nice and thanks for helping Davis and anyway I understand you cant help . . . I think you have done your best so do I!!!!

All we can do now is to let the Man die as we are both tired of helping him!! Take care and have a Good day bye I dont think i will be able to get to send you e-mails again because i have given up on Davis ok . . . bye bye for now

From: Tess

Sent: January 25, 2009 1:08:13 PM Hello Earl,

All I can say is I'm Sorry, When you see Davis, please can you tell him for me, I will always remember him, he gave me such wonderful feelings, I will never forget that. Take care of yourself Earl.

449

Thanks for everything you've done Tess

*I had to end this, and sending this card was the one way that I knew would put an end to this*

From: Tess

Sent: January 25, 2009 1:10:47 PM Hello Earl,

I have sent the card by Fed Ex, I will get the tracking number for you later today as it is at home, and I will send it to you

Tess

From: Tess

Sent: January 26, 2009 2:36:12 PM Hello Earl,

Maybe this will help, the tracking number for the envelope I sent to you for Davis is shipping order number 00370 this is the only number on the piece of paper from the FedEx place. Take care of yourself Duke, and again tell Davis I am sorry.

Tess

From: Earl Warleh

Sent: January 26, 2009 12:43:18 PM Hello Madam Tess,

I told Davis about the card and he said thats a nice thing you did but if you are willing to help him so that he will be saved and also to get him home the same way you can put the money into something like the pocket of a jacket and then zip it!!!

Think about it and tell me something!!!! Earl

From: Tess

Sent: January 26, 2009 10:57:45 PM Earl,

Please just give Davis the card I'm sending to him . . . It should be there on Tuesday or Wednesday

Thank You Tess

From: Earl Warleh

Sent: January 26, 2009 11:38:18 PM Hello Tess,

Thanks for the mail and i want you to know that mark my words i will always do anything you ask me to!!! i want you to tell me if you are willing to come forward with the idea i brought up by another means of getting the money here!!!

Thank you Earl

# 26

# MY FINAL GOODBYE

I think that Earl thought that I was sending Davis money inside the card; however what I sent was a sympathy card with two letters inside of it. The front of the card had the following caption printed across the top of it.

"Sincere Sympathy"

There is a picture of a tree in a field with beautiful sunset colours washing across the card.

The caption on the inside of the card read . . . Thoughts of deepest sympathy are with you in your time of loss I wrote on the inside . . . with deepest regrets, not saying goodbye . . . The first letter I wrote went like this . . .

Davis My Love, My Fantasy

I have known for a while now what is real and what has been fantasy or basically a lie.

I want to tell you that the words that you shared with me through your e-mails, your instant messages and your phone calls made me feel real and alive. I knew there was a chance that you weren't real, that you weren't the person you said you were but for me, again, the feelings were real.

I will never regret the feelings that you awakened in me.

What I do regret is not being able to have my fairy tale, no longer being able to read your words, or hear your voice, and I regret not having the chance to say goodbye.

I will never forget you Davis,

I will never forget you or what you did. Tess

And then I added the second letter:

There were several mistakes that you made that made me realize that you were not real and all you wanted was money out of me. There was a time when I thought I really meant something to you and that you wanted to tell me something, I was hoping the truth.

You see I have a friend who works for the special police force so I had him check a few things out. First off, there is no registration anywhere or proof that Davis lives in Whitehorse, also we found out that there is no Lungston Hospital in Accra Ghana and there is only a pharmacist by the name of Phil Byman, no Dr Phil Byman listed with the ministry of health.

There was also the fact that you could not or were not able to produce an invoice or passport with the name Davis on it, and your dates were wrong on the invoice. David Bagnad was also the name, (your name?) on the plane ticket.

Davis, David or Earl? No matter who you are, I again thank you for the memories.

I hope that you have put my money that I sent to you to good use to help others, could you at least send me a receipt so I can use it as a donation towards a tax deduction, it was close to $10, 000.00 that I personally gave to you. You can send it in an e-mail as well.

On that note I will say goodbye. I hope one day you will stop using and causing pain and hurt to us men and women who believe in love.

I would tell my friends that Davis is real, a wonderful man. I would tell them that he includes my daughter in our discussions and he talks with her on the phone, they have made plans together to go shopping when Davis comes home. No, Davis is real, he wouldn't do that if he wasn't real, only a monster would do that to a child, only a monster would be that cruel.

453

# 27

## LESSONS LEARNED

I haven't heard from Davis or Earl since I sent Davis the sympathy card and said my goodbye. To be honest, and completely truthful with myself, I did miss Davis's e-mails, and I did miss hearing his voice. Would I go to him if he showed up? No, he is what he is. When I talk of missing him, I guess I mean, I miss the attention that I received, 'you've got mail', the excitement of it all, it can draw a person in, it drew me in, and it has drawn in others. The hard part is breaking the connection, and as you can see by my story, even once I knew it was a complete scam, I had a hard time breaking the connection, so I played the game, knowing that I was playing, I kept telling myself, I just want to get more information out of them, which I did, but there were times when I felt that this game I was playing could turn into a dangerous one, what if Davis or the man calling himself Davis, did show up, I had ten different scenarios running through my head. It's a good thing that he didn't. When I did stop it, I was ready to stop, and being that it was Earl, made it a lot easier. I had no emotional connection to Earl.

I don't think Earl was Davis, I believe that Davis was a completely different person from Earl; the accent was completely different Davis had an Italian accent; Earl had a definite African accent. And Earl's writing was different. Towards the end of Davis's e-mails, I do feel that a couple of them were written by Earl. Where the abbrievitation Hmmmmmm, was used, Davis did not use that in his earlier e-mails. When I would talk to Earl on the phone and want to talk to Davis, Earl would tell me that Davis was sleeping. Had Earl been Davis, I feel he would have said just a minute and changed his voice. There were a couple of times when Davis got excited because the computer didn't show up or the money wasn't there when it was supposed to be and Davis did retain his Italian accent.

I suspect that Earl and Dr. Byman were the same person. There was one time when I called the phone number for the doctor that I had and the call didn't go through so I called Earl, when I mentioned to him that I had just tried calling the doctor, he asked me when did I try calling the doctor. I got the feeling from his remark that he was holding the doctor's phone in his hand.

I talked with Joseph Black when I had the $57, 000.00 in my account and was not moving it, he wanted to know what was happening with his money, I played the upset female and explained to him that Davis had collapsed and that everything was on hold, I then gave him the doctor's phone number because I told Joseph that Davis needed help and mentioned to Joseph that he may be able to help Davis, when I talked with Earl a few hours later he told me that Joseph had called him inquiring about Davis, once more confirming my belief that Earl and the doctor were one.

Joseph Black and Giovanni, they could have been the same person, they both had deep Italian accents. Joseph's voice did sound deeper in tone, so it is difficult to say as to whether or not they were one or two separate people, and both of their tones were completely different from Davis's. As for John Sigman, I am not sure about him, there was once when I was talking to him on the phone, that his accent changed. He didn't talk to me on the phone very often; most of my contact with John was through e-mail.

At any rate I was definitely dealing with more than one person throughout this scam.

One of the things that I did was I kept track of all of the phone numbers that these guys used, and there were several different numbers that showed up on my call display. I contacted Phone Busters with all of the numbers for each individual that I dealt with. At the end of the book I have listed the phone numbers for Phone Busters, along with their website. If you even think that the person you are talking with could be involving you in any type of a scam, call Phone Busters or contact them through their website, they have the ability to track some of these phone calls. I also contacted the credit bureaus, not just Equifax that is the popular one, but the other two as well, Trans Union and Experian and again I have listed their numbers at the end of the book. Call them and let them know that you think you've been a victim of fraud. If at anytime, you, or someone else tries to get a loan using your name. A red flag shows up on your file and you are contacted to verify that yes indeed you are the one requesting the loan.

I feel that I got away lucky so to say, in doing my research there have been both men and women that have lost thousands, hundreds of thousands of dollars, some their life savings, and in some cases people have lost their houses. The worst thing is other than loosing a lot of money, the trust and the person's feelings have been used and abused. And what about the person's picture that I fell in love with. What of those people, are they aware that their pictures are being used in these fraudulent scams? I sent my picture to these guys, will my picture be used in such a manner and how can that be stopped?

As for the $20, 000.00 that I could have been responsible for on my Visa, I have not heard anything further regarding the money that was placed fraudulently on my card, and I have never been asked to pay it back. Whether I was being treated by the bank as a victim of a crime and they were forgiving me this amount or my holding out and telling Davis to fix my Visa if he wanted me to accept the larger amount of money worked, I will never know. I am just glad that I haven't been held accountable for it. I do consider myself very lucky indeed given the circumstances that I found myself in.

My final act has been to phone the Canadian Embassy in Accra, Ghana. I explained what had happened to me. The receptionist told me that the local authorities were trying to shut down the internet fraud scams that were happening in Accra, so she asked me to send all of the information that I could to the immigration office of the embassy. She gave me both the e-mail address and the fax number. I'm not too sure if anything will or has come out of me sharing the information with them, but one never knows and hopefully the information that I was able to get from Earl and John was instrumental in some way to putting a stop to some of their illegal activities.

As for Steve and I, well I discovered that Steve does indeed have feelings for me; I know that I can consider him a friend, one that will be there for me. That to me means a lot. Whether or not we will ever figure out a relationship, I don't know, just the other day I was saying to Steve that alcohol will affect me more than him because I don't drink that much at all. Steve looked at me and said "I've said this to you before, you realize that when I quit drinking, I quit you" I smiled at him and asked "when are you going to quit?" Needless to say, I still check out my eharmony matches, one must never give up, I just plan on being a lot wiser and I have to get the man that I meet to get checked out by my friends, and family before I can get excited about him. Another thing that was reiterated to me was 'Listen to Your Friends" no matter how much you don't want to . . . LISTEN . . . Because they care about you and love you. And don't ever be afraid to talk to someone if you feel that something is not sitting right with you in any type of relationship that you are in.

One of the frightening things that I discovered once I had ended this charade with Earl was that these scam organizations are considered to be operated by organized crime syndicates, not only are they diffucult to take down, but they can be very dangerous. When I think about some of the things I have read online, I feel scared, scared of the danger that I may have put not only me but my family into. Even today whenever I think of it, I catch myself looking around, wondering if someone is watching me.

A lot of lessons learned, a new chapter to add to my life's experiences and one that I wanted to share with others so that they may understand in some way as to why I got caught up in this scam and how my wanting to feel love and be loved was used to the scammers benefit . . . Love is a powerful emotion that may need some guidance once in a while. I still believe in Love, that is something I will never give up on and hopefully one day I will meet the man of my dreams. Someone who will love me for who I am and take my family as his own . . . and who knows maybe I will get my fairy tale, and that might just be another story . . .

I don't know what the answer is to stopping these scammers that are attacking us through the internet. I guess the best thing that we, as individuals can do is to be aware of what is happening around us. It comes down to always asking questions and never take things at face value. Gone are the days when a 'man's handshake' was his word. We are in a new era with a new set of rules. I always wanted to believe in people and trust in others, now I have to move into the future and realise that before I give my trust to someone who is a stanger to me, I need to know who it is that I'm dealing with and again I need to ask the questions and get the answers, also check the answers to make sure that they are real. Before this happened, I never realized that scams like this existed to such a magnitude as they do. I was naieve. I had heard of people being taken for money online, but never did I think that it would happen to me . . . that ol' cliché . . . unfortunately those ol'clichés we need to listen to . . . because it can happen to us and we need to protect ourselves.

1. Analogy of a Romance Scam April 21, 2008 by romancescams Romance Scams Blog http://www.romancescams.org

2. You can report any suspicious calls to Phone Busters at the same toll free number in the Canada or the United States

Toll Free:1 (888) 495-8501

Overseas and Local: 1 (705) 495-8501

Toll Free Fax:1 (888) 654-9426 Mailing Address:

Box 686

North Bay, Ontario P1B 8J8

E-mail: info@phonebusters.com Copies of Advanced Fee Letter Fraud (419 / West African / Nigerian Letters) should be e-mailed directly to: wafl@phonebusters.com

If you feel that you are a victim of identity theft, or any type of fraudulent activity call the following Credit Bureaus and let them know what has happened and they will keep track of anyone using your name and information to gain credit or loans.

These are the major credit bureaus that should be contacted as well if you feel that you have been a victim of a scam or fraud or identity theft.

Equifax 1 888 766 0008 this phone number has been taken from their web site

www.fraudalerts.equifax.com For Canadian and US Resident's

Trans Union Canada For Residents living outside of Quebec 1-800-663-9980 between 8am – 8pm ET

For Residents of Quebec 1-877-713-3393 or 514-335-0374 between 8:30am – 4:30pm Mon – Thur,and 8:30am – 4:30pm Fri

For Resident's of the United States

Experian 1 888-397-3742 this phone number has been taken from their web site www.experian.com

And it is important as well to contact your local authorities and let them know that you think you are a victim of identity theft, fraudulent or scam type activity.

Hopefully, one day, there will be a way to stop these criminals, until then, we need to be aware and be prepared.

# EPILOGUE

## A HAPPY NEW BEGINNING

A year and a half has gone by since I met the man called Davis and his group of scammers and a lot has happened since then. I did continue to spend time with Steve. At first Steve was caring and seemed to be considerate of my feelings, I felt as if we had finally achieved a friendship that was beyond being one of convenience. I was able to keep my feelings in check as Steve kept telling me all he needed as a place, meaning me, I knew I would be nothing more. I did not want to be in a relationship that was so one sided and empty. I was very leery of going online looking for that someone special, I would get so hurt by Steve that I would find myself online just to talk to someone. I still believed that love had to exist somewhere; I wasn't ready to give up hope. So after a year and a half, I took the risk and went onto a couple of date sites. One was matchmaker.com the other was match. com. I would get an interest notification sent to me by different men and I would send an interest notification back to them or an instant message through the date site. I received such an interest notification from a gentleman going by the name of Maxwell Brooks, his profile stated that he was from Florida and that he was a business man, self employed. He liked to hunt and fish and his picture on his profile page showed the appearance of a hunter and fisherman. It also said that he had a daughter and that he was a widower. His profile picture attracted me, so I contacted him and it just so happened that he was online as we were able to talk through the instant messenger on the date site.

After about five minutes of conversing through the instant messenger he asked me if I had MSN messenger as it would be easier to converse through as he was having difficulty with the site. I agreed to give him my email and set him up on my MSN messenger site. While we were conversing I was asking him certain questions about what he did for a living and his fondness for hunting and fishing. It was clear that after only a few questions he was not a hunter or a fisherman and definitely not one from Florida. One question I asked him was what did he like to hunt and he replied "fish" I also asked him what type of game was there in Florida and his response was "golf, basketball, etc". Finally I couldn't take anymore and I told him that he was really bad at this and asked him if he would answer a few questions that I had of how a person such as himself, scams others. At first he was quite belligerent about my questions, but finally he did tell me that he was in Nigeria and that he was 23 years old. He had been recruited by a friend of his who was showing him how to set up the different profiles on the date sites. He told me that they look for, (this is how he put it) "rich greedy white women"; women who are between 35 and 65 years of age, women who state that they are looking for the "man of their dreams" and women that sound vulnerable. He sets his different profiles up to reflect ordinary men by using pictures off of the internet and making these men self employed, world travelers, they are either business consultants or entrepreneurs and they are portrayed as being rich. The male profiles used are also men who are divorced with kids or widowed with kids. This is the type of man that these scammers feel North American women want.

The scammer I talked with told me that he was doing this to make money as there were no jobs available in Nigeria and he had to take care of his mother, brothers and sisters. He also needed to get money to get out of Nigeria so he could get a work Visa and find a good job in a different country, which would help his family a lot. These guys don't give up. I agreed to meet this scammer who now had told me that his name was Otaga, the following evening as I had more questions to ask him, I also may have insinuated that if he answered my questions I would pay him for his answers. The next evening I met Otaga on line at our pre-arranged time and we talked for approximately two minutes, the usual greetings, when Otaga wrote to me saying that someone was coming and that he had to go. I waited for about ten minutes before he came back online. When he did come back online there was a different feel to the conversation, he immediately asked me if I was sending him the money and I told him that I only agreed to that if he answered my questions. I was then told that I was a wicked woman for not sending any money and the conversation coming from this man just kept getting nastier. He finally said that he was not Otaga, Otaga had left and that he was the man. He told me that they would never be stopped as they were everywhere and would continue to go after "rich white women bitches". The way he stated this was almost frightening. At one time during our conversation he said he could see me, that he was watching me. I was also told that they now have my picture, my address, my phone number and my profile and would use these to scam others.

I ended my conversation and proceeded to contact the customer service department of the date site I was on and told them about this guy who was an actual scammer. It took about a week, but his profile was removed from that date site. During this time I was also contacted by about ten other men who had read my profile and wanted to get to know me. Out of the ten men that contacted me I got eight kicked off of the date site because they weren't able to answer my direct questions. I also would ask them where they lived and would go to the white pages on line for that town and try and locate the address or check the phone number and name with the phone directory, or I would Google their name. I would ask them about their profile and if they said they were from my home town, I asked an exact location. If they couldn't answer my questions I reported them to the customer service department and they were removed from the site. Their profile descriptions matched what my scammer Otaga had told me. Most of these men were self-employed, well off, entrepreneurs, divorced or widowed with kids.

It was while I was on the lookout for these scammers that I received an interest notice from a gentleman whose profile showed he lived in Whitehorse. He was one man who was able to answer one of my direct questions. We sent about four emails back and forth before he asked me if we could meet for a coffee, and he was able to state an exact location in Whitehorse. I thought about meeting this gentleman for a day or two and then I agreed to meet for a coffee. Coffee is always safer as it is easy to get up and leave if it doesn't work out and there are no feelings hurt and maybe a new friend has been met. Anyhow I met this gentleman for coffee, Kent is his name. Let's just say that that was the best tasting coffee I've had in a very long time and now I know for sure that the letters that Davis wrote to me and the feelings that these letters gave me was what I wanted, however it was only an illusion of what I wanted. After meeting Kent, he has given me more than the feelings that I wanted to feel, he has given to me my dream. I truly believe that I have the man that I have always wished for. I believed in love, in its

462

existence and I am so glad that I never gave up believing. I kept my faith in my belief and now it has come to me.

There is true love that can be found on the internet with online dating, the lesson for me was to ask the direct questions and get the correct answers, be careful about giving out any information even your hotmail account can be harmful to you if it should fall into the wrong hands. Most importantly, if anyone asks you for money, no matter how sincere they seem to be, don't send it to them. If the person truly loves you, they would never ask for money and should never make you feel that you are the only person who can help them. If they are worldly travelers, a business man of any type, then they should have their own accountants and lawyers who can help them out; not to mention friends and family members. Beware the person who has no friends or family members that they can turn to for help. And of course believe in yourself, believe in love, never give up believing and never give up on your dream.

I feel that I have come full circle and I can now close this book and begin another, a love story. My fairytale has come true, I consider myself as having a new beginning and it feels wonderful.

On January 19th 2010, I invited to be a quest on a radio-internet talk show called Mission Unstoppable with Frankie Picasso; the topic was online dating scams. During the talk show I met a couple of people who have their own websites and are trying to stop these scammers or at the very least, they are trying to educate people on how to protect themselves from scammers as well as helping those who have been scammed. I wish that I would have known about these two groups while I was going through my meeting of Davis and his band of scammer men. Mary Leal a police officer, who at the time of the talk show was online as one of the quests while she was teaching a criminology course, the topic of her class that evening was dealing with scams. Mary has been dealing with people who have been scammed for awhile now and she stated that my story sounds very familiar to the other stories she has heard. She also stated that a lot of people are ashamed of what has happened to them when they find out they have been scammed and tend to not tell anyone and not get help. I guess that is another lesson that I did learn, tell someone and don't be afraid to ask for help, once you do that the weight comes off of your shoulders and you don't feel alone anymore. If you don't have someone such as a friend or a family member to tell, Mary is willing to listen to your story and help as well as Jeff Hoffman the gentleman that I met through

Frankie Picasso's show; he too is willing to help those who have been scammed. I have added both Jeff's website and Mary's email addresses for those looking for information and/or help.

www.pigbusters.com mleal@woh.rr.com

Remember to keep yourself safe while online, and to never give up on true love.

CPSIA information can be obtained
at www.ICGtesting.com
Printed in the USA
LVHW011149240521
688313LV00005B/77

9 781649 089861